D0508333

For anyone who ever got lost and followed
their own winding road home, no matter how
dark the night or indecipherable the directions.
CHRISTOPHER

———✦❉✦———

To Peggy and Marla. For rescuing me and
putting me on my path to art. I wouldn't be
where I am today without you both.
JOSHUA

———✦❉✦———

As always thanks go to Helen for being the voice to
tell me that a sound effect isn't working or splitting
a balloon didn't work. And for telling me lettering
comics might actually not be a bad idea.
HASSAN

IMAGE COMICS, INC. • **Robert Kirkman:** Chief Operating Officer • **Erik Larsen:** Chief Financial Officer • **Todd McFarlane:** President • **Marc Silvestri:** Chief Executive Officer • **Jim Valentino:** Vice President • **Eric Stephenson:** Publisher / Chief Creative Officer • **Corey Hart:** Director of Sales • **Jeff Boison:** Director of Publishing Planning & Book Trade Sales • **Chris Ross:** Director of Digital Sales • **Jeff Stang:** Director of Specialty Sales • **Kat Salazar:** Director of PR & Marketing • **Drew Gill:** Art Director • **Heather Doornink:** Production Director • **Nicole Lapalme:** Controller • **IMAGECOMICS.COM**

Deanna Phelps: Production Artist for SHANGAHAI RED

SHANGHAI RED. First printing. January 2019. Published by Image Comics, Inc. Office of publication: 2701 NW Vaughn St., Suite 780, Portland, OR 97210. Copyright © 2019 Christopher Sebela, Joshua Hixson & Hassan Otsmane-Elhaou. All rights reserved. Contains material originally published in single magazine form as SHANGHAI RED #1-5. "Shanghai Red," its logos, and the likenesses of all characters herein are trademarks of Christopher Sebela, Joshua Hixson & Hassan Otsmane-Elhaou, unless otherwise noted. "Image" and the Image Comics logos are registered trademarks of Image Comics, Inc. No part of this publication may be reproduced or transmitted, in any form or by any means (except for short excerpts for journalistic or review purposes), without the express written permission of Christopher Sebela, Joshua Hixson & Hassan Otsmane-Elhaou, or Image Comics, Inc. All names, characters, events, and locales in this publication are entirely fictional. Any resemblance to actual persons (living or dead), events, or places, without satirical intent, is coincidental. Printed in the USA. For information regarding the CPSIA on this printed material call: 203-595-3636. For international rights, contact: foreignlicensing@imagecomics.com.
ISBN: 978-1-5343-1034-6.

SHANGHAI RED

CHRISTOPHER SEBELA
Script & Design

JOSHUA HIXSON
Art & Colors

HASSAN OTSMANE-ELHAOU
Lettering

ROMAN STEVENS
Color Flatting

ANDREA SHOCKLING
Editorial

DYLAN TODD
Logo

SHANGHAI RED
created by
Sebela, Hixson & Otsmane-Elhaou

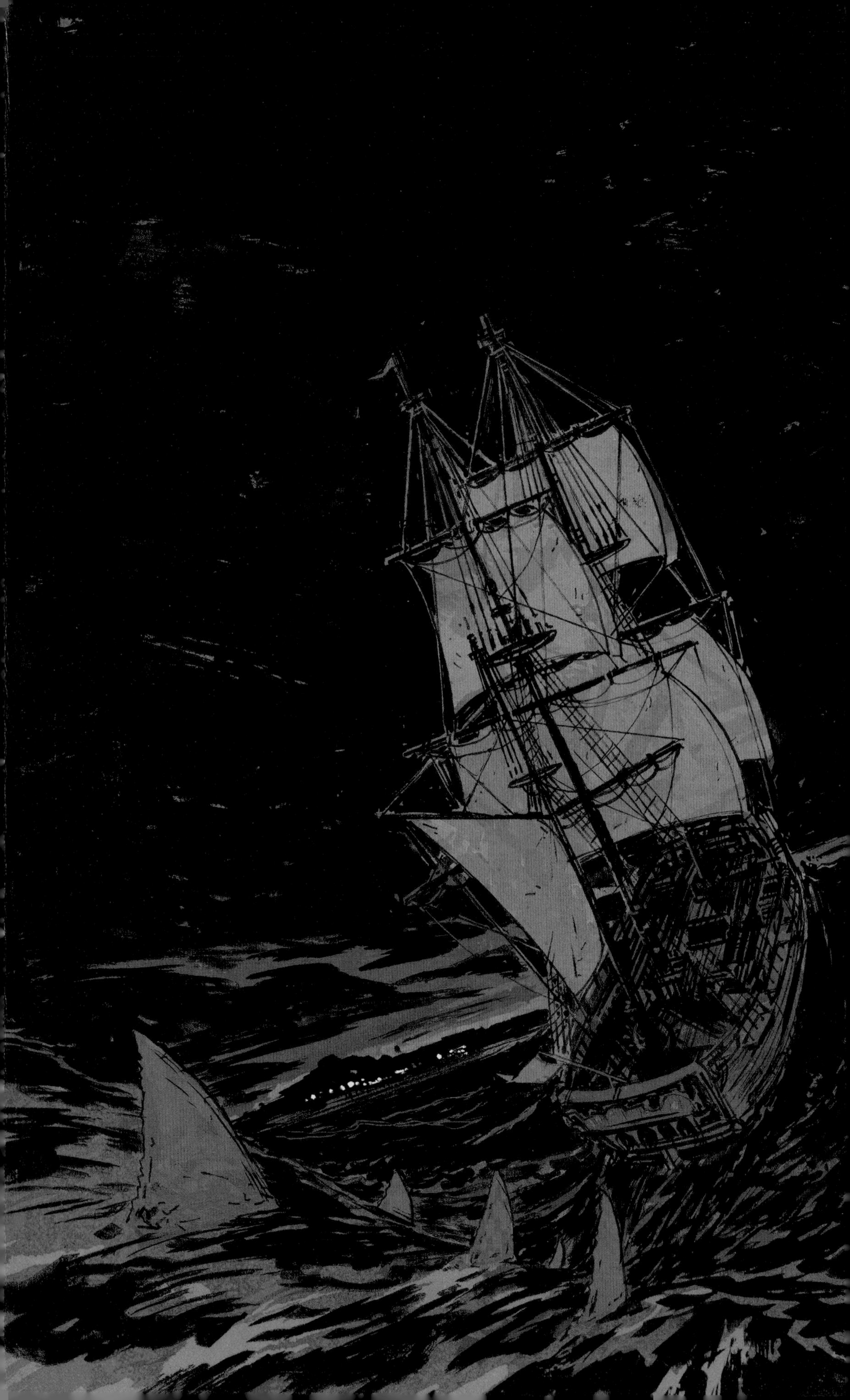

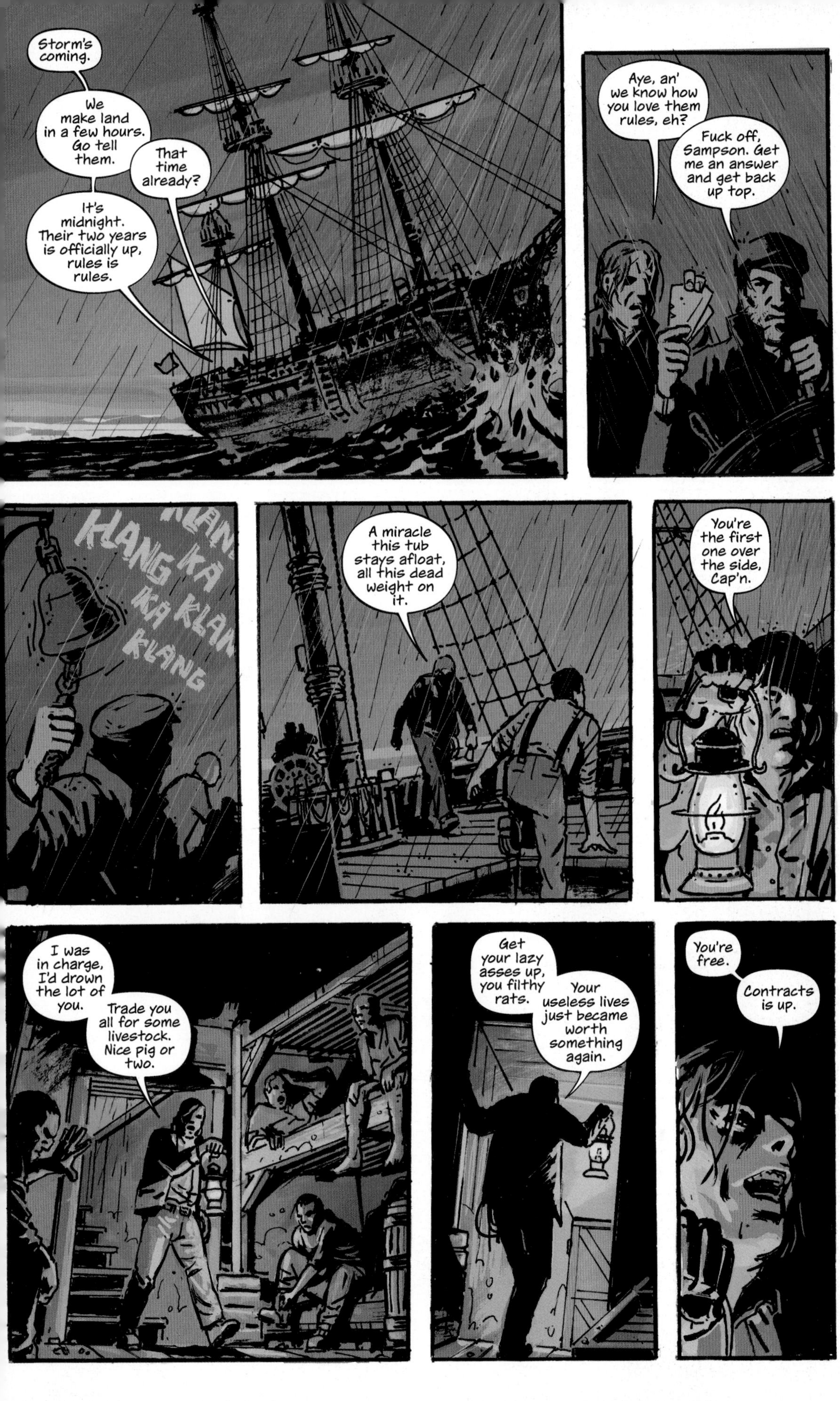
Storm's coming.
We make land in a few hours. Go tell them.
That time already?
It's midnight. Their two years is officially up, rules is rules.
Aye, an' we know how you love them rules, eh?
Fuck off, Sampson. Get me an answer and get back up top.
KLANG KA KA KLANG KLANG
A miracle this tub stays afloat, all this dead weight on it.
You're the first one over the side, Cap'n.
I was in charge, I'd drown the lot of you.
Trade you all for some livestock. Nice pig or two.
Get your lazy asses up, you filthy rats.
Your useless lives just became worth something again.
You're free.
Contracts is up.

The captain took on your debts when he bought you, a fair bit of coin. Now you're all paid up.

Started with a dozen of you. I been cracking the whip across your backs, trying to teach you somethin' and now comes the day of reckoning.

You got a choice to make, boys.

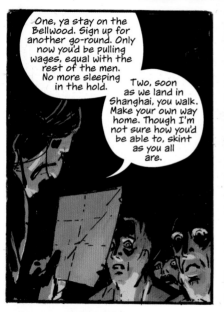

One, ya stay on the Bellwood. Sign up for another go-round. Only now you'd be pulling wages, equal with the rest of the men. No more sleeping in the hold.

Two, soon as we land in Shanghai, you walk. Make your own way home. Though I'm not sure how you'd be able to, skint as you all are.

You got two minutes to decide. Captain wants me back on deck.

You'll sign it if you're smart.

Smile, boys. You're sailors now.

Just need all five of your names on--

Where the hell's Jack?

Off in one of his little cubby-holes.

You rats must like the abuse, as much as you keep forcin' my hand.

If you like, I can cross all your names off the contract. No one missed the others.

That what you want? On account of Jack?

Get him out here or you're all-- AAGH!

Sampson. I thought about your offer.

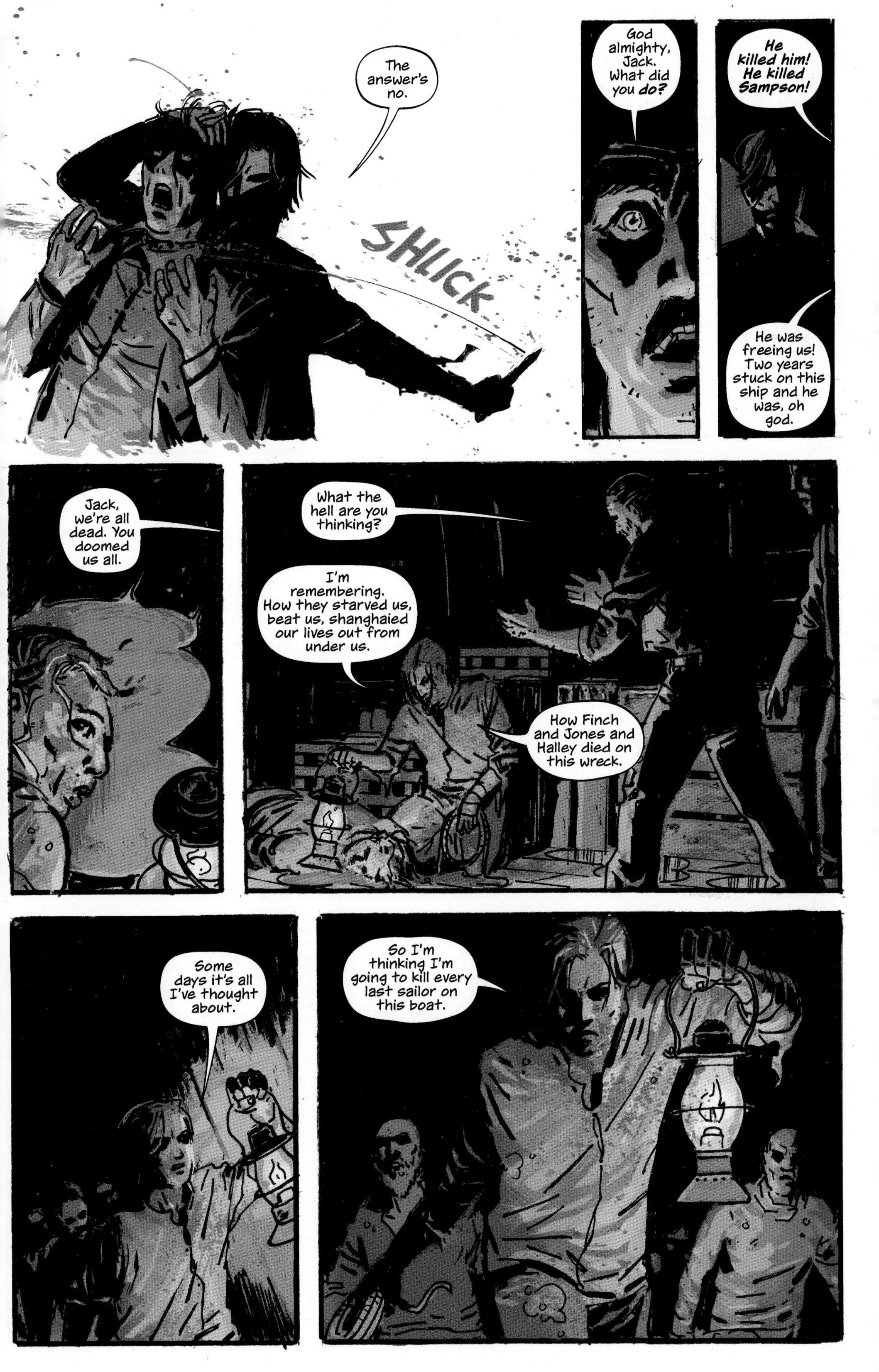

The answer's no.
SHLICK
God almighty, Jack. What did you *do?*
He killed him! He killed Sampson!
He was freeing us! Two years stuck on this ship and he was, oh god.
Jack, we're all dead. You doomed us all.
What the hell are you thinking?
I'm remembering. How they starved us, beat us, shanghaied our lives out from under us.
How Finch and Jones and Halley died on this wreck.
Some days it's all I've thought about.
So I'm thinking I'm going to kill every last sailor on this boat.

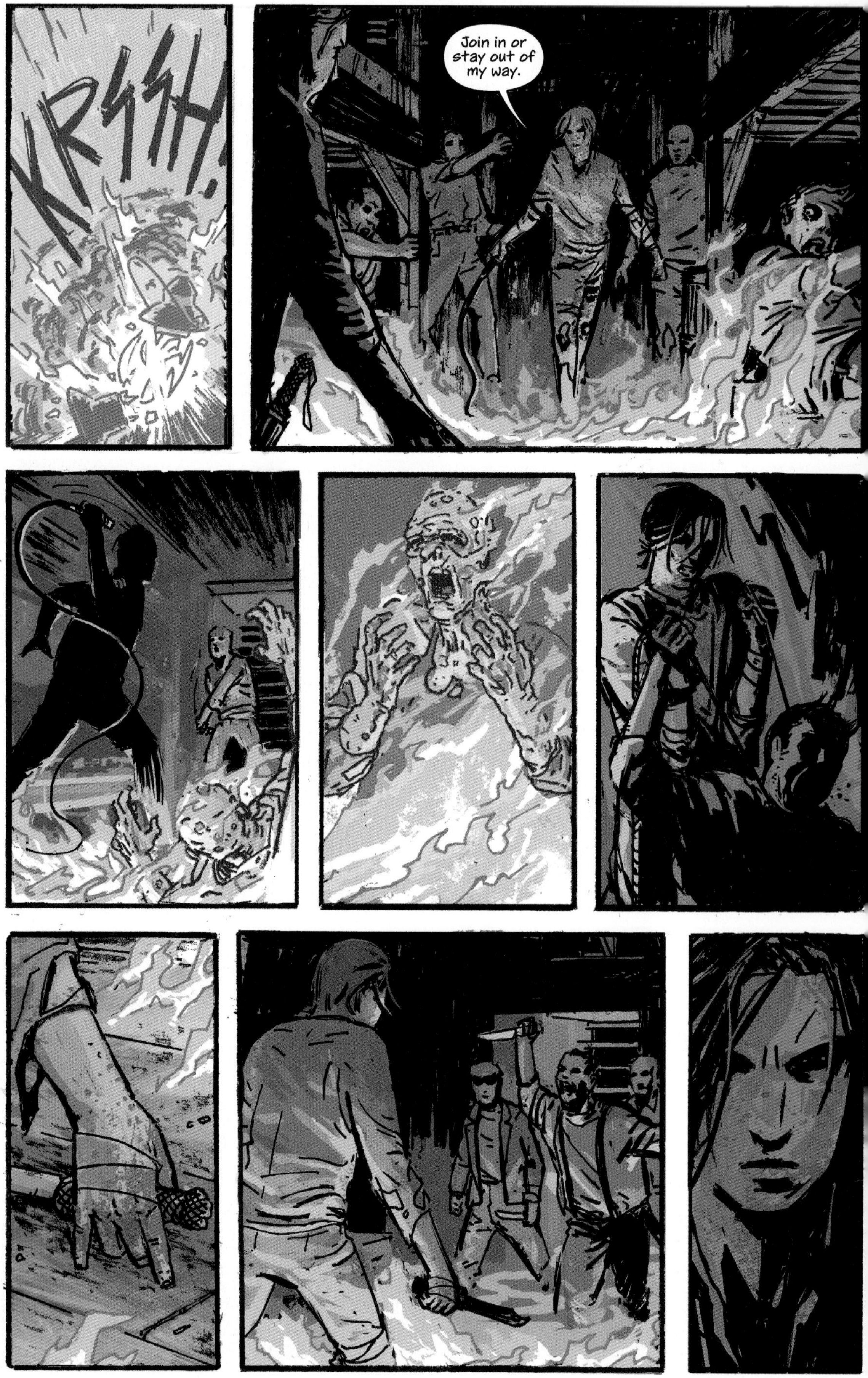
KRSSH!
Join in or stay out of my way.

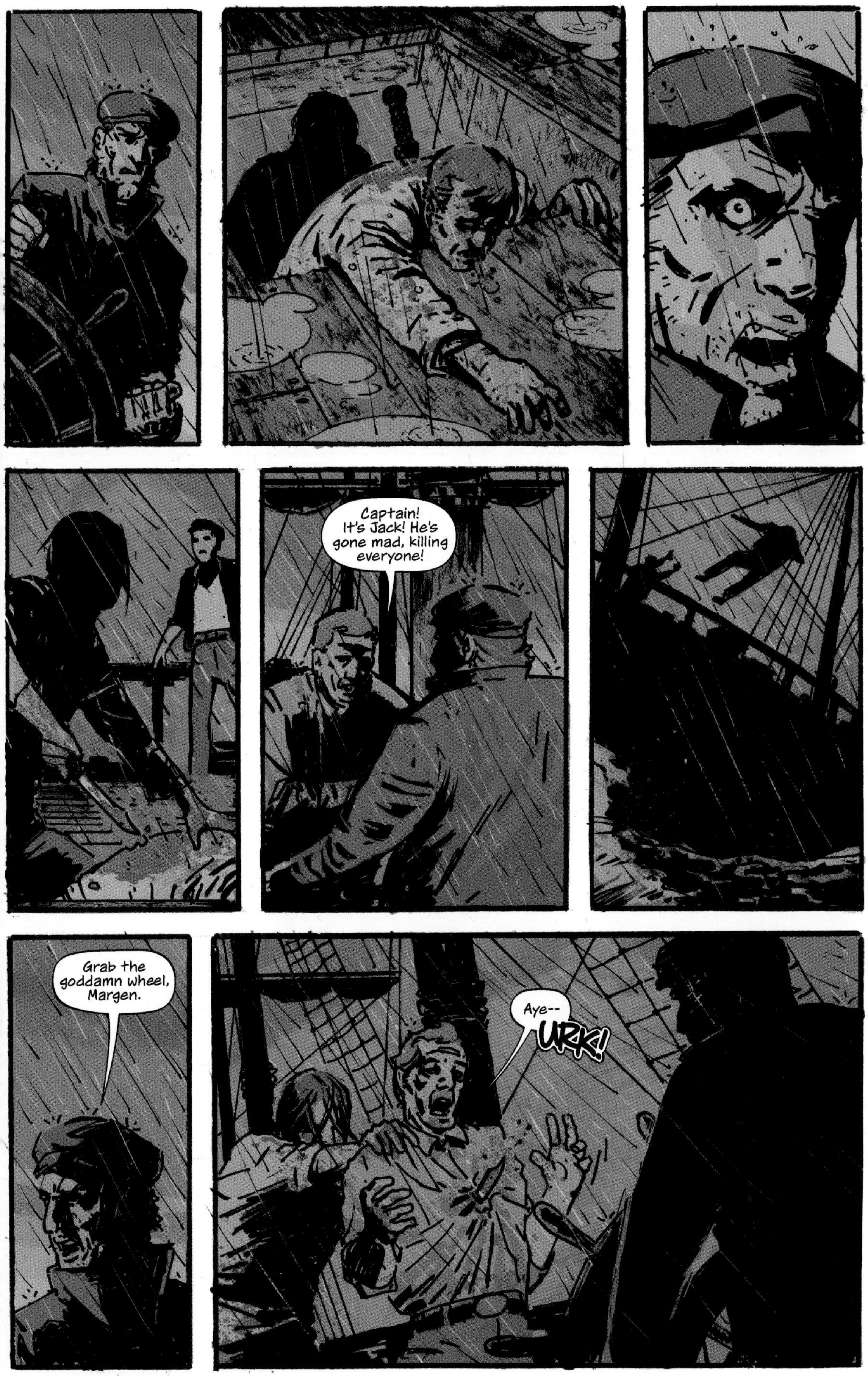
Captain! It's Jack! He's gone mad, killing everyone!
Grab the goddamn wheel, Margen.
Aye--
URK!

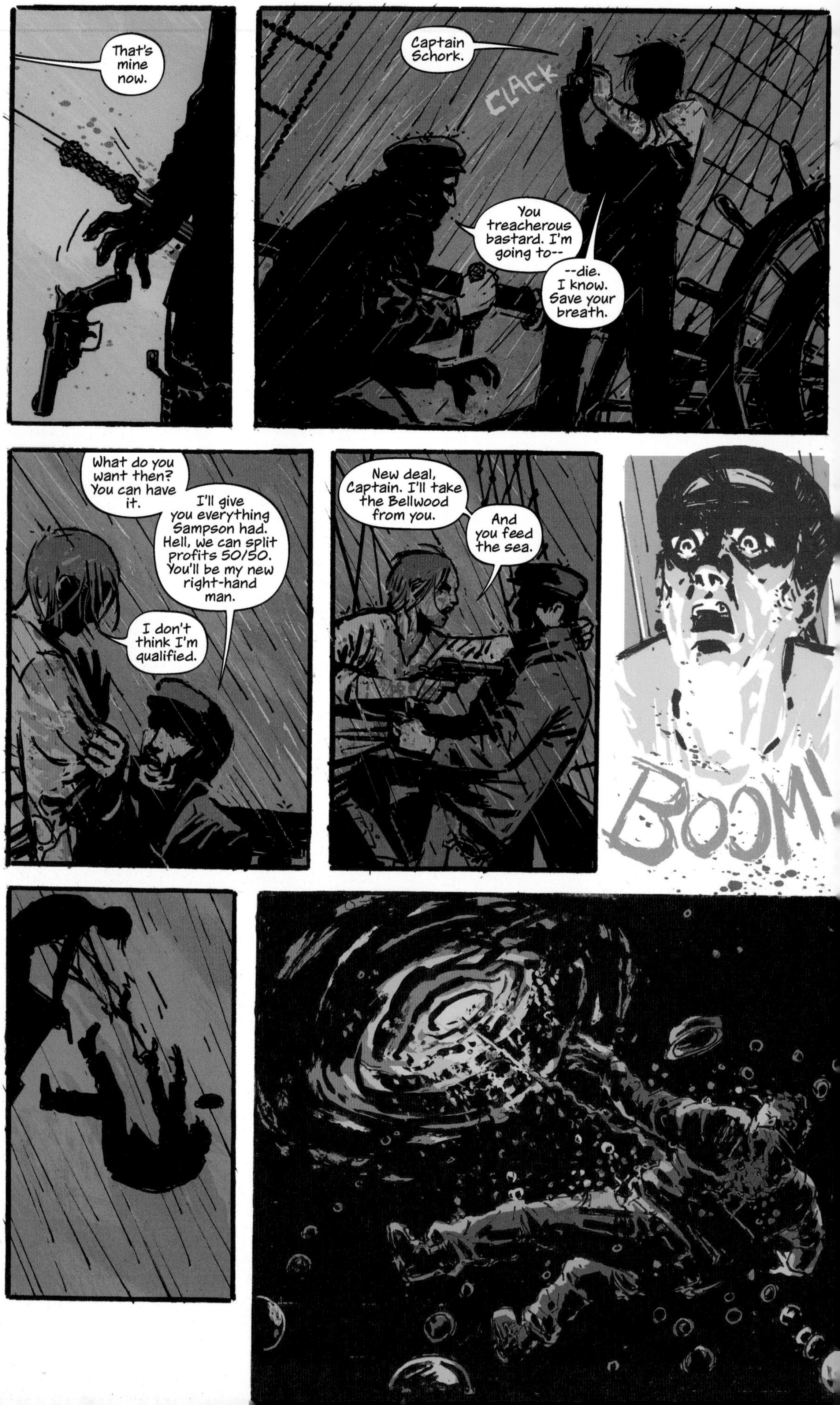

That's mine now.
Captain Schork.
CLACK
You treacherous bastard. I'm going to--
--die. I know. Save your breath.
What do you want then? You can have it.
I'll give you everything Sampson had. Hell, we can split profits 50/50. You'll be my new right-hand man.
I don't think I'm qualified.
New deal, Captain. I'll take the Bellwood from you.
And you feed the sea.
BOOM

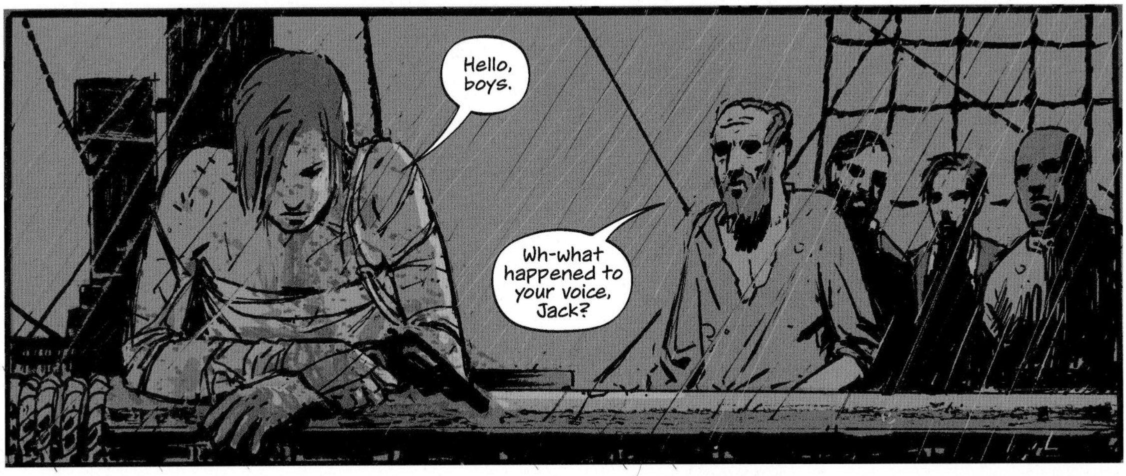
Hello, boys.
Wh-what happened to your voice, Jack?

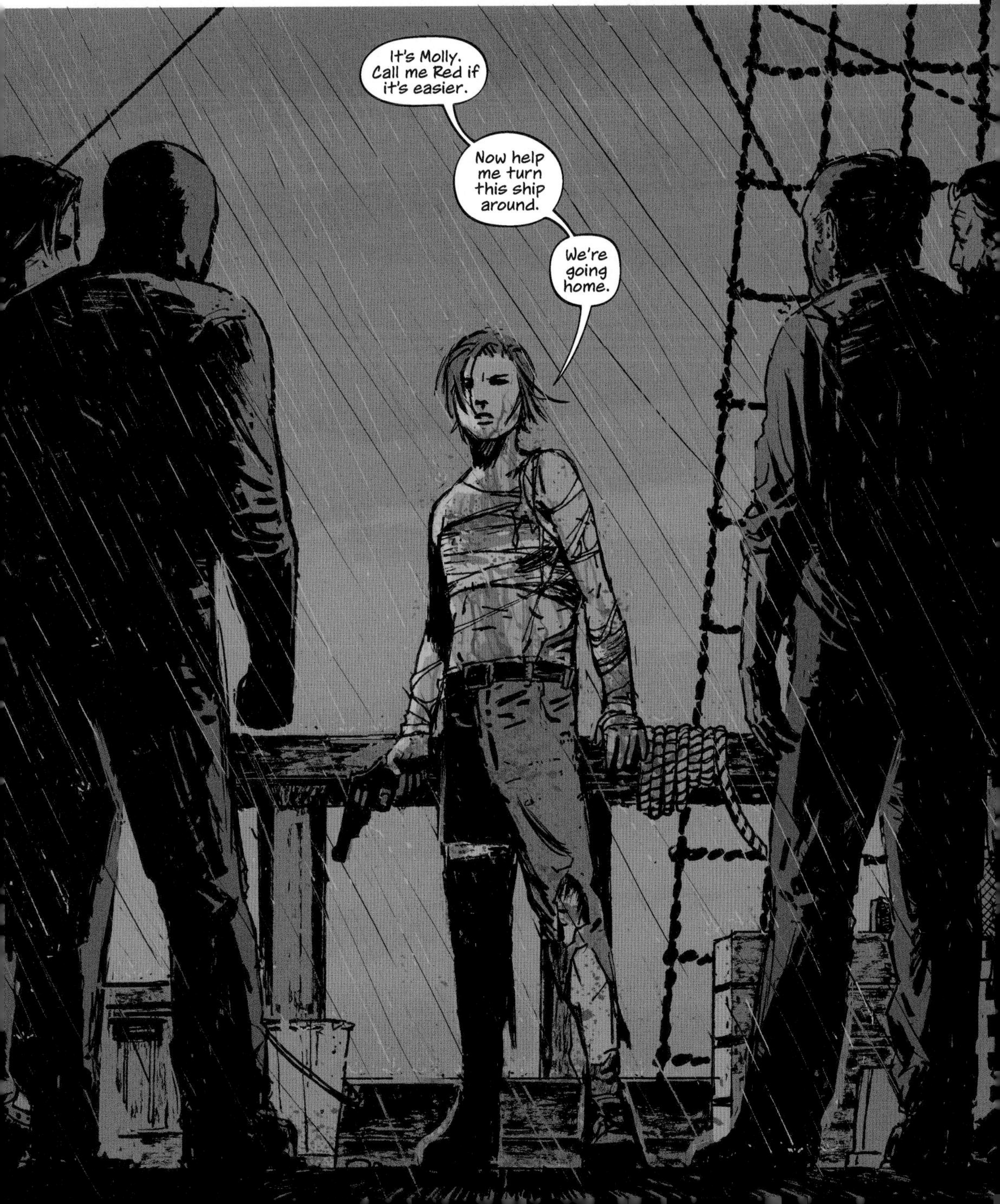
It's Molly. Call me Red if it's easier.
Now help me turn this ship around.
We're going home.

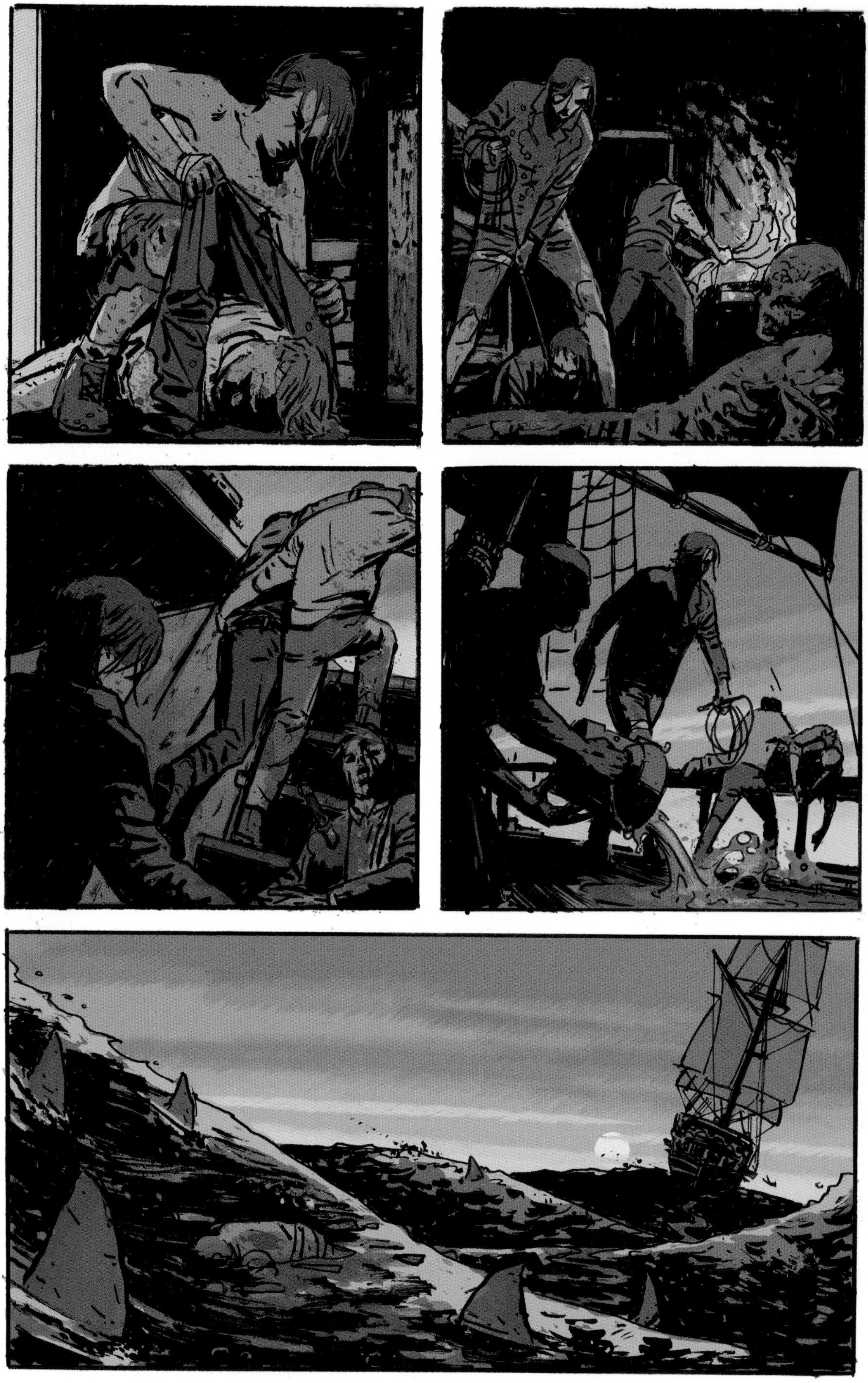

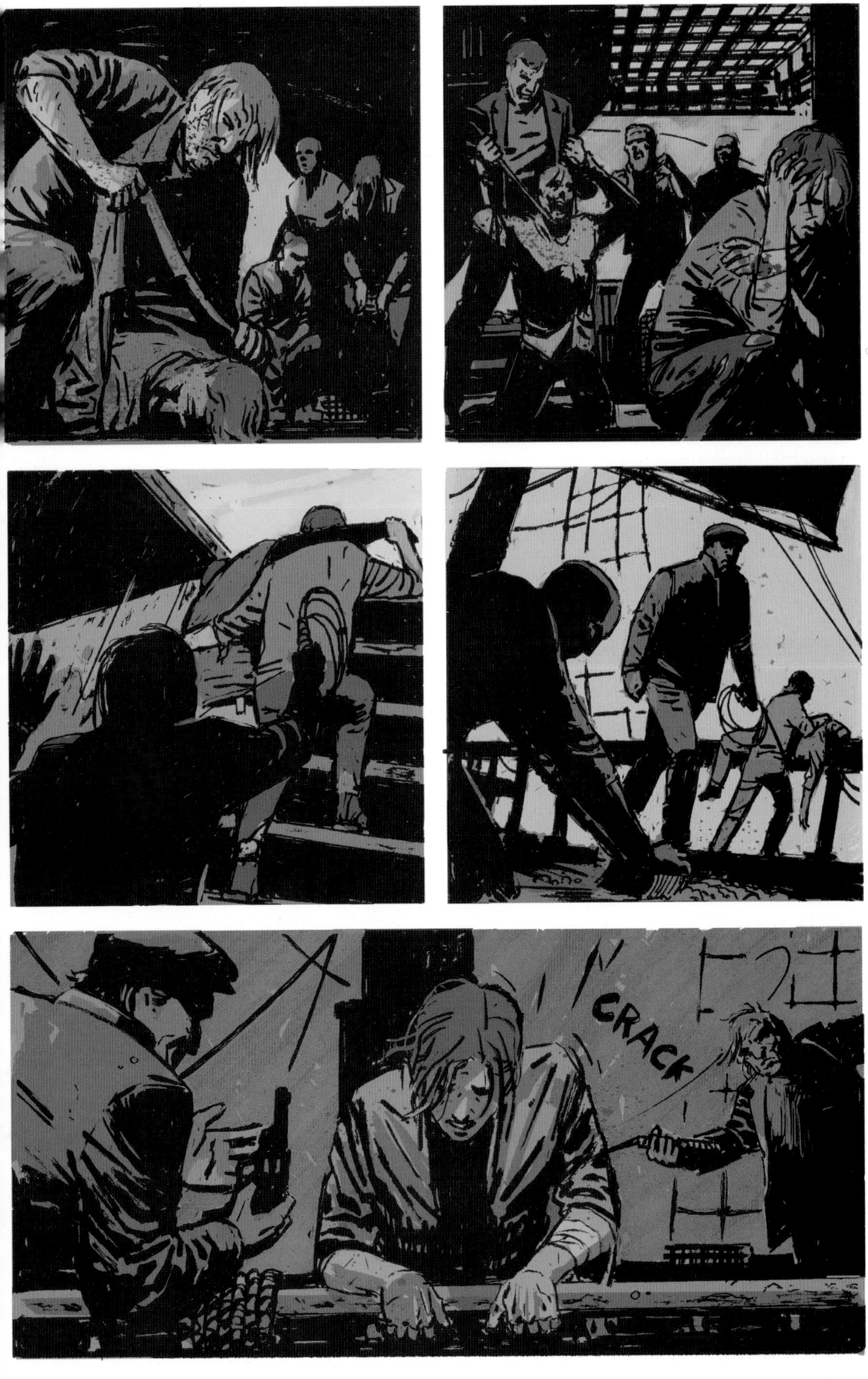
CRACK

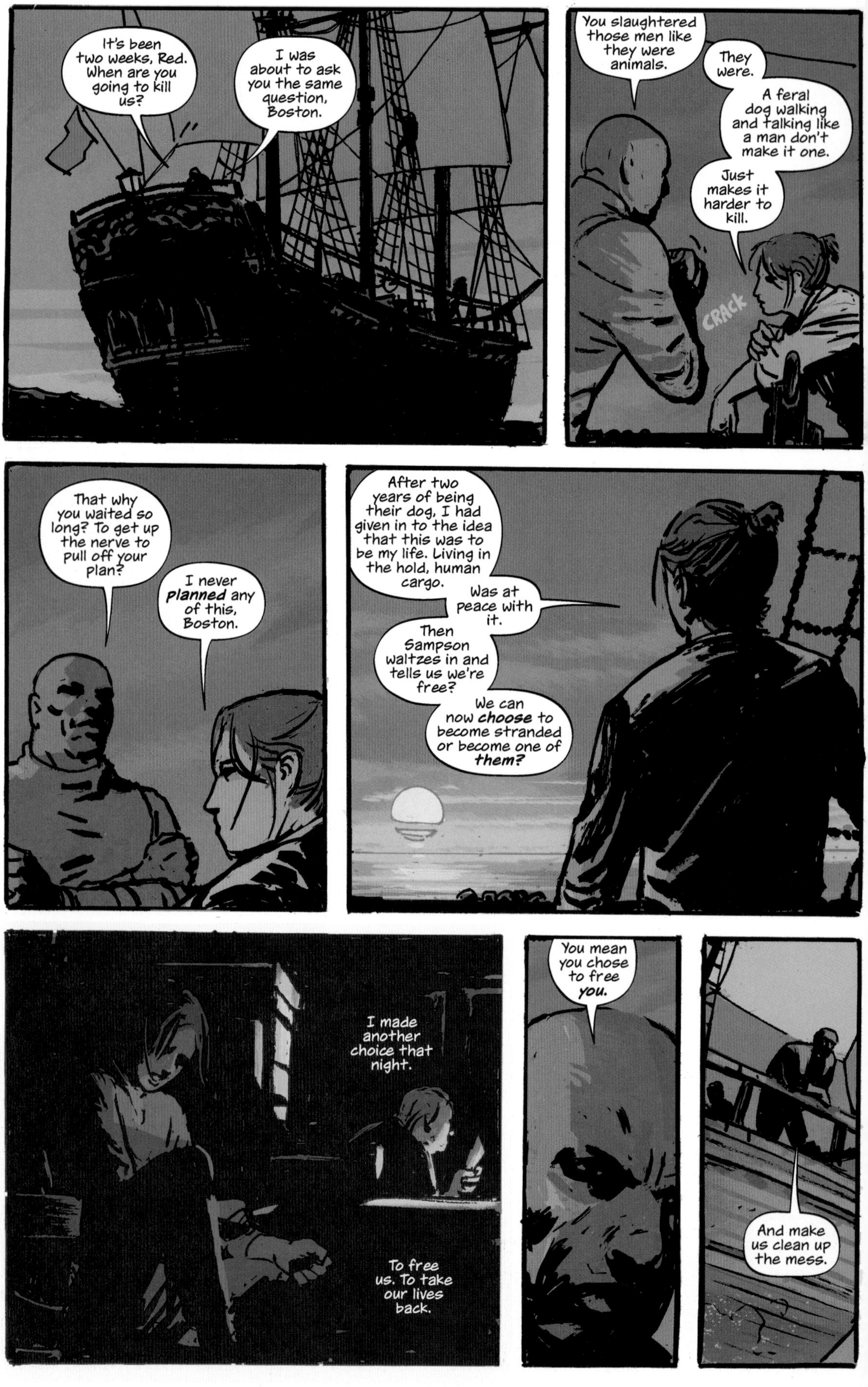
It's been two weeks, Red. When are you going to kill us?
I was about to ask you the same question, Boston.
You slaughtered those men like they were animals.
They were.
A feral dog walking and talking like a man don't make it one.
Just makes it harder to kill.
CRACK
That why you waited so long? To get up the nerve to pull off your plan?
I never **planned** any of this, Boston.
After two years of being their dog, I had given in to the idea that this was to be my life. Living in the hold, human cargo.
Was at peace with it.
Then Sampson waltzes in and tells us we're free?
We can now **choose** to become stranded or become one of **them?**
I made another choice that night.
To free us. To take our lives back.
You mean you chose to free **you.**
And make us clean up the mess.

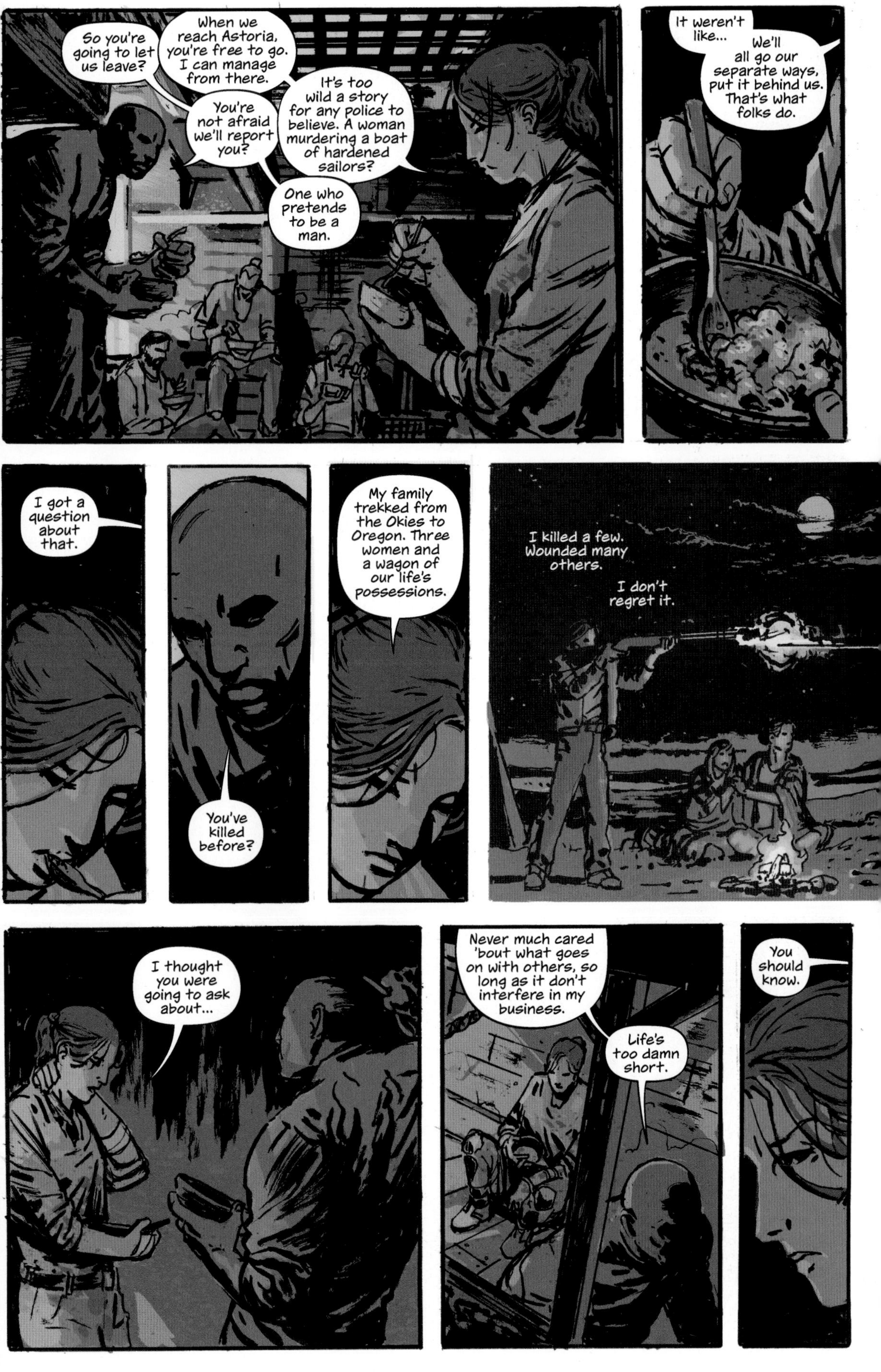
So you're going to let us leave?
When we reach Astoria, you're free to go. I can manage from there.
You're not afraid we'll report you?
It's too wild a story for any police to believe. A woman murdering a boat of hardened sailors?
One who pretends to be a man.
It weren't like...
We'll all go our separate ways, put it behind us. That's what folks do.
I got a question about that.
You've killed before?
My family trekked from the Okies to Oregon. Three women and a wagon of our life's possessions.
I killed a few. Wounded many others.
I don't regret it.
I thought you were going to ask about...
Never much cared 'bout what goes on with others, so long as it don't interfere in my business.
Life's too damn short.
You should know.

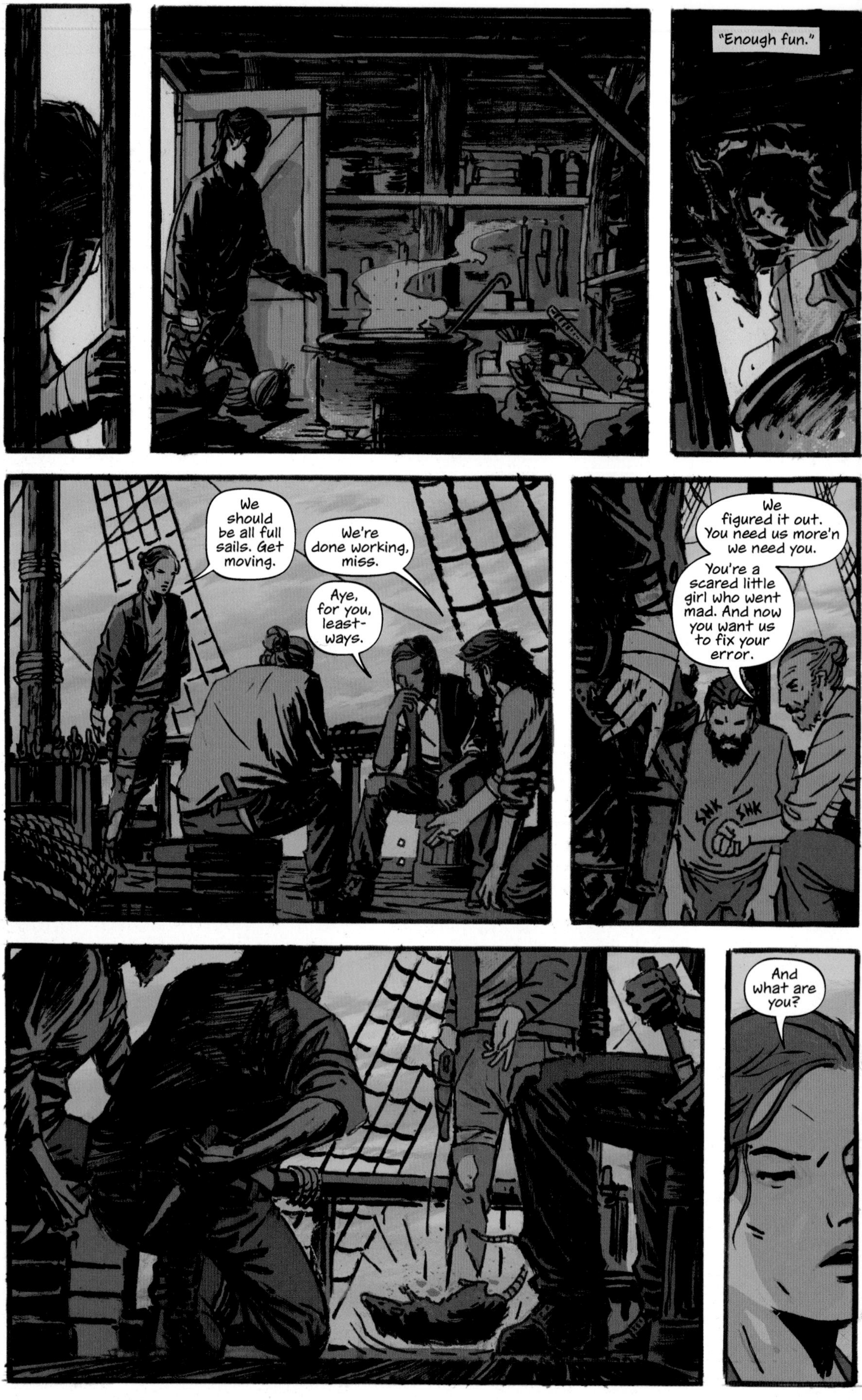

"Enough fun."
We should be all full sails. Get moving.
We're done working, miss.
Aye, for you, least-ways.
We figured it out. You need us more'n we need you.
You're a scared little girl who went mad. And now you want us to fix your error.
SHK
SHK
And what are you?

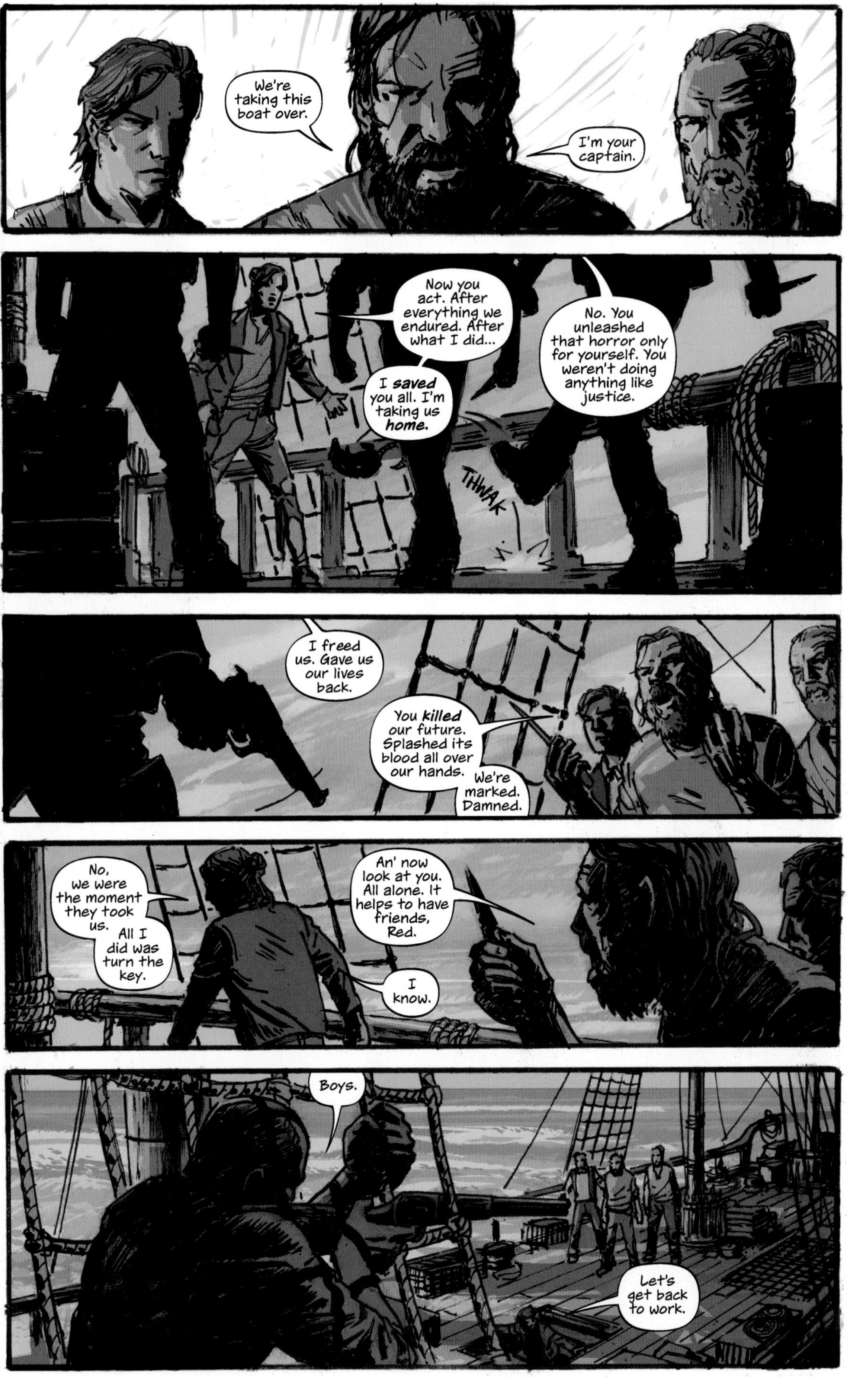
We're taking this boat over.
I'm your captain.
Now you act. After everything we endured. After what I did...
I saved you all. I'm taking us home.
No. You unleashed that horror only for yourself. You weren't doing anything like justice.
THWAK
I freed us. Gave us our lives back.
You killed our future. Splashed its blood all over our hands.
We're marked. Damned.
No, we were the moment they took us.
All I did was turn the key.
An' now look at you. All alone. It helps to have friends, Red.
I know.
Boys.
Let's get back to work.

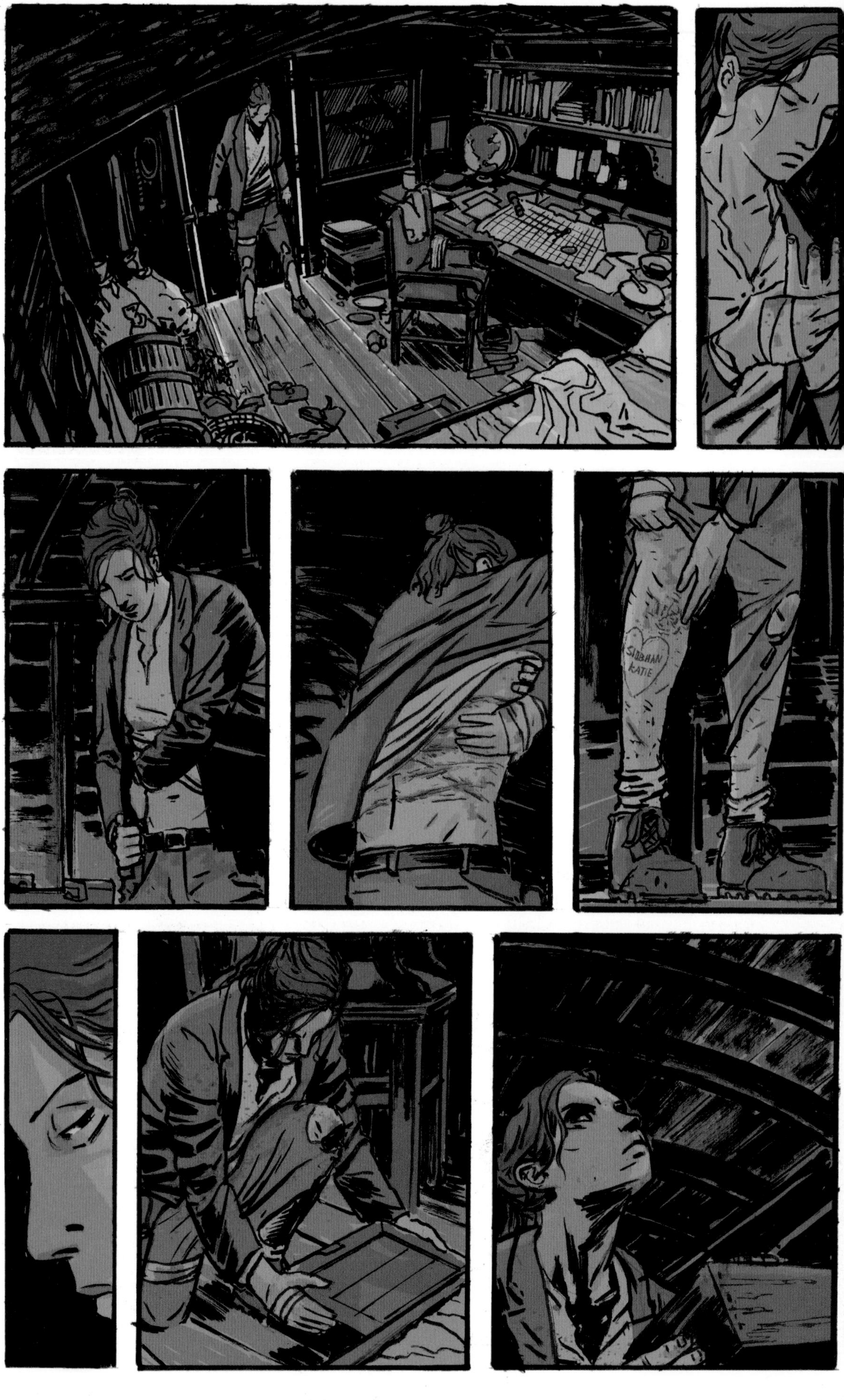
SIOBHAN
KATIE

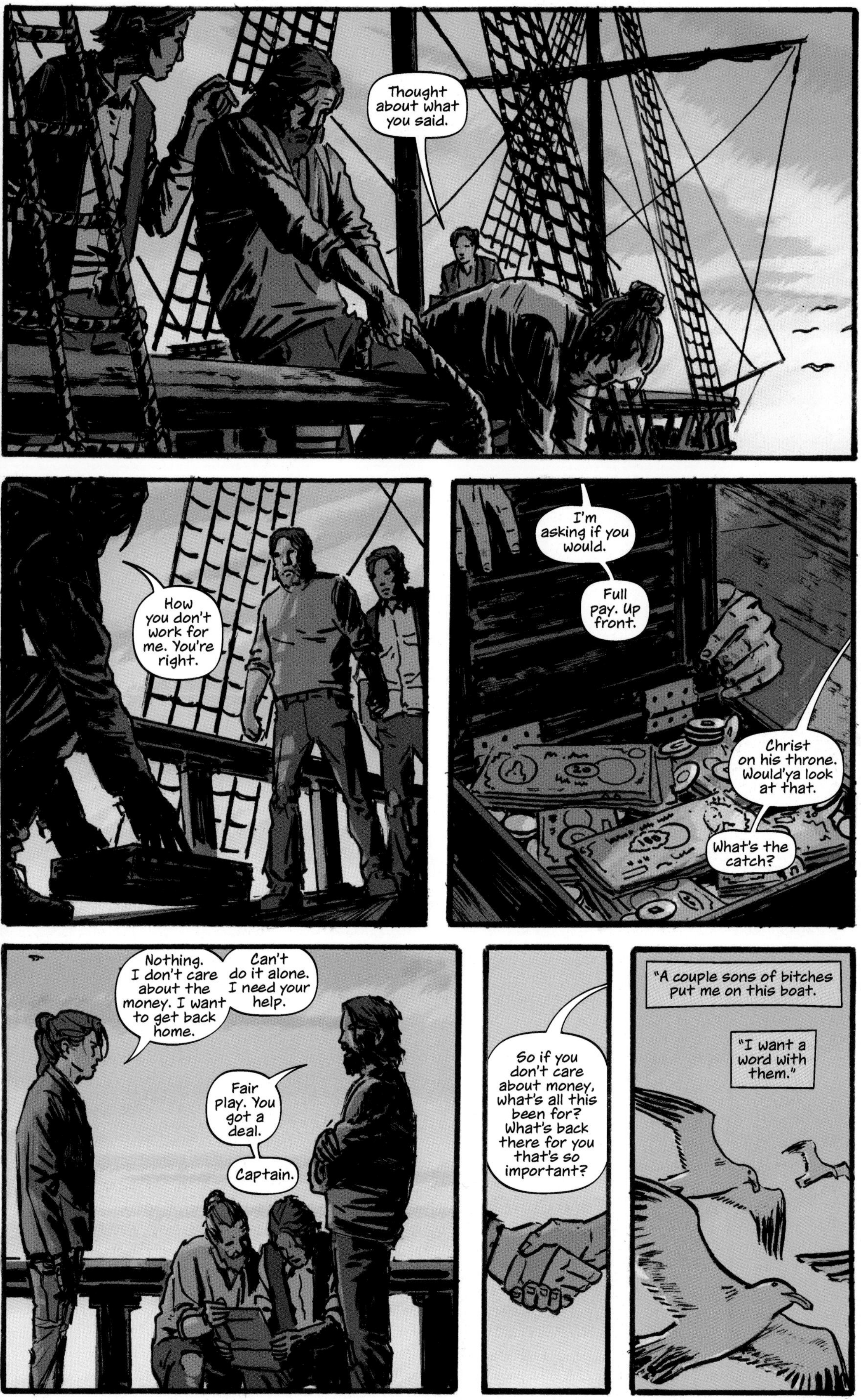
Thought about what you said.
How you don't work for me. You're right.
I'm asking if you would.
Full pay. Up front.
Christ on his throne. Would'ya look at that.
What's the catch?
Nothing. I don't care about the money. I want to get back home.
Can't do it alone. I need your help.
Fair play. You got a deal.
Captain.
So if you don't care about money, what's all this been for? What's back there for you that's so important?
"A couple sons of bitches put me on this boat.
"I want a word with them."

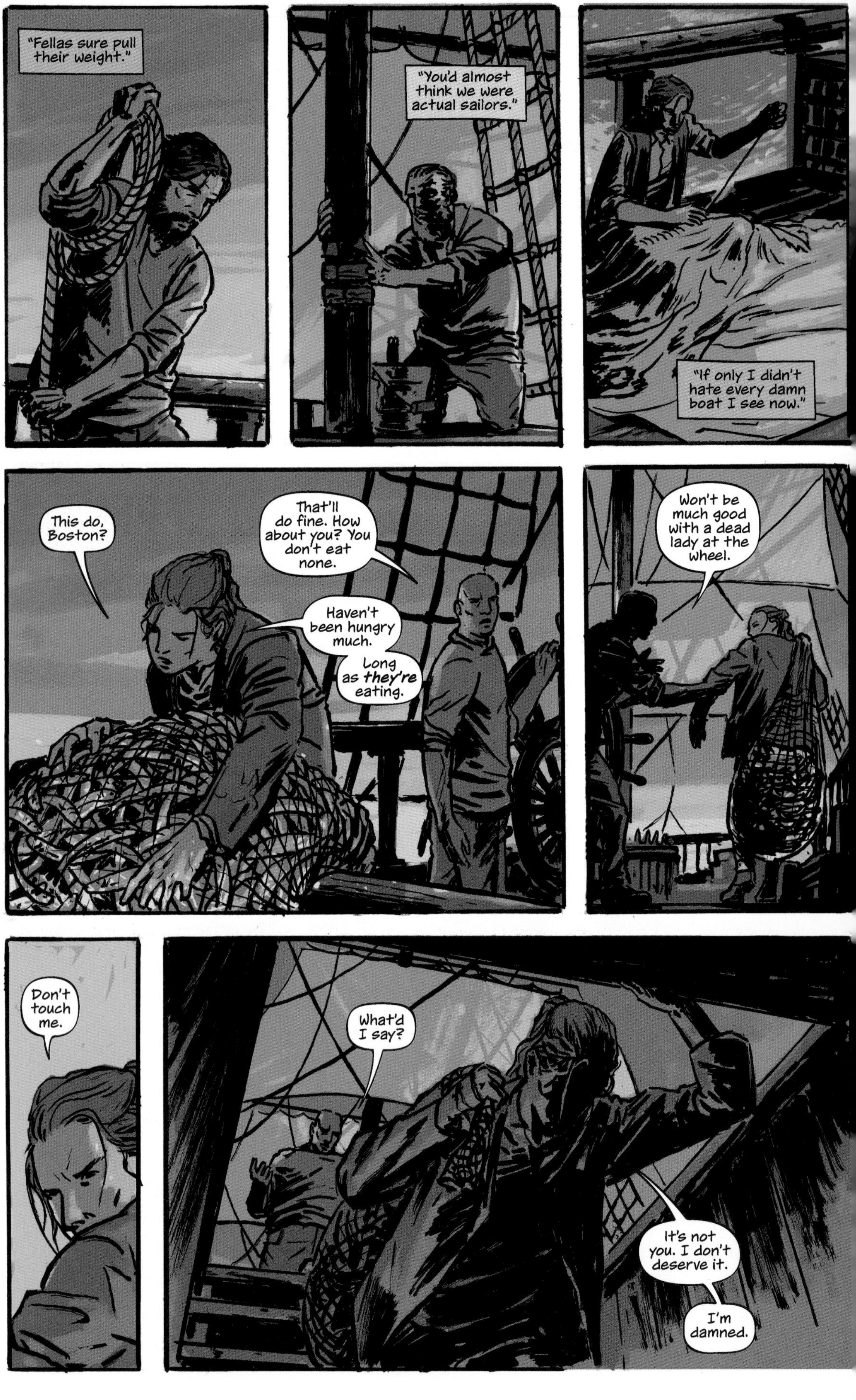
"Fellas sure pull their weight."
"You'd almost think we were actual sailors."
"If only I didn't hate every damn boat I see now."
This do, Boston?
That'll do fine. How about you? You don't eat none.
Haven't been hungry much.
Long as *they're* eating.
Won't be much good with a dead lady at the wheel.
Don't touch me.
What'd I say?
It's not you. I don't deserve it.
I'm damned.

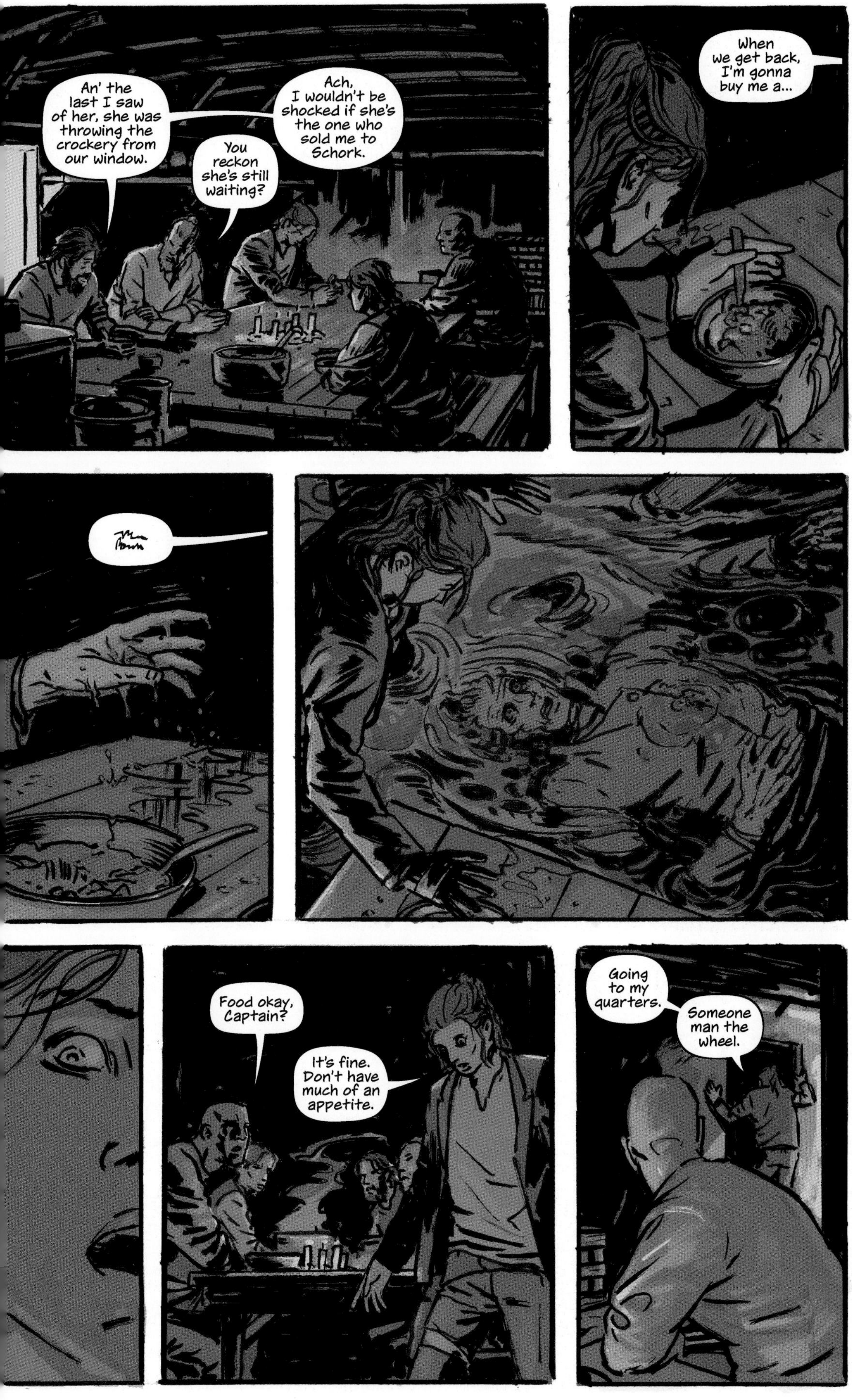
An' the last I saw of her, she was throwing the crockery from our window.
You reckon she's still waiting?
Ach, I wouldn't be shocked if she's the one who sold me to Schork.
When we get back, I'm gonna buy me a...
Food okay, Captain?
It's fine. Don't have much of an appetite.
Going to my quarters.
Someone man the wheel.

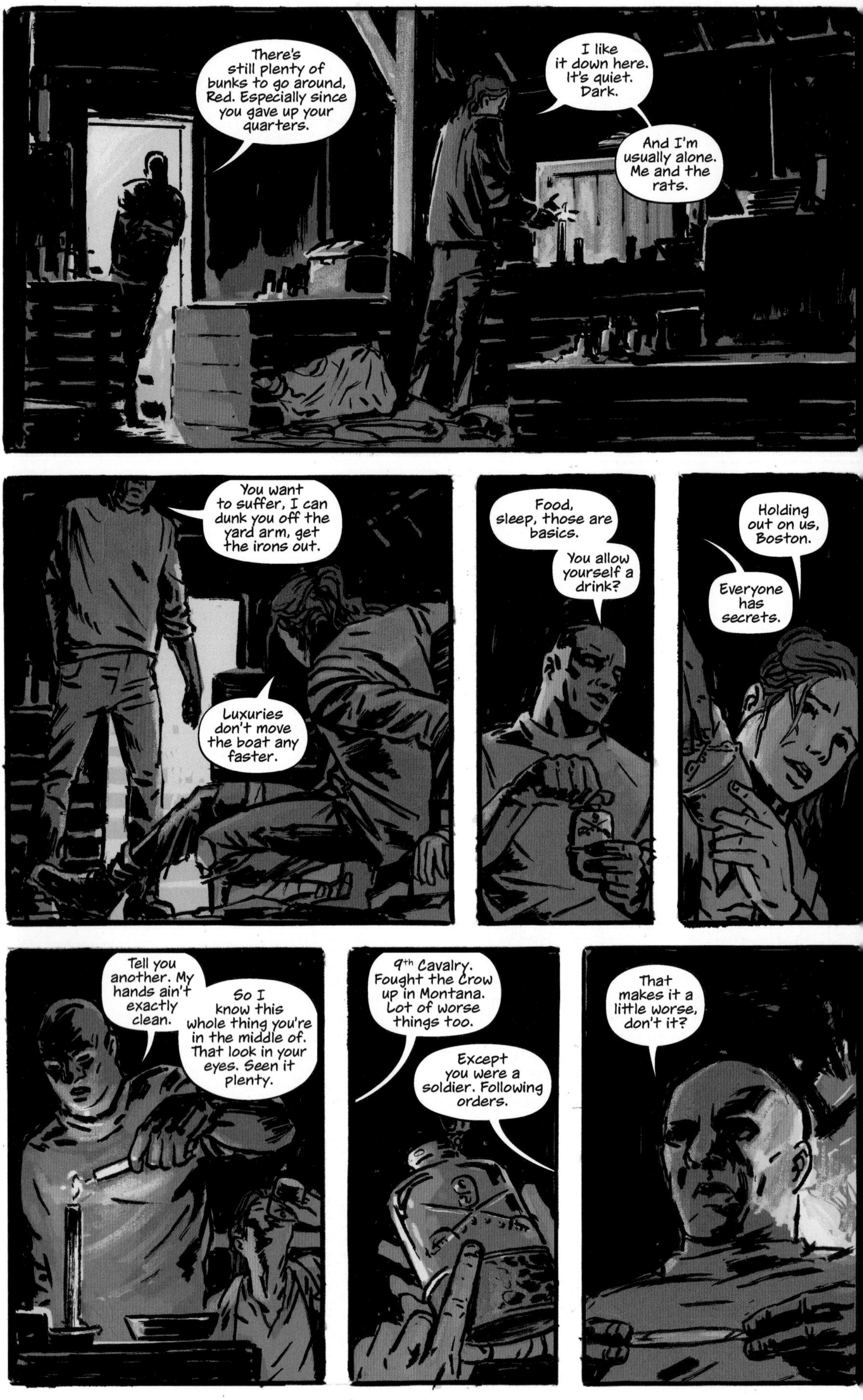
There's still plenty of bunks to go around, Red. Especially since you gave up your quarters.
I like it down here. It's quiet. Dark.
And I'm usually alone. Me and the rats.
You want to suffer, I can dunk you off the yard arm, get the irons out.
Luxuries don't move the boat any faster.
Food, sleep, those are basics.
You allow yourself a drink?
Holding out on us, Boston.
Everyone has secrets.
Tell you another. My hands ain't exactly clean.
So I know this whole thing you're in the middle of. That look in your eyes. Seen it plenty.
9th Cavalry. Fought the Crow up in Montana. Lot of worse things too.
Except you were a soldier. Following orders.
That makes it a little worse, don't it?

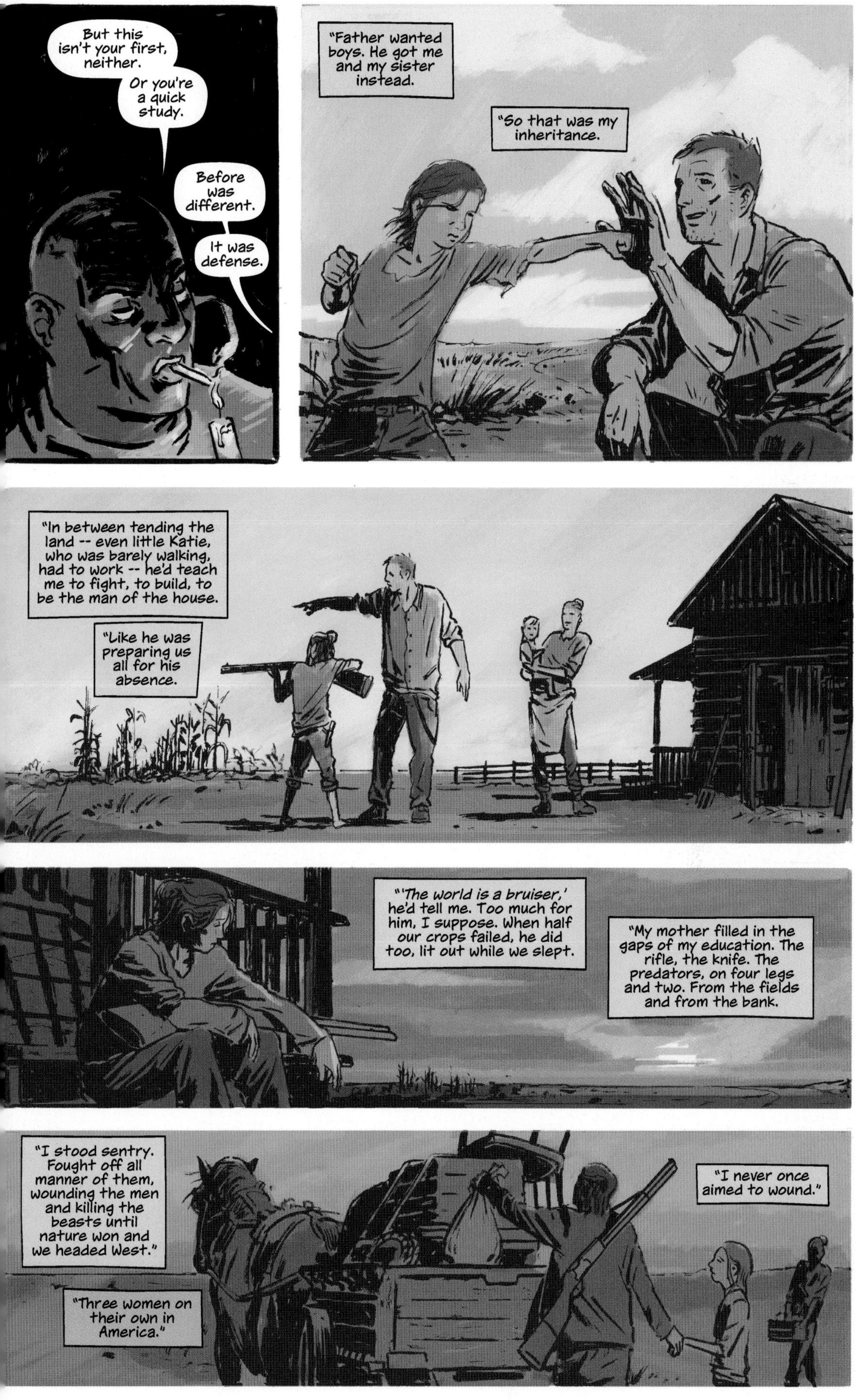
But this isn't your first, neither.
Or you're a quick study.
Before was different.
It was defense.
"Father wanted boys. He got me and my sister instead.
"So that was my inheritance.
"In between tending the land -- even little Katie, who was barely walking, had to work -- he'd teach me to fight, to build, to be the man of the house.
"Like he was preparing us all for his absence.
"'The world is a bruiser,' he'd tell me. Too much for him, I suppose. When half our crops failed, he did too, lit out while we slept.
"My mother filled in the gaps of my education. The rifle, the knife. The predators, on four legs and two. From the fields and from the bank.
"I stood sentry. Fought off all manner of them, wounding the men and killing the beasts until nature won and we headed West."
"Three women on their own in America."
"I never once aimed to wound."

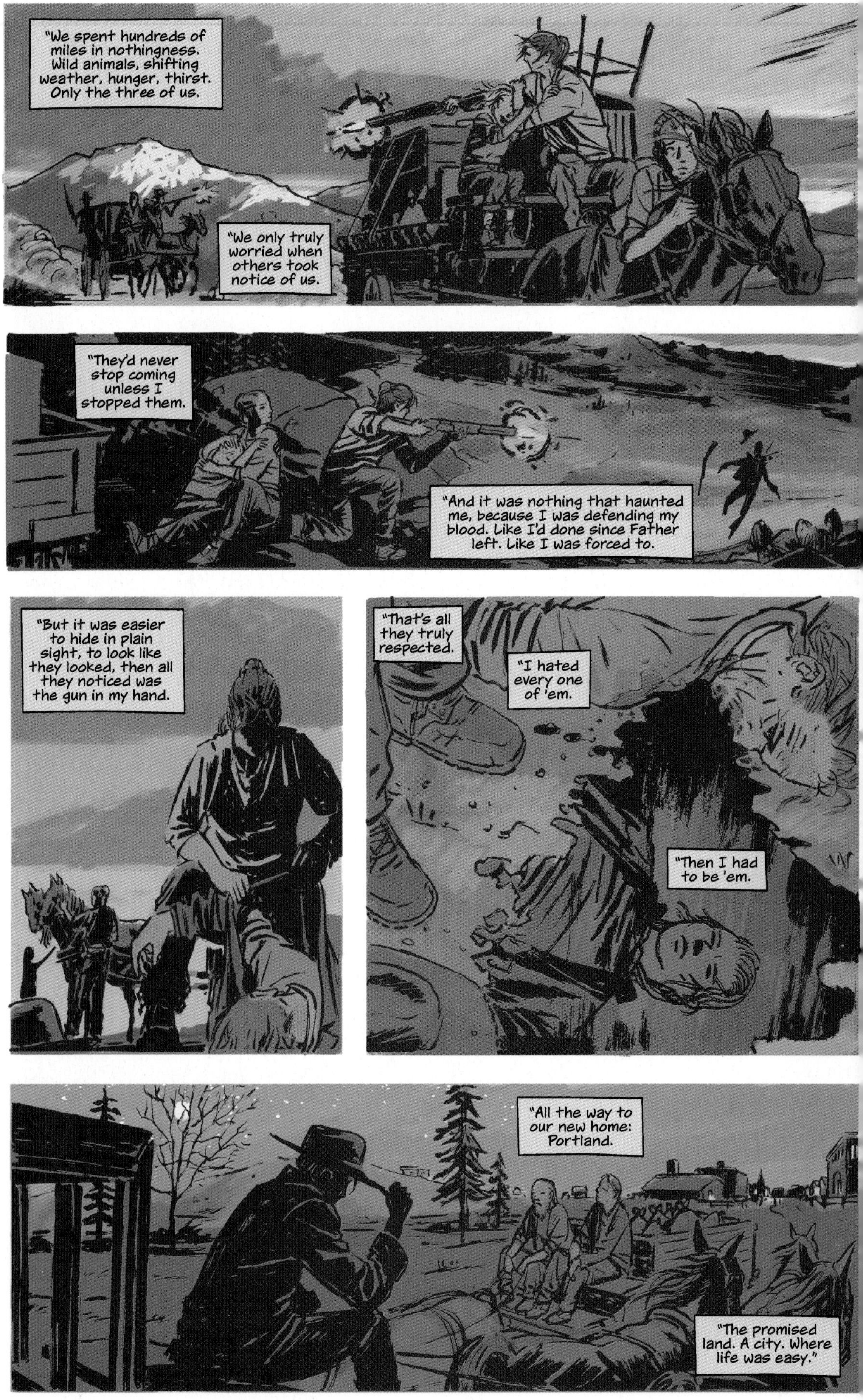
"We spent hundreds of miles in nothingness. Wild animals, shifting weather, hunger, thirst. Only the three of us.
"We only truly worried when others took notice of us.
"They'd never stop coming unless I stopped them.
"And it was nothing that haunted me, because I was defending my blood. Like I'd done since Father left. Like I was forced to.
"But it was easier to hide in plain sight, to look like they looked, then all they noticed was the gun in my hand.
"That's all they truly respected.
"I hated every one of 'em.
"Then I had to be 'em.
"All the way to our new home: Portland.
"The promised land. A city. Where life was easy."

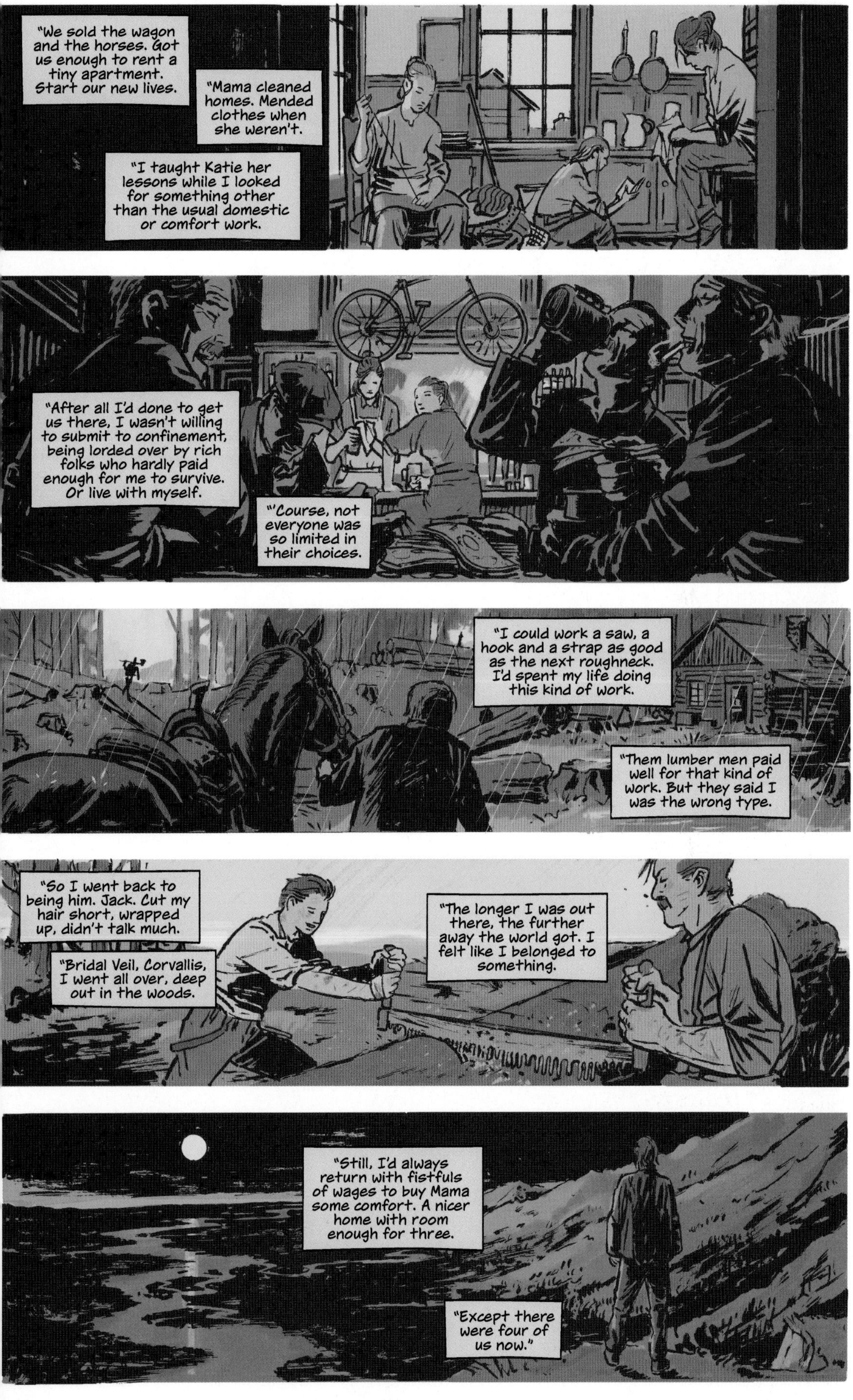
"We sold the wagon and the horses. Got us enough to rent a tiny apartment. Start our new lives.
"Mama cleaned homes. Mended clothes when she weren't.
"I taught Katie her lessons while I looked for something other than the usual domestic or comfort work.
"After all I'd done to get us there, I wasn't willing to submit to confinement, being lorded over by rich folks who hardly paid enough for me to survive. Or live with myself.
"'Course, not everyone was so limited in their choices.
"I could work a saw, a hook and a strap as good as the next roughneck. I'd spent my life doing this kind of work.
"Them lumber men paid well for that kind of work. But they said I was the wrong type.
"So I went back to being him. Jack. Cut my hair short, wrapped up, didn't talk much.
"Bridal Veil, Corvallis, I went all over, deep out in the woods.
"The longer I was out there, the further away the world got. I felt like I belonged to something.
"Still, I'd always return with fistfuls of wages to buy Mama some comfort. A nicer home with room enough for three.
"Except there were four of us now."

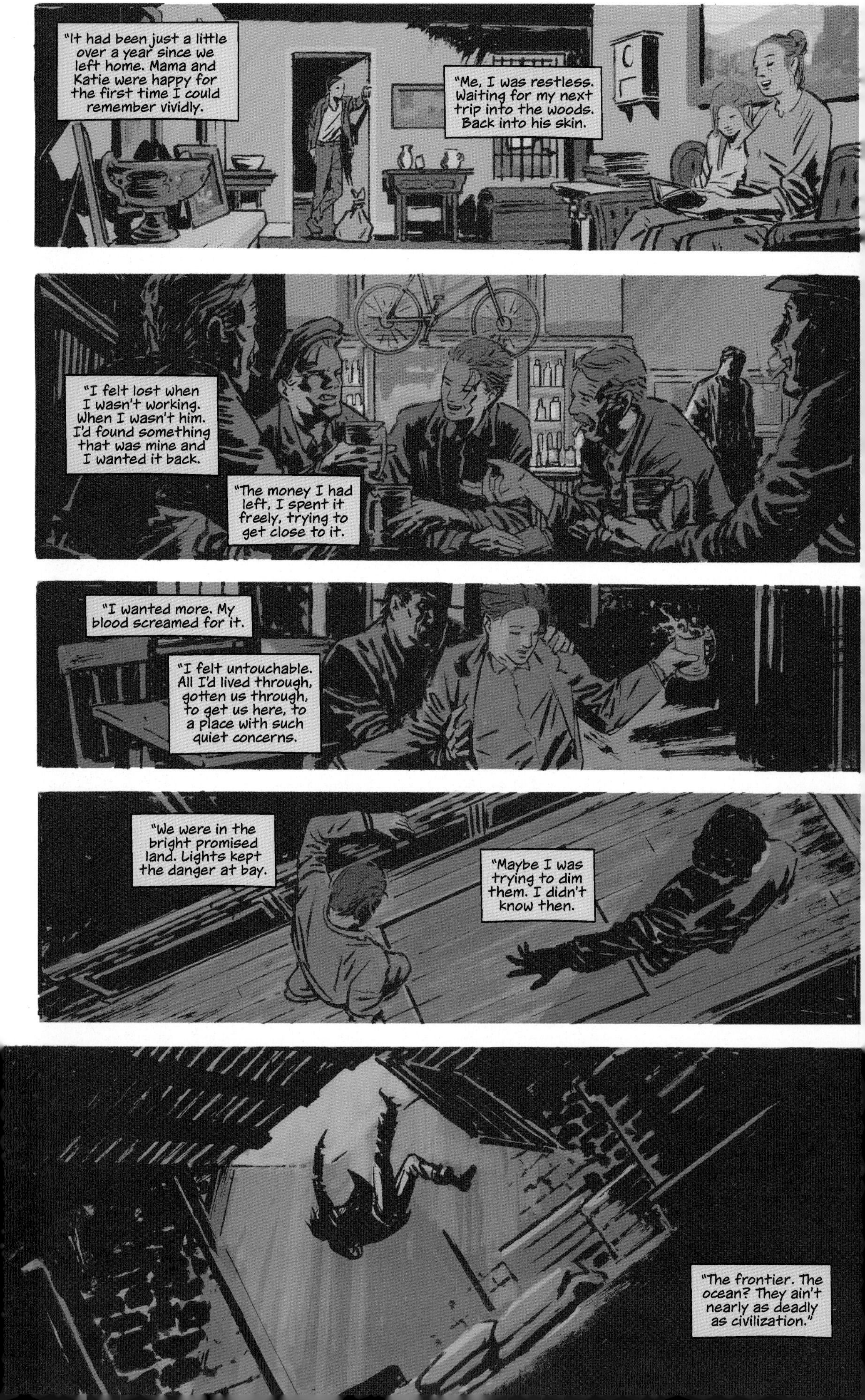
"It had been just a little over a year since we left home. Mama and Katie were happy for the first time I could remember vividly.
"Me, I was restless. Waiting for my next trip into the woods. Back into his skin.
"I felt lost when I wasn't working. When I wasn't him. I'd found something that was mine and I wanted it back.
"The money I had left, I spent it freely, trying to get close to it.
"I wanted more. My blood screamed for it.
"I felt untouchable. All I'd lived through, gotten us through, to get us here, to a place with such quiet concerns.
"We were in the bright promised land. Lights kept the danger at bay.
"Maybe I was trying to dim them. I didn't know then.
"The frontier. The ocean? They ain't nearly as deadly as civilization."

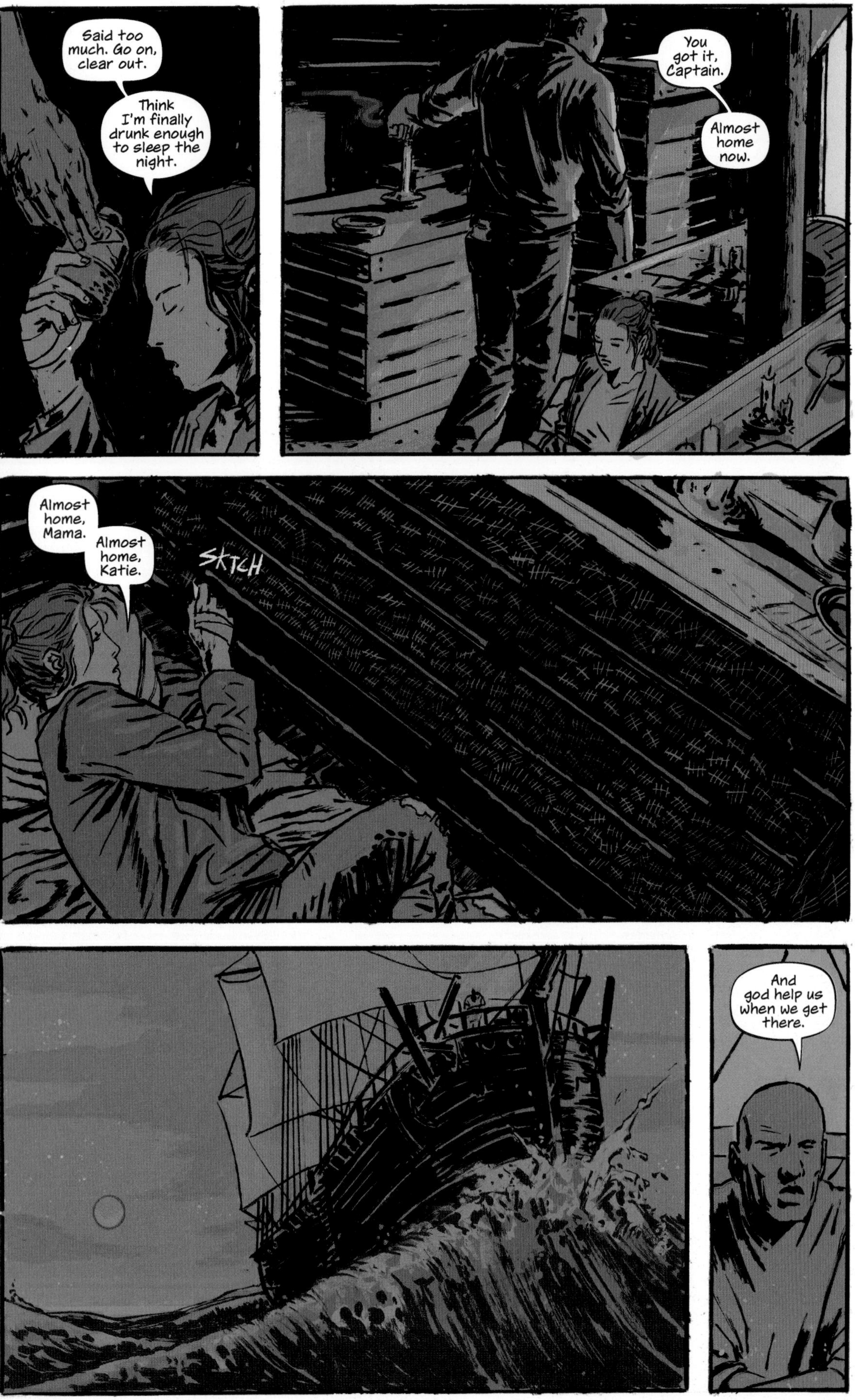
Said too much. Go on, clear out.
Think I'm finally drunk enough to sleep the night.
You got it, Captain.
Almost home now.
Almost home, Mama.
Almost home, Katie.
SKTCH
And god help us when we get there.

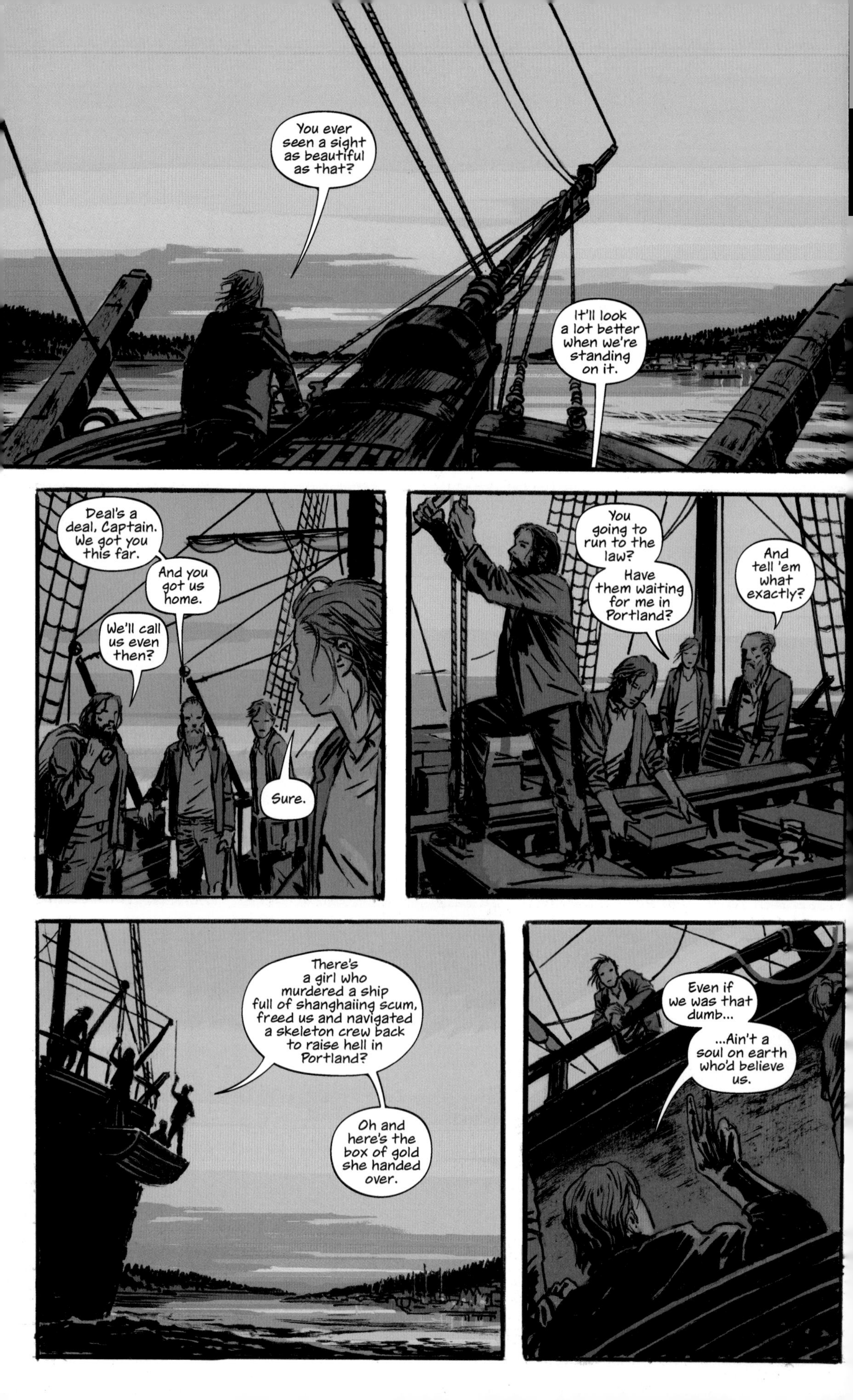
You ever seen a sight as beautiful as that?
It'll look a lot better when we're standing on it.
Deal's a deal, Captain. We got you this far.
And you got us home.
We'll call us even then?
Sure.
You going to run to the law?
Have them waiting for me in Portland?
And tell 'em what exactly?
There's a girl who murdered a ship full of shanghaiing scum, freed us and navigated a skeleton crew back to raise hell in Portland?
Oh and here's the box of gold she handed over.
Even if we was that dumb...
...Ain't a soul on earth who'd believe us.

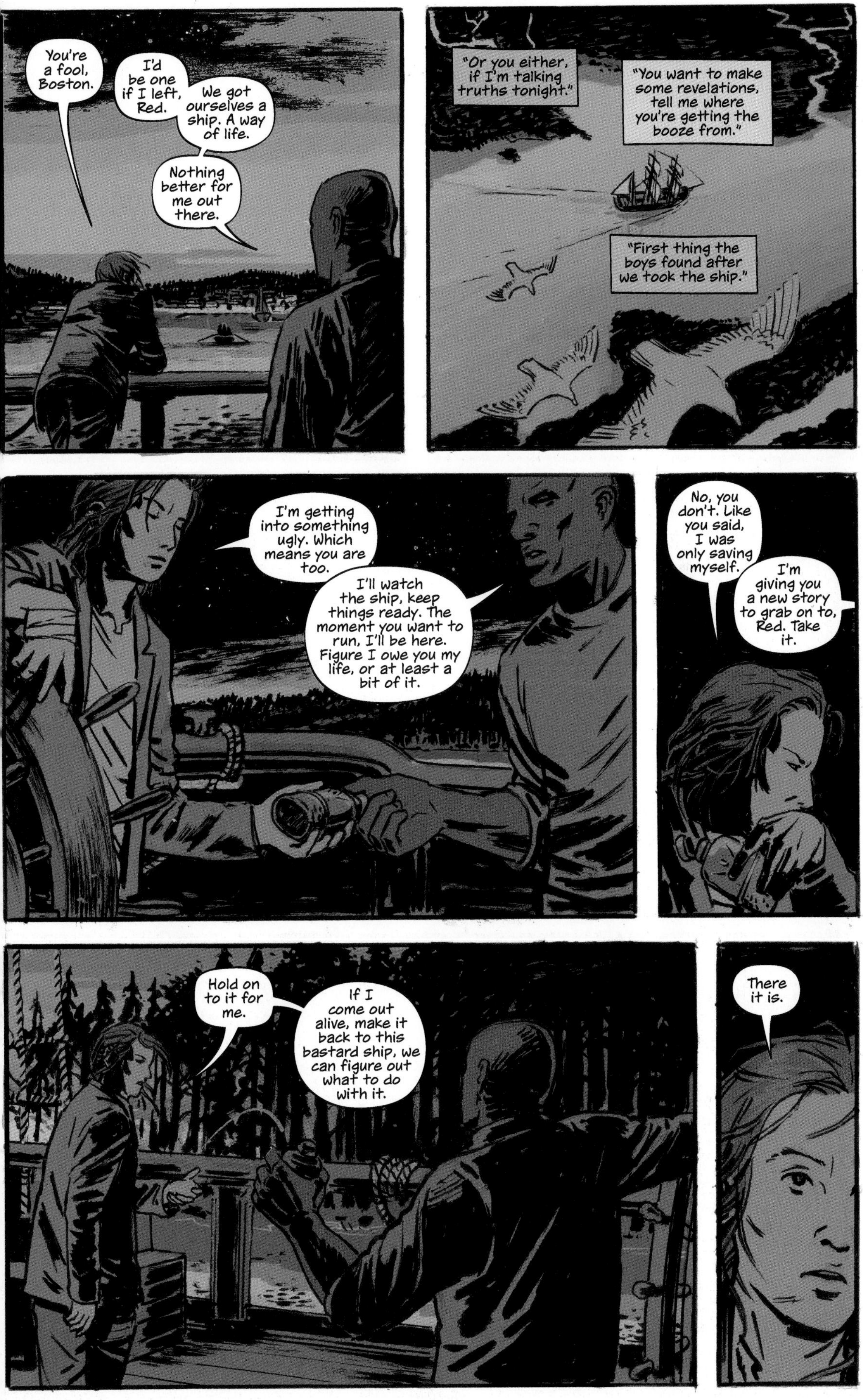
You're a fool, Boston.
I'd be one if I left, Red.
We got ourselves a ship. A way of life.
Nothing better for me out there.
"Or you either, if I'm talking truths tonight."
"You want to make some revelations, tell me where you're getting the booze from."
"First thing the boys found after we took the ship."
I'm getting into something ugly. Which means you are too.
I'll watch the ship, keep things ready. The moment you want to run, I'll be here. Figure I owe you my life, or at least a bit of it.
No, you don't. Like you said, I was only saving myself.
I'm giving you a new story to grab on to, Red. Take it.
Hold on to it for me.
If I come out alive, make it back to this bastard ship, we can figure out what to do with it.
There it is.

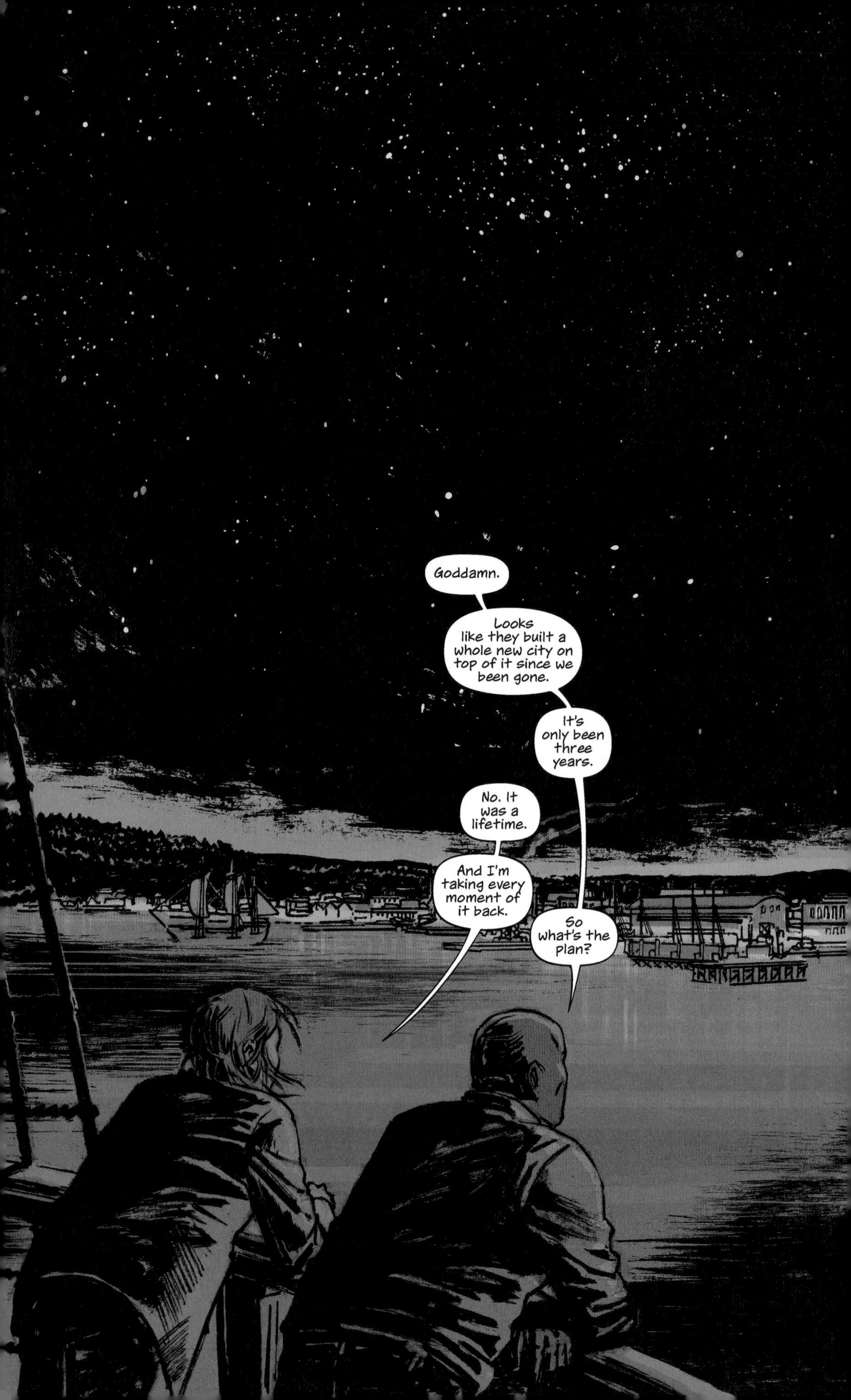
Goddamn.
Looks like they built a whole new city on top of it since we been gone.
It's only been three years.
No. It was a lifetime.
And I'm taking every moment of it back.
So what's the plan?

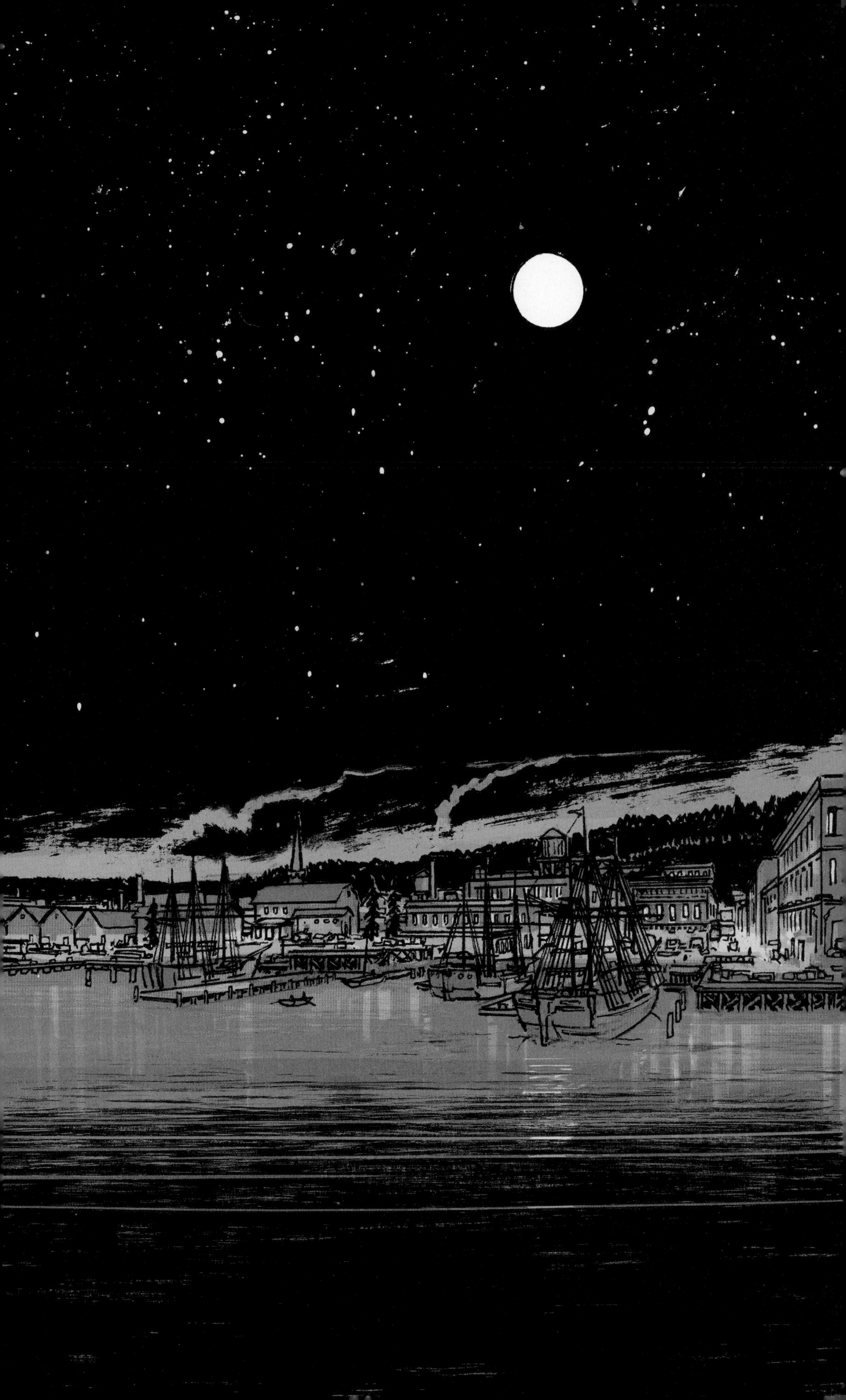

"I find my mother. My sister. They stole that from me too. Only thing that was ever mine."

"Then I go find the ones who did this to me."

"And do what? Rob 'em? Arrest 'em?"

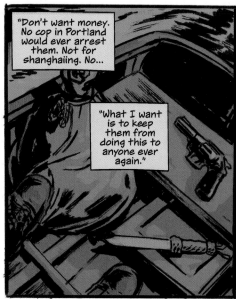

"Don't want money. No cop in Portland would ever arrest them. Not for shanghaiing. No..."

"What I want is to keep them from doing this to anyone ever again."

"Murder, you mean. You came all this way to kill a man."

"Men. As many of them as I can get on the other end of my gun."

"You ain't afraid?"

"Of doing this? No.

"But then, I'm not the one who should be scared."

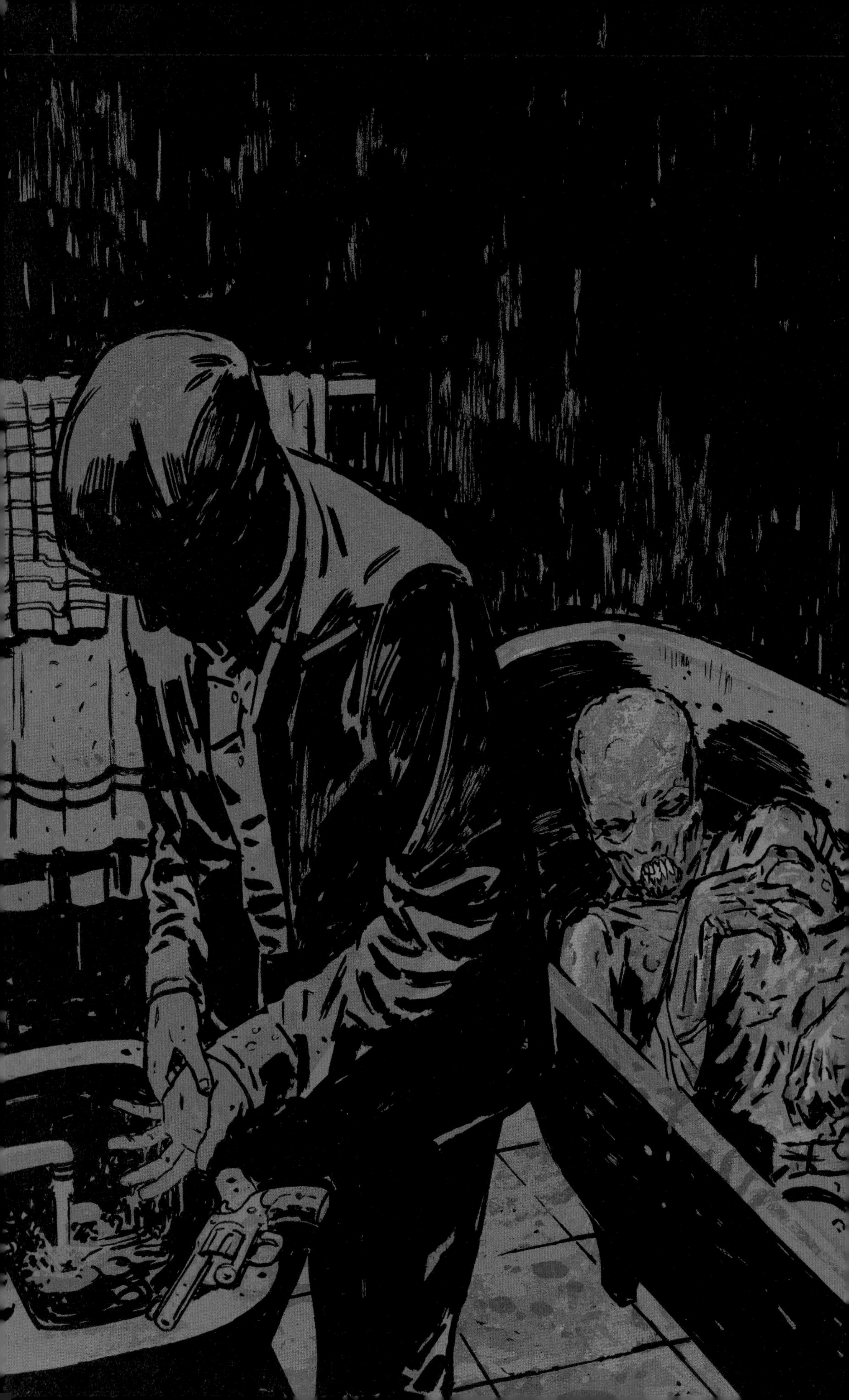

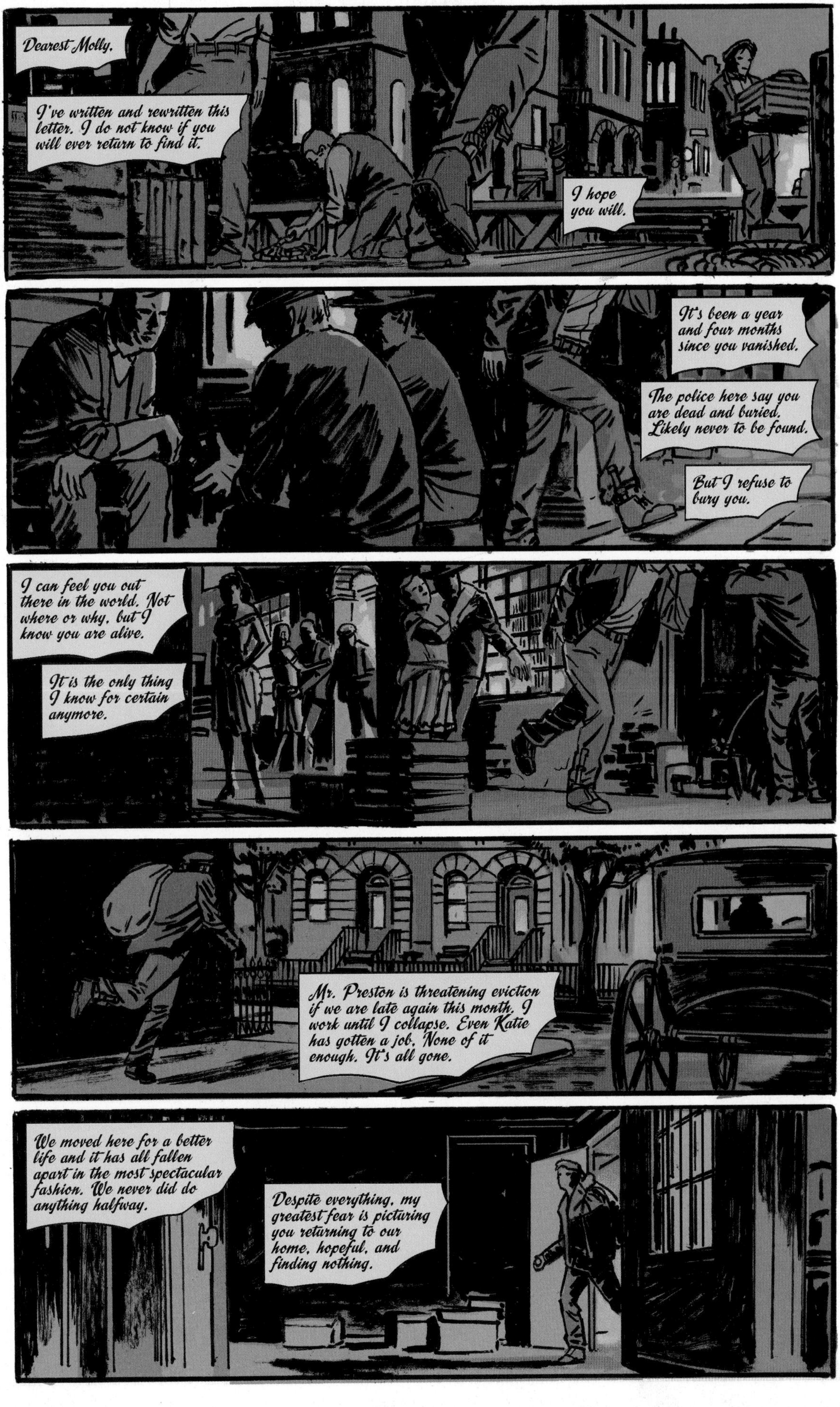
Dearest Molly.
I've written and rewritten this letter. I do not know if you will ever return to find it.
I hope you will.
It's been a year and four months since you vanished.
The police here say you are dead and buried. Likely never to be found.
But I refuse to bury you.
I can feel you out there in the world. Not where or why, but I know you are alive.
It is the only thing I know for certain anymore.
Mr. Preston is threatening eviction if we are late again this month. I work until I collapse. Even Katie has gotten a job. None of it enough. It's all gone.
We moved here for a better life and it has all fallen apart in the most spectacular fashion. We never did do anything halfway.
Despite everything, my greatest fear is picturing you returning to our home, hopeful, and finding nothing.

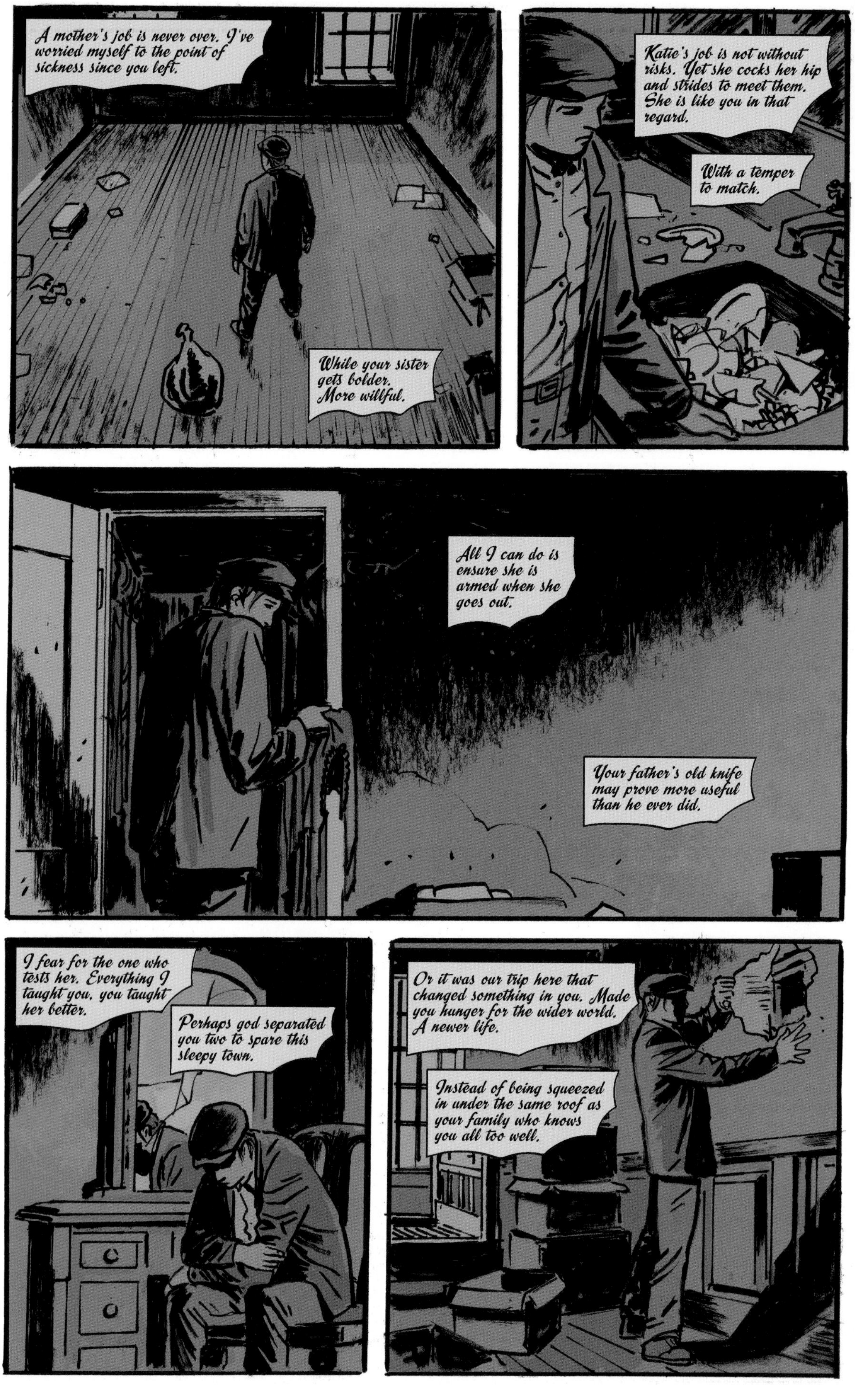
A mother's job is never over. I've worried myself to the point of sickness since you left.
While your sister gets bolder. More willful.
Katie's job is not without risks. Yet she cocks her hip and strides to meet them. She is like you in that regard.
With a temper to match.
All I can do is ensure she is armed when she goes out.
Your father's old knife may prove more useful than he ever did.
I fear for the one who tests her. Everything I taught you, you taught her better.
Perhaps god separated you two to spare this sleepy town.
Or it was our trip here that changed something in you. Made you hunger for the wider world. A newer life.
Instead of being squeezed in under the same roof as your family who knows you all too well.

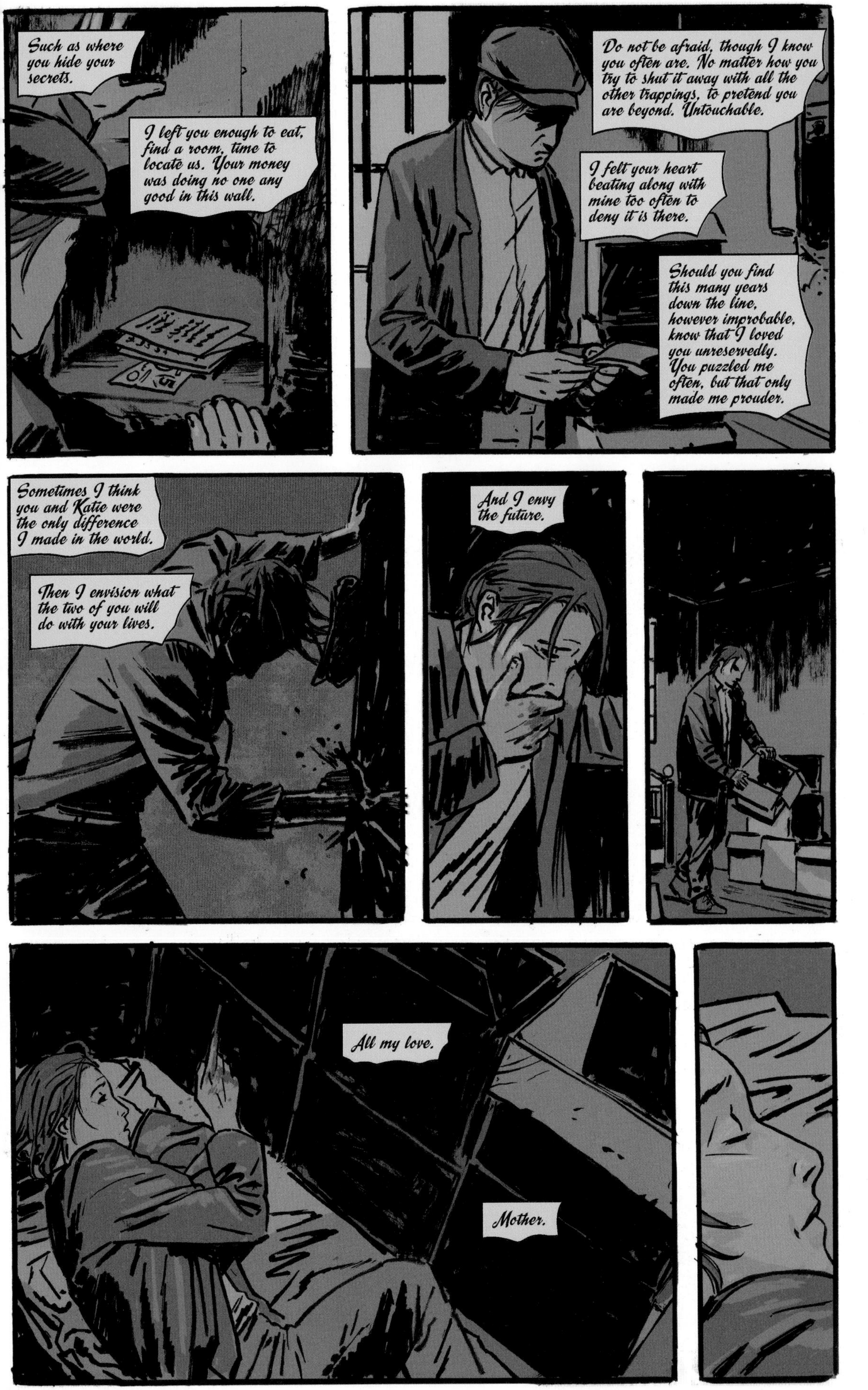
Such as where you hide your secrets.
I left you enough to eat, find a room, time to locate us. Your money was doing no one any good in this wall.
Do not be afraid, though I know you often are. No matter how you try to shut it away with all the other trappings, to pretend you are beyond. Untouchable.
I felt your heart beating along with mine too often to deny it is there.
Should you find this many years down the line, however improbable, know that I loved you unreservedly. You puzzled me often, but that only made me prouder.
Sometimes I think you and Katie were the only difference I made in the world.
Then I envision what the two of you will do with your lives.
And I envy the future.
All my love.
Mother.

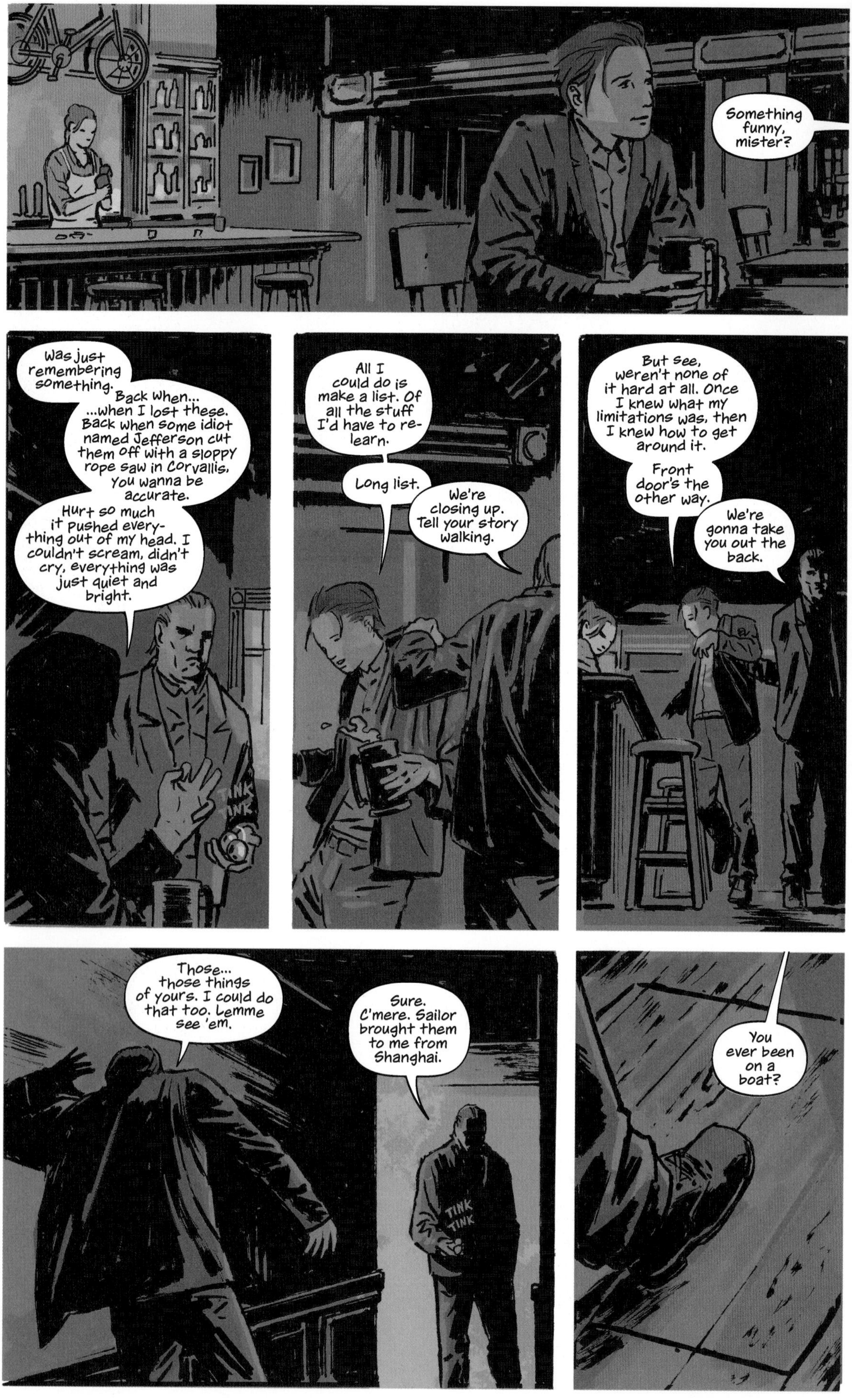
Something funny, mister?
Was just remembering something.
Back when... ...when I lost these. Back when some idiot named Jefferson cut them off with a sloppy rope saw in Corvallis, You wanna be accurate.
Hurt so much it pushed everything out of my head. I couldn't scream, didn't cry, everything was just quiet and bright.
TINK TINK
All I could do is make a list. Of all the stuff I'd have to relearn.
Long list.
We're closing up. Tell your story walking.
But see, weren't none of it hard at all. Once I knew what my limitations was, then I knew how to get around it.
Front door's the other way.
We're gonna take you out the back.
Those... those things of yours. I could do that too. Lemme see 'em.
Sure. C'mere. Sailor brought them to me from Shanghai.
TINK TINK
You ever been on a boat?

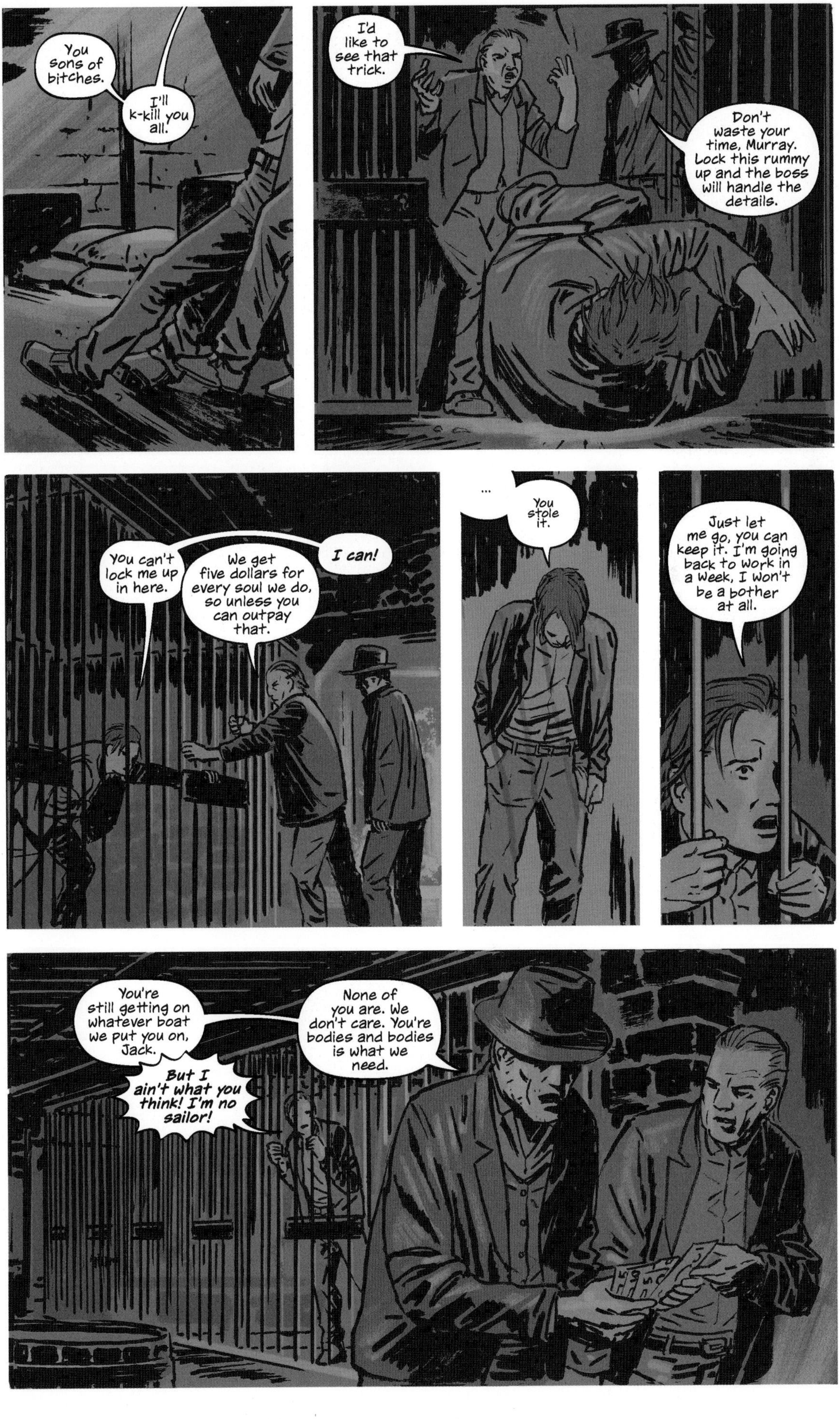
You sons of bitches.
I'll k-kill you all.
I'd like to see that trick.
Don't waste your time, Murray. Lock this rummy up and the boss will handle the details.
You can't lock me up in here.
I can!
We get five dollars for every soul we do, so unless you can outpay that.
...
You stole it.
Just let me go, you can keep it. I'm going back to work in a week, I won't be a bother at all.
You're still getting on whatever boat we put you on, Jack.
But I ain't what you think! I'm no sailor!
None of you are. We don't care. You're bodies and bodies is what we need.

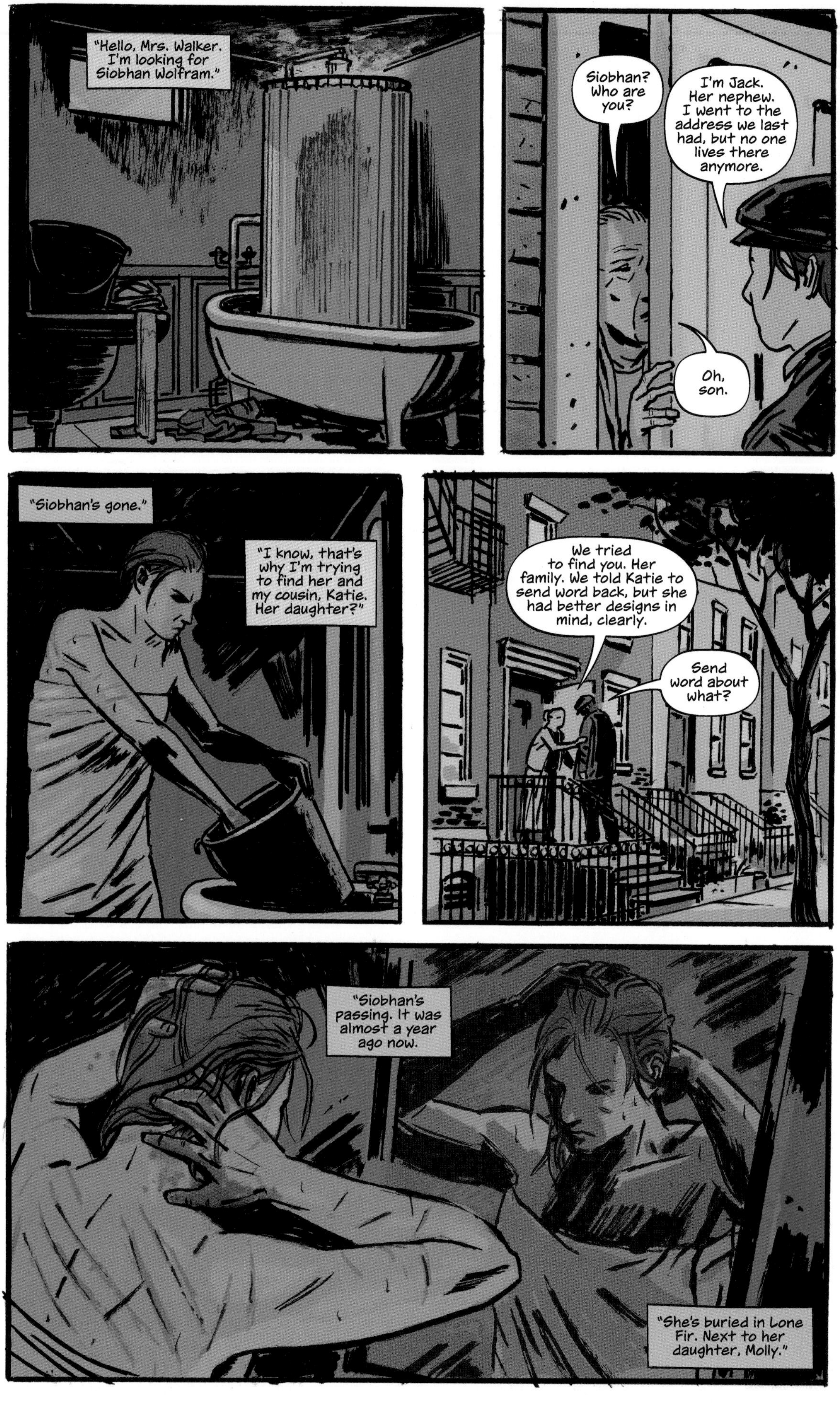
"Hello, Mrs. Walker. I'm looking for Siobhan Wolfram."
Siobhan? Who are you?
I'm Jack. Her nephew. I went to the address we last had, but no one lives there anymore.
Oh, son.
"Siobhan's gone."
"I know, that's why I'm trying to find her and my cousin, Katie. Her daughter?"
We tried to find you. Her family. We told Katie to send word back, but she had better designs in mind, clearly.
Send word about what?
"Siobhan's passing. It was almost a year ago now.
"She's buried in Lone Fir. Next to her daughter, Molly."

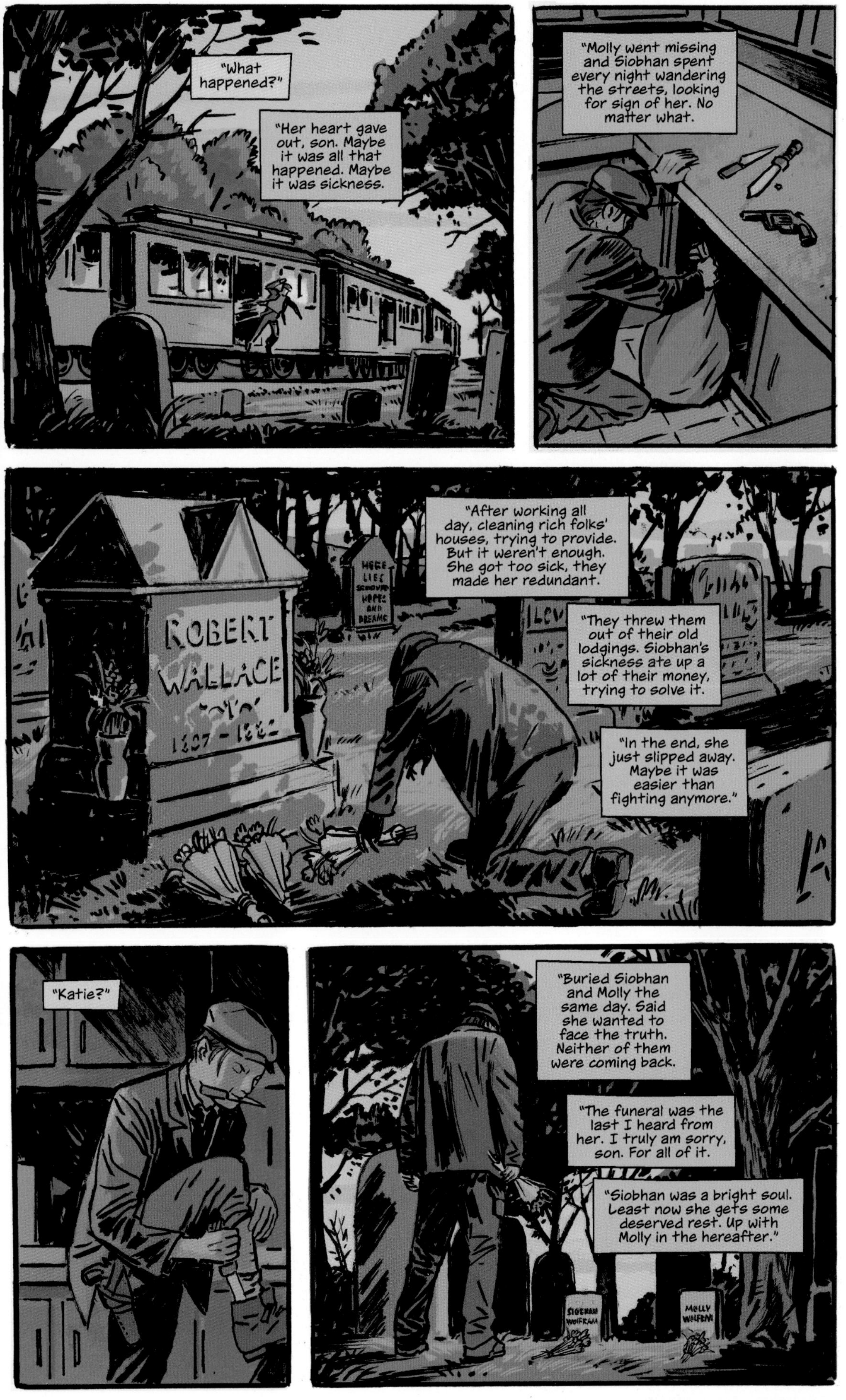
"What happened?"
"Her heart gave out, son. Maybe it was all that happened. Maybe it was sickness.
"Molly went missing and Siobhan spent every night wandering the streets, looking for sign of her. No matter what.
"After working all day, cleaning rich folks' houses, trying to provide. But it weren't enough. She got too sick, they made her redundant.
ROBERT WALLACE
"They threw them out of their old lodgings. Siobhan's sickness ate up a lot of their money, trying to solve it.
"In the end, she just slipped away. Maybe it was easier than fighting anymore."
"Katie?"
"Buried Siobhan and Molly the same day. Said she wanted to face the truth. Neither of them were coming back.
"The funeral was the last I heard from her. I truly am sorry, son. For all of it.
"Siobhan was a bright soul. Least now she gets some deserved rest. Up with Molly in the hereafter."
SIOBHAN WOLFRAM
MOLLY WOLFRAM

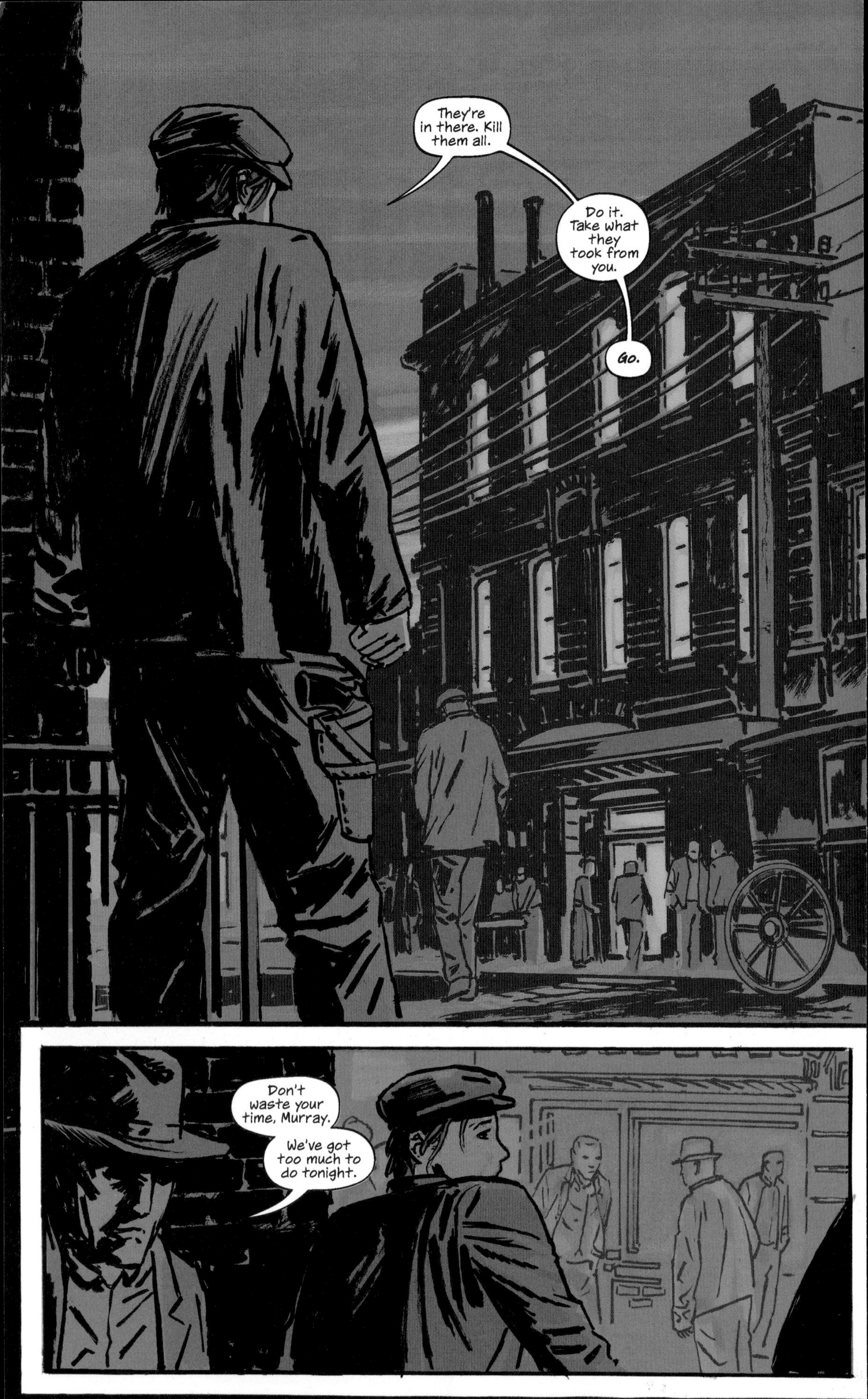
They're in there. Kill them all.
Do it. Take what they took from you.
Go.
Don't waste your time, Murray.
We've got too much to do tonight.

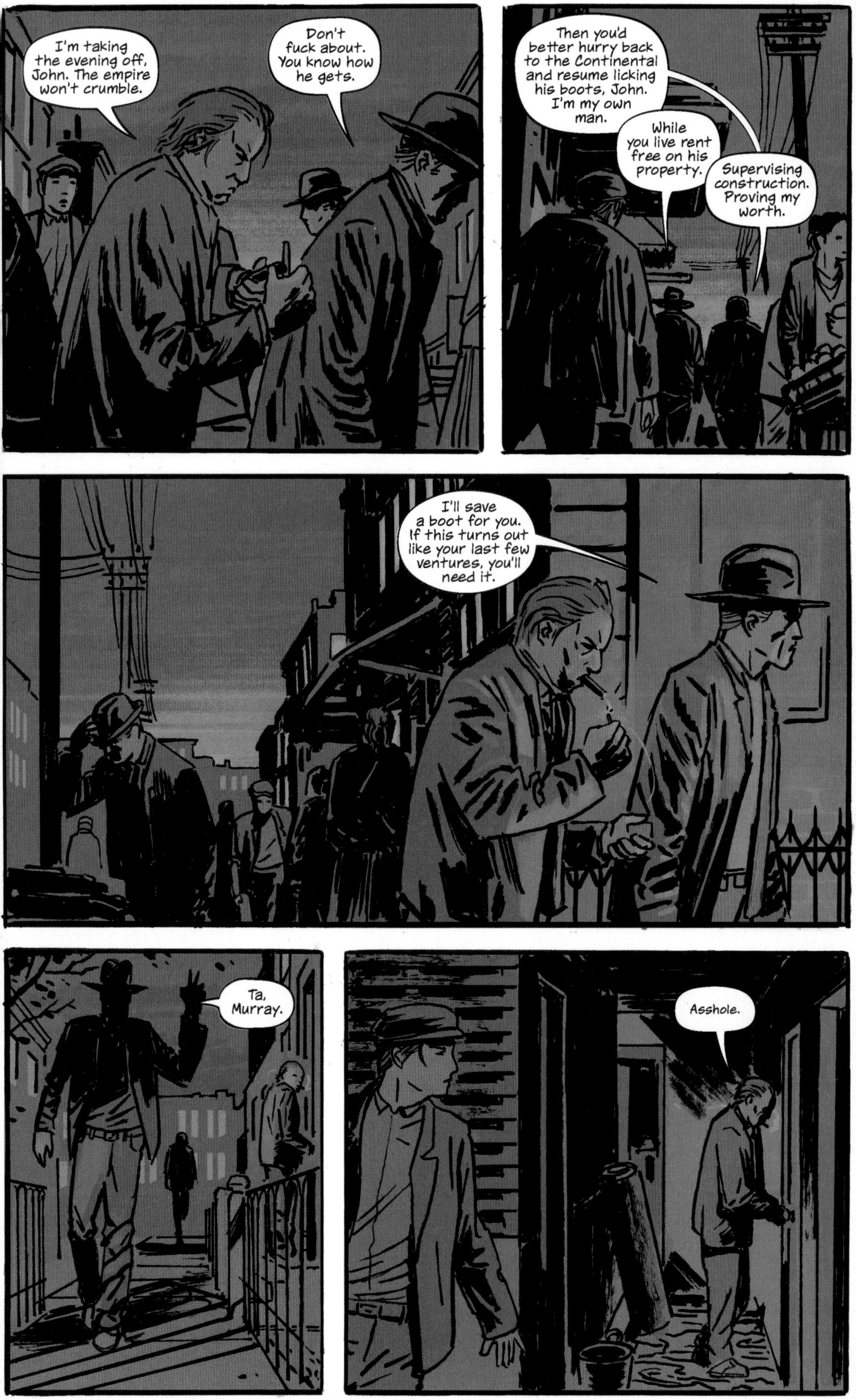
I'm taking the evening off, John. The empire won't crumble.
Don't fuck about. You know how he gets.
Then you'd better hurry back to the Continental and resume licking his boots, John. I'm my own man.
While you live rent free on his property.
Supervising construction. Proving my worth.
I'll save a boot for you. If this turns out like your last few ventures, you'll need it.
Ta, Murray.
Asshole.

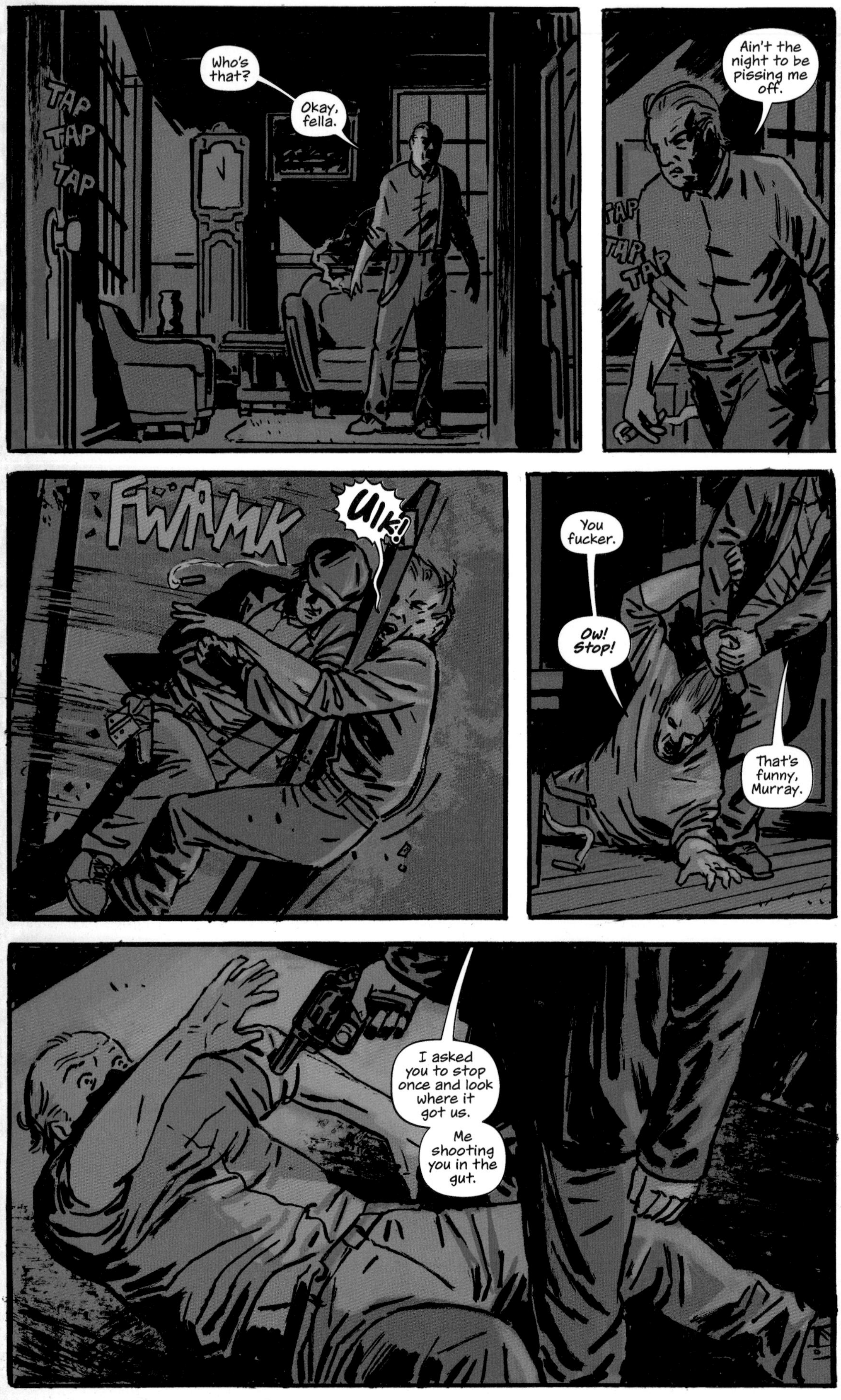
TAP
TAP
TAP
Who's that?
Okay, fella.
Ain't the night to be pissing me off.
TAP
TAP
TAP
FWAMK
UIK!
You fucker.
Ow! Stop!
That's funny, Murray.
I asked you to stop once and look where it got us.
Me shooting you in the gut.

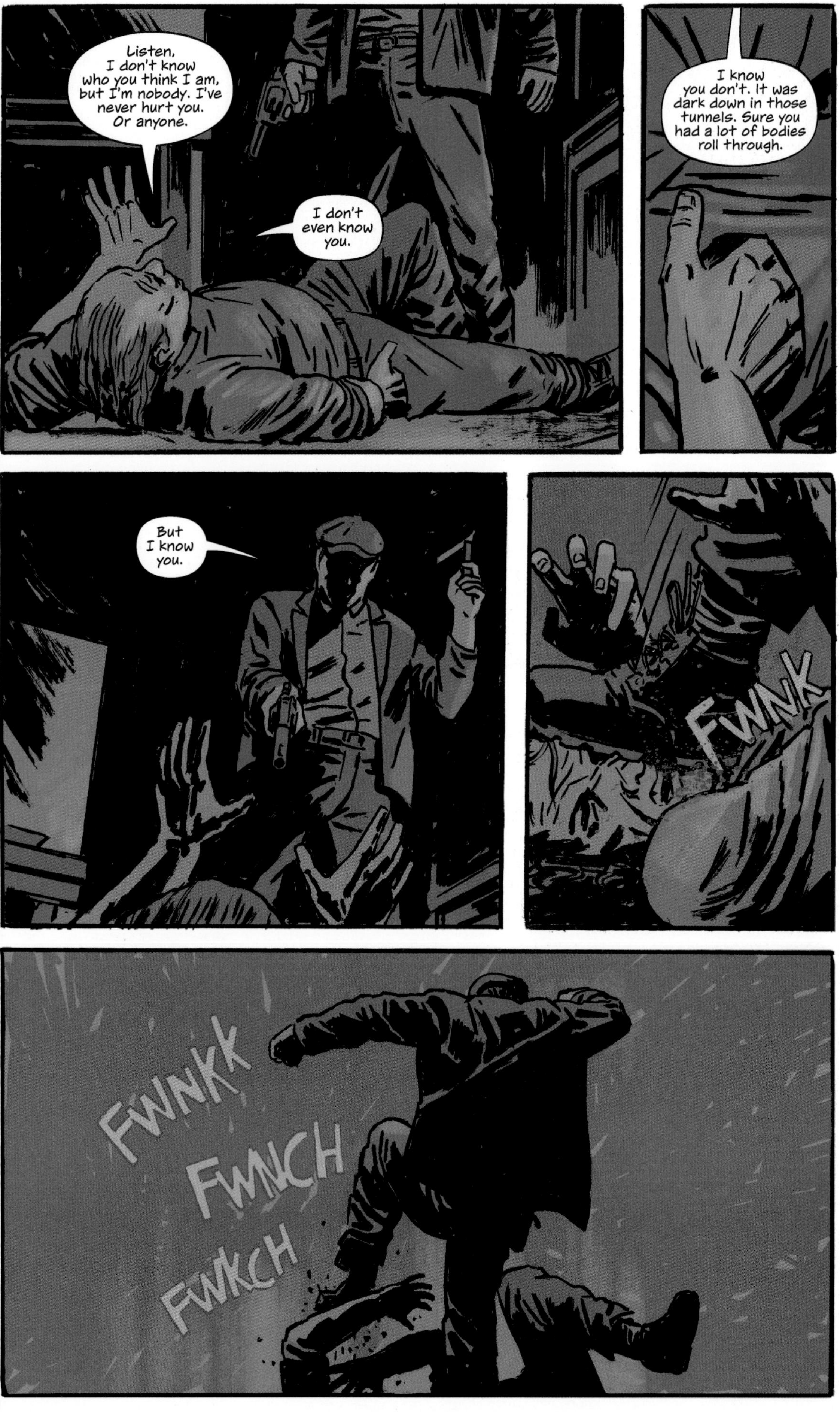

Listen, I don't know who you think I am, but I'm nobody. I've never hurt you. Or anyone.
I don't even know you.
I know you don't. It was dark down in those tunnels. Sure you had a lot of bodies roll through.
But I know you.
FWNK
FWNKK
FWNCH
FWKCH

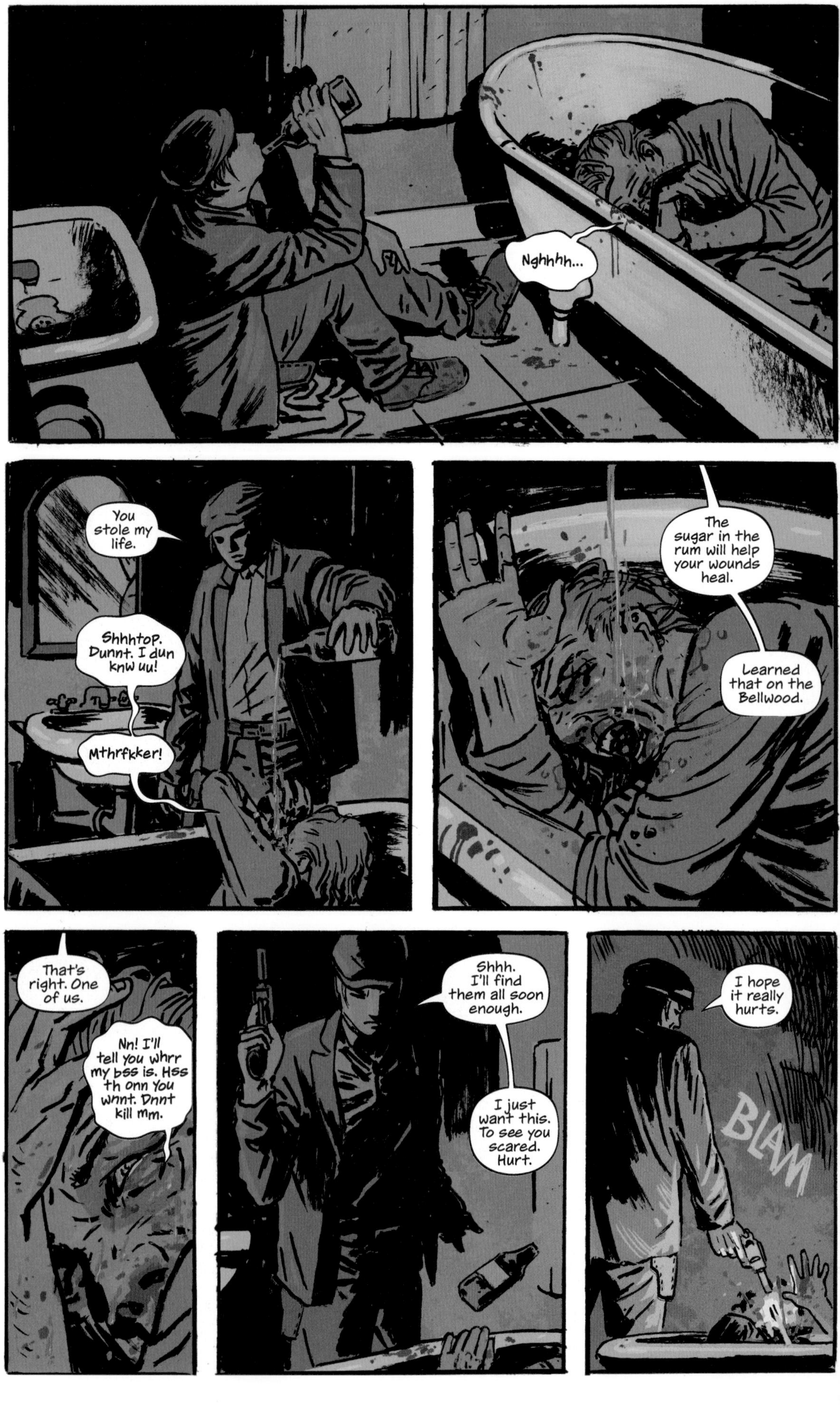
Nghhhh...
You stole my life.
Shhhtop. Dunnt. I dun knw uu!
Mthrfkker!
The sugar in the rum will help your wounds heal.
Learned that on the Bellwood.
That's right. One of us.
Nn! I'll tell you whrr my bss is. Hss th onn You wnnt. Dnnt kill mm.
Shhh. I'll find them all soon enough.
I just want this. To see you scared. Hurt.
I hope it really hurts.
BLAM

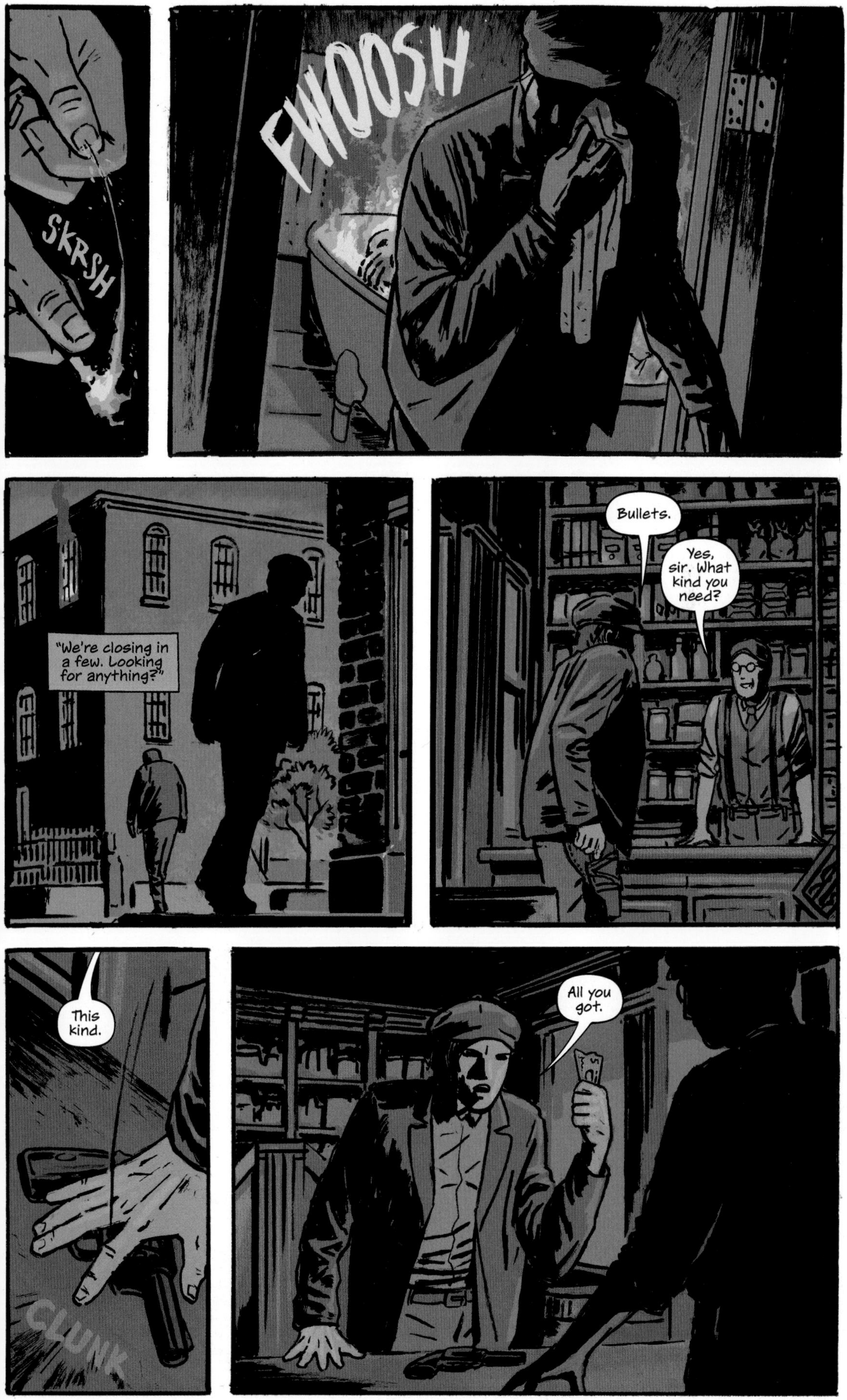
SKRSH
FWOOSH
"We're closing in a few. Looking for anything?"
Bullets.
Yes, sir. What kind you need?
This kind.
CLUNK
All you got.

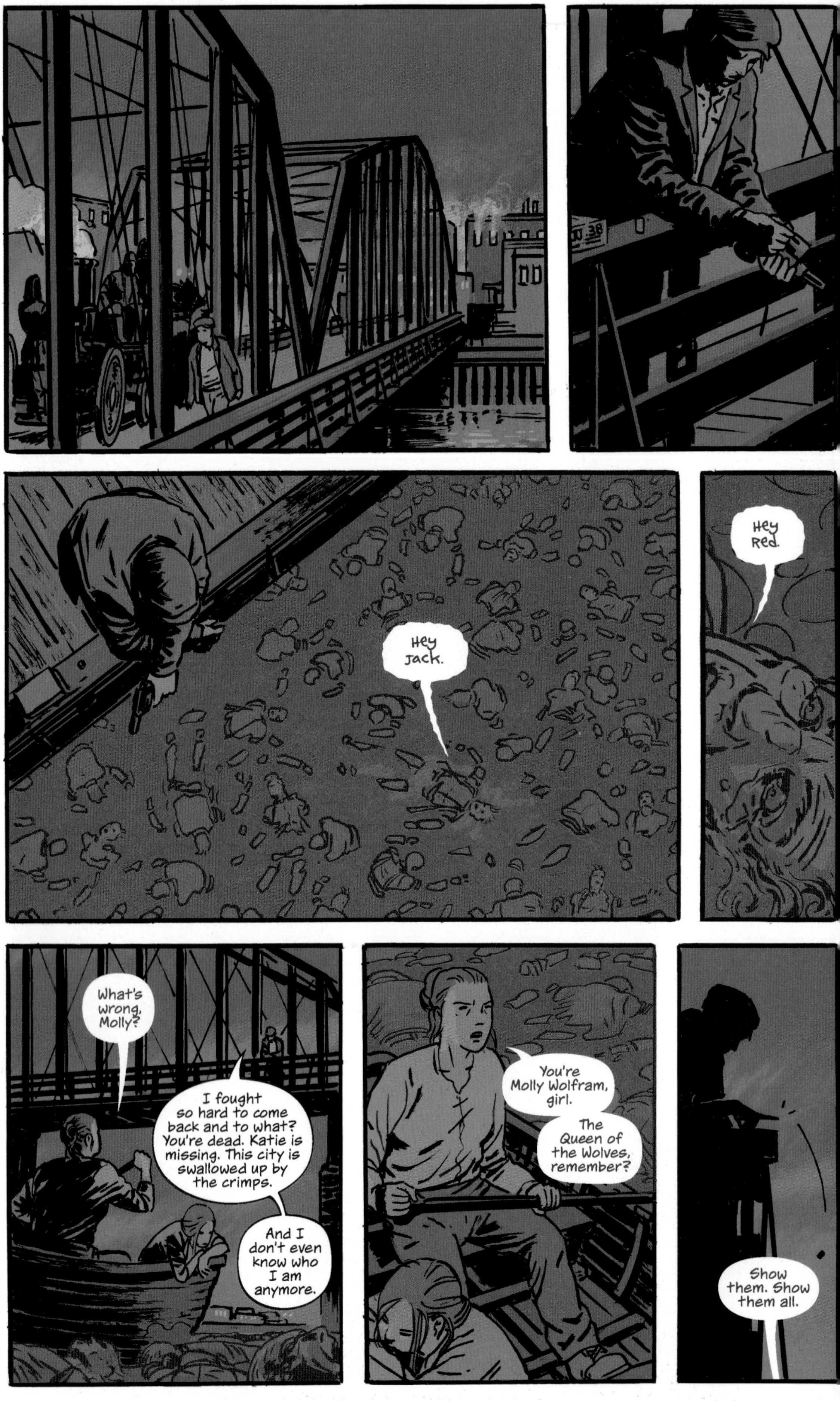
Hey Jack.
Hey Red.
What's wrong, Molly?
I fought so hard to come back and to what? You're dead. Katie is missing. This city is swallowed up by the crimps.
And I don't even know who I am anymore.
You're Molly Wolfram, girl.
The Queen of the Wolves, remember?
Show them. Show them all.

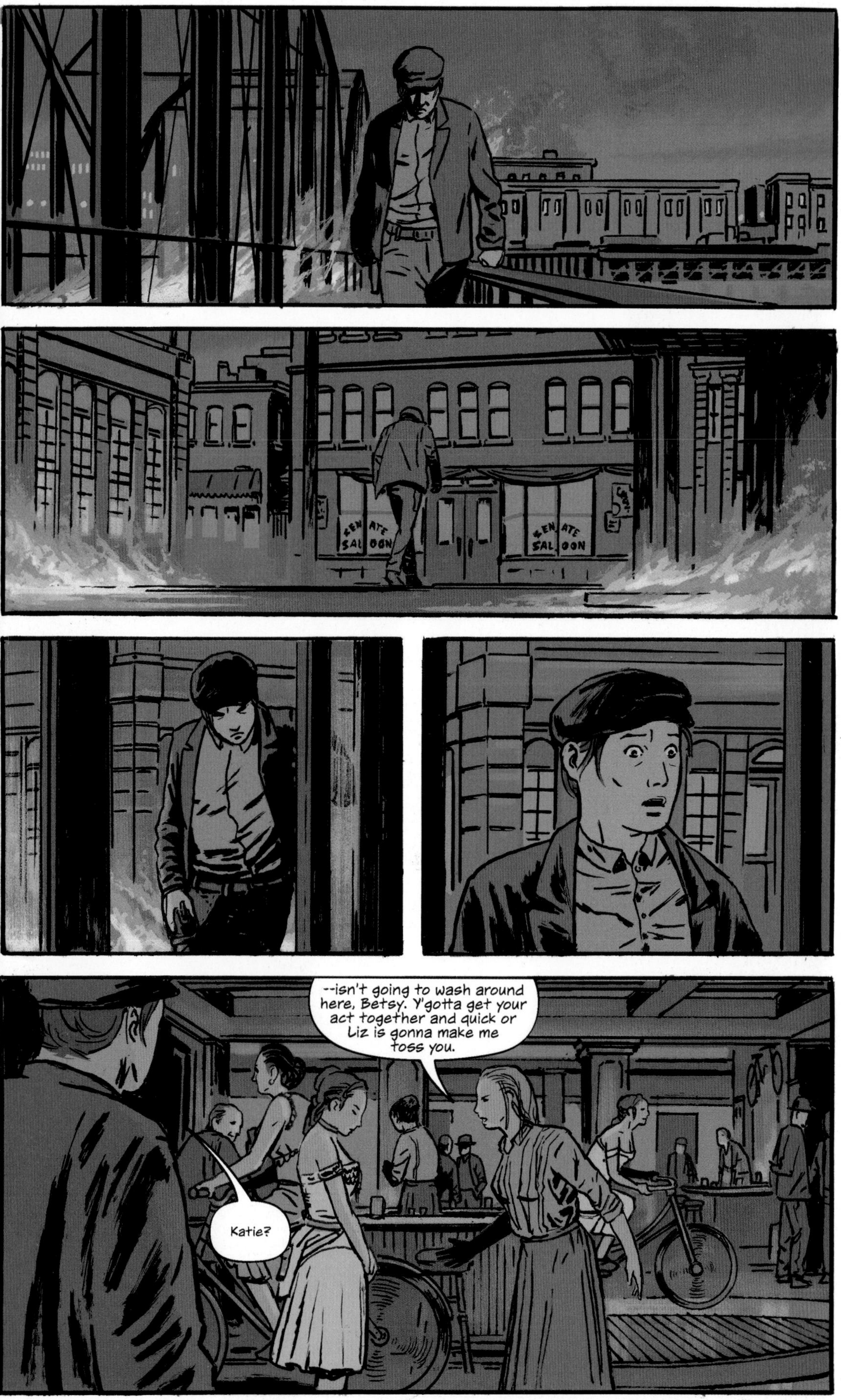
SENATE SALOON
SENATE SALOON
--isn't going to wash around here, Betsy. Y'gotta get your act together and quick or Liz is gonna make me toss you.
Katie?

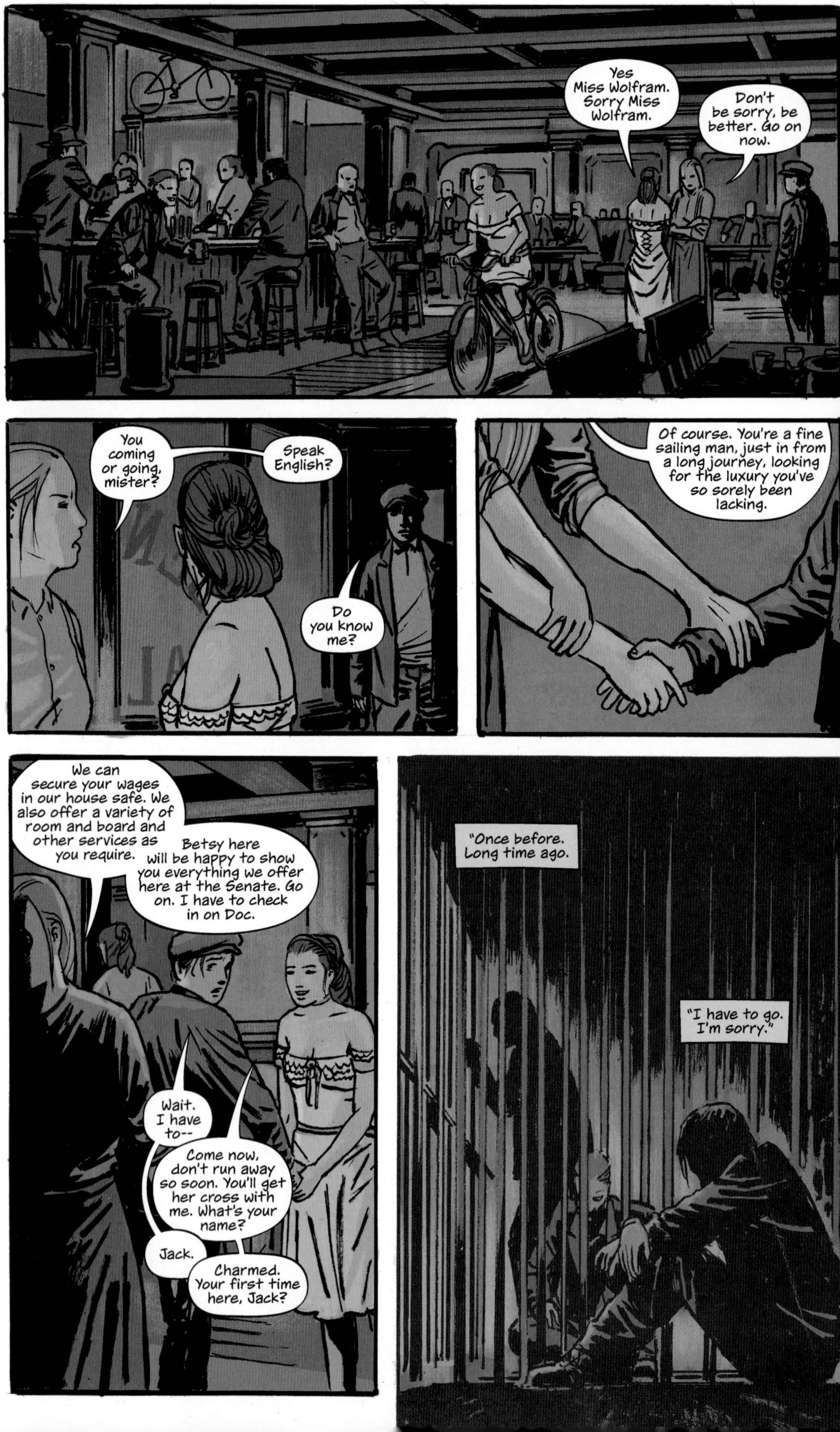
Yes Miss Wolfram. Sorry Miss Wolfram.
Don't be sorry, be better. Go on now.
You coming or going, mister?
Speak English?
Do you know me?
Of course. You're a fine sailing man, just in from a long journey, looking for the luxury you've so sorely been lacking.
We can secure your wages in our house safe. We also offer a variety of room and board and other services as you require.
Betsy here will be happy to show you everything we offer here at the Senate. Go on. I have to check in on Doc.
Wait. I have to--
Come now, don't run away so soon. You'll get her cross with me. What's your name?
Jack.
Charmed. Your first time here, Jack?
"Once before. Long time ago.
"I have to go. I'm sorry."

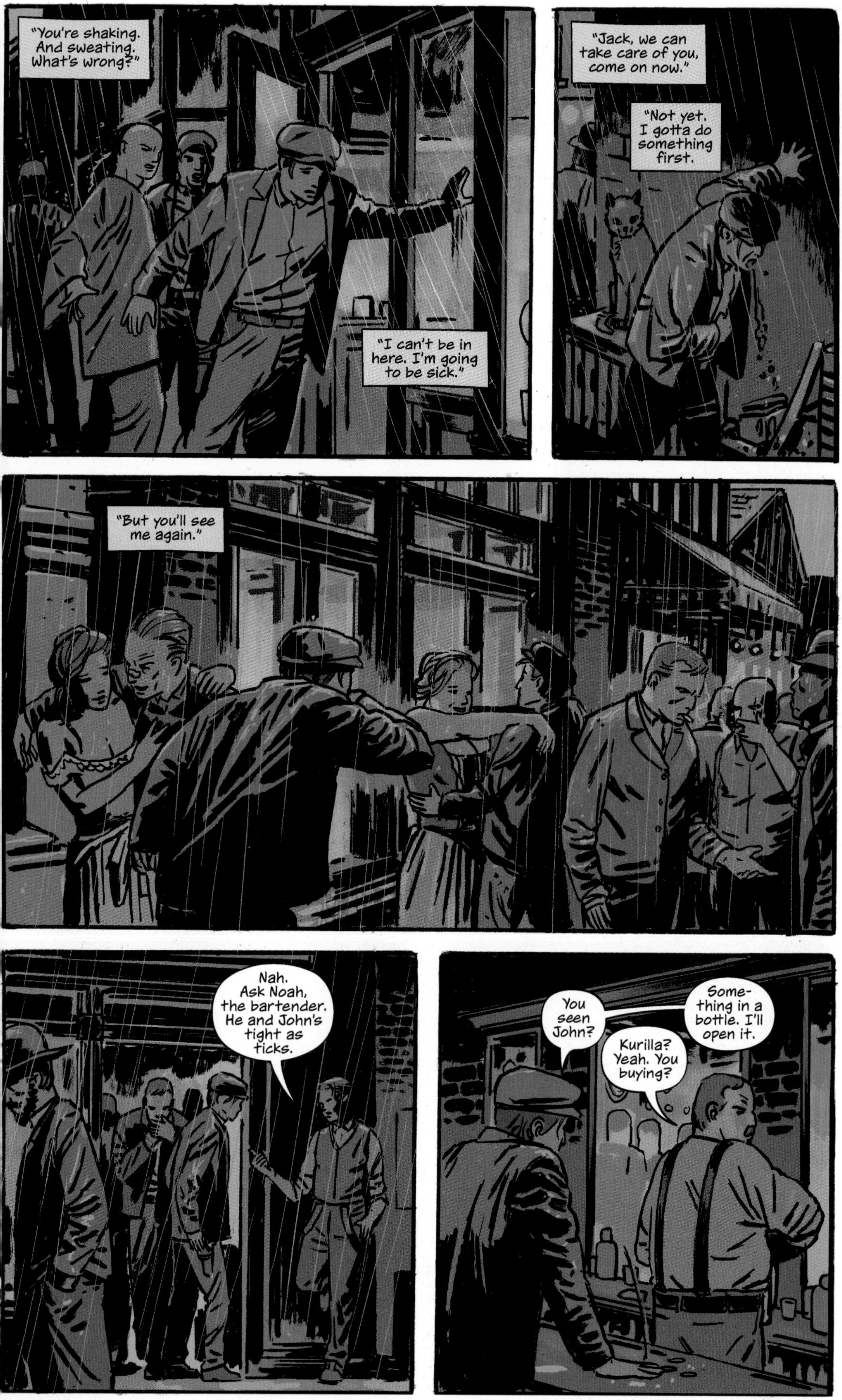
"You're shaking. And sweating. What's wrong?"
"I can't be in here. I'm going to be sick."
"Jack, we can take care of you, come on now."
"Not yet. I gotta do something first.
"But you'll see me again."
Nah. Ask Noah, the bartender. He and John's tight as ticks.
You seen John?
Kurilla? Yeah. You buying?
Some-thing in a bottle. I'll open it.

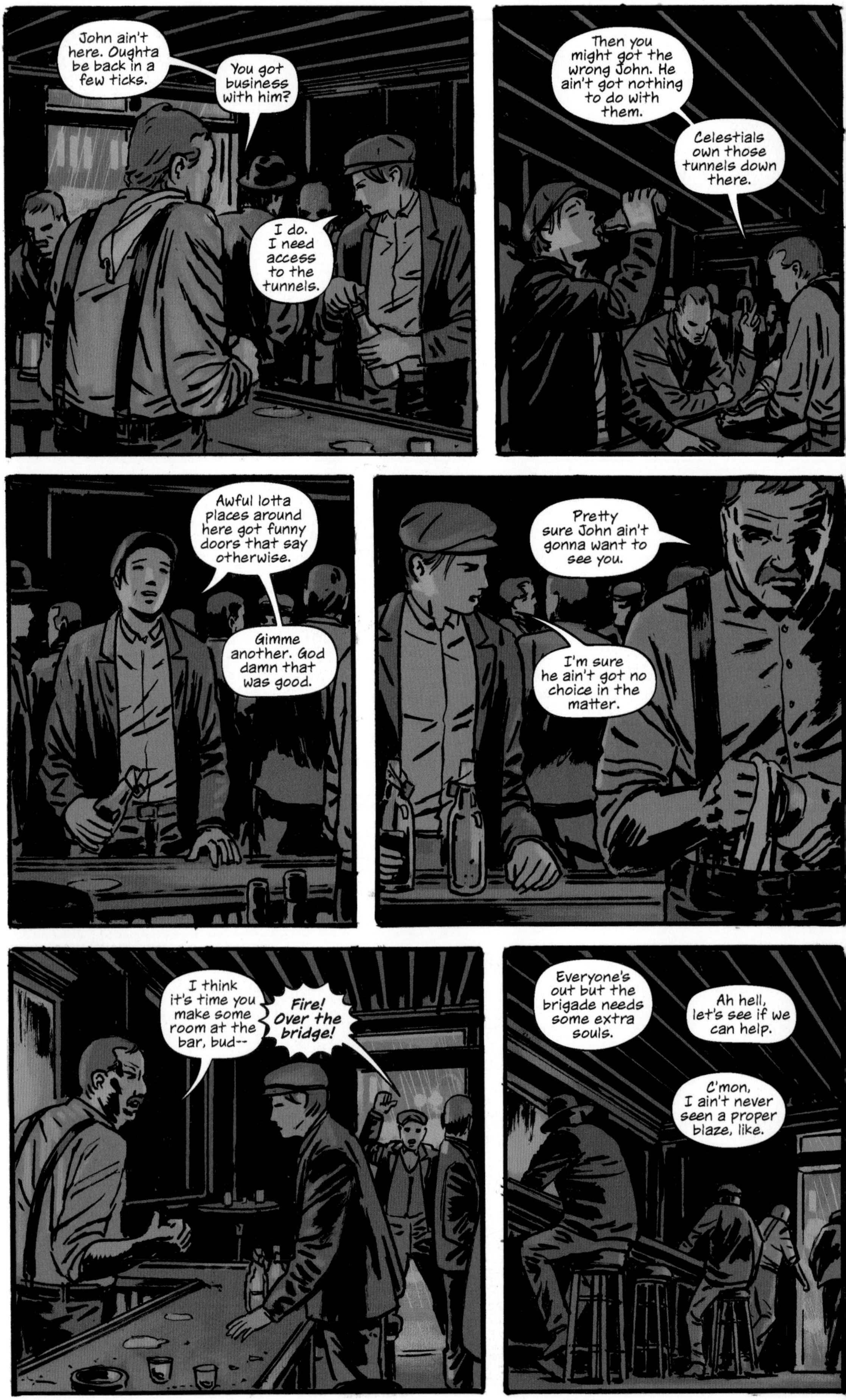
John ain't here. Oughta be back in a few ticks.
You got business with him?
I do. I need access to the tunnels.
Then you might got the wrong John. He ain't got nothing to do with them.
Celestials own those tunnels down there.
Awful lotta places around here got funny doors that say otherwise.
Gimme another. God damn that was good.
Pretty sure John ain't gonna want to see you.
I'm sure he ain't got no choice in the matter.
I think it's time you make some room at the bar, bud--
Fire! Over the bridge!
Everyone's out but the brigade needs some extra souls.
Ah hell, let's see if we can help.
C'mon, I ain't never seen a proper blaze, like.

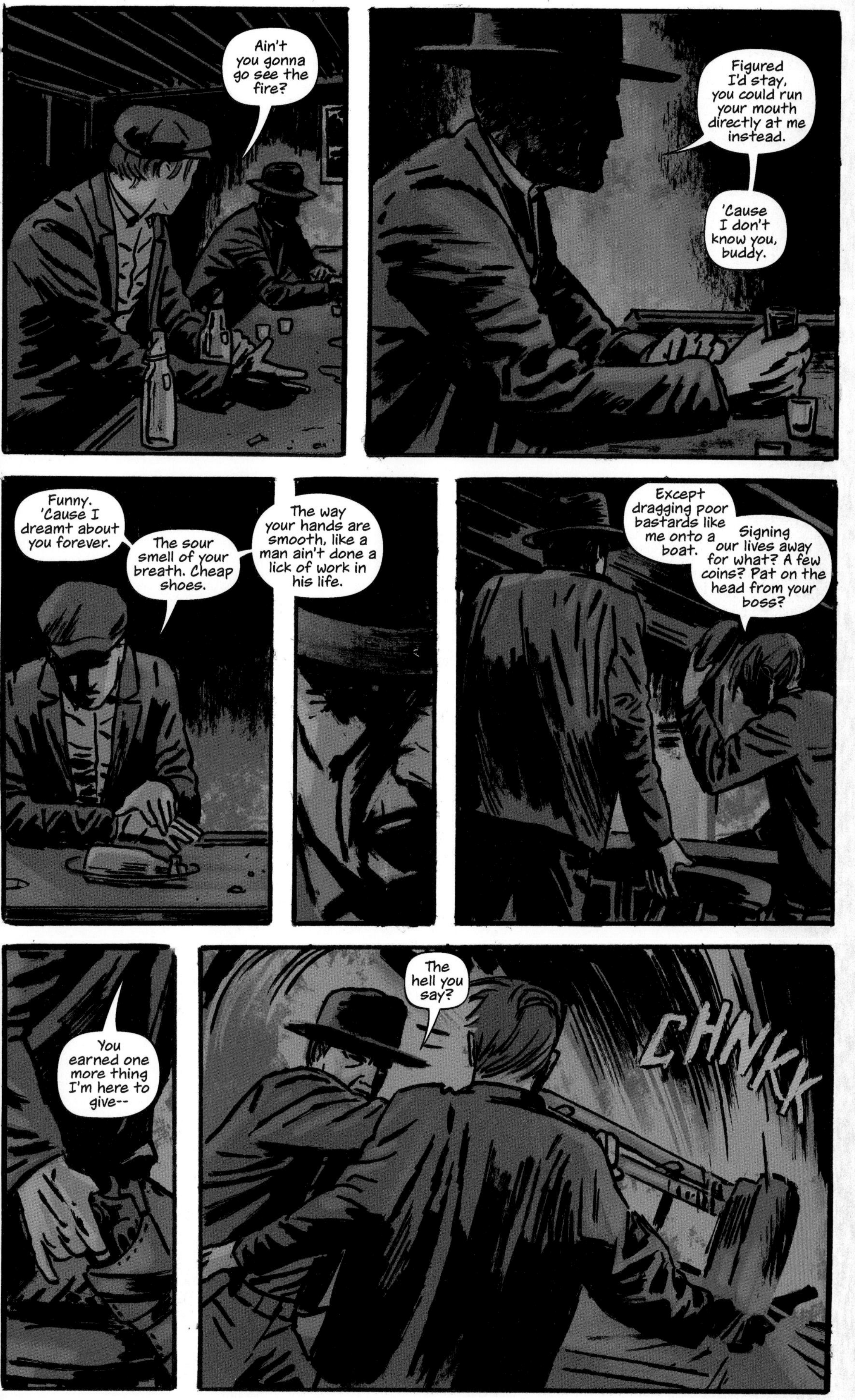
Ain't you gonna go see the fire?
Figured I'd stay, you could run your mouth directly at me instead.
'Cause I don't know you, buddy.
Funny. 'Cause I dreamt about you forever.
The sour smell of your breath. Cheap shoes.
The way your hands are smooth, like a man ain't done a lick of work in his life.
Except dragging poor bastards like me onto a boat.
Signing our lives away for what? A few coins? Pat on the head from your boss?
You earned one more thing I'm here to give--
The hell you say?
CHNKK

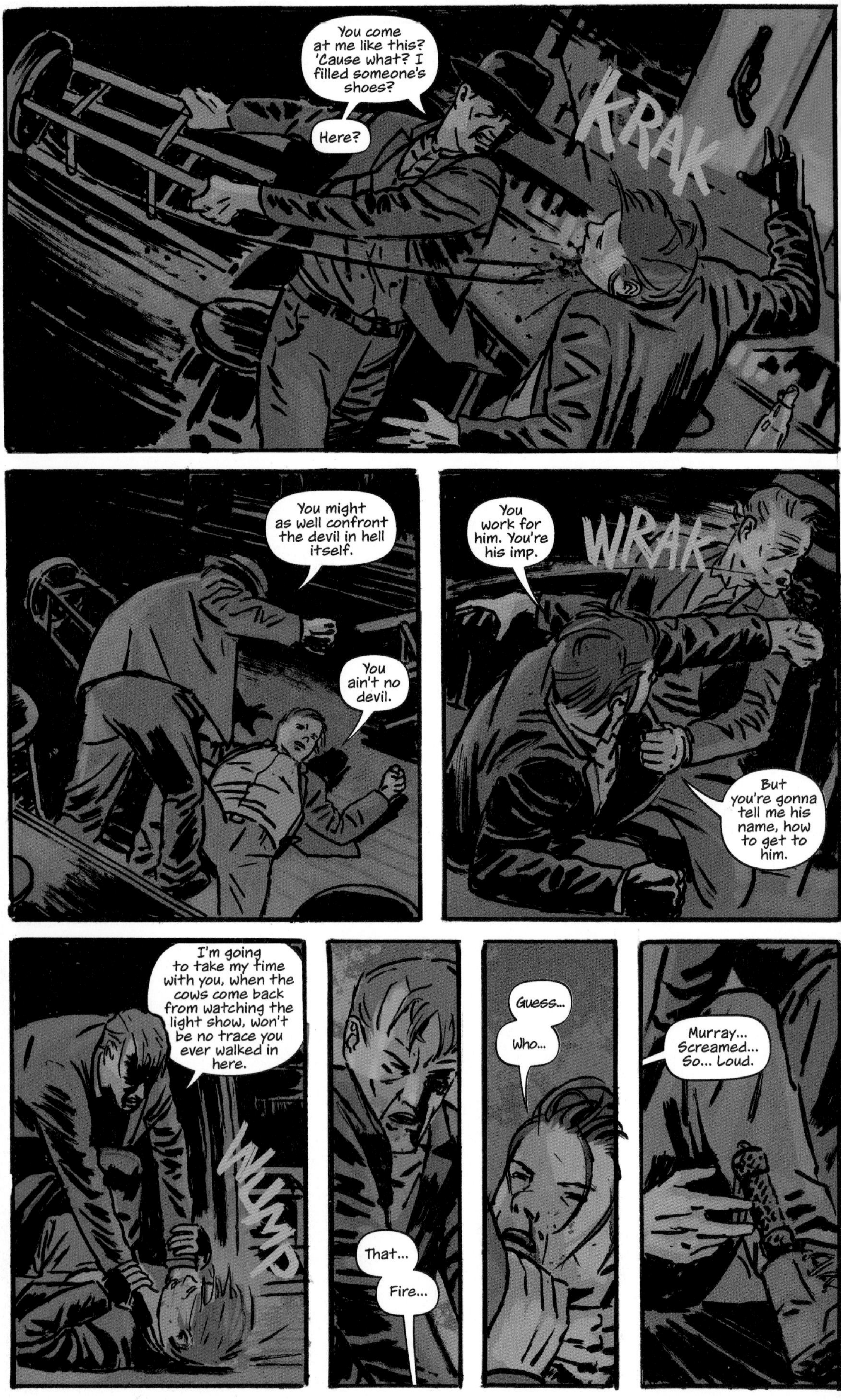
You come at me like this? 'Cause what? I filled someone's shoes?
Here?
KRAK
You might as well confront the devil in hell itself.
You ain't no devil.
You work for him. You're his imp.
WRAK
But you're gonna tell me his name, how to get to him.
I'm going to take my time with you, when the cows come back from watching the light show, won't be no trace you ever walked in here.
WUMP
That...
Fire...
Guess...
Who...
Murray... Screamed... So... Loud.

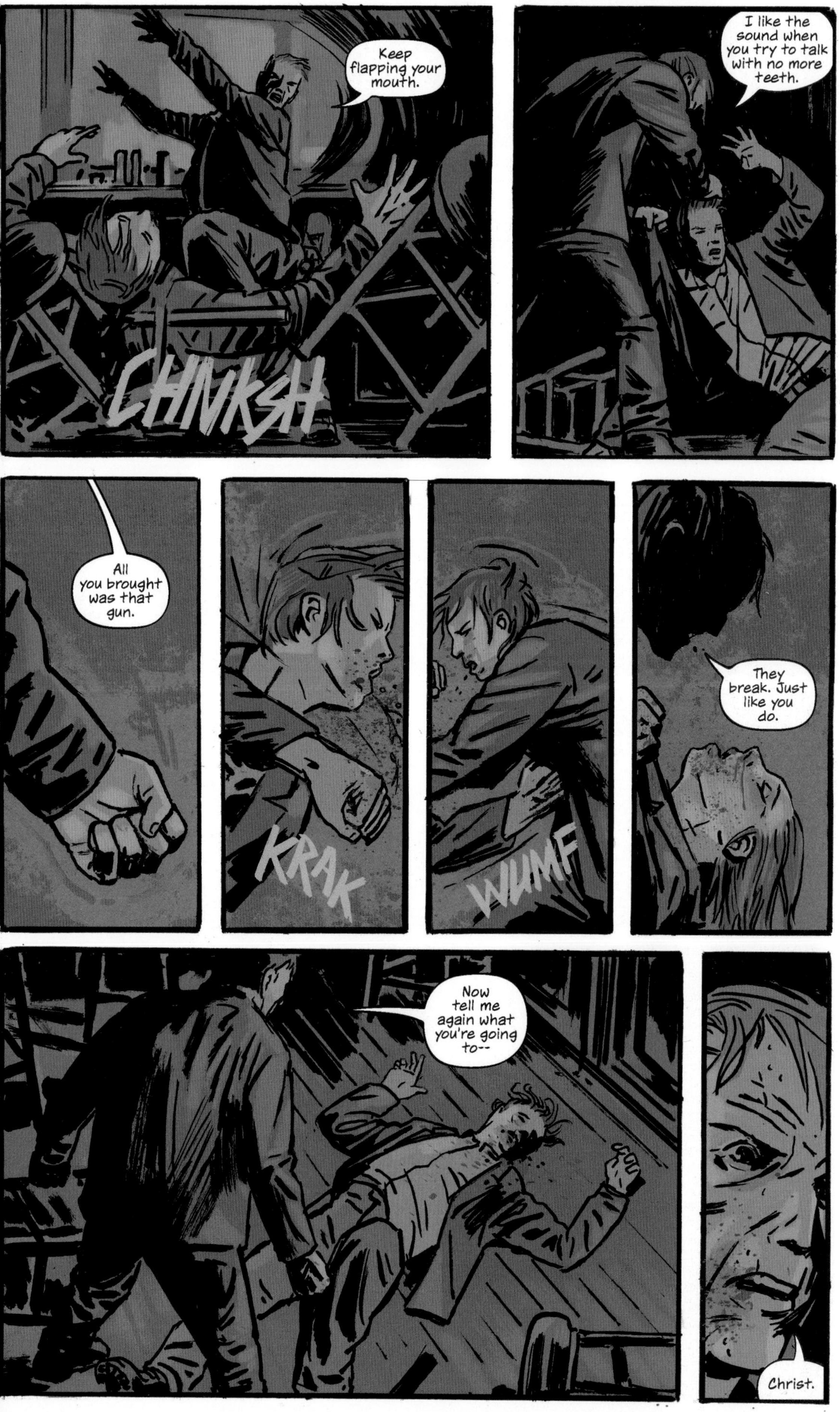
Keep flapping your mouth.
CHNKSH
I like the sound when you try to talk with no more teeth.
All you brought was that gun.
KRAK
WUMF
They break. Just like you do.
Now tell me again what you're going to--
Christ.

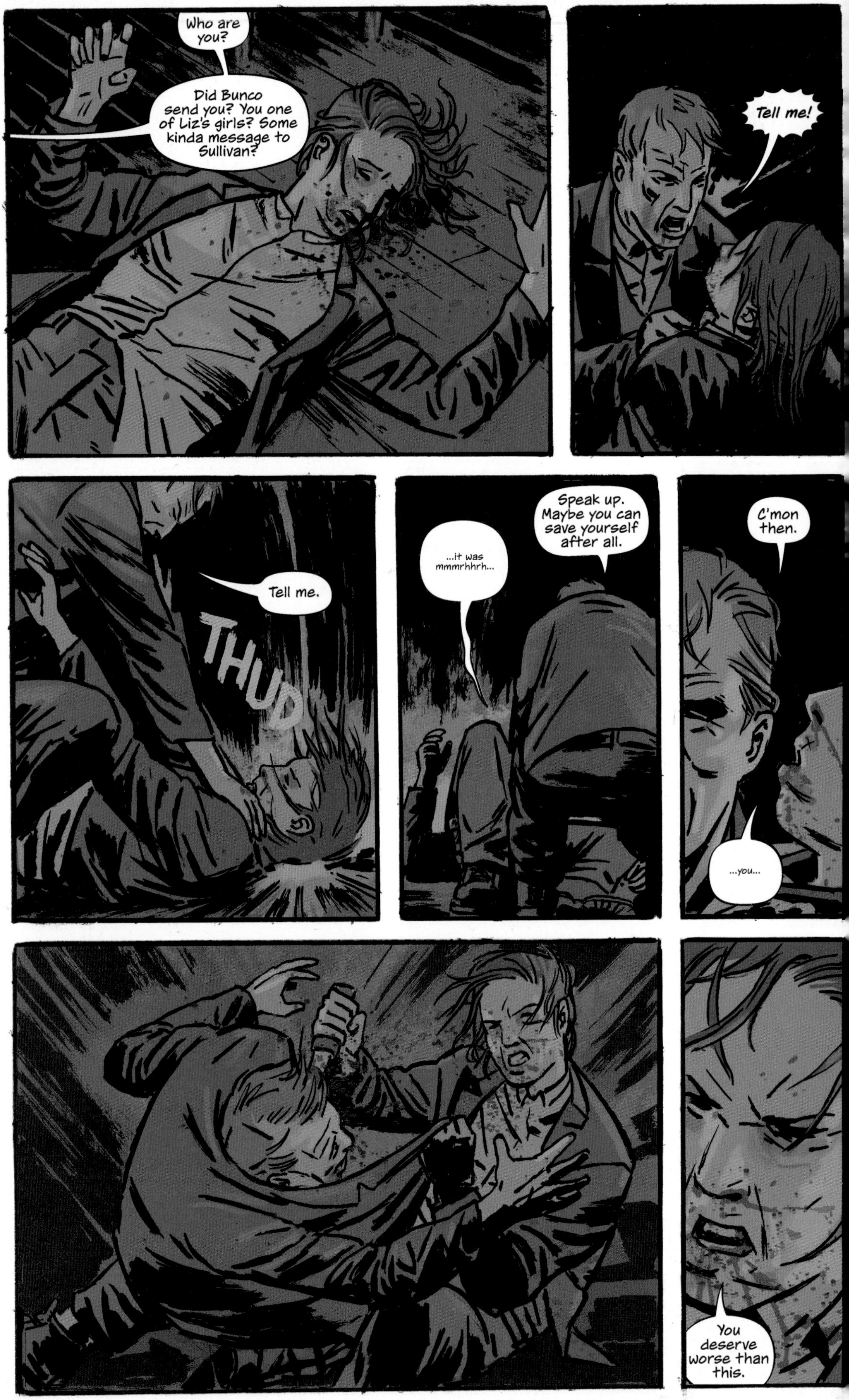
Who are you?
Did Bunco send you? You one of Liz's girls? Some kinda message to Sullivan?
Tell me!
Tell me.
THUD
...it was mmmrhhrh...
Speak up. Maybe you can save yourself after all.
C'mon then.
...you...
You deserve worse than this.

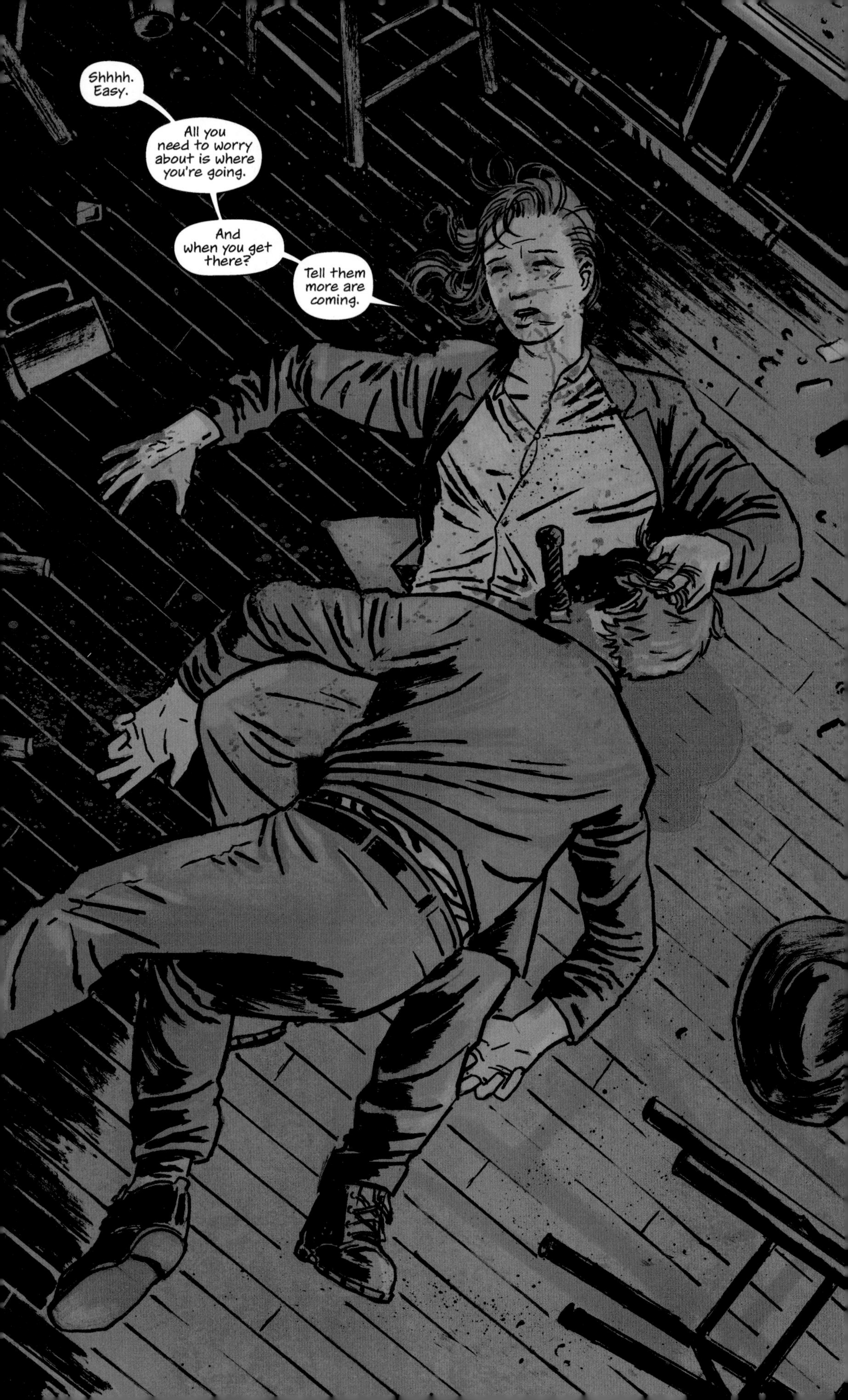
Shhhh. Easy.
All you need to worry about is where you're going.
And when you get there?
Tell them more are coming.

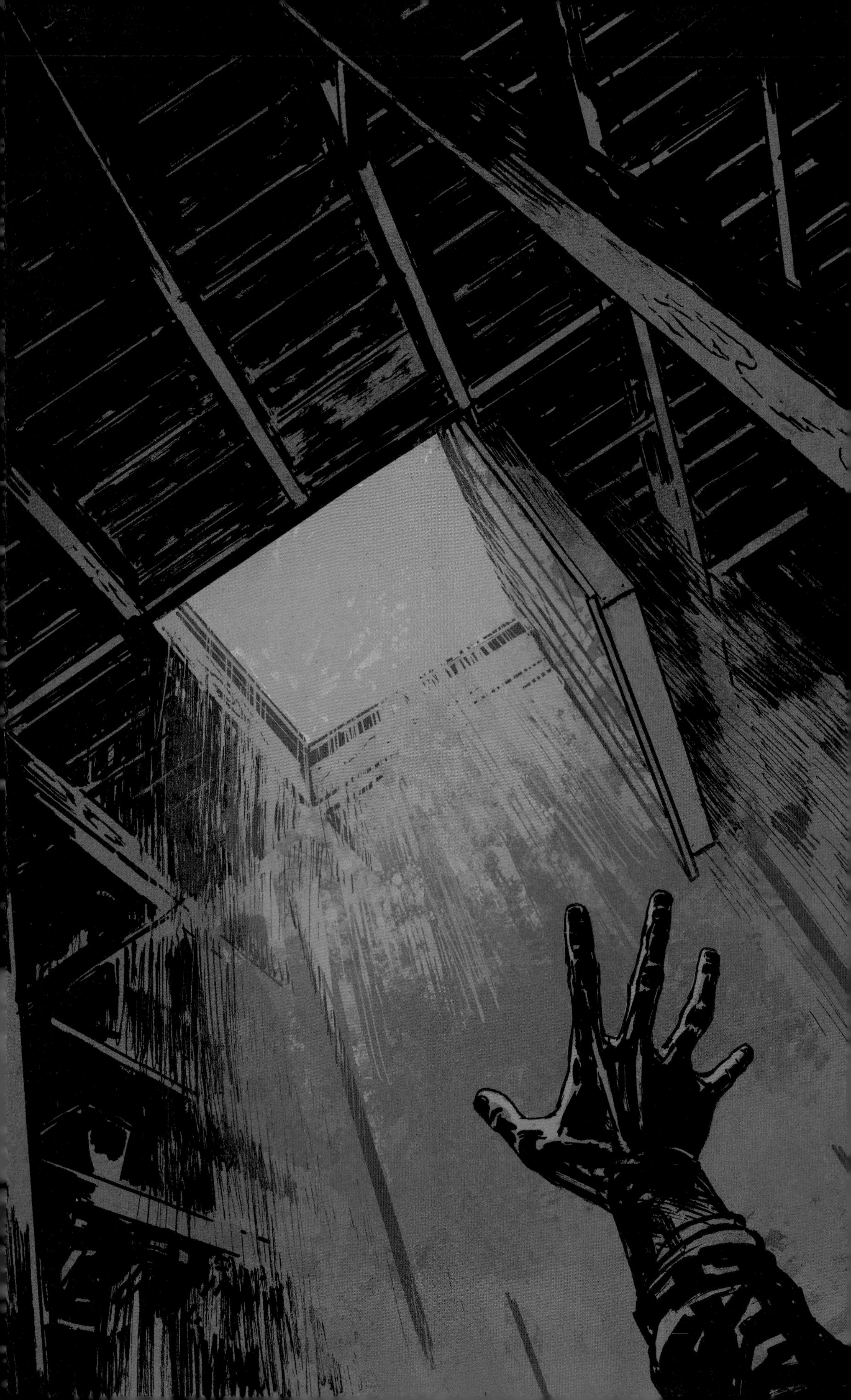

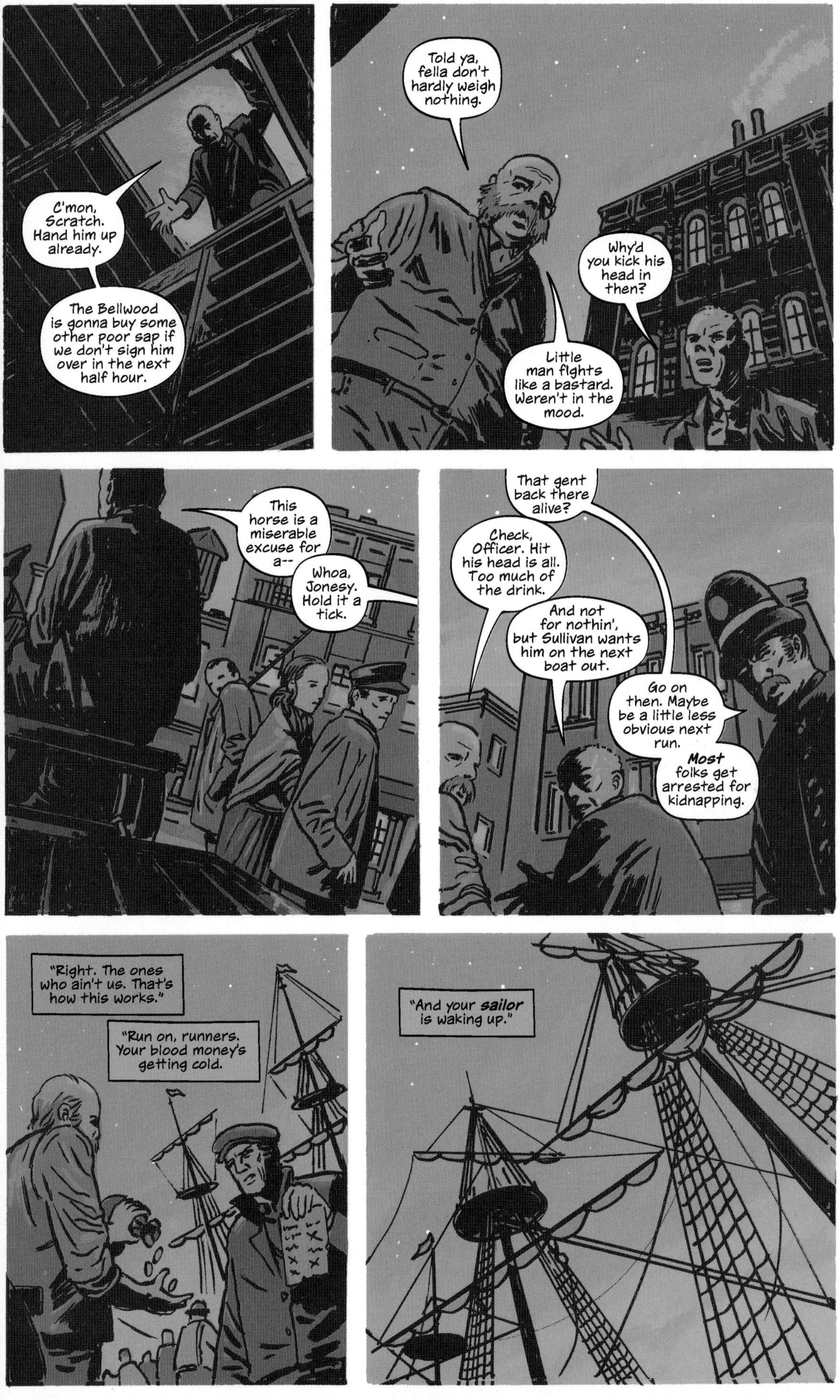
C'mon, Scratch. Hand him up already.
The Bellwood is gonna buy some other poor sap if we don't sign him over in the next half hour.
Told ya, fella don't hardly weigh nothing.
Why'd you kick his head in then?
Little man fights like a bastard. Weren't in the mood.
This horse is a miserable excuse for a--
Whoa, Jonesy. Hold it a tick.
That gent back there alive?
Check, Officer. Hit his head is all. Too much of the drink.
And not for nothin', but Sullivan wants him on the next boat out.
Go on then. Maybe be a little less obvious next run.
Most folks get arrested for kidnapping.
"Right. The ones who ain't us. That's how this works."
"Run on, runners. Your blood money's getting cold.
"And your **sailor** is waking up."

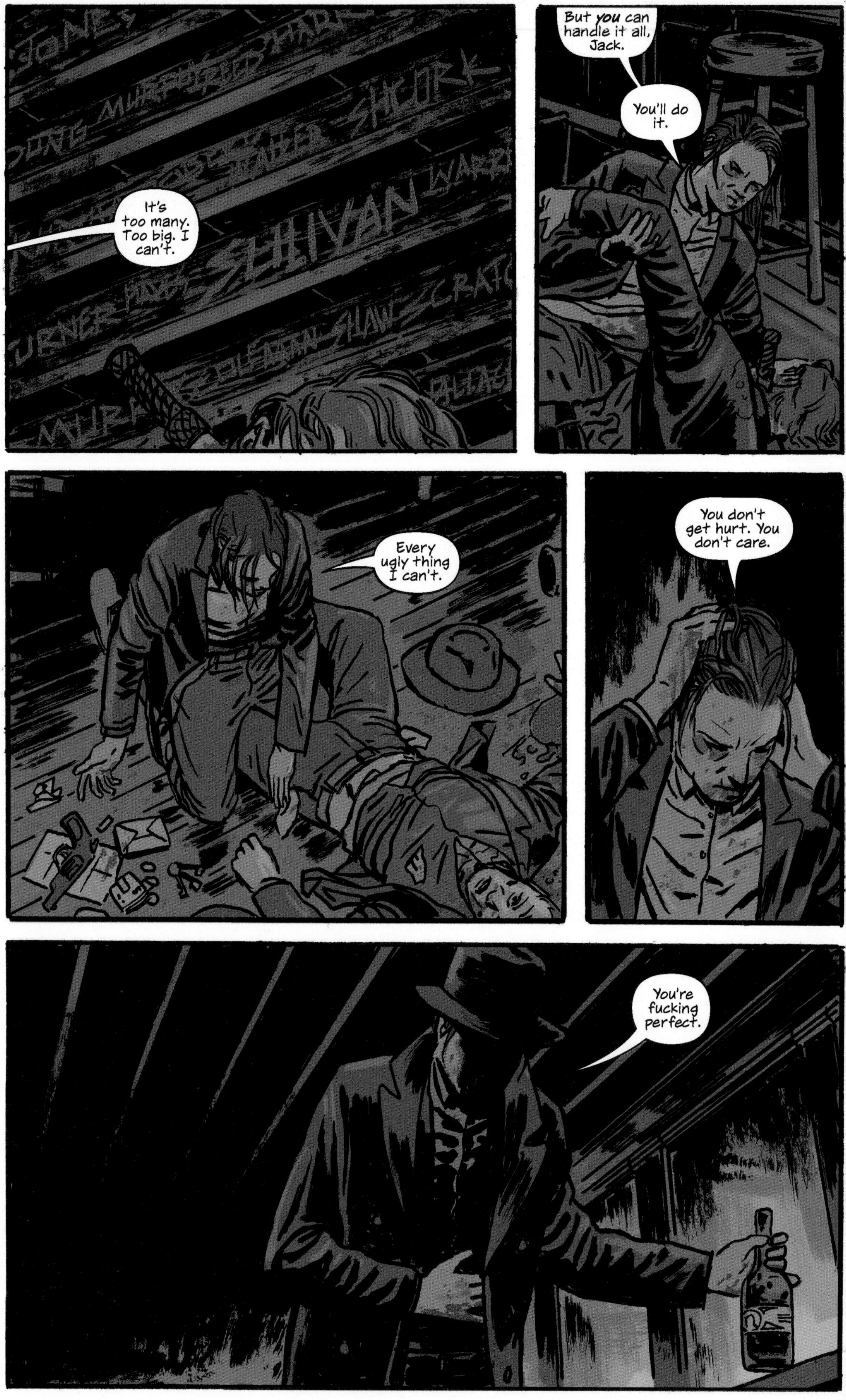
It's too many. Too big. I can't.
But *you* can handle it all, Jack.
You'll do it.
Every ugly thing I can't.
You don't get hurt. You don't care.
You're fucking perfect.

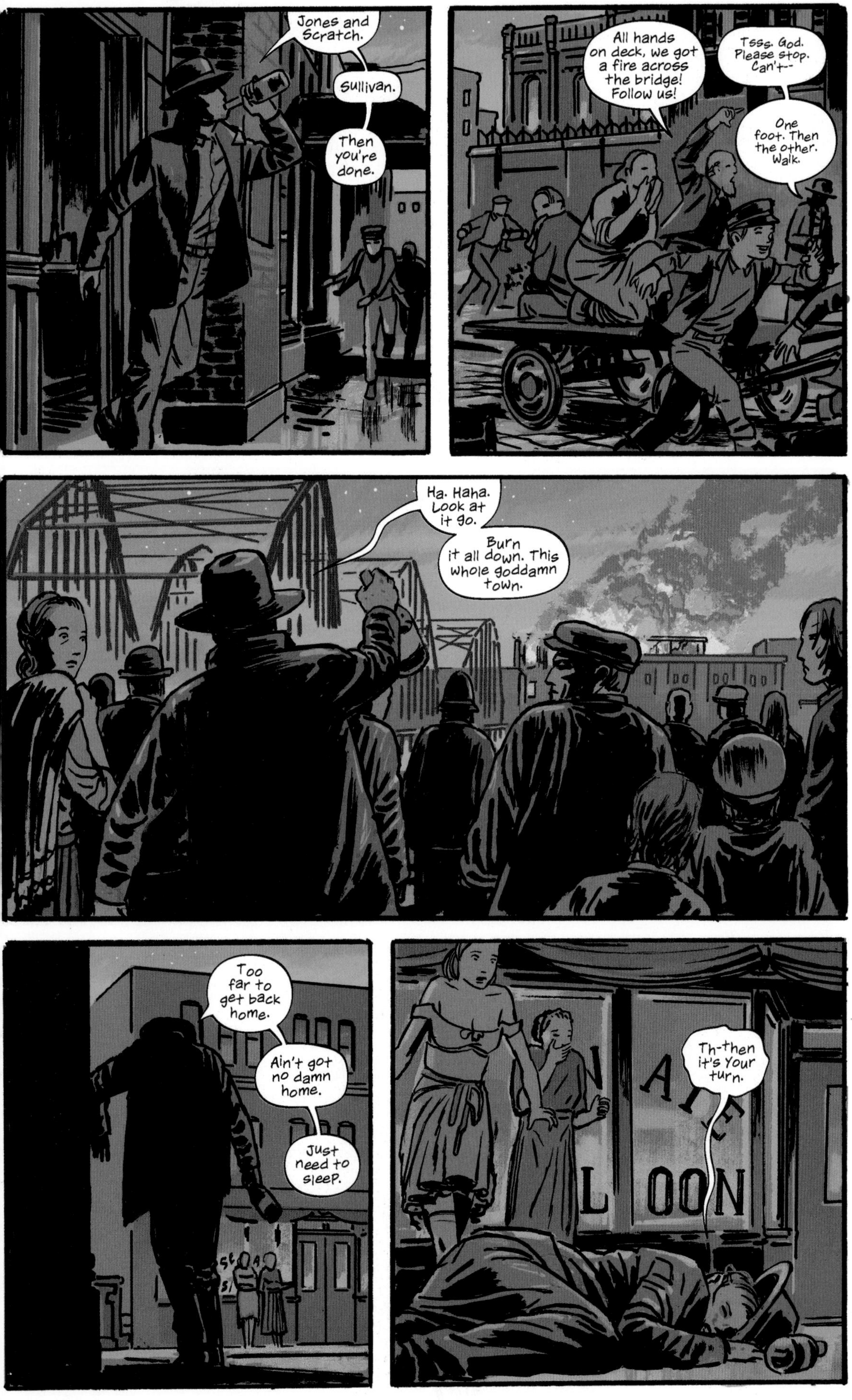
Jones and Scratch.
Sullivan.
Then you're done.
All hands on deck, we got a fire across the bridge! Follow us!
Tsss. God. Please stop. Can't--
One foot. Then the other. Walk.
Ha. Haha. Look at it go.
Burn it all down. This whole goddamn town.
Too far to get back home.
Ain't got no damn home.
Just need to sleep.
Th-then it's your turn.

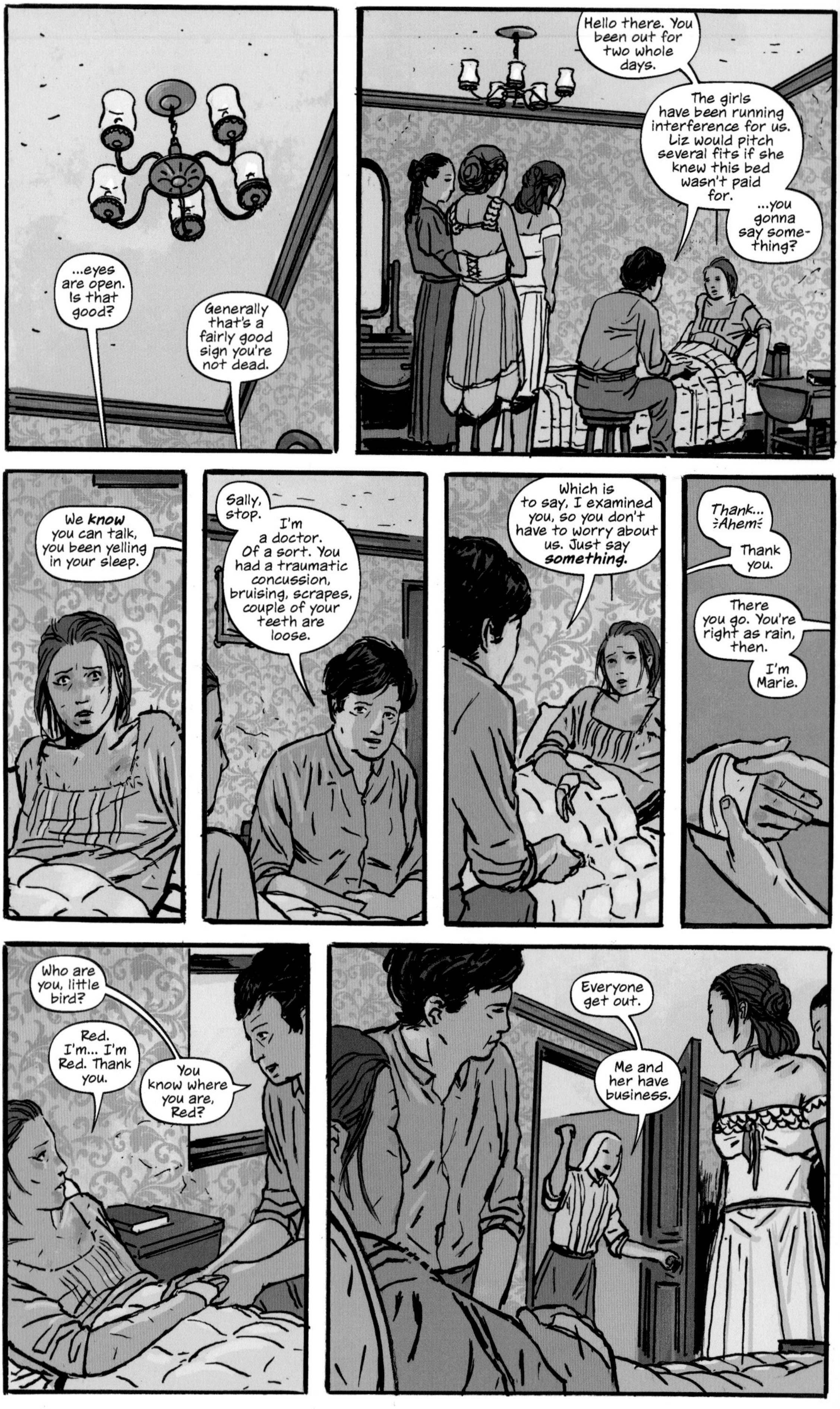

...eyes are open. Is that good?
Generally that's a fairly good sign you're not dead.
Hello there. You been out for two whole days.
The girls have been running interference for us. Liz would pitch several fits if she knew this bed wasn't paid for.
...you gonna say some-thing?
We **know** you can talk, you been yelling in your sleep.
Sally, stop.
I'm a doctor. Of a sort. You had a traumatic concussion, bruising, scrapes, couple of your teeth are loose.
Which is to say, I examined you, so you don't have to worry about us. Just say **something.**
Thank... Ahem
Thank you.
There you go. You're right as rain, then.
I'm Marie.
Who are you, little bird?
Red. I'm... I'm Red. Thank you.
You know where you are, Red?
Everyone get out.
Me and her have business.

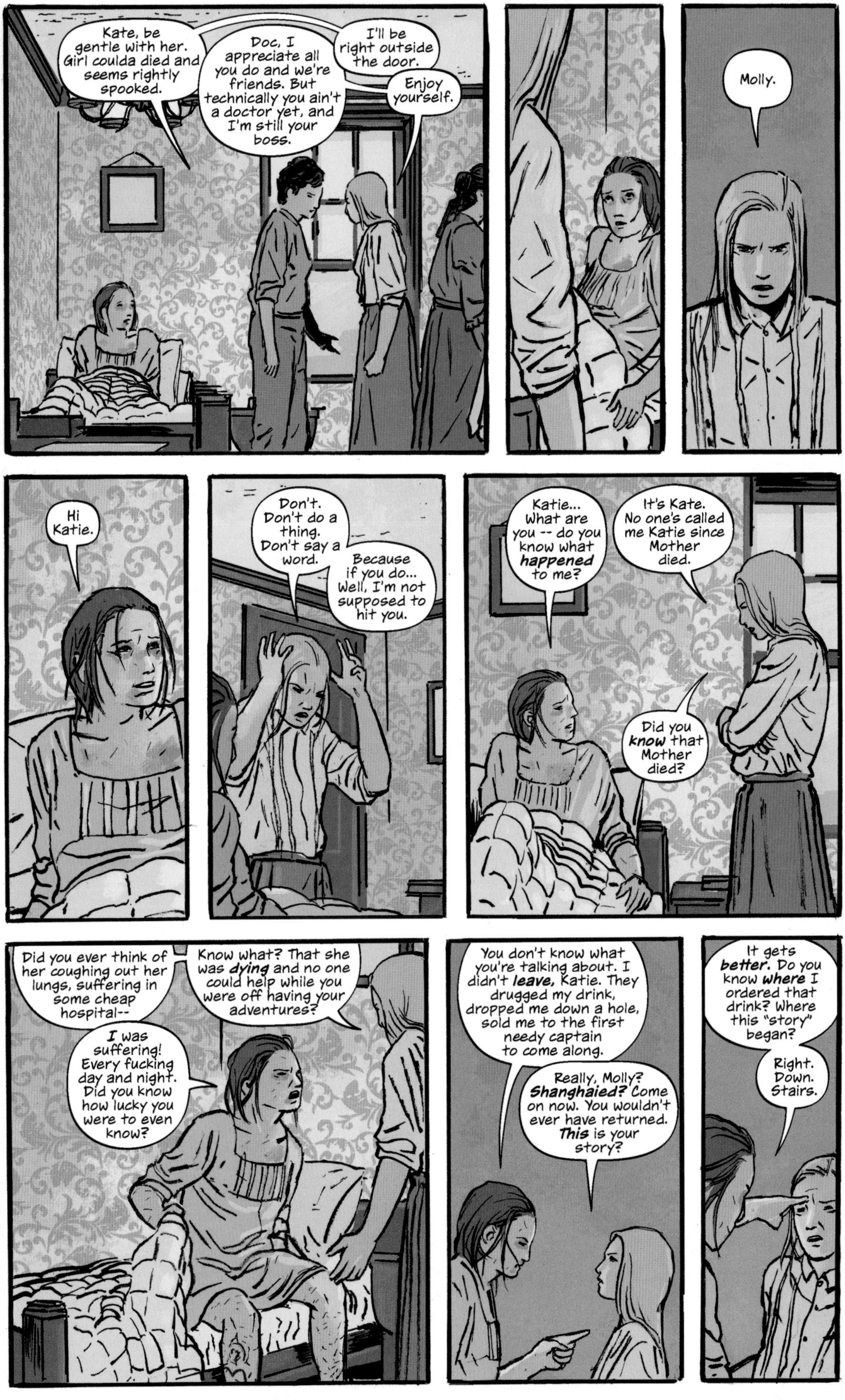
Kate, be gentle with her. Girl coulda died and seems rightly spooked.
Doc, I appreciate all you do and we're friends. But technically you ain't a doctor yet, and I'm still your boss.
I'll be right outside the door.
Enjoy yourself.
Molly.
Hi Katie.
Don't. Don't do a thing. Don't say a word.
Because if you do... Well, I'm not supposed to hit you.
Katie... What are you -- do you know what happened to me?
It's Kate. No one's called me Katie since Mother died.
Did you know that Mother died?
Did you ever think of her coughing out her lungs, suffering in some cheap hospital--
Know what? That she was dying and no one could help while you were off having your adventures?
I was suffering! Every fucking day and night. Did you know how lucky you were to even know?
You don't know what you're talking about. I didn't leave, Katie. They drugged my drink, dropped me down a hole, sold me to the first needy captain to come along.
Really, Molly? Shanghaied? Come on now. You wouldn't ever have returned. This is your story?
It gets better. Do you know where I ordered that drink? Where this "story" began?
Right. Down. Stairs.

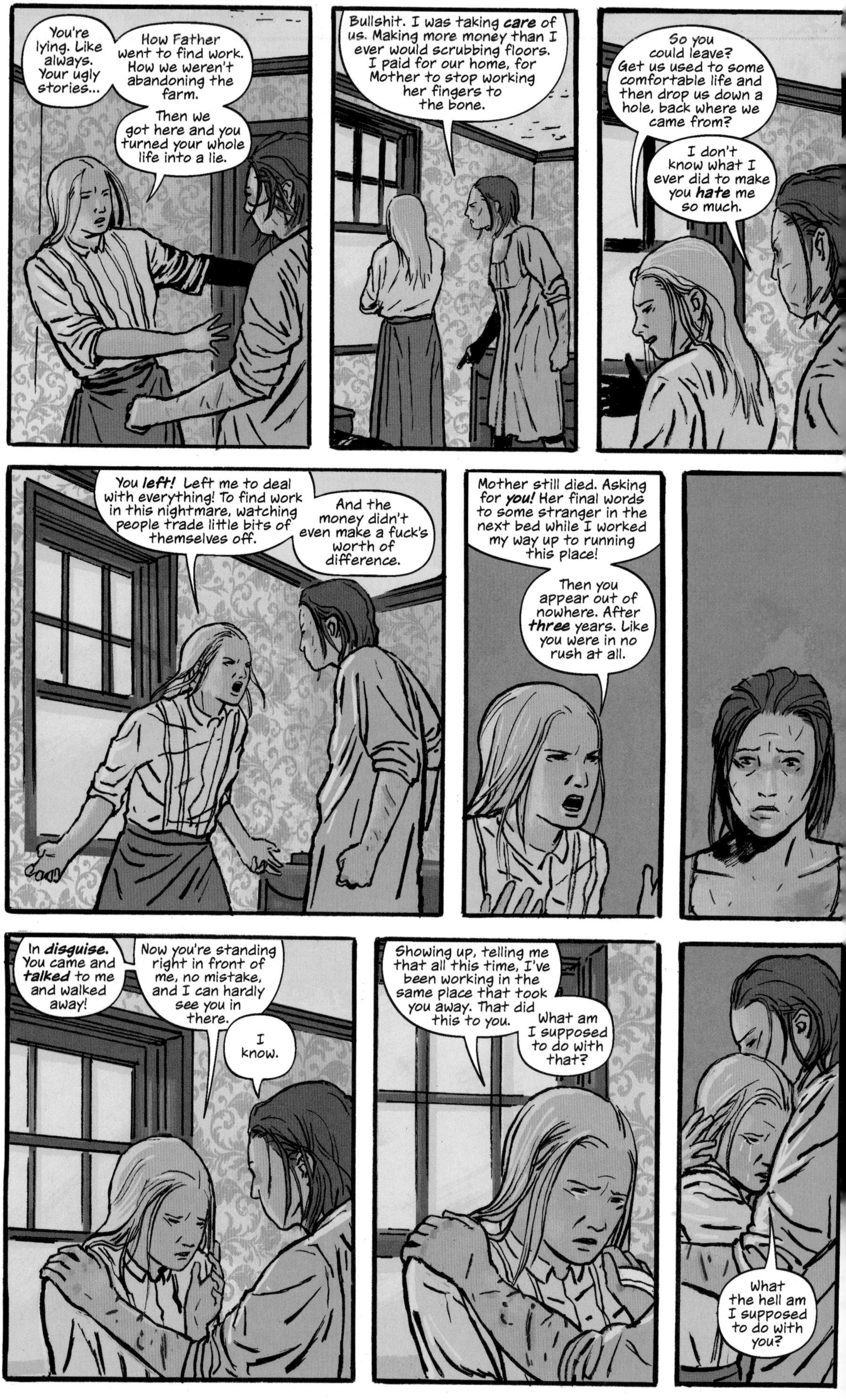
You're lying. Like always. Your ugly stories...
How Father went to find work. How we weren't abandoning the farm.
Then we got here and you turned your whole life into a lie.
Bullshit. I was taking *care* of us. Making more money than I ever would scrubbing floors. I paid for our home, for Mother to stop working her fingers to the bone.
So you could leave? Get us used to some comfortable life and then drop us down a hole, back where we came from?
I don't know what I ever did to make you *hate* me so much.
You *left!* Left me to deal with everything! To find work in this nightmare, watching people trade little bits of themselves off.
And the money didn't even make a fuck's worth of difference.
Mother still died. Asking for *you!* Her final words to some stranger in the next bed while I worked my way up to running this place!
Then you appear out of nowhere. After *three* years. Like you were in no rush at all.
In *disguise.* You came and *talked* to me and walked away!
Now you're standing right in front of me, no mistake, and I can hardly see you in there.
I know.
Showing up, telling me that all this time, I've been working in the same place that took you away. That did this to you.
What am I supposed to do with that?
What the hell am I supposed to do with you?

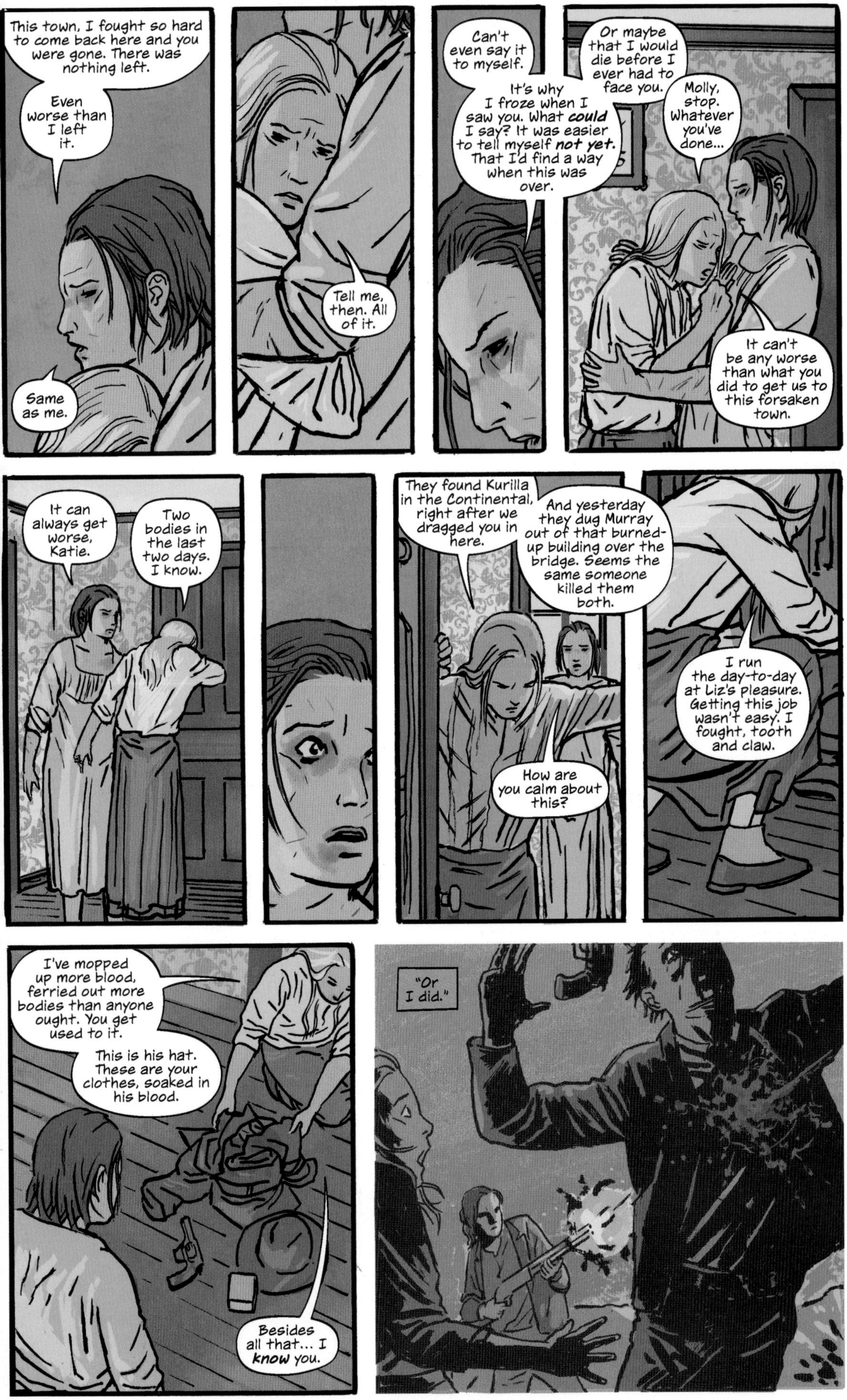
This town, I fought so hard to come back here and you were gone. There was nothing left.
Even worse than I left it.
Same as me.
Tell me, then. All of it.
Can't even say it to myself.
It's why I froze when I saw you. What **could** I say? It was easier to tell myself **not yet**. That I'd find a way when this was over.
Or maybe that I would die before I ever had to face you.
Molly, stop. Whatever you've done...
It can't be any worse than what you did to get us to this forsaken town.
It can always get worse, Katie.
Two bodies in the last two days. I know.
They found Kurilla in the Continental, right after we dragged you in here.
And yesterday they dug Murray out of that burned-up building over the bridge. Seems the same someone killed them both.
How are you calm about this?
I run the day-to-day at Liz's pleasure. Getting this job wasn't easy. I fought, tooth and claw.
I've mopped up more blood, ferried out more bodies than anyone ought. You get used to it.
This is his hat. These are your clothes, soaked in his blood.
Besides all that... I **know** you.
"Or I did."

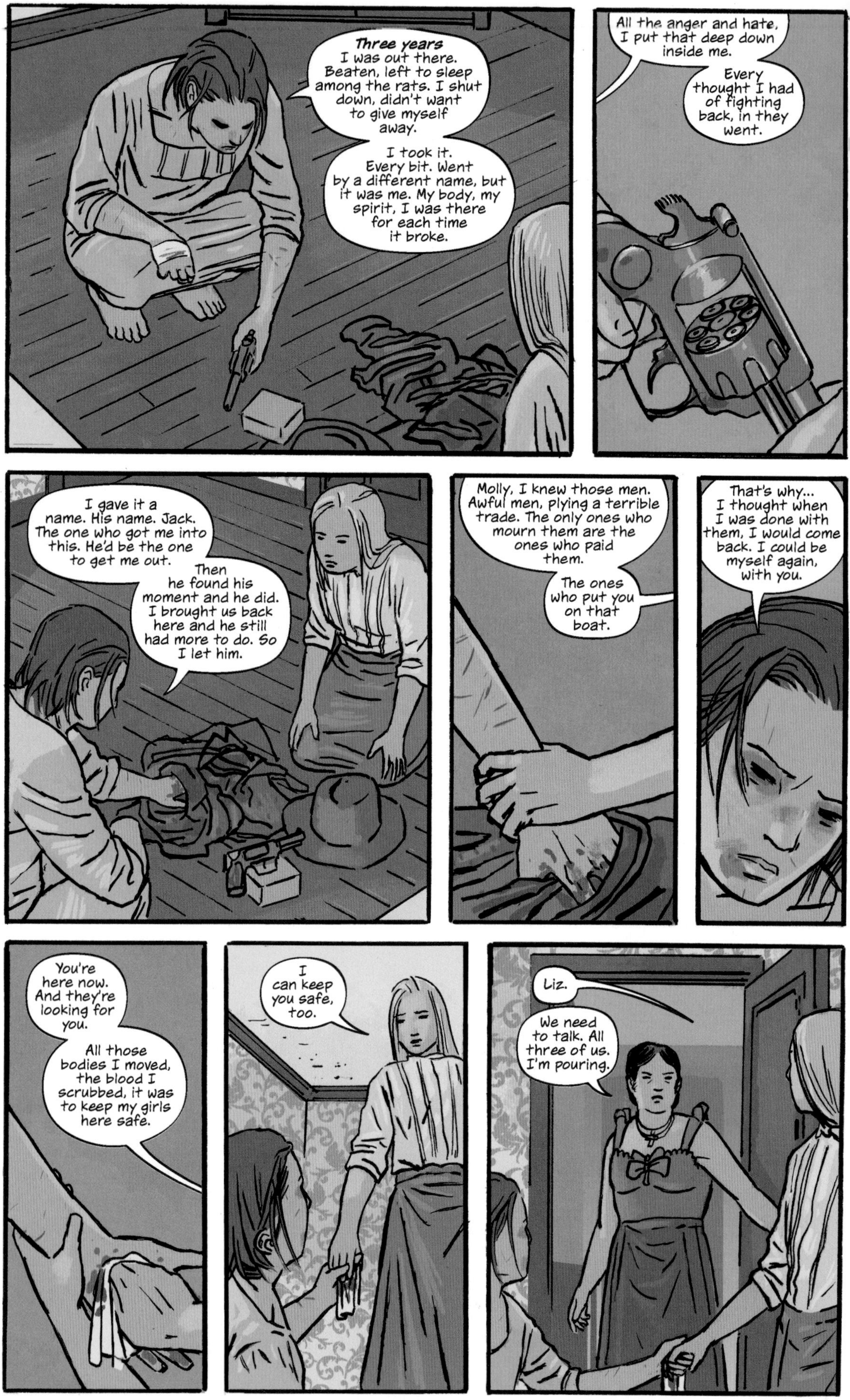

Three years I was out there. Beaten, left to sleep among the rats. I shut down, didn't want to give myself away.
I took it. Every bit. Went by a different name, but it was me. My body, my spirit, I was there for each time it broke.
All the anger and hate, I put that deep down inside me.
Every thought I had of fighting back, in they went.
I gave it a name. His name. Jack. The one who got me into this. He'd be the one to get me out.
Then he found his moment and he did. I brought us back here and he still had more to do. So I let him.
Molly, I knew those men. Awful men, plying a terrible trade. The only ones who mourn them are the ones who paid them.
The ones who put you on that boat.
That's why... I thought when I was done with them, I would come back. I could be myself again, with you.
You're here now. And they're looking for you.
All those bodies I moved, the blood I scrubbed, it was to keep my girls here safe.
I can keep you safe, too.
Liz.
We need to talk. All three of us. I'm pouring.

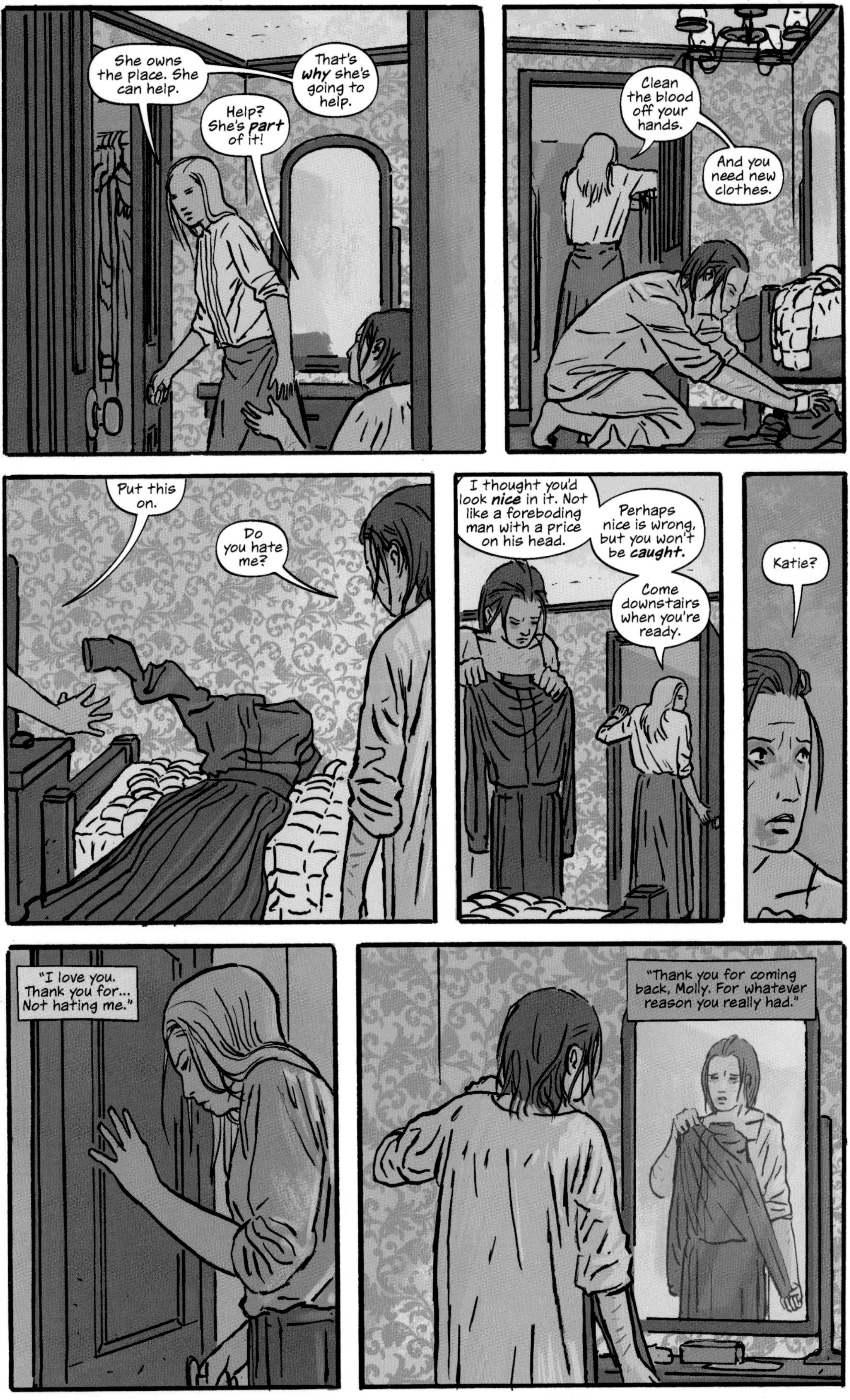

She owns the place. She can help.
That's *why* she's going to help.
Help? She's *part* of it!
Clean the blood off your hands.
And you need new clothes.
Put this on.
Do you hate me?
I thought you'd look *nice* in it. Not like a foreboding man with a price on his head.
Perhaps nice is wrong, but you won't be *caught.*
Come downstairs when you're ready.
Katie?
"I love you. Thank you for... Not hating me."
"Thank you for coming back, Molly. For whatever reason you really had."

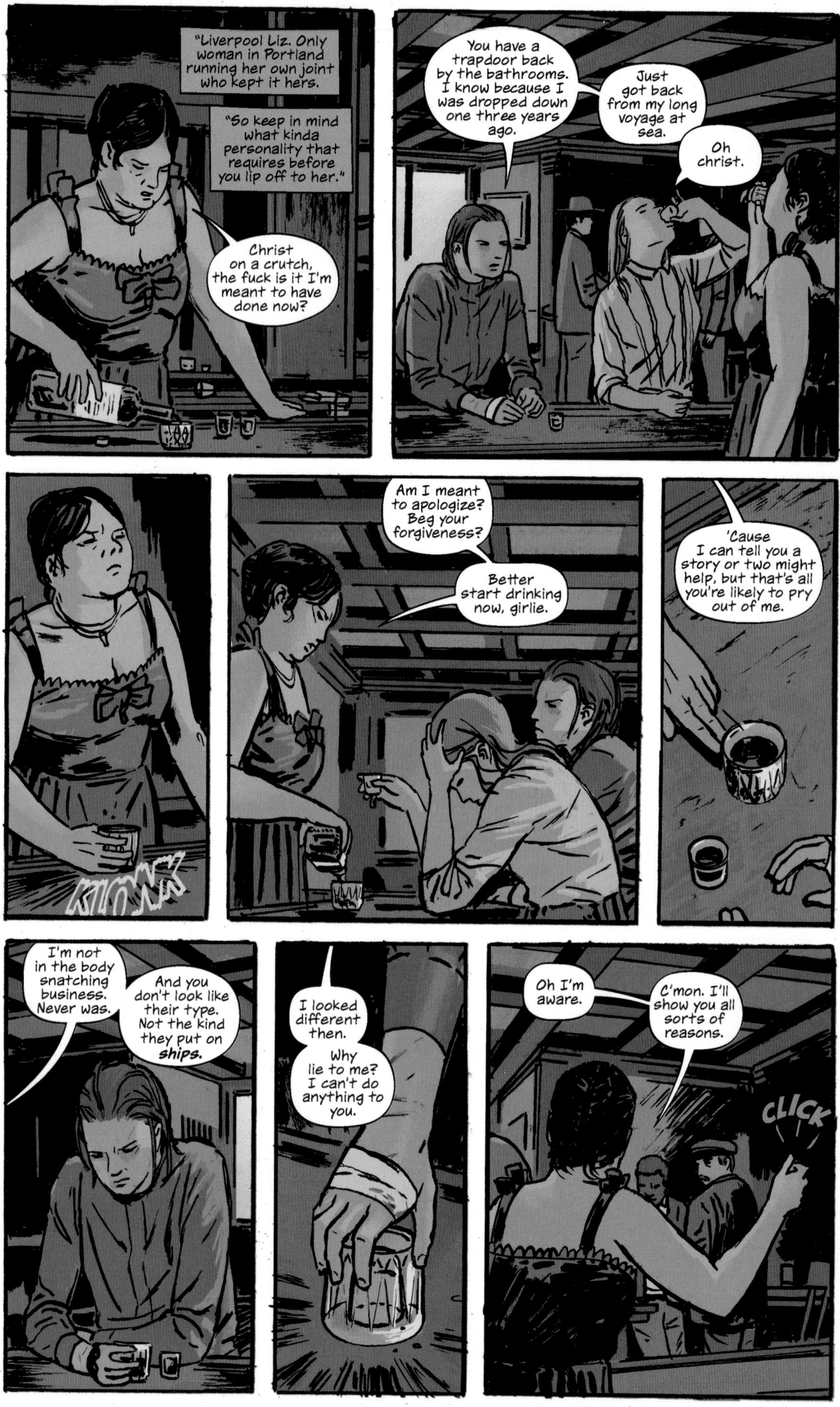
"Liverpool Liz. Only woman in Portland running her own joint who kept it hers.
"So keep in mind what kinda personality that requires before you lip off to her."
Christ on a crutch, the fuck is it I'm meant to have done now?
You have a trapdoor back by the bathrooms. I know because I was dropped down one three years ago.
Just got back from my long voyage at sea.
Oh christ.
KLONK
Am I meant to apologize? Beg your forgiveness?
Better start drinking now, girlie.
'Cause I can tell you a story or two might help, but that's all you're likely to pry out of me.
I'm not in the body snatching business. Never was.
And you don't look like their type. Not the kind they put on ***ships.***
I looked different then.
Why lie to me? I can't do anything to you.
Oh I'm aware.
C'mon. I'll show you all sorts of reasons.
CLICK

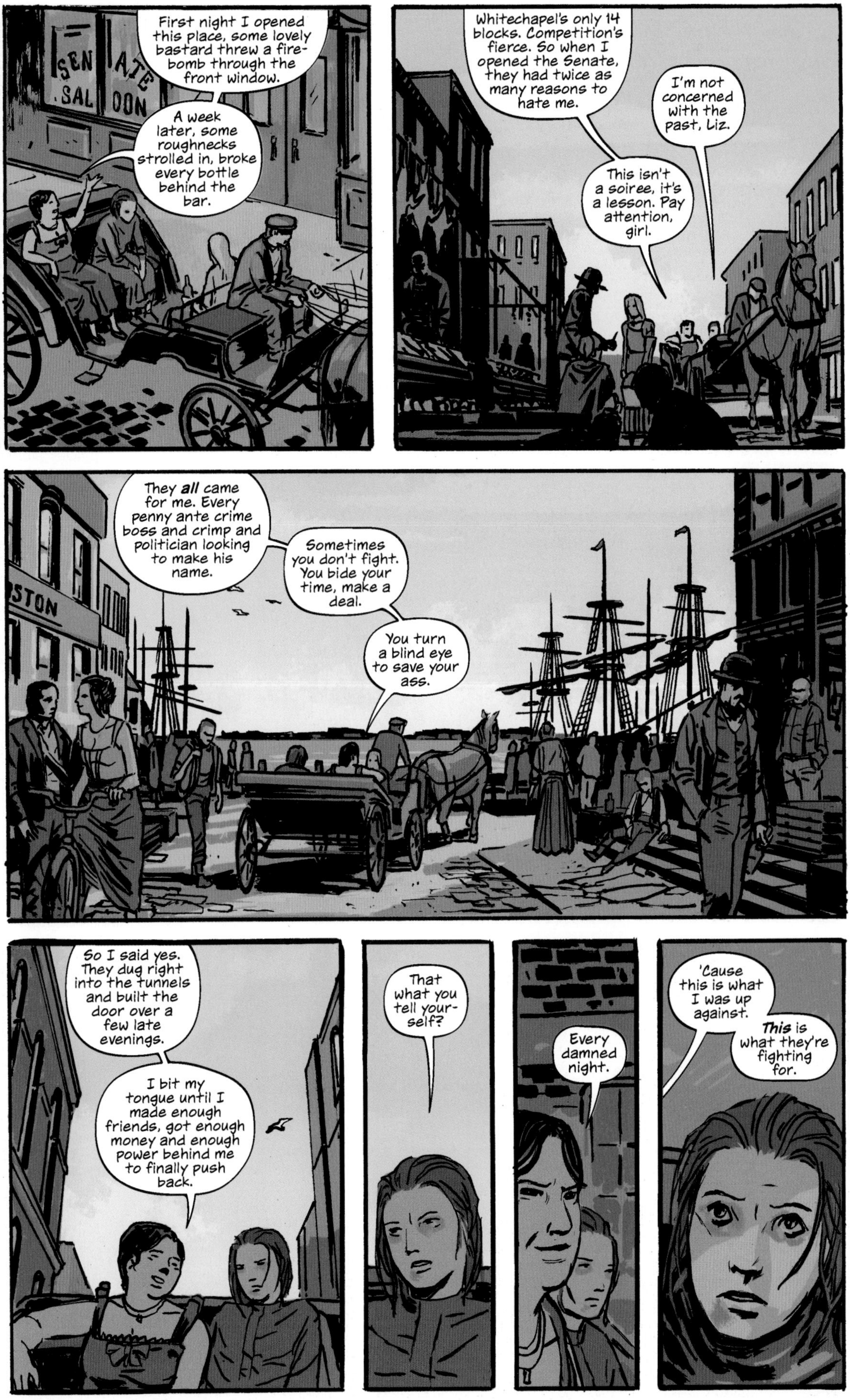
SENATE SALOON
First night I opened this place, some lovely bastard threw a fire-bomb through the front window.
A week later, some roughnecks strolled in, broke every bottle behind the bar.
Whitechapel's only 14 blocks. Competition's fierce. So when I opened the Senate, they had twice as many reasons to hate me.
This isn't a soiree, it's a lesson. Pay attention, girl.
I'm not concerned with the past, Liz.
They all came for me. Every penny ante crime boss and crimp and politician looking to make his name.
Sometimes you don't fight. You bide your time, make a deal.
You turn a blind eye to save your ass.
So I said yes. They dug right into the tunnels and built the door over a few late evenings.
I bit my tongue until I made enough friends, got enough money and enough power behind me to finally push back.
That what you tell your-self?
Every damned night.
'Cause this is what I was up against.
This is what they're fighting for.

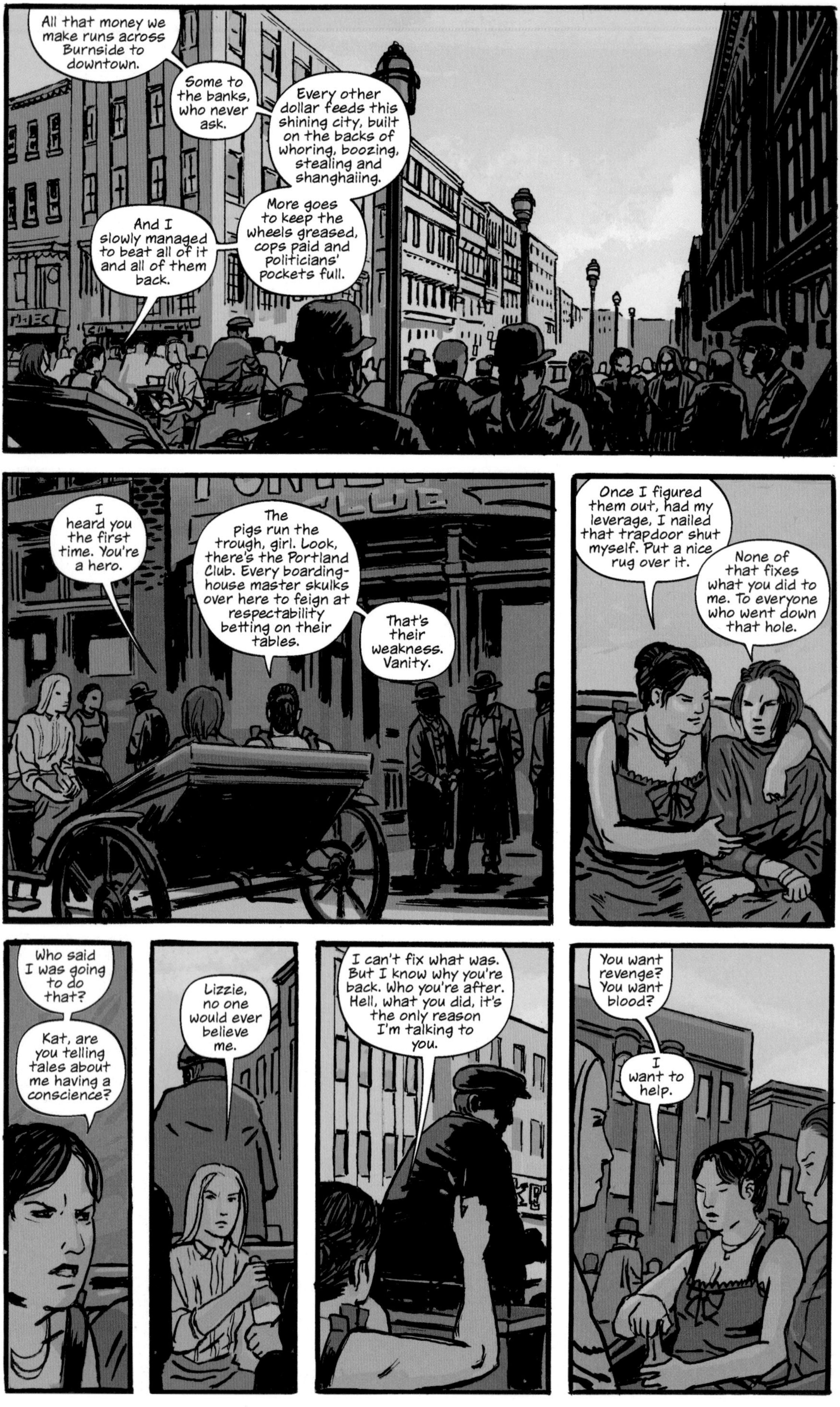
All that money we make runs across Burnside to downtown.
Some to the banks, who never ask.
Every other dollar feeds this shining city, built on the backs of whoring, boozing, stealing and shanghaiing.
More goes to keep the wheels greased, cops paid and politicians' pockets full.
And I slowly managed to beat all of it and all of them back.
I heard you the first time. You're a hero.
The pigs run the trough, girl. Look, there's the Portland Club. Every boarding-house master skulks over here to feign at respectability betting on their tables.
That's their weakness. Vanity.
Once I figured them out, had my leverage, I nailed that trapdoor shut myself. Put a nice rug over it.
None of that fixes what you did to me. To everyone who went down that hole.
Who said I was going to do that?
Kat, are you telling tales about me having a conscience?
Lizzie, no one would ever believe me.
I can't fix what was. But I know why you're back. Who you're after. Hell, what you did, it's the only reason I'm talking to you.
You want revenge? You want blood?
I want to help.

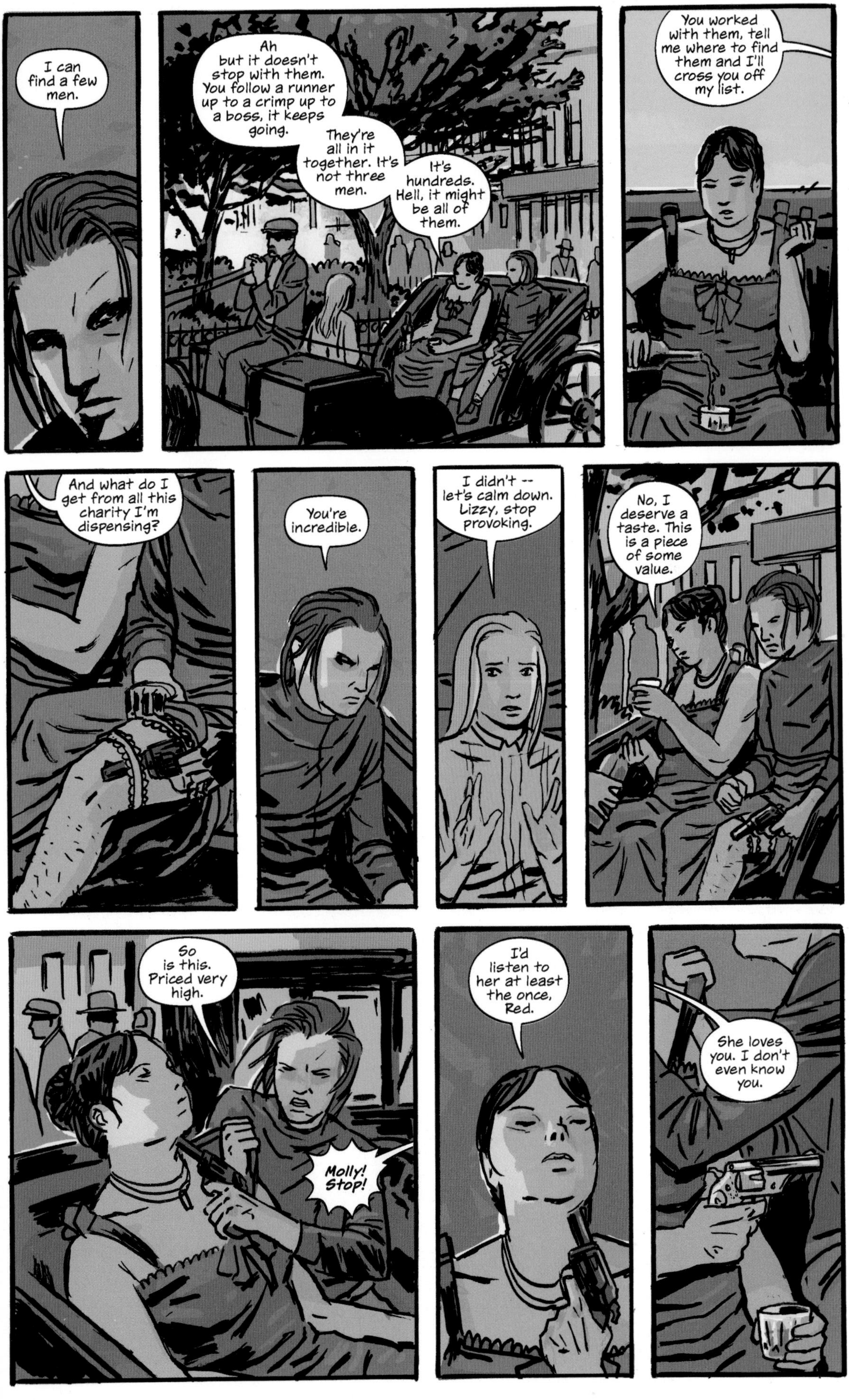
I can find a few men.
Ah but it doesn't stop with them. You follow a runner up to a crimp up to a boss, it keeps going.
They're all in it together. It's not three men.
It's hundreds. Hell, it might be all of them.
You worked with them, tell me where to find them and I'll cross you off my list.
And what do I get from all this charity I'm dispensing?
You're incredible.
I didn't -- let's calm down. Lizzy, stop provoking.
No, I deserve a taste. This is a piece of some value.
So is this. Priced very high.
Molly! Stop!
I'd listen to her at least the once, Red.
She loves you. I don't even know you.

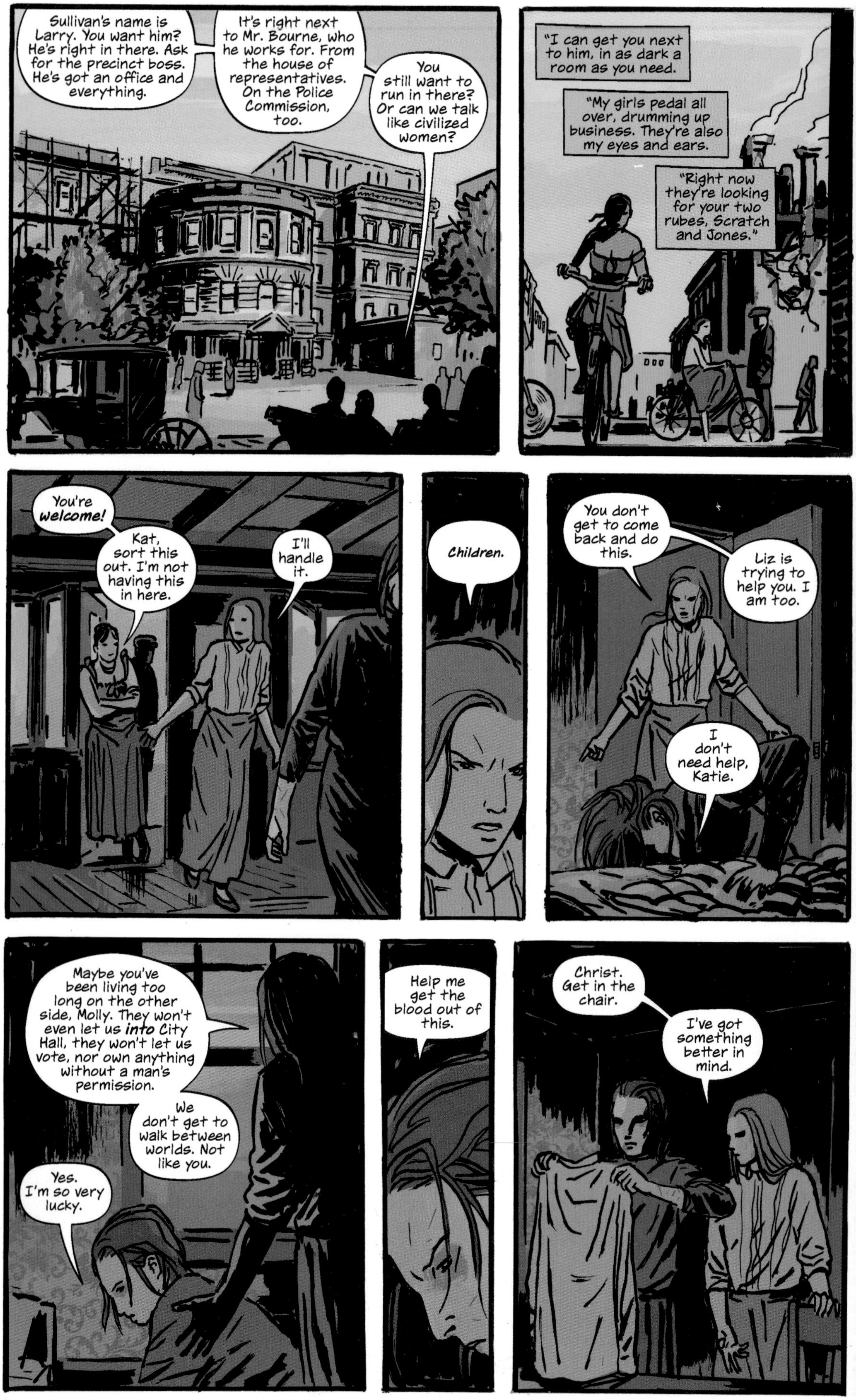
Sullivan's name is Larry. You want him? He's right in there. Ask for the precinct boss. He's got an office and everything.
It's right next to Mr. Bourne, who he works for. From the house of representatives. On the Police Commission, too.
You still want to run in there? Or can we talk like civilized women?
"I can get you next to him, in as dark a room as you need.
"My girls pedal all over, drumming up business. They're also my eyes and ears.
"Right now they're looking for your two rubes, Scratch and Jones."
You're *welcome!*
Kat, sort this out. I'm not having this in here.
I'll handle it.
Children.
You don't get to come back and do this.
Liz is trying to help you. I am too.
I don't need help, Katie.
Maybe you've been living too long on the other side, Molly. They won't even let us *into* City Hall, they won't let us vote, nor own anything without a man's permission.
We don't get to walk between worlds. Not like you.
Yes. I'm so very lucky.
Help me get the blood out of this.
Christ. Get in the chair.
I've got something better in mind.

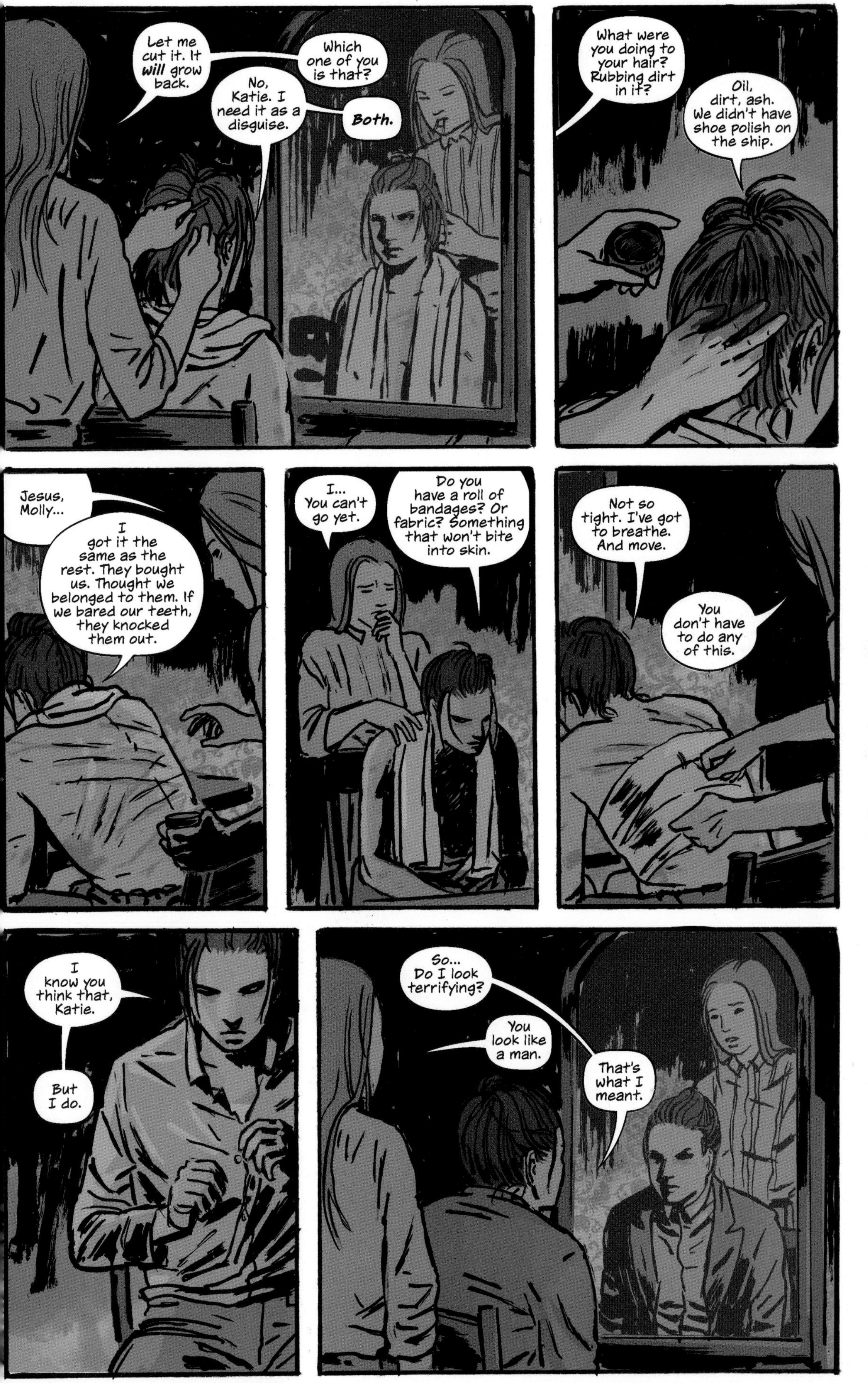
Let me cut it. It *will* grow back.
Which one of you is that?
No, Katie. I need it as a disguise.
Both.
What were you doing to your hair? Rubbing dirt in it?
Oil, dirt, ash. We didn't have shoe polish on the ship.
Jesus, Molly...
I got it the same as the rest. They bought us. Thought we belonged to them. If we bared our teeth, they knocked them out.
I... You can't go yet.
Do you have a roll of bandages? Or fabric? Something that won't bite into skin.
Not so tight. I've got to breathe. And move.
You don't have to do any of this.
I know you think that, Katie.
But I do.
So... Do I look terrifying?
You look like a man.
That's what I meant.

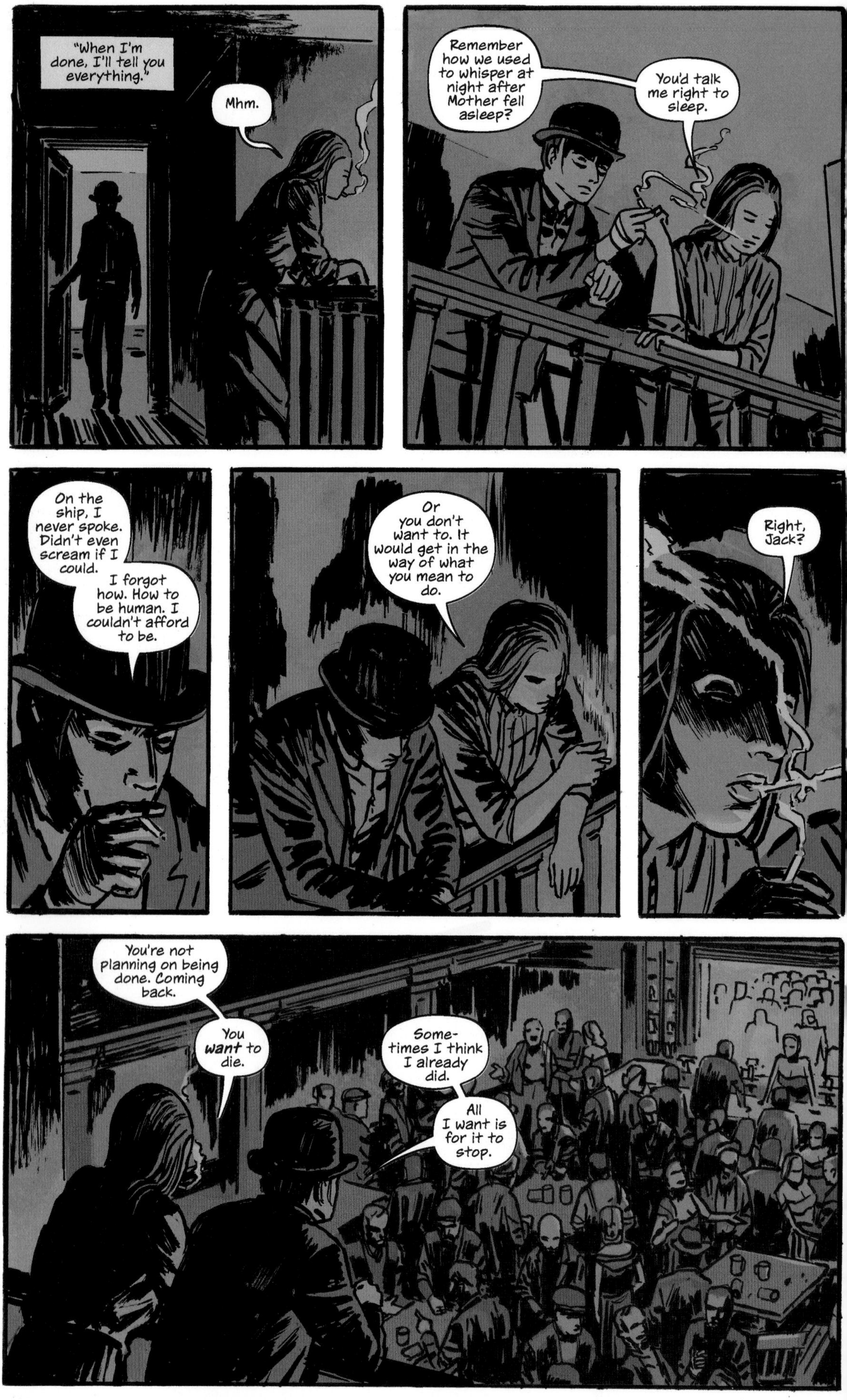
"When I'm done, I'll tell you everything."
Mhm.
Remember how we used to whisper at night after Mother fell asleep?
You'd talk me right to sleep.
On the ship, I never spoke. Didn't even scream if I could.
I forgot how. How to be human. I couldn't afford to be.
Or you don't want to. It would get in the way of what you mean to do.
Right, Jack?
You're not planning on being done. Coming back.
You *want* to die.
Some-times I think I already did.
All I want is for it to stop.

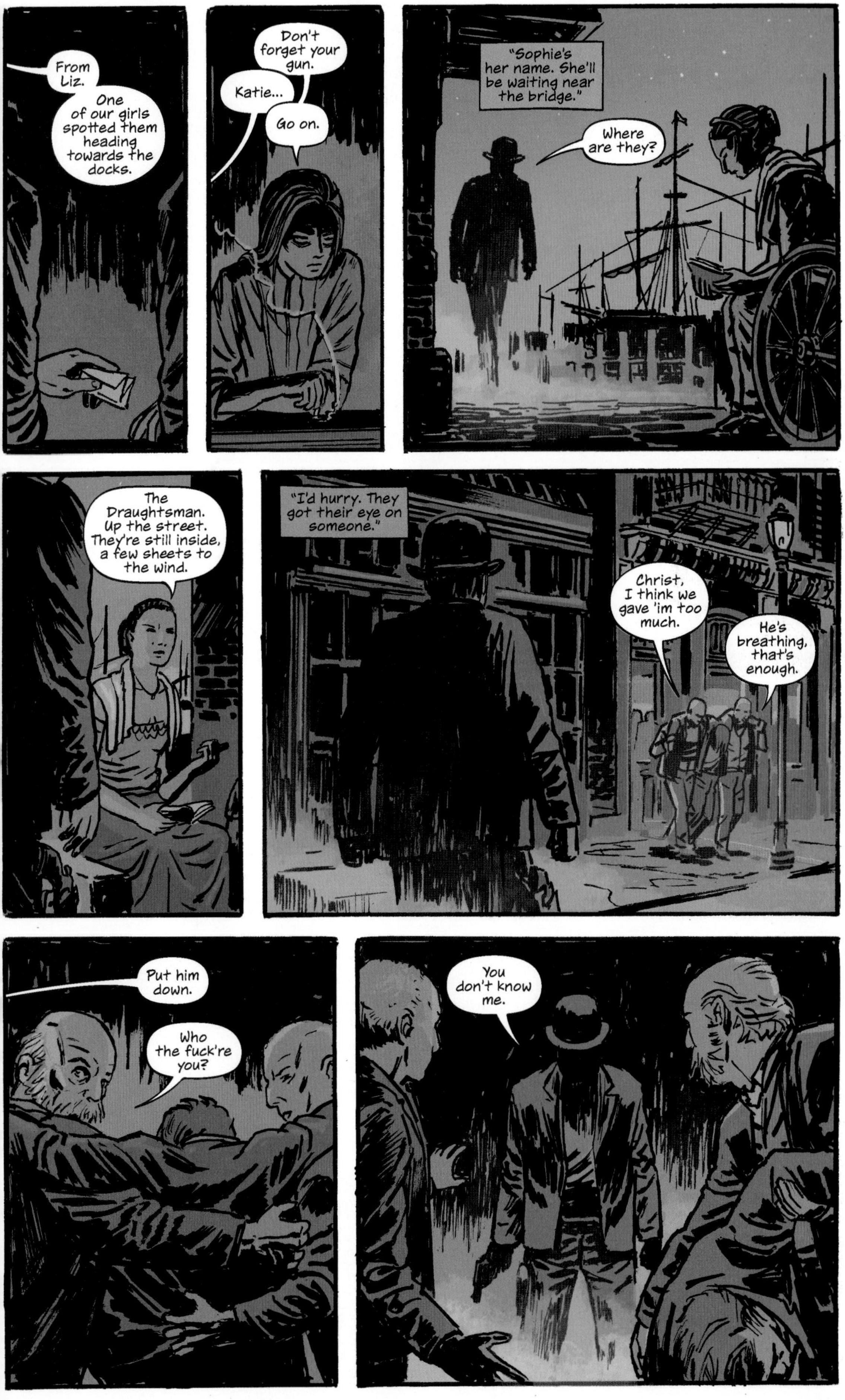
From Liz.
One of our girls spotted them heading towards the docks.
Katie...
Don't forget your gun.
Go on.
"Sophie's her name. She'll be waiting near the bridge."
Where are they?
The Draughtsman. Up the street. They're still inside, a few sheets to the wind.
"I'd hurry. They got their eye on someone."
Christ, I think we gave 'im too much.
He's breathing, that's enough.
Put him down.
Who the fuck're you?
You don't know me.

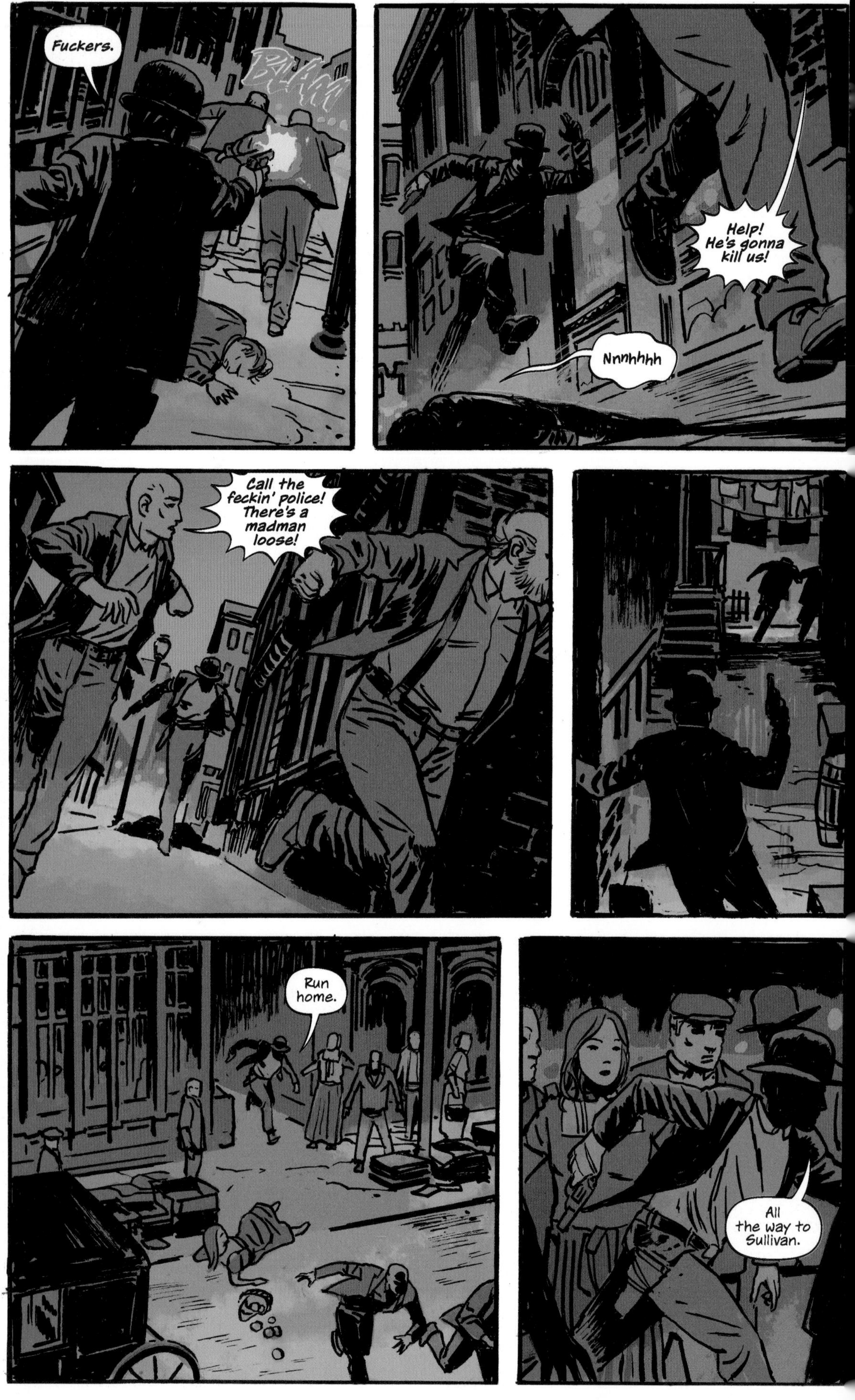
Fuckers.
BLAM
Help! He's gonna kill us!
Nnnhhhh
Call the feckin' police! There's a madman loose!
Run home.
All the way to Sullivan.

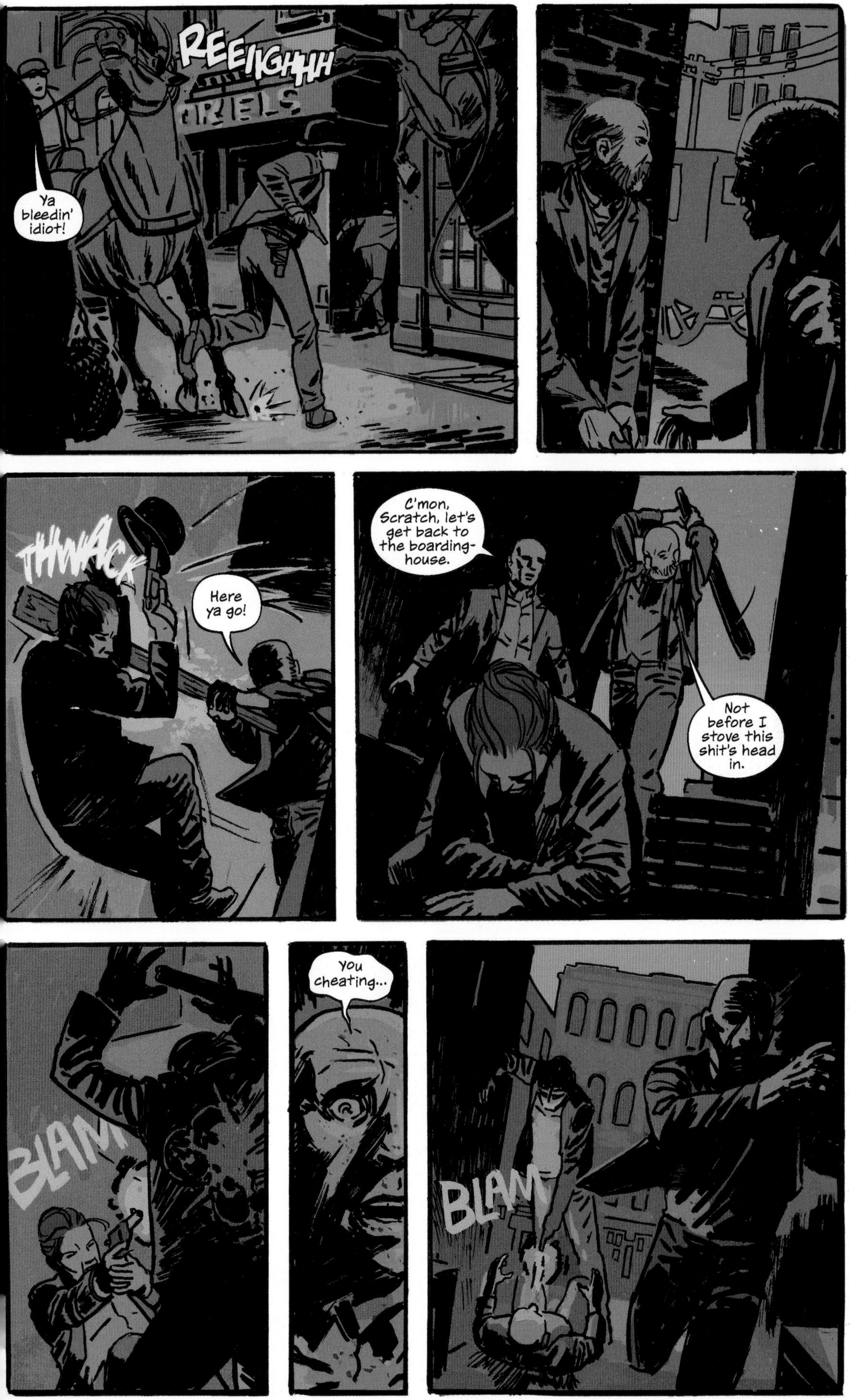
REEIGHHH
RELS
Ya bleedin' idiot!
THWACK
Here ya go!
C'mon, Scratch, let's get back to the boarding-house.
Not before I stove this shit's head in.
BLAM
You cheating...
BLAM

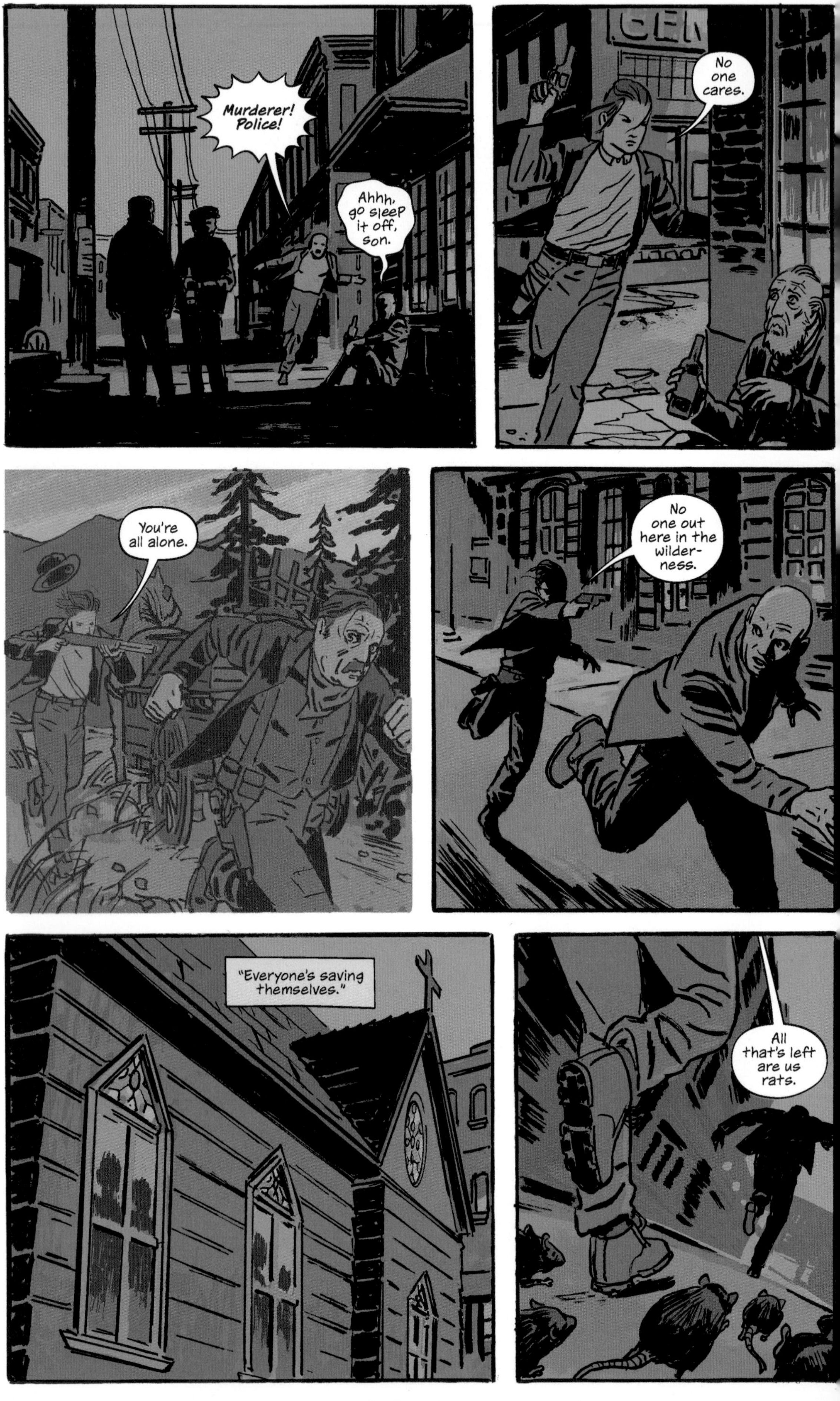
Murderer! Police!
Ahhh, go sleep it off, son.
No one cares.
You're all alone.
No one out here in the wilder-ness.
"Everyone's saving themselves."
All that's left are us rats.

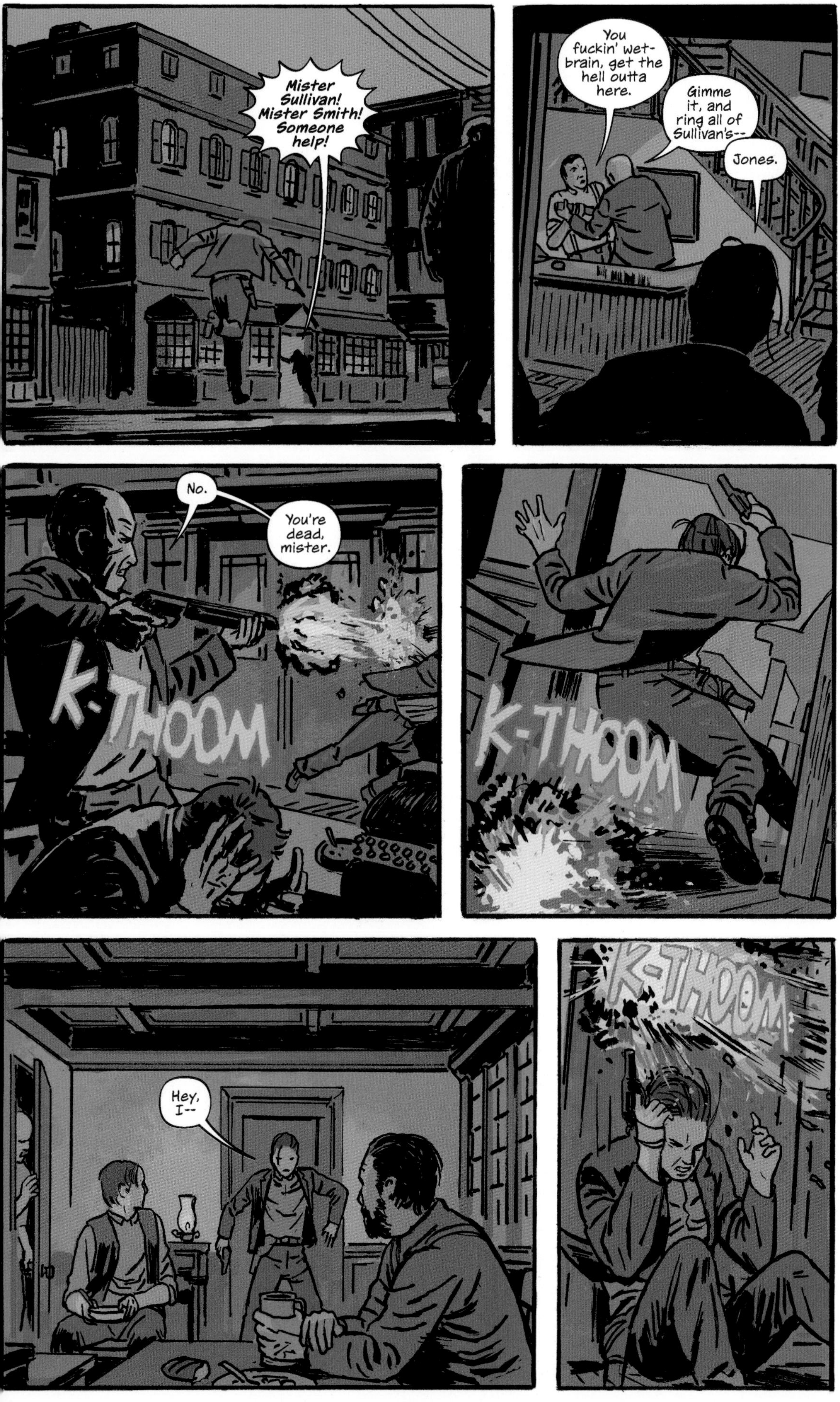
Mister Sullivan! Mister Smith! Someone help!
You fuckin' wet-brain, get the hell outta here.
Gimme it, and ring all of Sullivan's--
Jones.
No.
You're dead, mister.
K-THOOM
K-THOOM
Hey, I--
K-THOOM

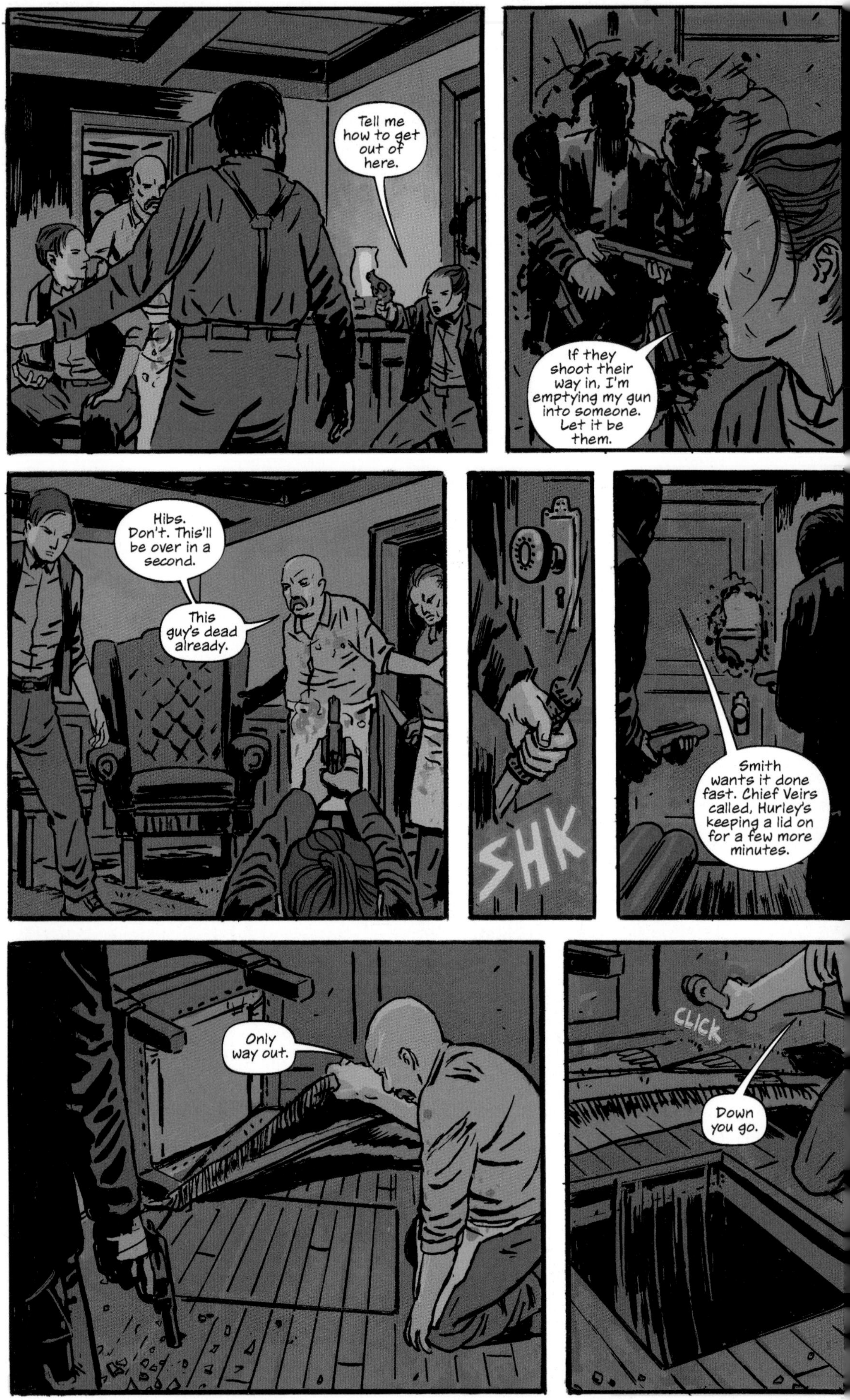
Tell me how to get out of here.
If they shoot their way in, I'm emptying my gun into someone. Let it be them.
Hibs. Don't. This'll be over in a second.
This guy's dead already.
SHK
Smith wants it done fast. Chief Veirs called, Hurley's keeping a lid on for a few more minutes.
Only way out.
CLICK
Down you go.

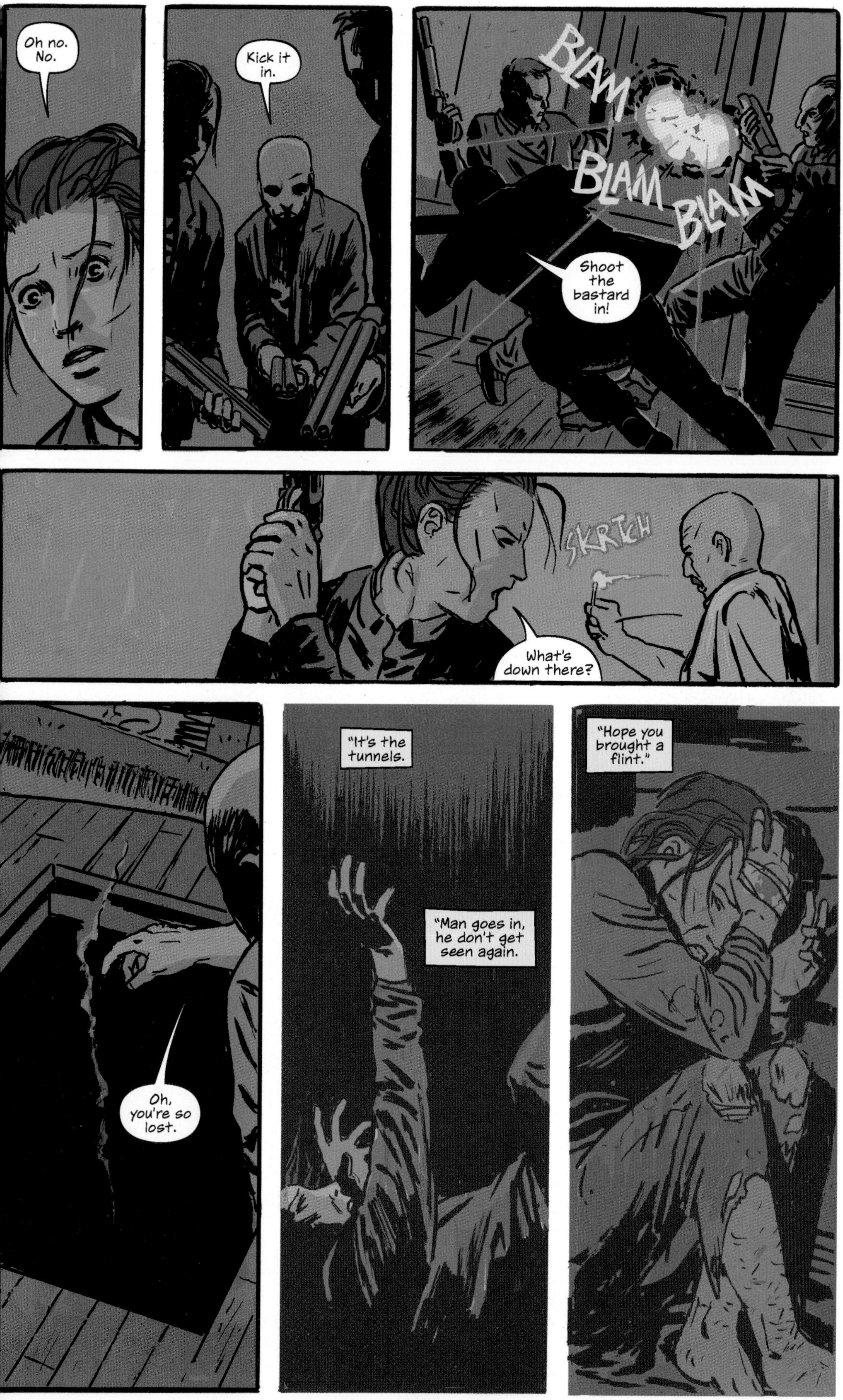
Oh no. No.
Kick it in.
BLAM
BLAM
BLAM
Shoot the bastard in!
SKRTCH
What's down there?
Oh, you're so lost.
"It's the tunnels.
"Man goes in, he don't get seen again.
"Hope you brought a flint."

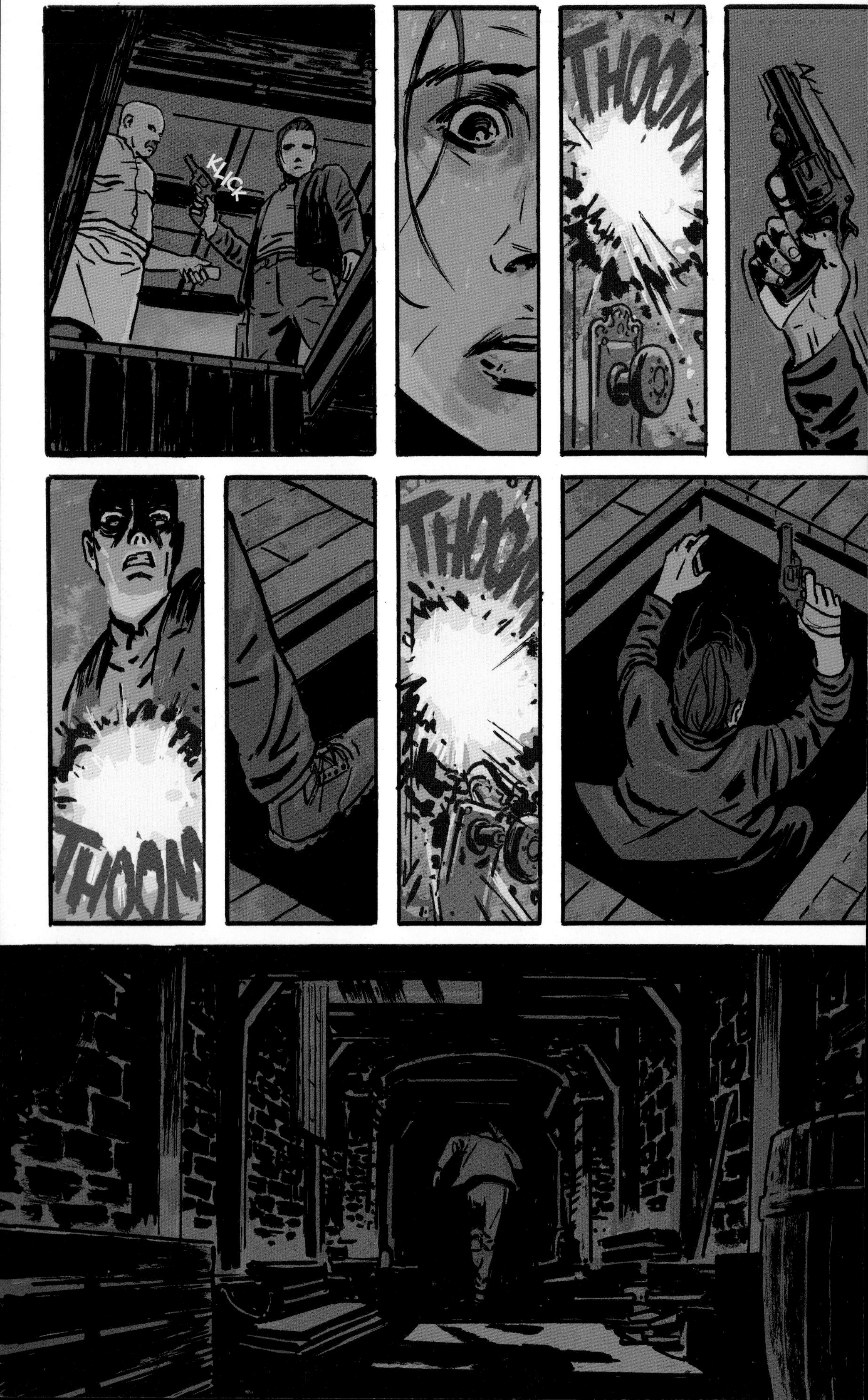
KLICK
THOOM
THOOM
THOOM

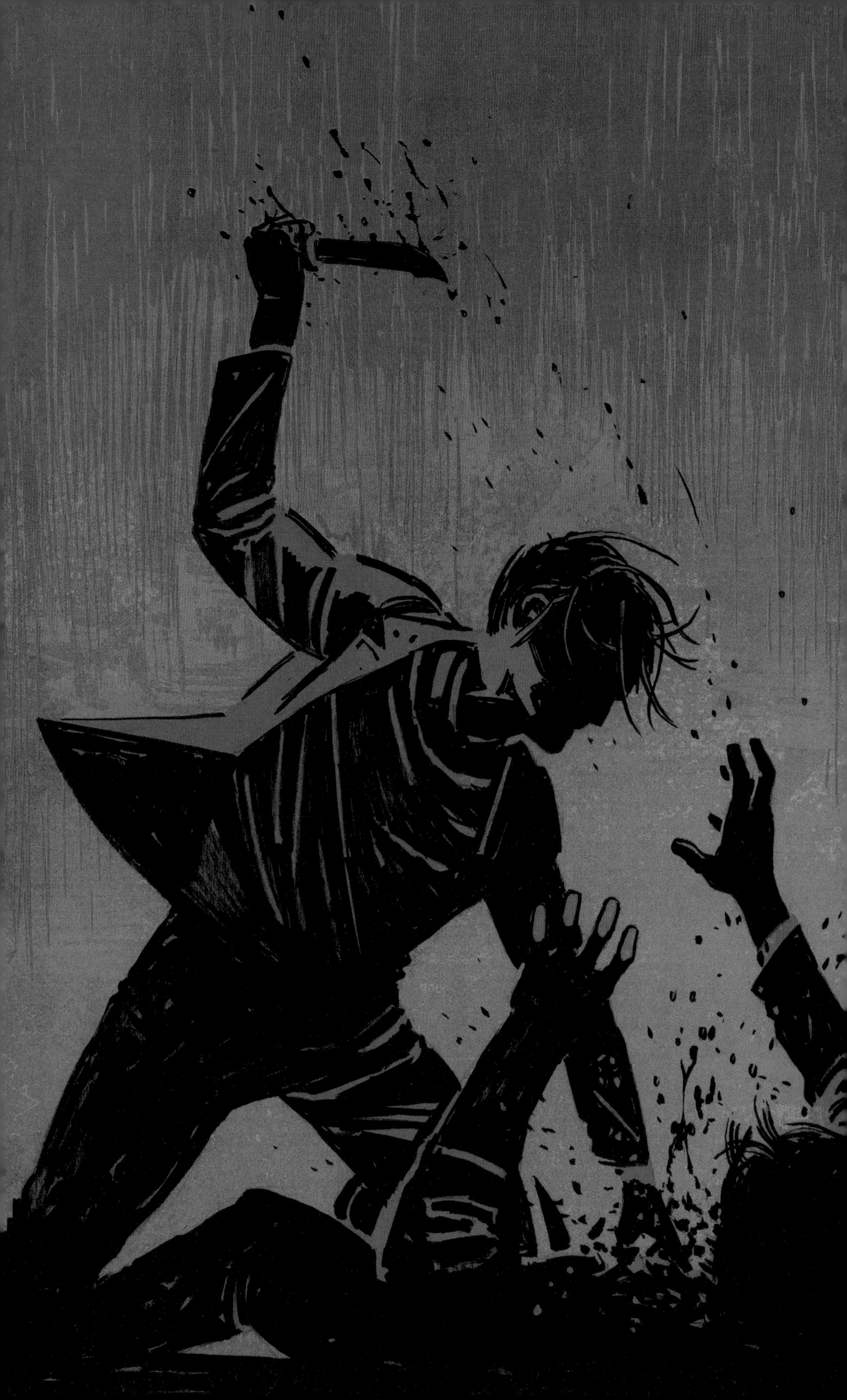

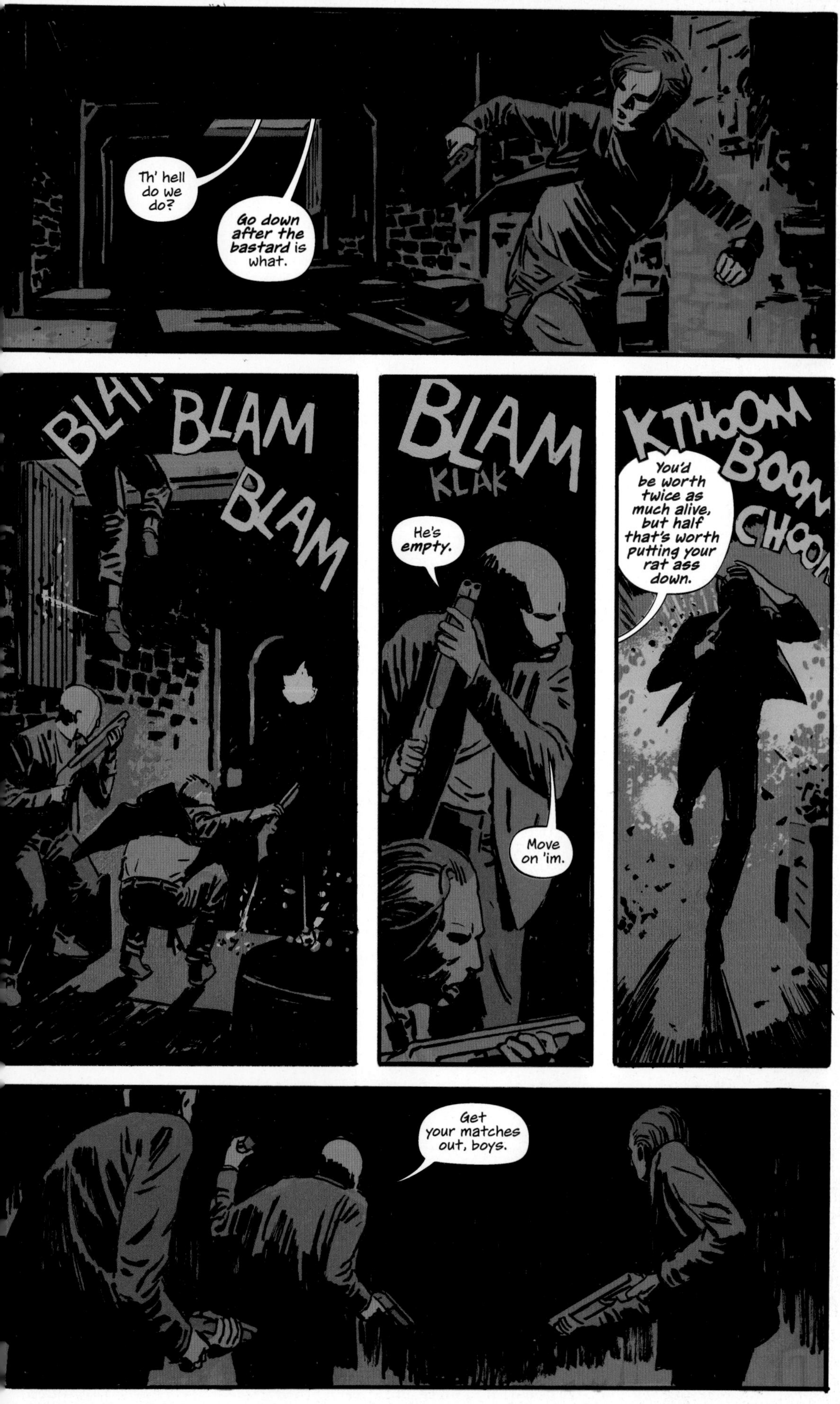
Th' hell do we do?
Go down after the bastard is what.
BLAM
BLAM
BLAM
KLAK
He's empty.
Move on 'im.
KTHOOM
You'd be worth twice as much alive, but half that's worth putting your rat ass down.
Get your matches out, boys.

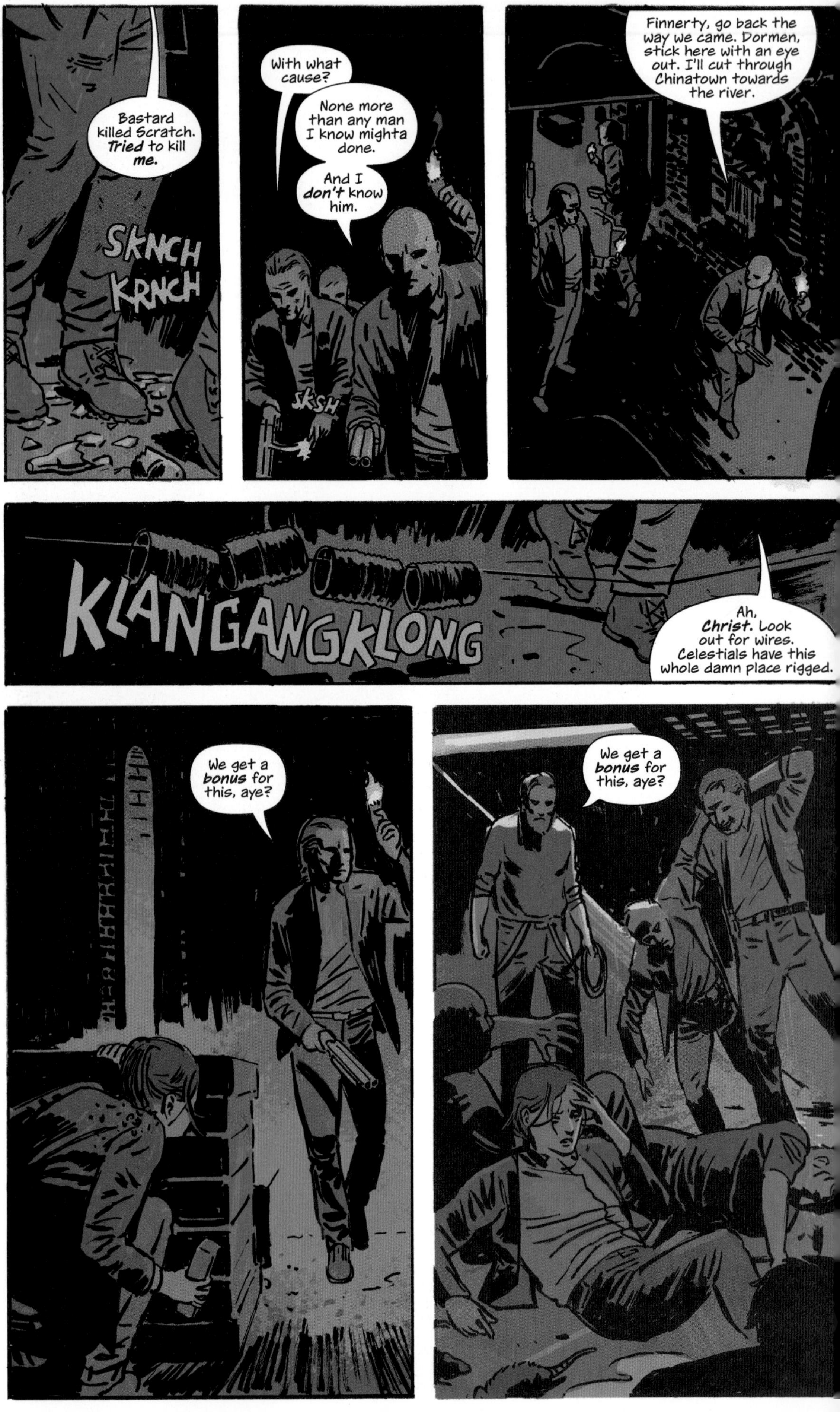
Bastard killed Scratch. Tried to kill me.
SKNCH KRNCH
With what cause?
None more than any man I know mighta done.
And I don't know him.
SKSH
Finnerty, go back the way we came. Dormen, stick here with an eye out. I'll cut through Chinatown towards the river.
KLANGANGKLONG
Ah, Christ. Look out for wires. Celestials have this whole damn place rigged.
We get a bonus for this, aye?
We get a bonus for this, aye?

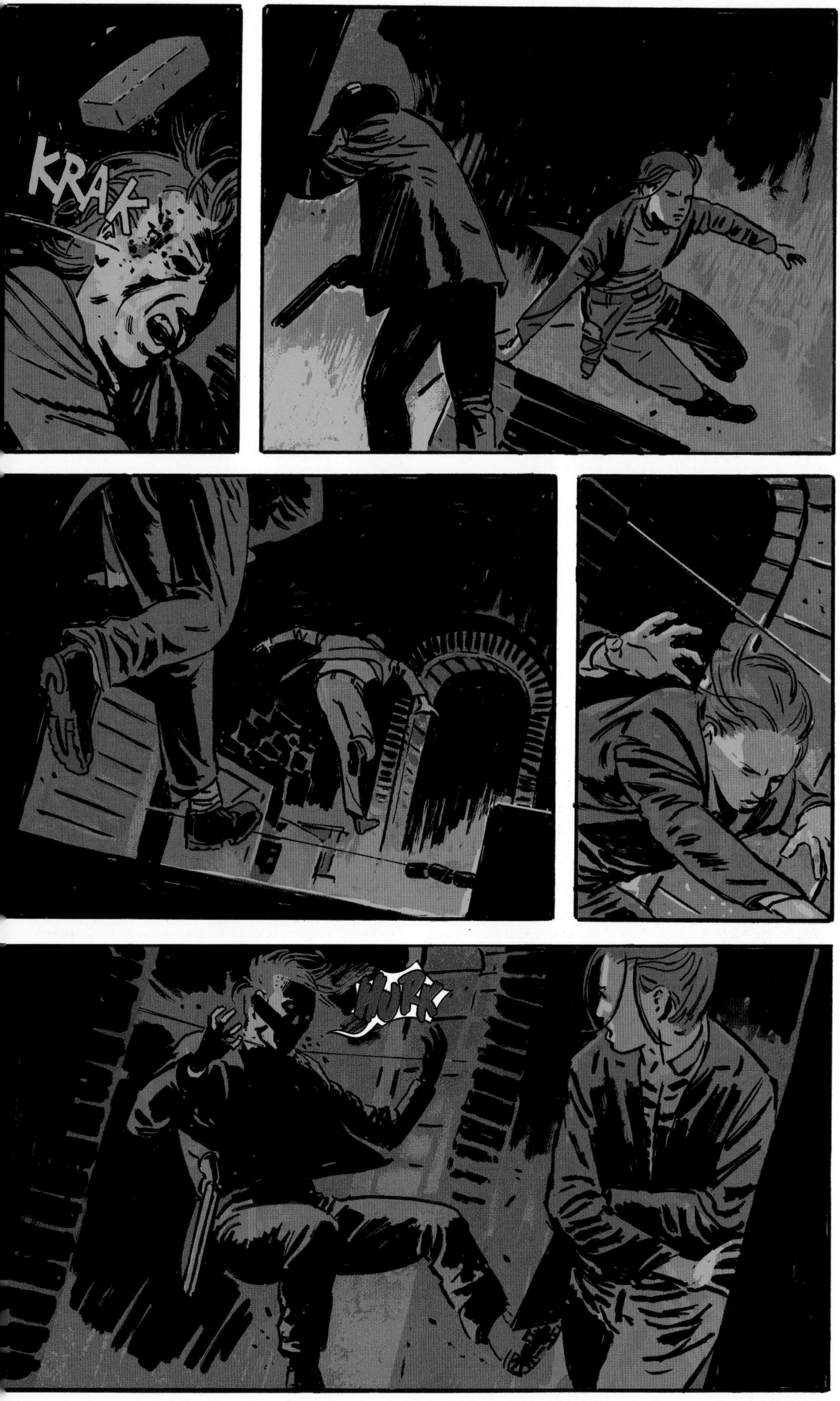
KRAK
HURK

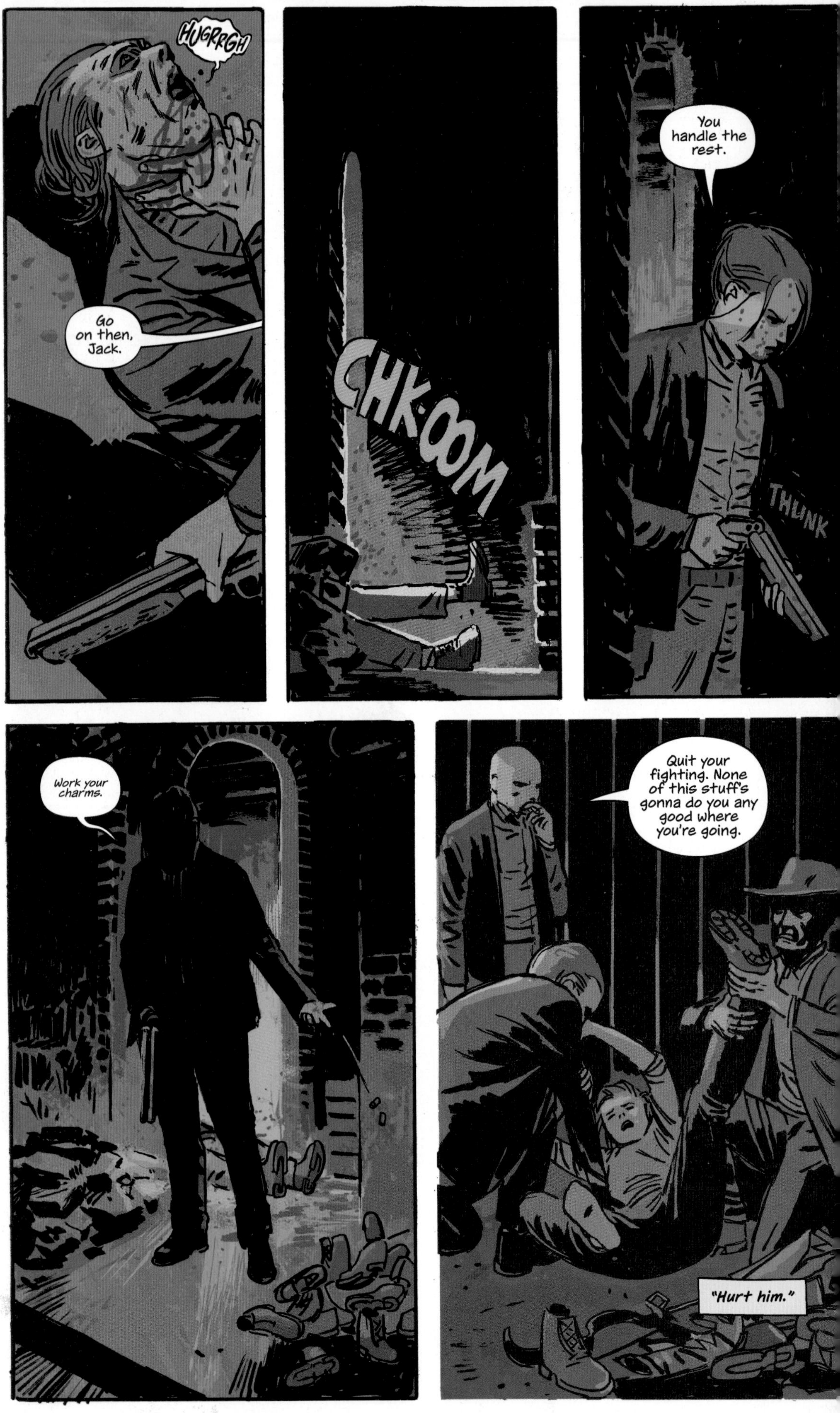
HUGRRGH
Go on then, Jack.
CHK-OOM
You handle the rest.
THUNK
Work your charms.
Quit your fighting. None of this stuff's gonna do you any good where you're going.
"Hurt him."

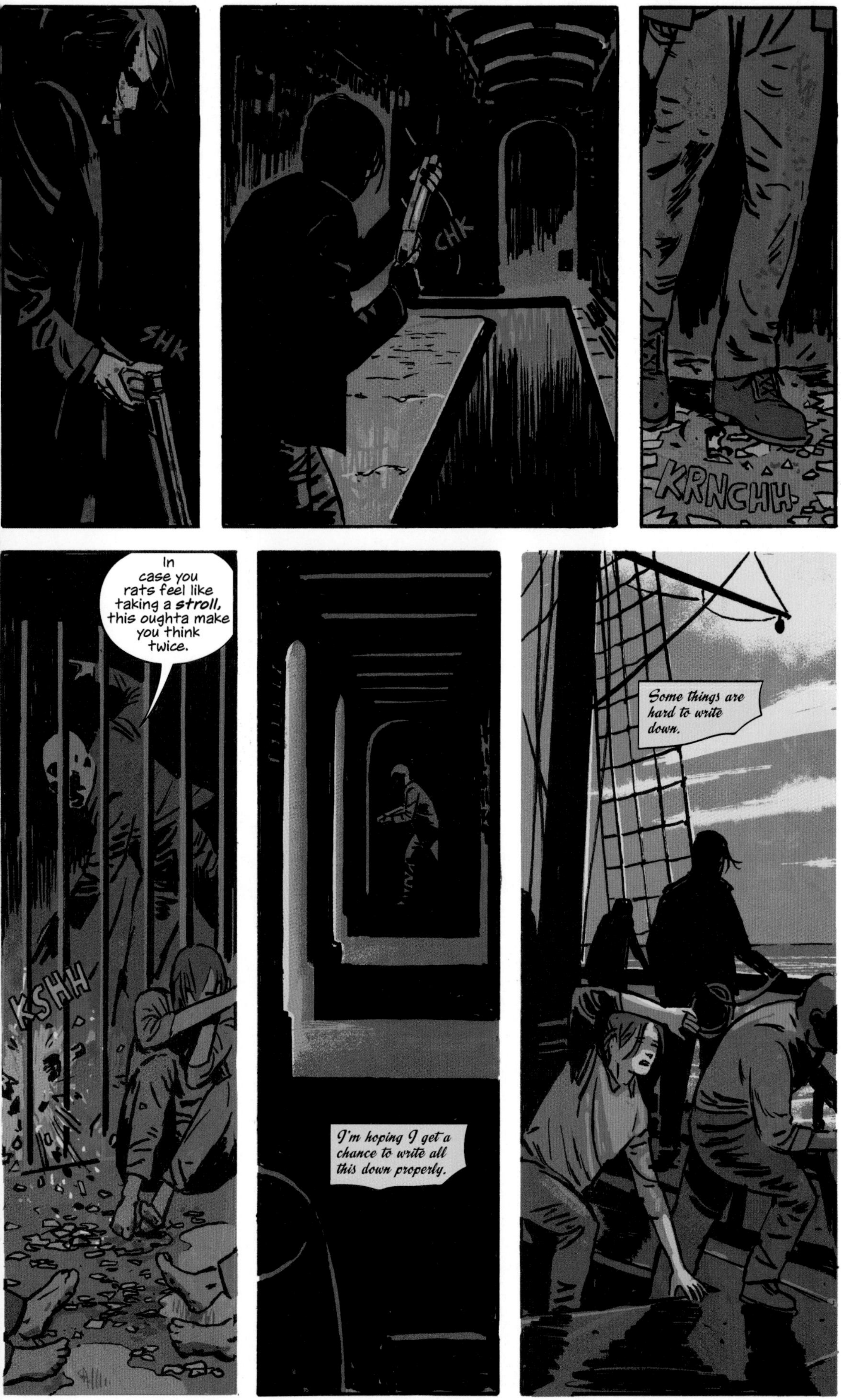

SHK
CHK
KRNCHH
In case you rats feel like taking a **stroll,** this oughta make you think twice.
KSHH
I'm hoping I get a chance to write all this down properly.
Some things are hard to write down.

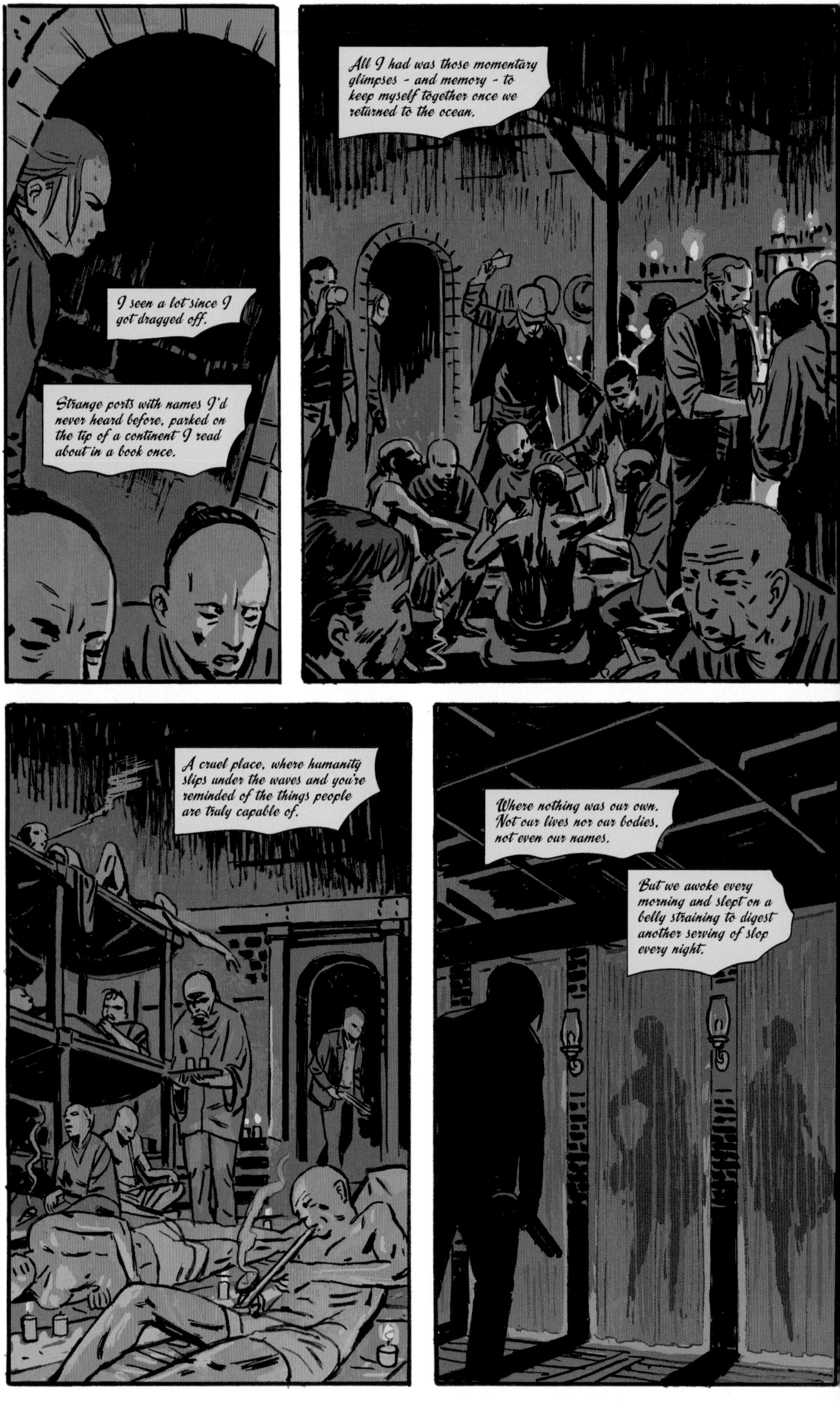
I seen a lot since I got dragged off.
Strange ports with names I'd never heard before, parked on the tip of a continent I read about in a book once.
All I had was those momentary glimpses - and memory - to keep myself together once we returned to the ocean.
A cruel place, where humanity slips under the waves and you're reminded of the things people are truly capable of.
Where nothing was our own. Not our lives nor our bodies, not even our names.
But we awoke every morning and slept on a belly straining to digest another serving of slop every night.

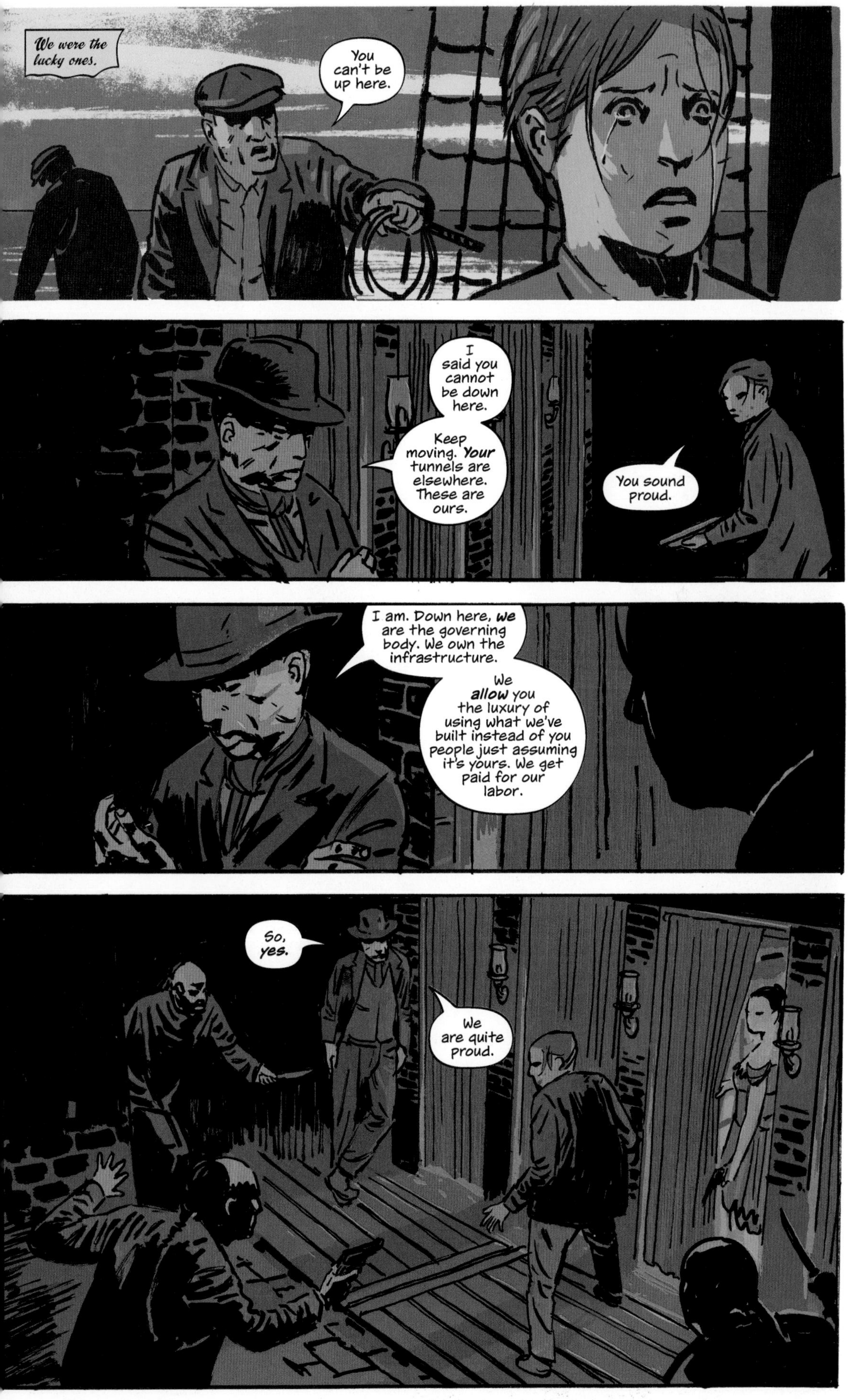
We were the lucky ones.
You can't be up here.
I said you cannot be down here.
Keep moving. Your tunnels are elsewhere. These are ours.
You sound proud.
I am. Down here, we are the governing body. We own the infrastructure.
We allow you the luxury of using what we've built instead of you people just assuming it's yours. We get paid for our labor.
So, yes.
We are quite proud.

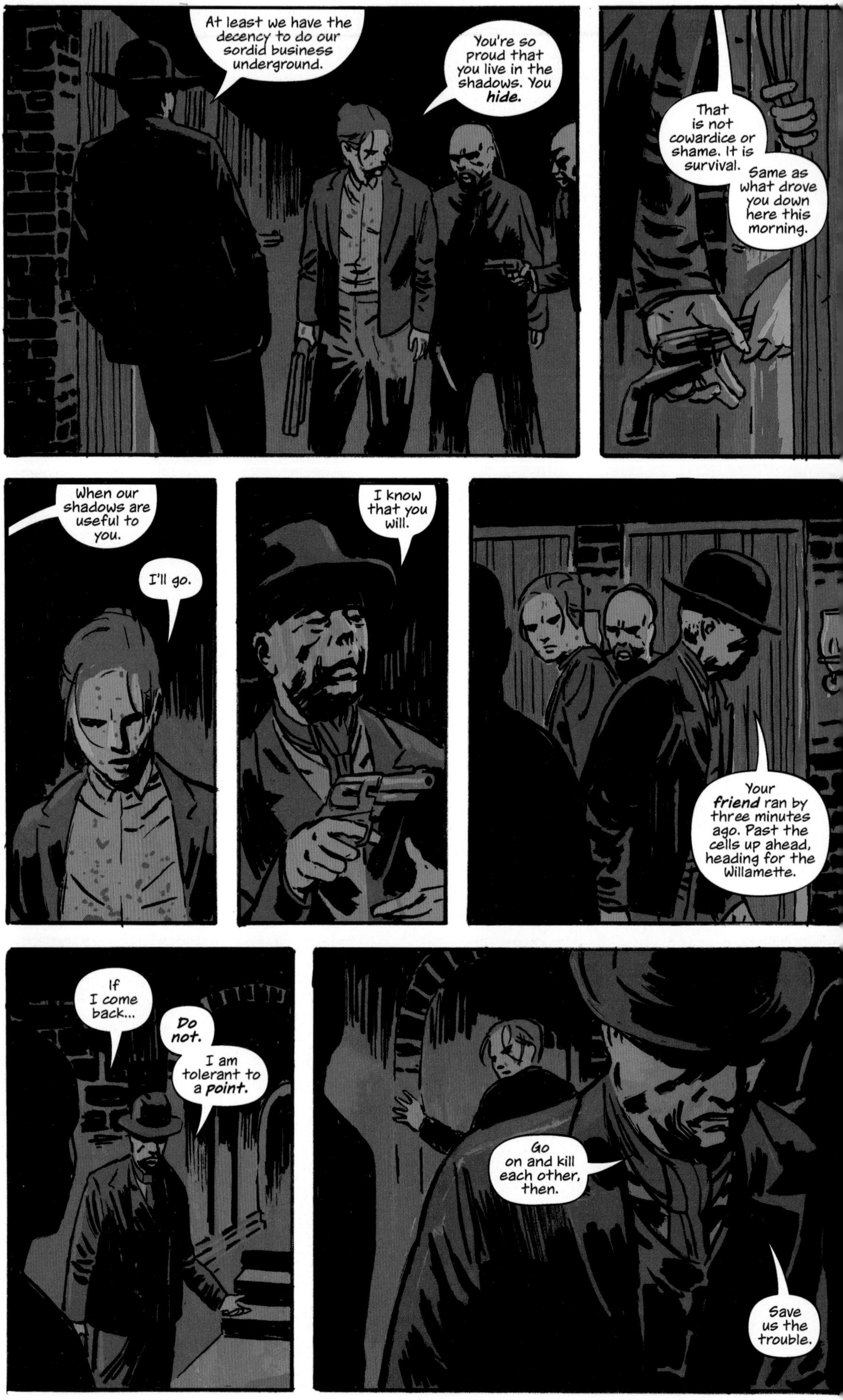
At least we have the decency to do our sordid business underground.
You're so proud that you live in the shadows. You **hide.**
That is not cowardice or shame. It is survival.
Same as what drove you down here this morning.
When our shadows are useful to you.
I'll go.
I know that you will.
Your **friend** ran by three minutes ago. Past the cells up ahead, heading for the Willamette.
If I come back...
Do not.
I am tolerant to a **point.**
Go on and kill each other, then.
Save us the trouble.

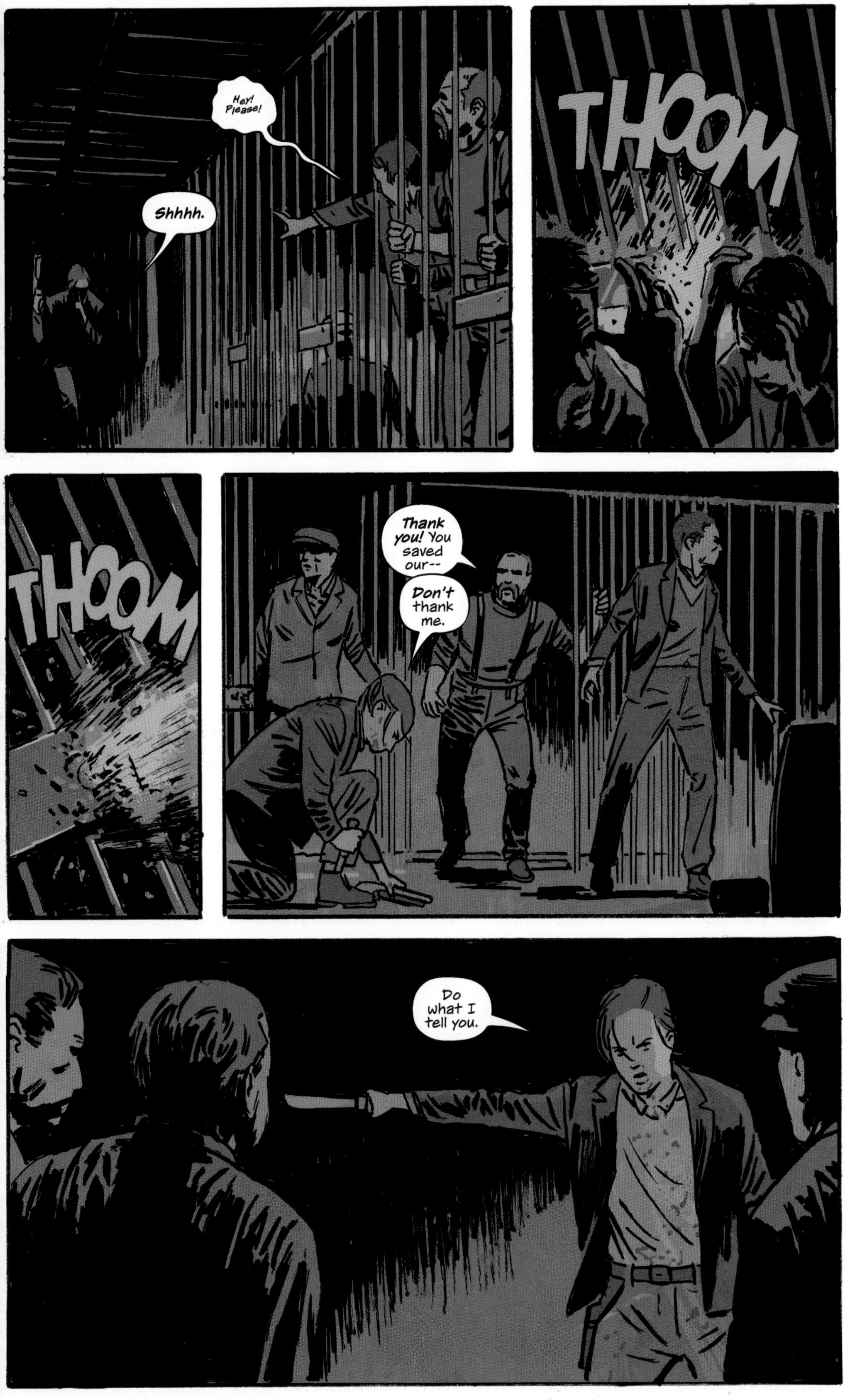
Hey! Please!
Shhhh.
THOOM
THOOM
Thank you! You saved our--
Don't thank me.
Do what I tell you.

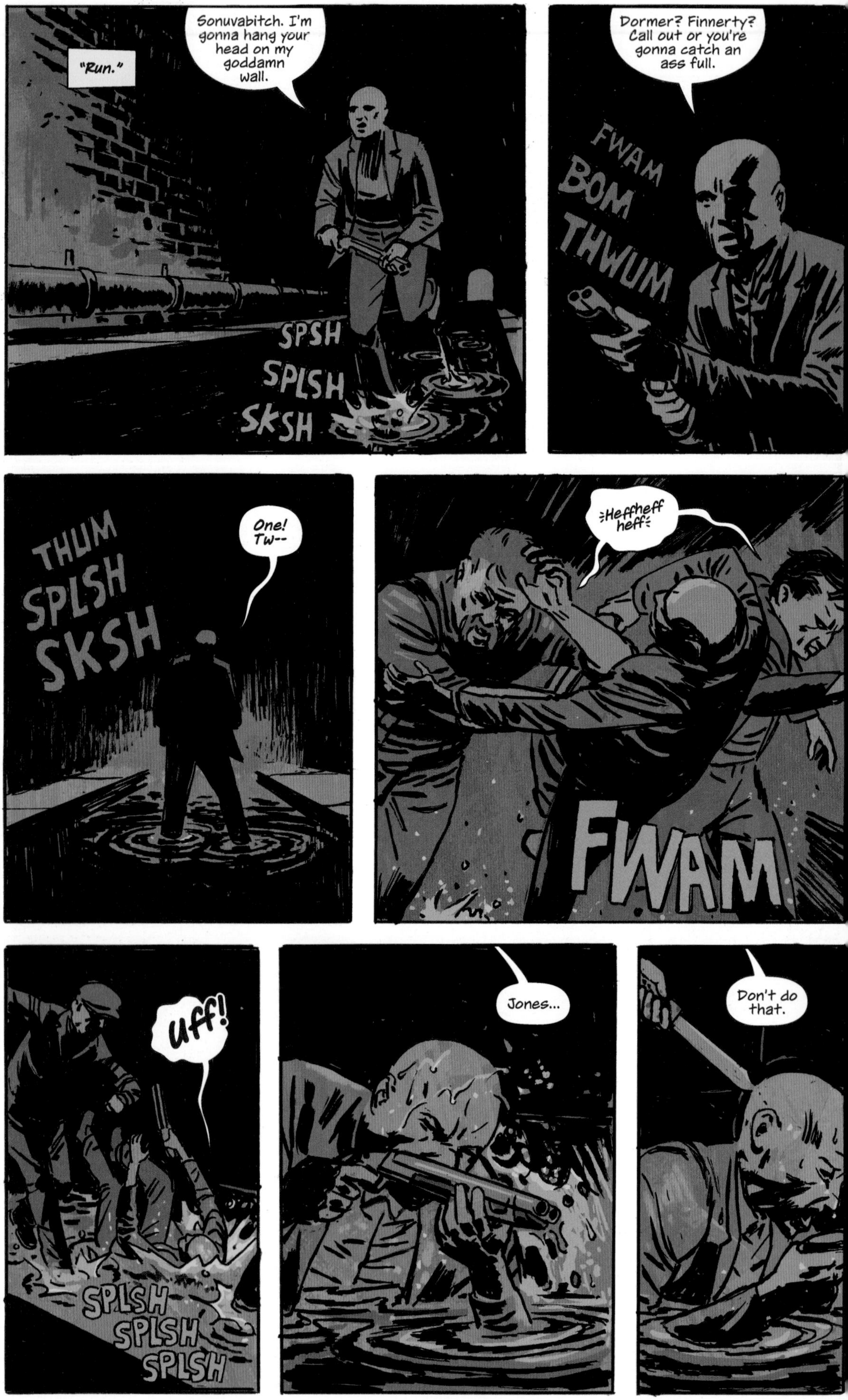
"Run."
Sonuvabitch. I'm gonna hang your head on my goddamn wall.
SPSH
SPLSH
SKSH
Dormer? Finnerty? Call out or you're gonna catch an ass full.
FWAM
BOM
THWUM
THUM
SPLSH
SKSH
One! Tw--
Heffheff heff
FWAM
Uff!
SPLSH
SPLSH
SPLSH
Jones...
Don't do that.

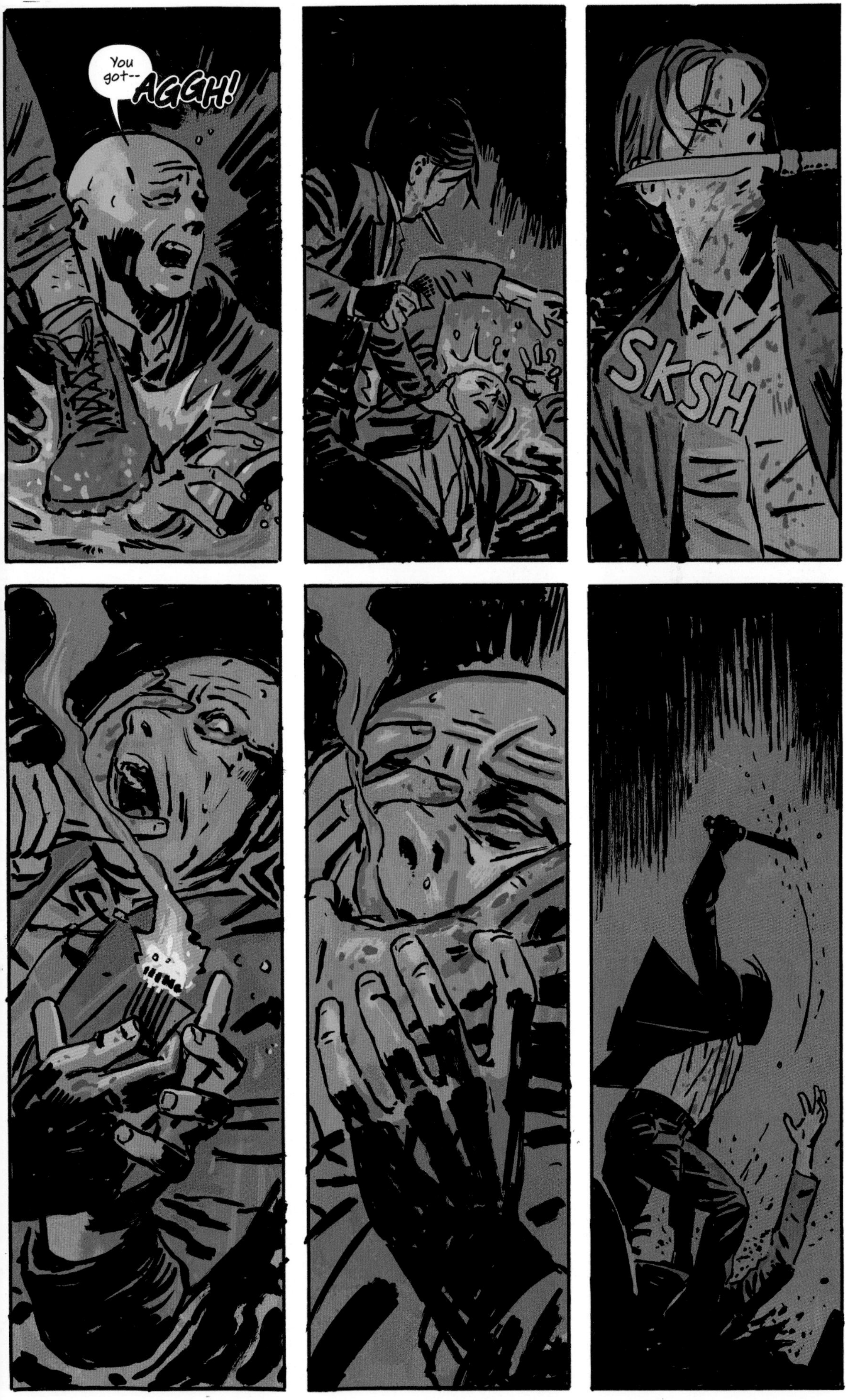
You got-- AGGH!
SKSH

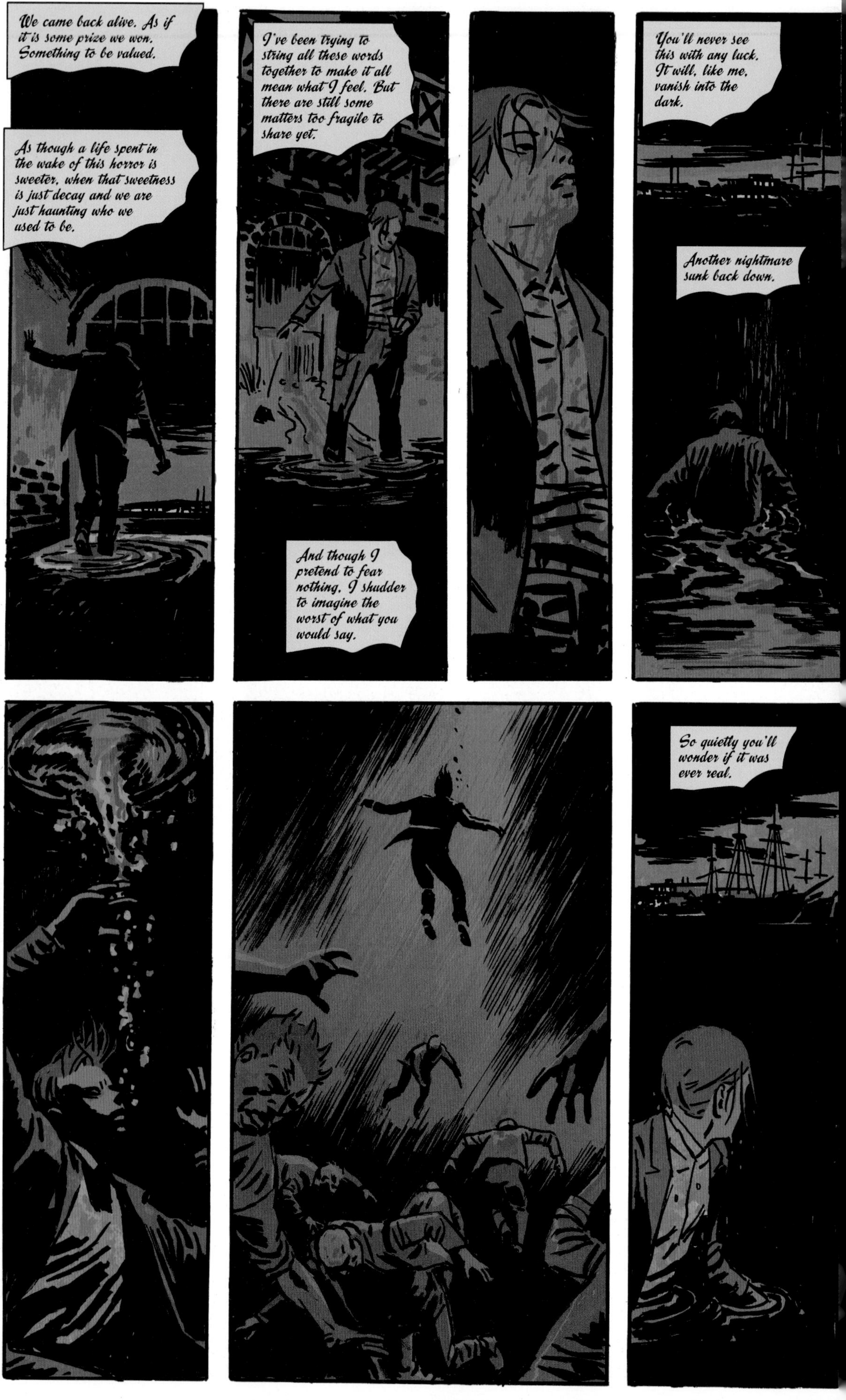
We came back alive. As if it is some prize we won. Something to be valued.
As though a life spent in the wake of this horror is sweeter, when that sweetness is just decay and we are just haunting who we used to be.
I've been trying to string all these words together to make it all mean what I feel. But there are still some matters too fragile to share yet.
And though I pretend to fear nothing, I shudder to imagine the worst of what you would say.
You'll never see this with any luck. It will, like me, vanish into the dark.
Another nightmare sunk back down.
So quietly you'll wonder if it was ever real.

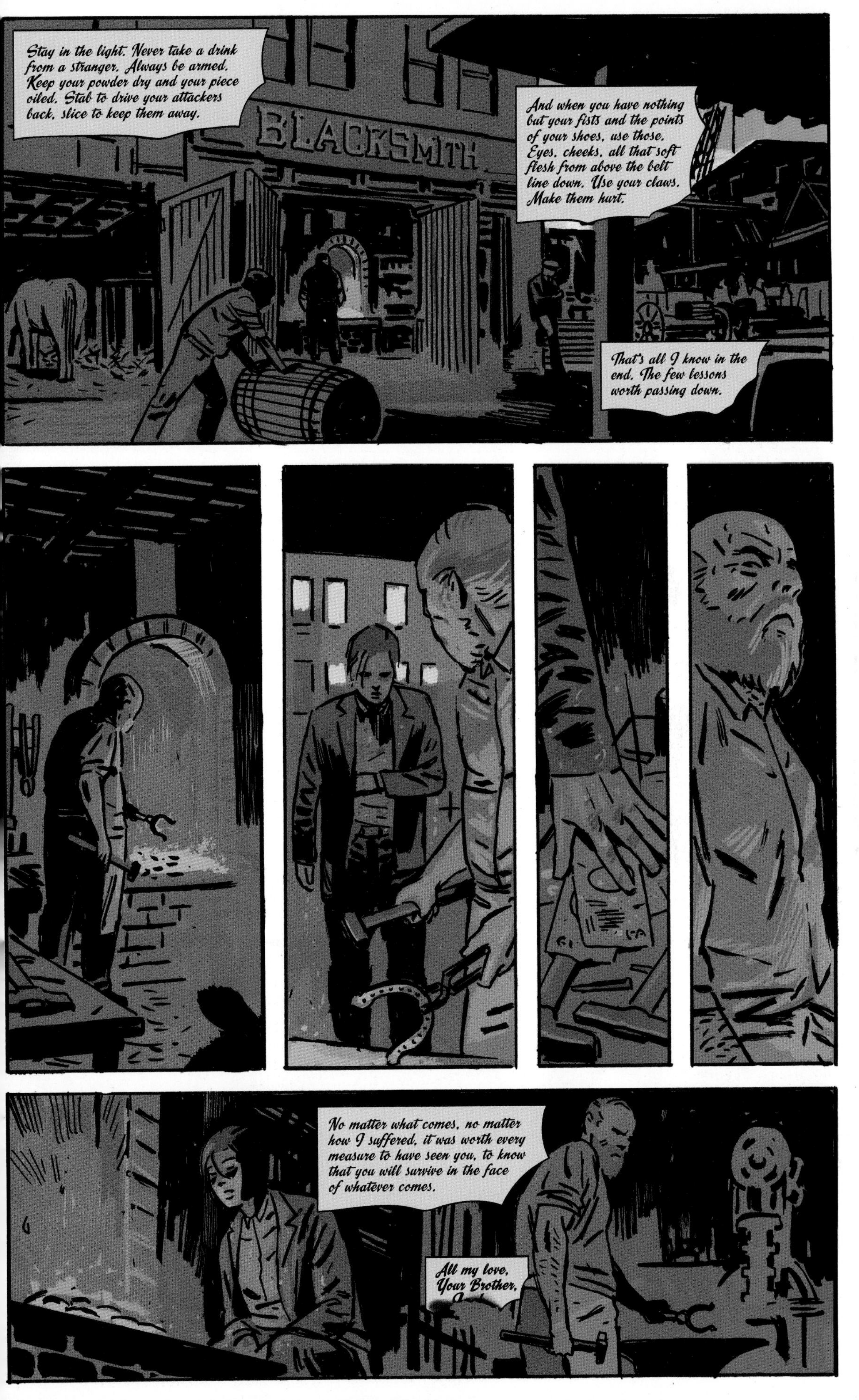
Stay in the light. Never take a drink from a stranger. Always be armed. Keep your powder dry and your piece oiled. Stab to drive your attackers back, slice to keep them away.
BLACKSMITH
And when you have nothing but your fists and the points of your shoes, use those. Eyes, cheeks, all that soft flesh from above the belt line down. Use your claws. Make them hurt.
That's all I know in the end. The few lessons worth passing down.
No matter what comes, no matter how I suffered, it was worth every measure to have seen you, to know that you will survive in the face of whatever comes.
All my love, Your Brother,

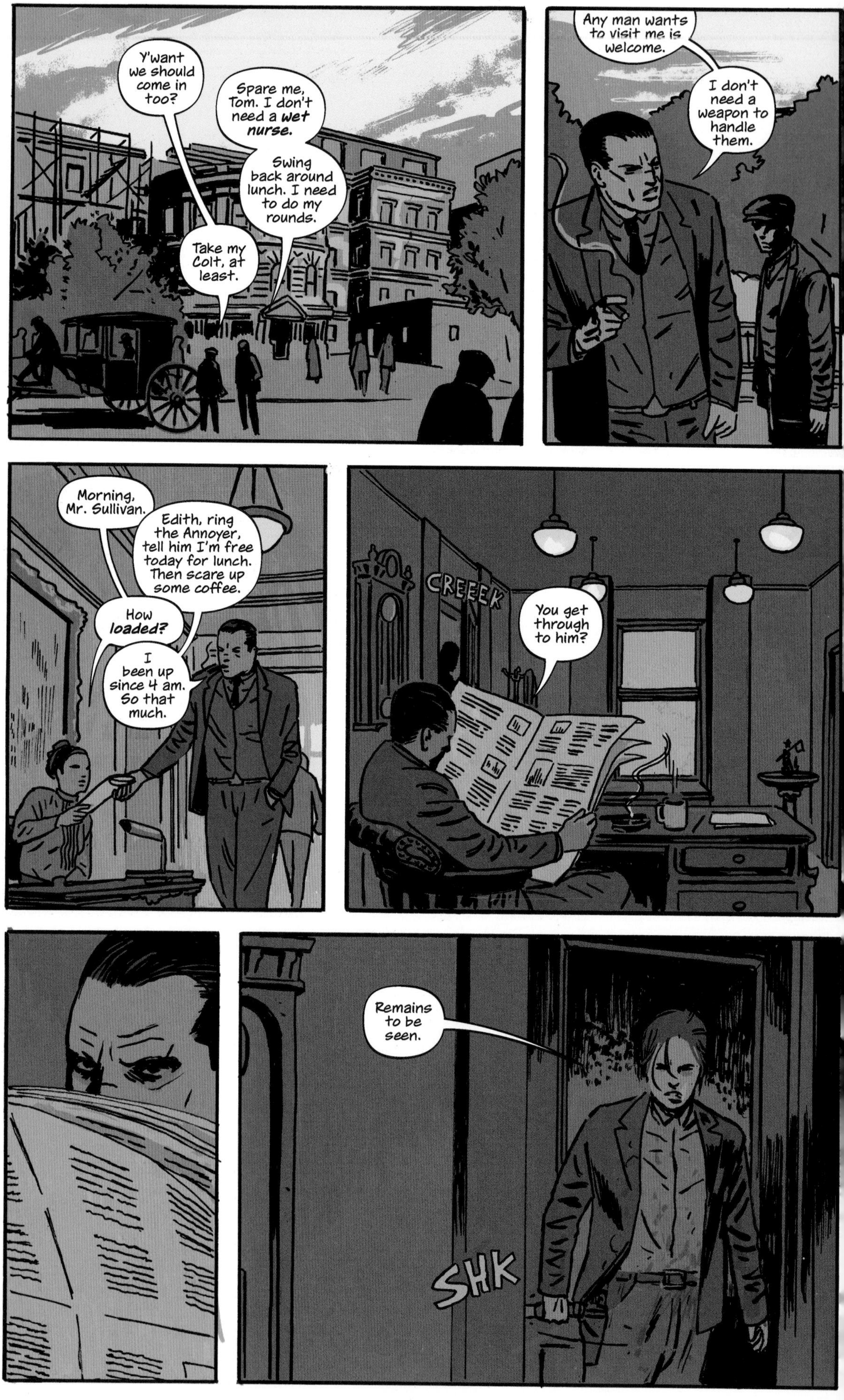
Y'want we should come in too?
Spare me, Tom. I don't need a **wet nurse.**
Swing back around lunch. I need to do my rounds.
Take my Colt, at least.
Any man wants to visit me is welcome.
I don't need a weapon to handle them.
Morning, Mr. Sullivan.
Edith, ring the Annoyer, tell him I'm free today for lunch. Then scare up some coffee.
How ***loaded?***
I been up since 4 am. So that much.
CREEEK
You get through to him?
Remains to be seen.
SHK

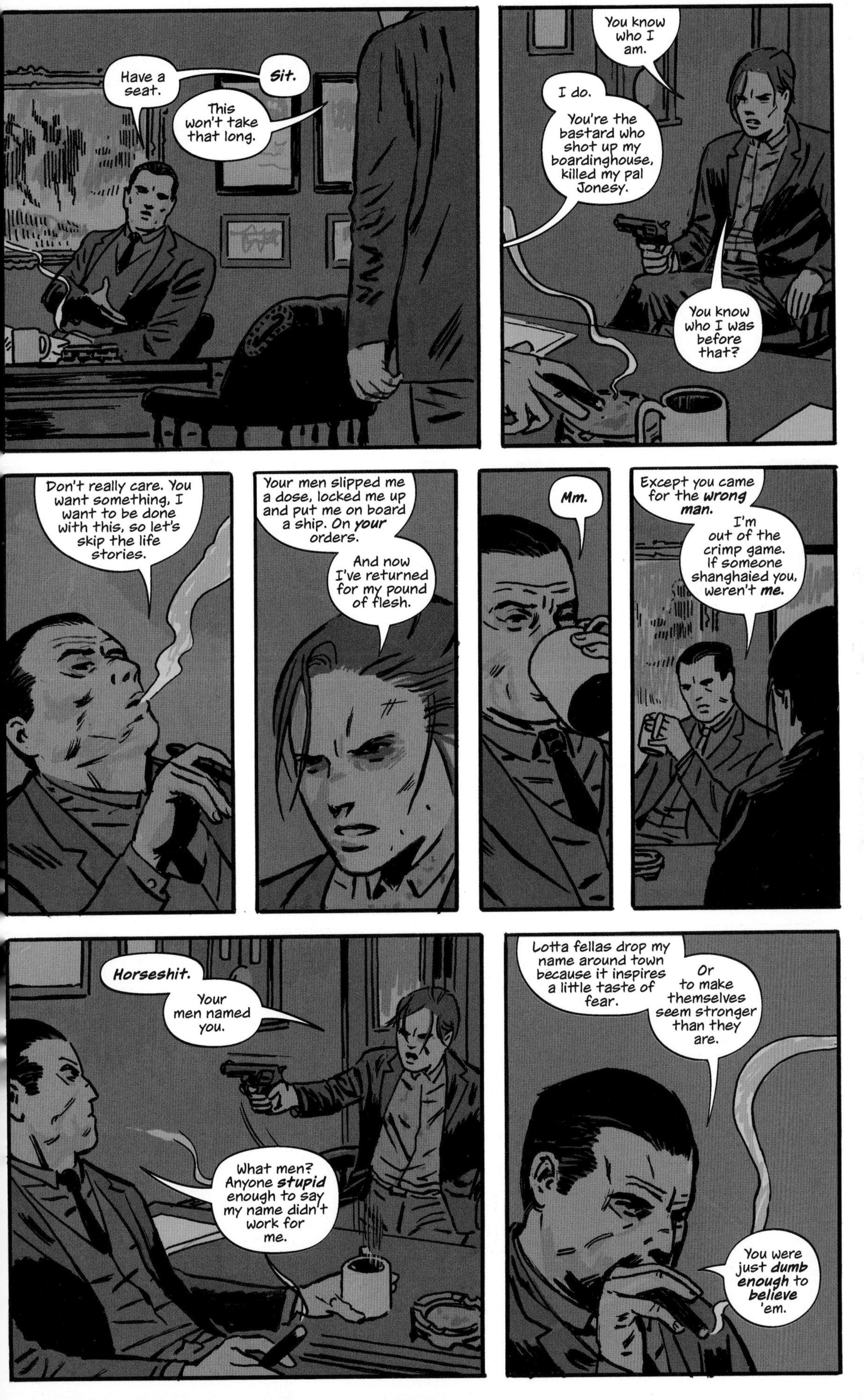
Have a seat.
Sit.
This won't take that long.
You know who I am.
I do.
You're the bastard who shot up my boardinghouse, killed my pal Jonesy.
You know who I was before that?
Don't really care. You want something, I want to be done with this, so let's skip the life stories.
Your men slipped me a dose, locked me up and put me on board a ship. On your orders.
And now I've returned for my pound of flesh.
Mm.
Except you came for the wrong man.
I'm out of the crimp game. If someone shanghaied you, weren't me.
Horseshit.
Your men named you.
What men? Anyone stupid enough to say my name didn't work for me.
Lotta fellas drop my name around town because it inspires a little taste of fear.
Or to make themselves seem stronger than they are.
You were just dumb enough to believe 'em.

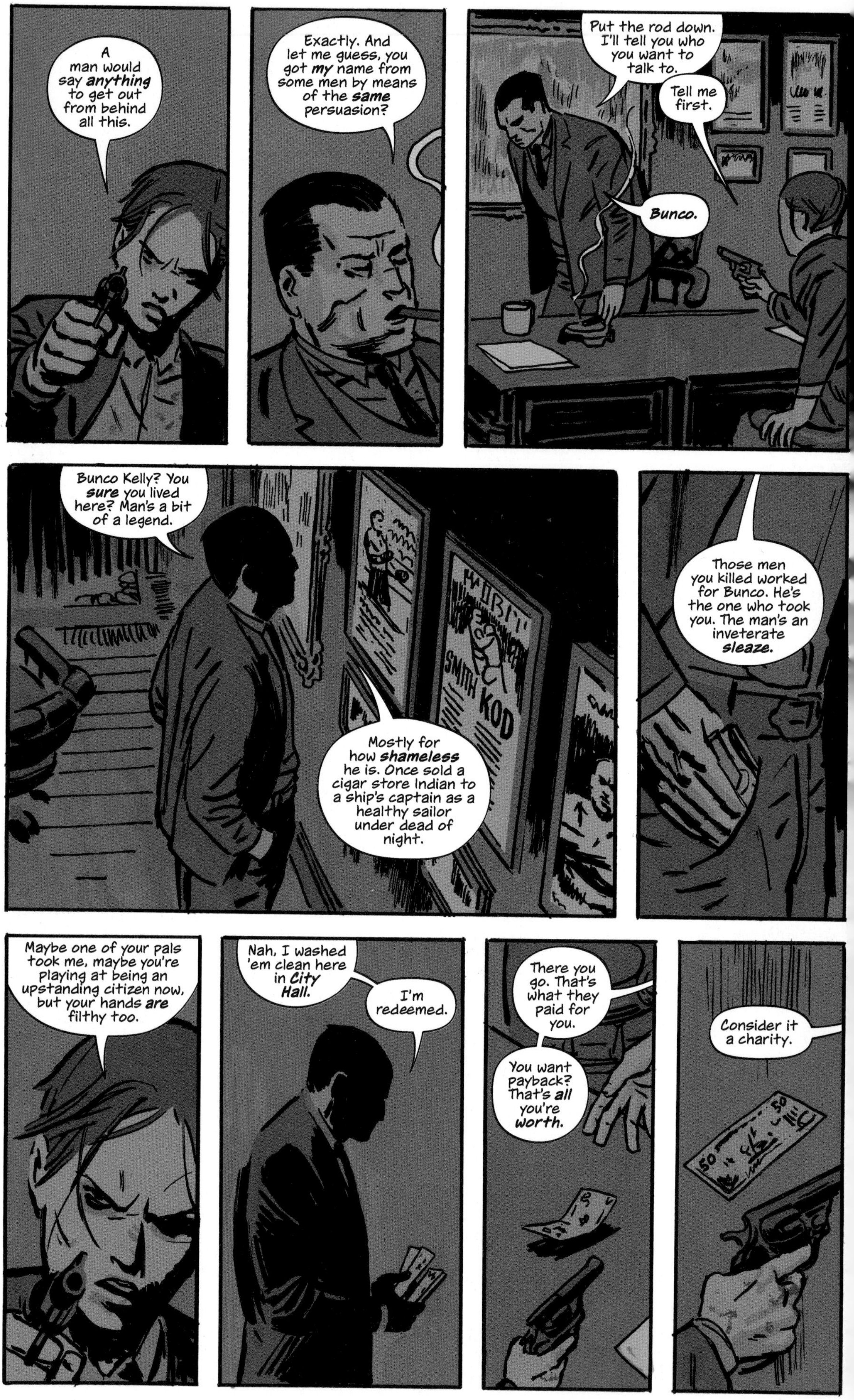
A man would say *anything* to get out from behind all this.
Exactly. And let me guess, you got *my* name from some men by means of the *same* persuasion?
Put the rod down. I'll tell you who you want to talk to.
Tell me first.
Bunco.
Bunco Kelly? You *sure* you lived here? Man's a bit of a legend.
Mostly for how *shameless* he is. Once sold a cigar store Indian to a ship's captain as a healthy sailor under dead of night.
Those men you killed worked for Bunco. He's the one who took you. The man's an inveterate *sleaze.*
Maybe one of your pals took me, maybe you're playing at being an upstanding citizen now, but your hands *are* filthy too.
Nah, I washed 'em clean here in *City Hall.*
I'm redeemed.
There you go. That's what they paid for you.
You want payback? That's *all* you're *worth.*
Consider it a charity.

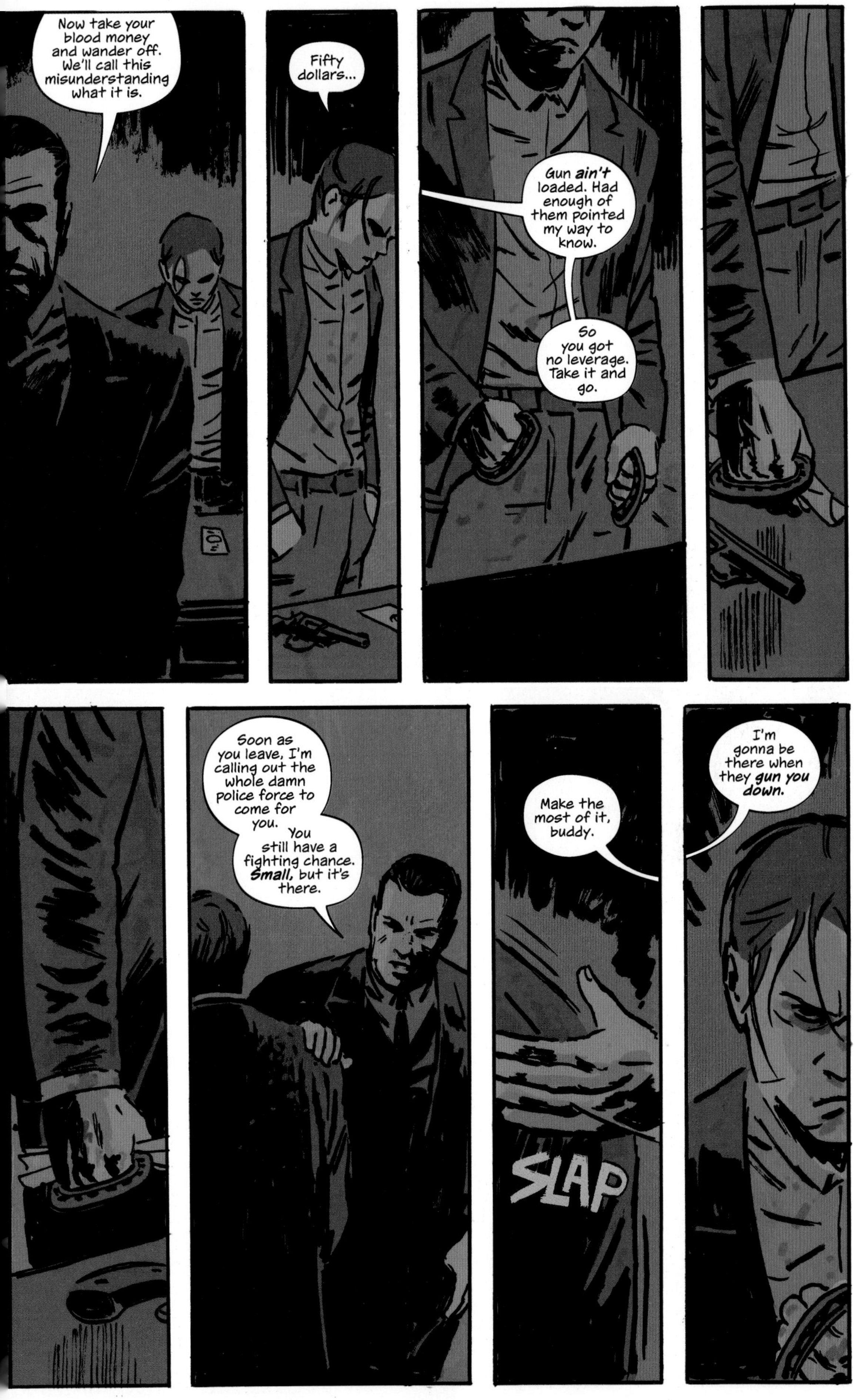
Now take your blood money and wander off. We'll call this misunderstanding what it is.
Fifty dollars...
Gun **ain't** loaded. Had enough of them pointed my way to know.
So you got no leverage. Take it and go.
Soon as you leave, I'm calling out the whole damn police force to come for you.
You still have a fighting chance. **Small,** but it's there.
Make the most of it, buddy.
SLAP
I'm gonna be there when they **gun you down.**

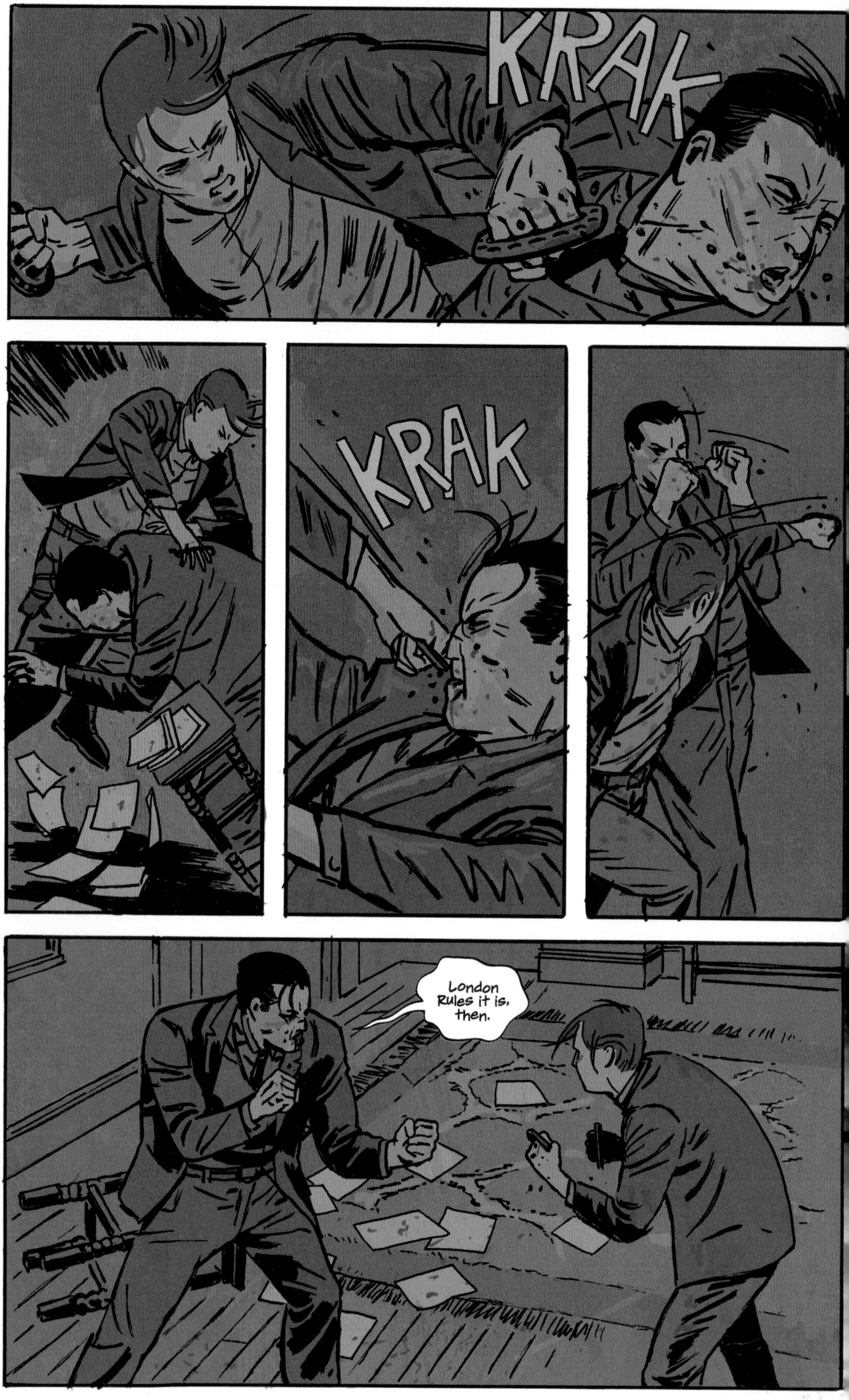
KRAK
KRAK
London Rules it is, then.

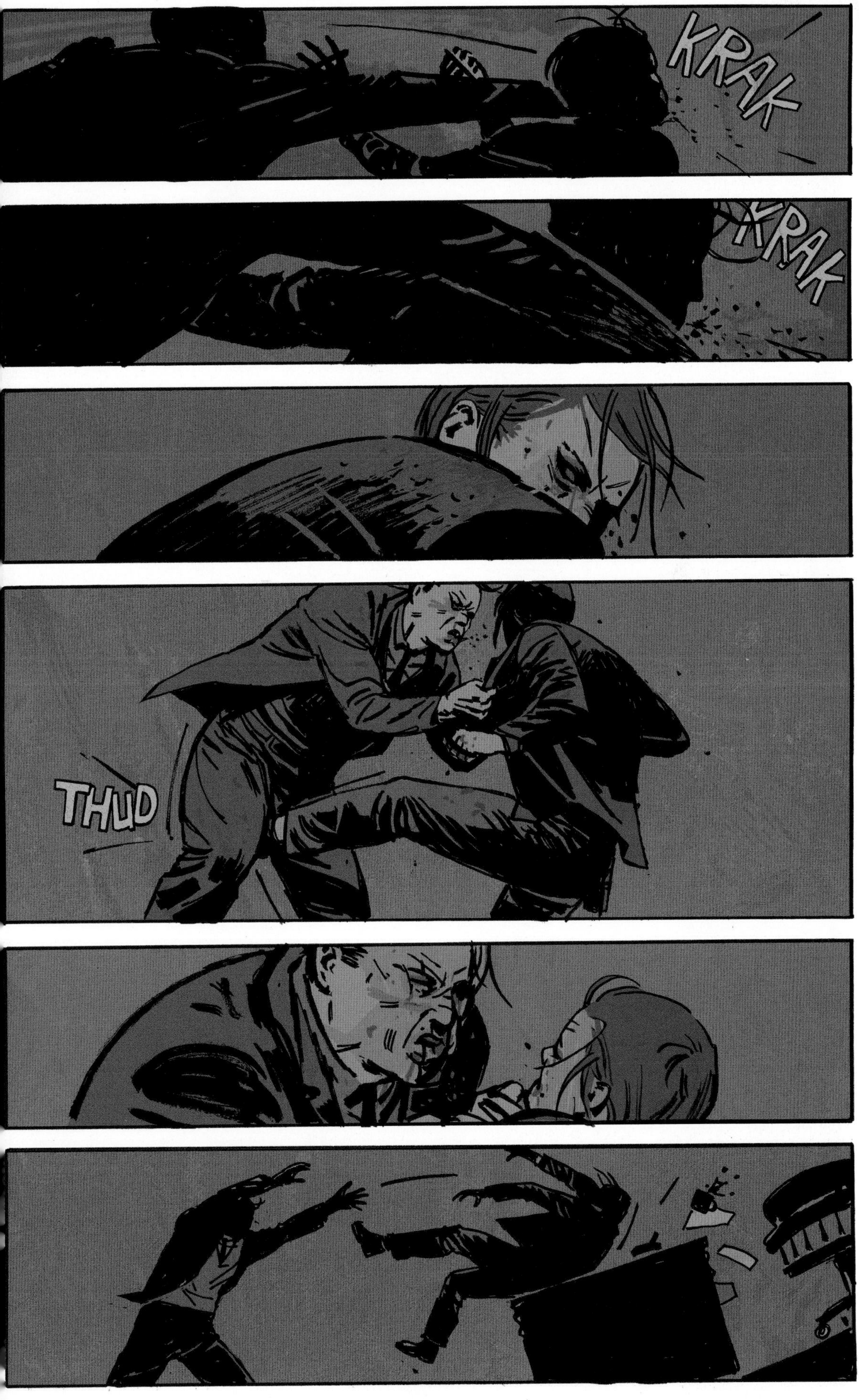
KRAK
KRAK
THUD

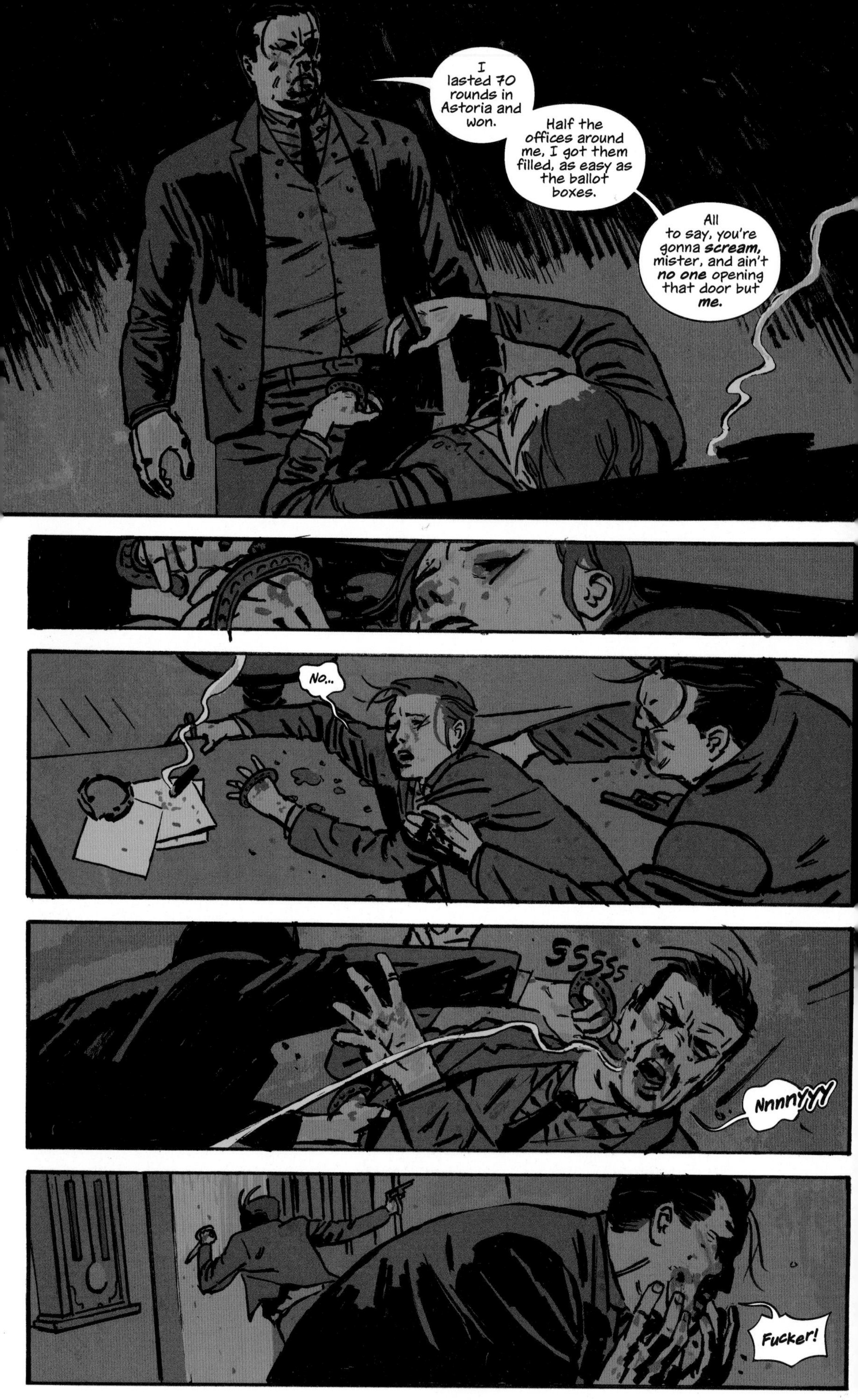
I lasted 70 rounds in Astoria and won.
Half the offices around me, I got them filled, as easy as the ballot boxes.
All to say, you're gonna *scream,* mister, and ain't *no one* opening that door but *me.*
No...
SSSSS
NnnnYYY
Fucker!

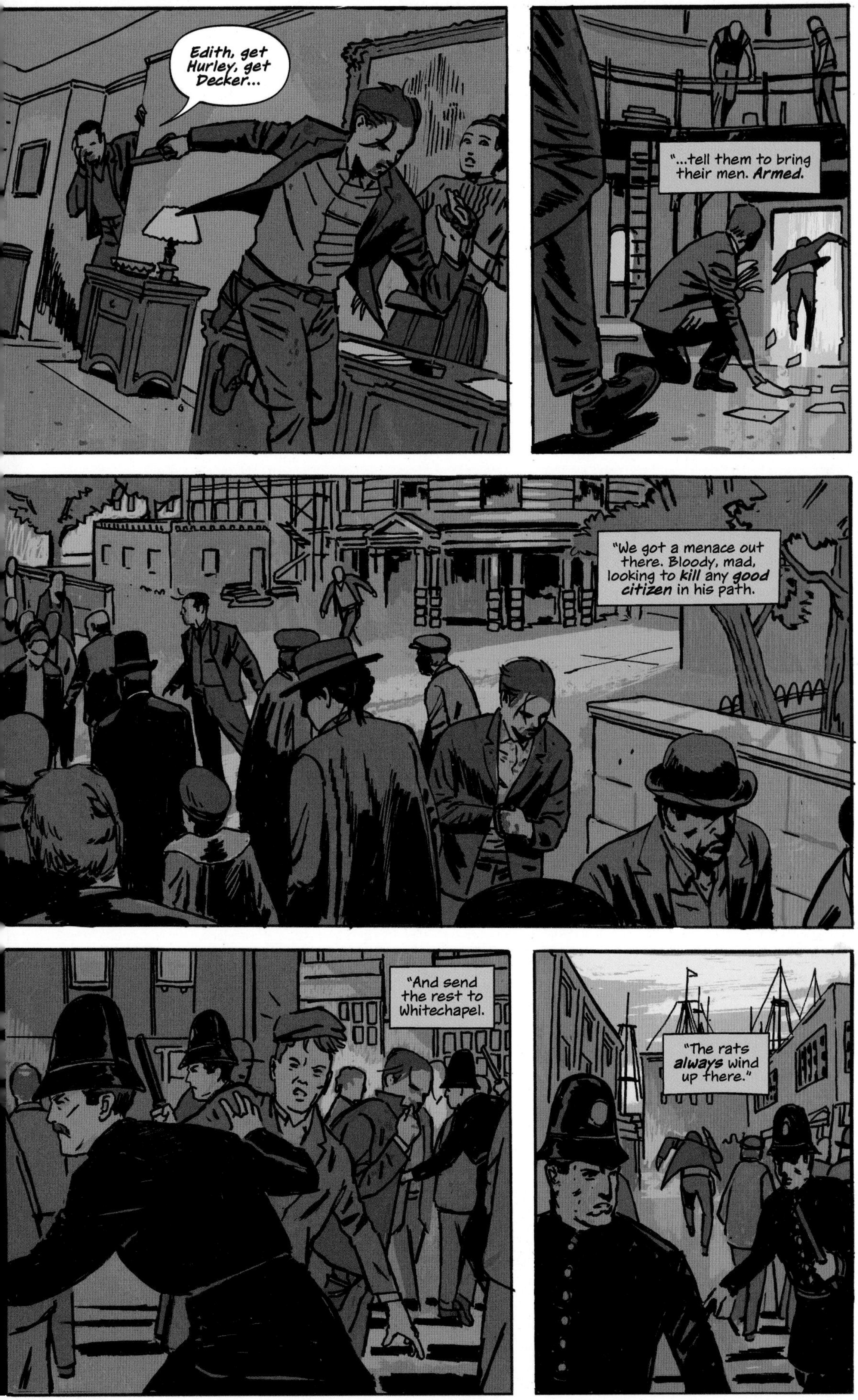
Edith, get Hurley, get Decker...
"...tell them to bring their men. Armed.
"We got a menace out there. Bloody, mad, looking to kill any good citizen in his path.
"And send the rest to Whitechapel.
"The rats always wind up there."

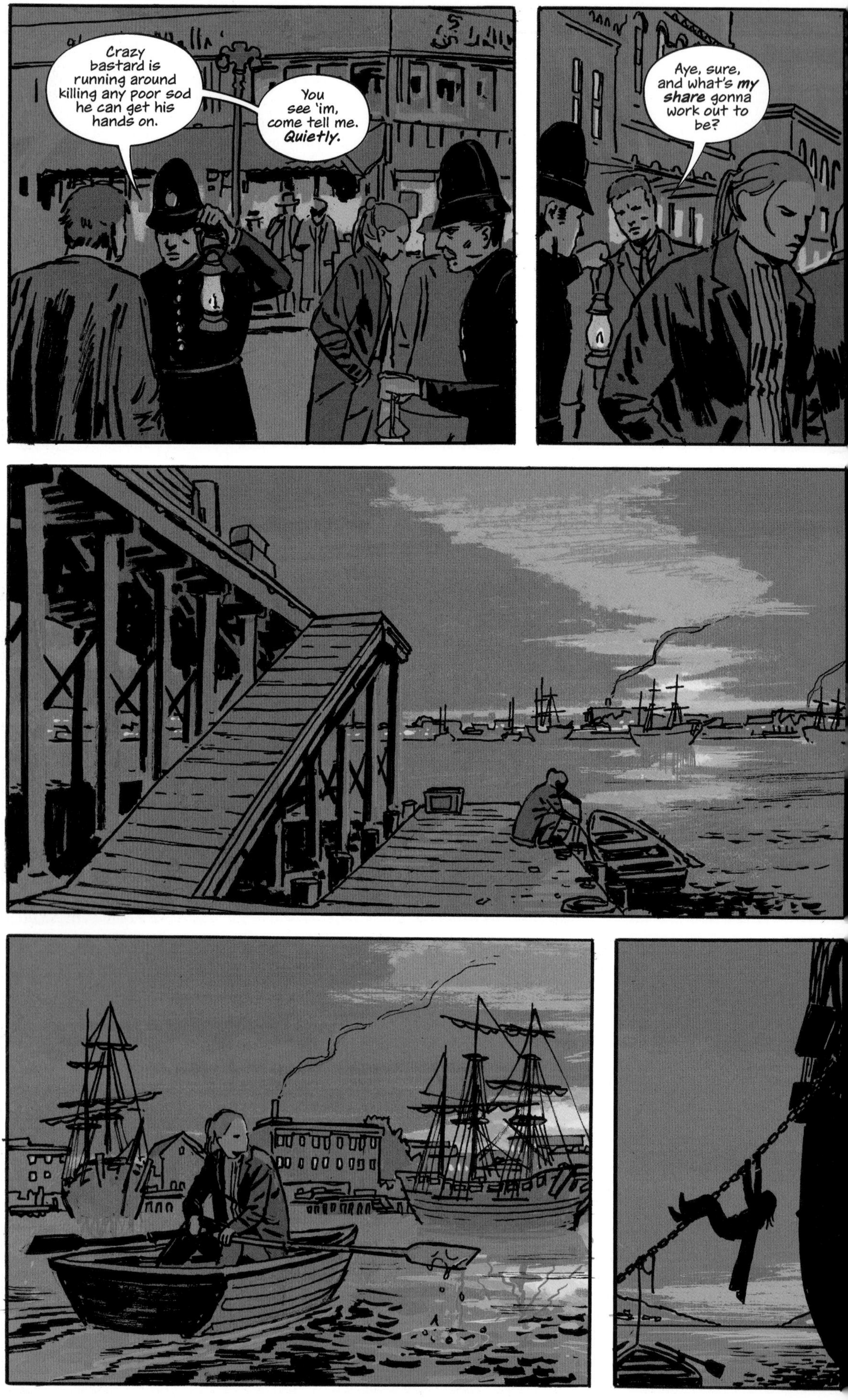

Crazy bastard is running around killing any poor sod he can get his hands on.
You see 'im, come tell me. *Quietly.*
Aye, sure, and what's *my share* gonna work out to be?

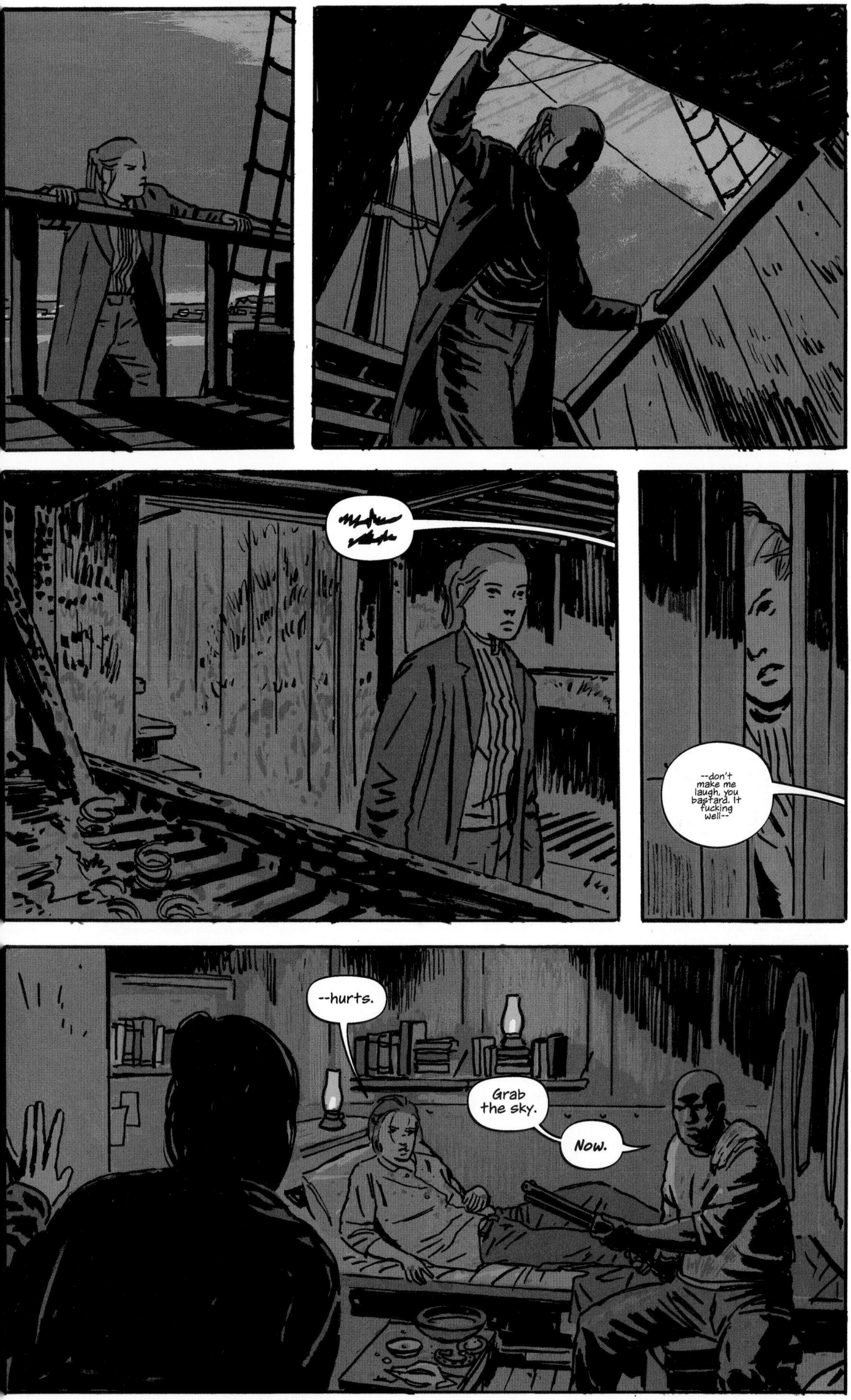
--don't make me laugh, you bastard. It fucking well--
--hurts.
Grab the sky.
Now.

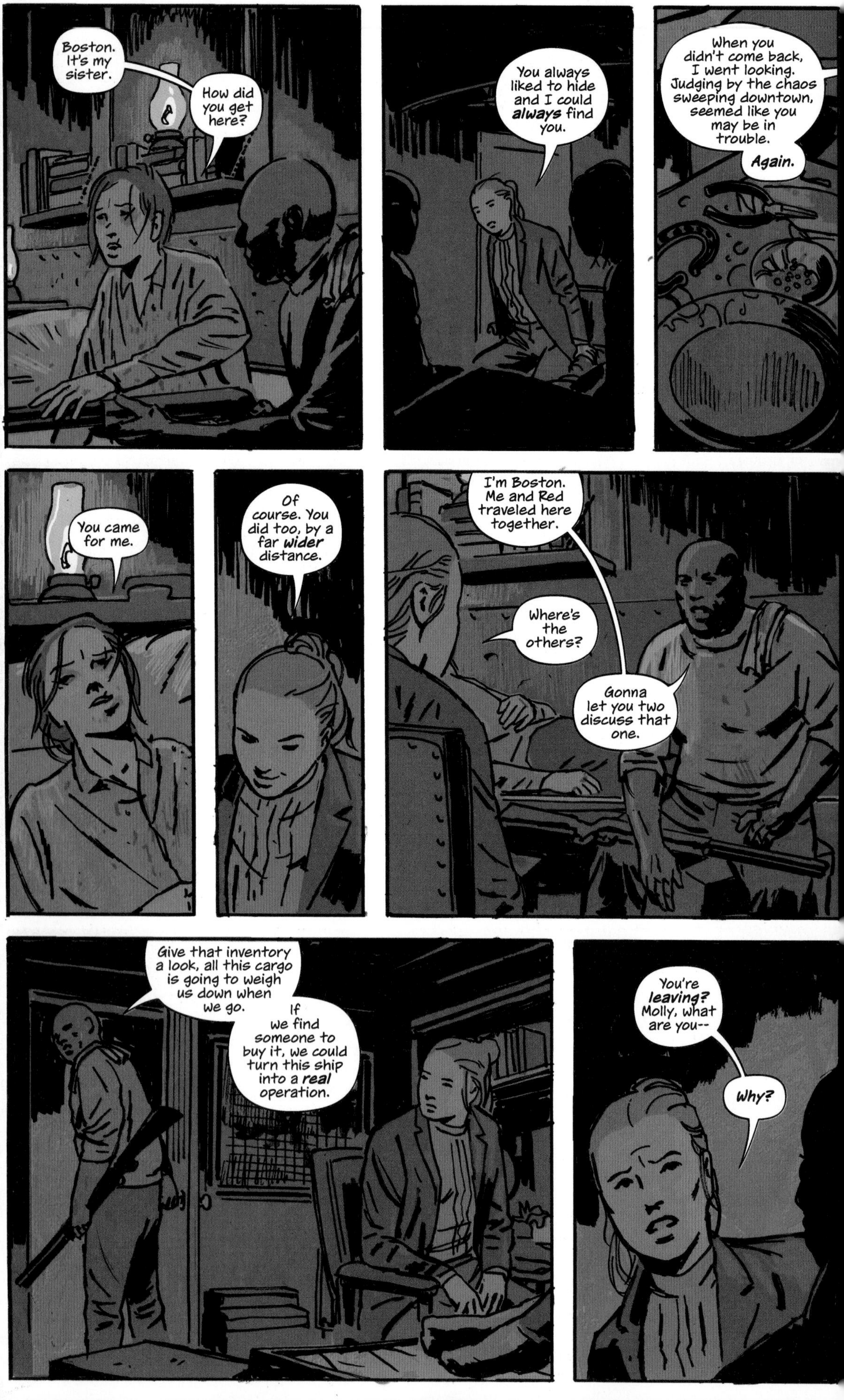
Boston. It's my sister.
How did you get here?
You always liked to hide and I could always find you.
When you didn't come back, I went looking. Judging by the chaos sweeping downtown, seemed like you may be in trouble.
Again.
You came for me.
Of course. You did too, by a far wider distance.
I'm Boston. Me and Red traveled here together.
Where's the others?
Gonna let you two discuss that one.
Give that inventory a look, all this cargo is going to weigh us down when we go.
If we find someone to buy it, we could turn this ship into a real operation.
You're leaving? Molly, what are you--
Why?

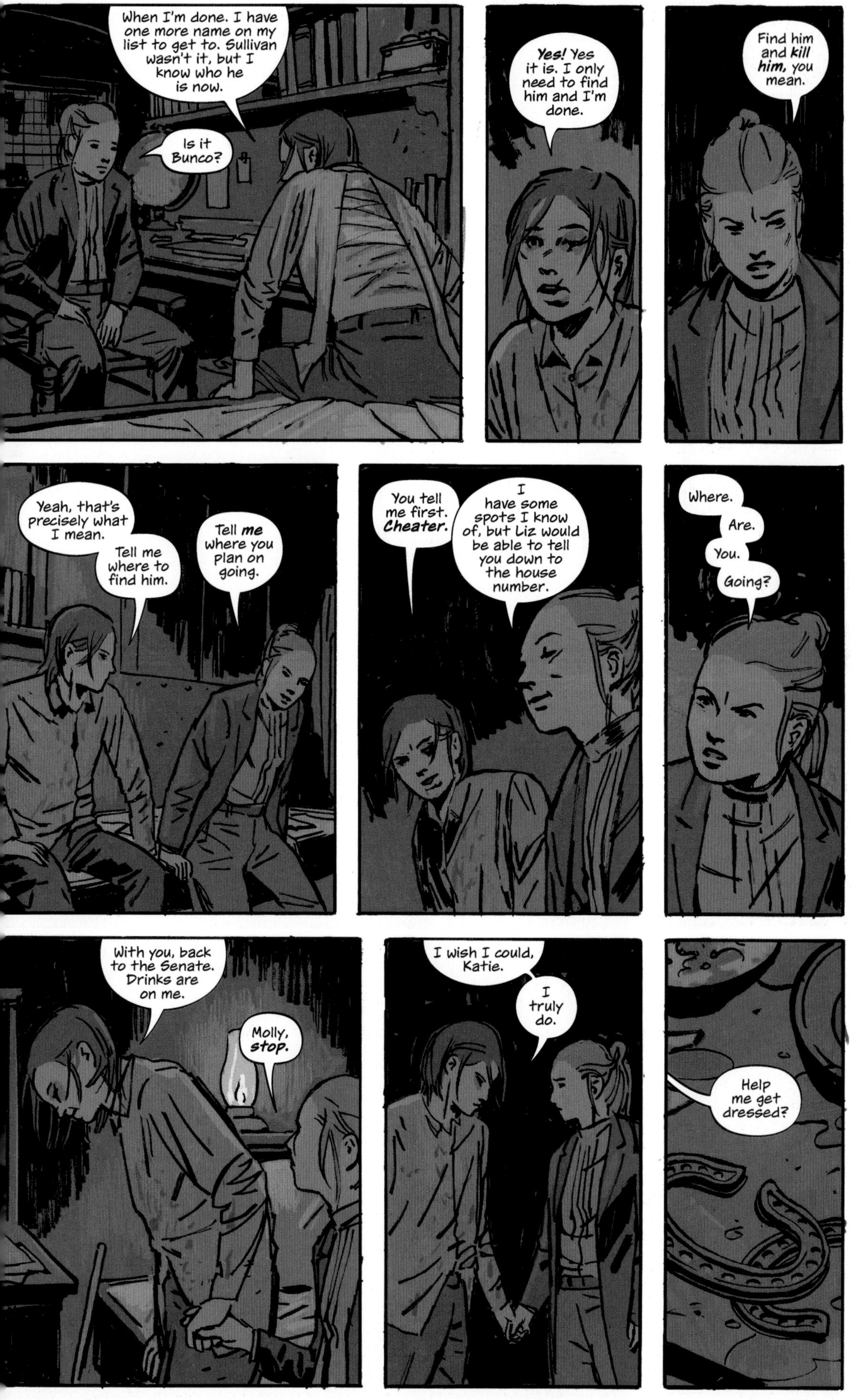
When I'm done. I have one more name on my list to get to. Sullivan wasn't it, but I know who he is now.
Is it Bunco?
Yes! Yes it is. I only need to find him and I'm done.
Find him and **kill him,** you mean.
Yeah, that's precisely what I mean.
Tell me where to find him.
Tell **me** where you plan on going.
You tell me first. **Cheater.**
I have some spots I know of, but Liz would be able to tell you down to the house number.
Where.
Are.
You.
Going?
With you, back to the Senate. Drinks are on me.
Molly, **stop.**
I wish I could, Katie.
I truly do.
Help me get dressed?

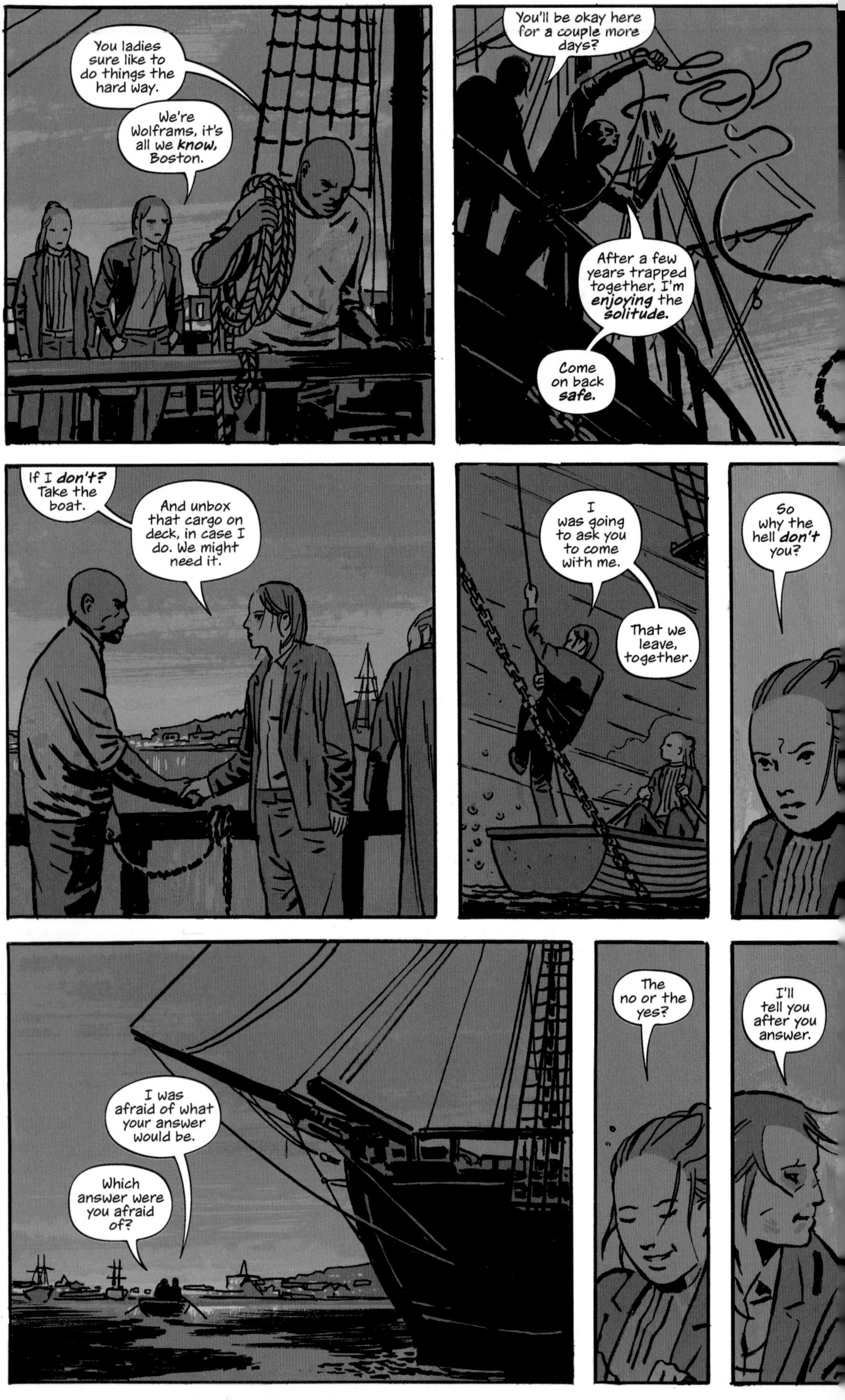
You ladies sure like to do things the hard way.
We're Wolframs, it's all we **know,** Boston.
You'll be okay here for a couple more days?
After a few years trapped together, I'm ***enjoying*** the ***solitude.***
Come on back ***safe.***
If I ***don't?*** Take the boat.
And unbox that cargo on deck, in case I do. We might need it.
I was going to ask you to come with me.
That we leave, together.
So why the hell ***don't*** you?
I was afraid of what your answer would be.
Which answer were you afraid of?
The no or the yes?
I'll tell you after you answer.

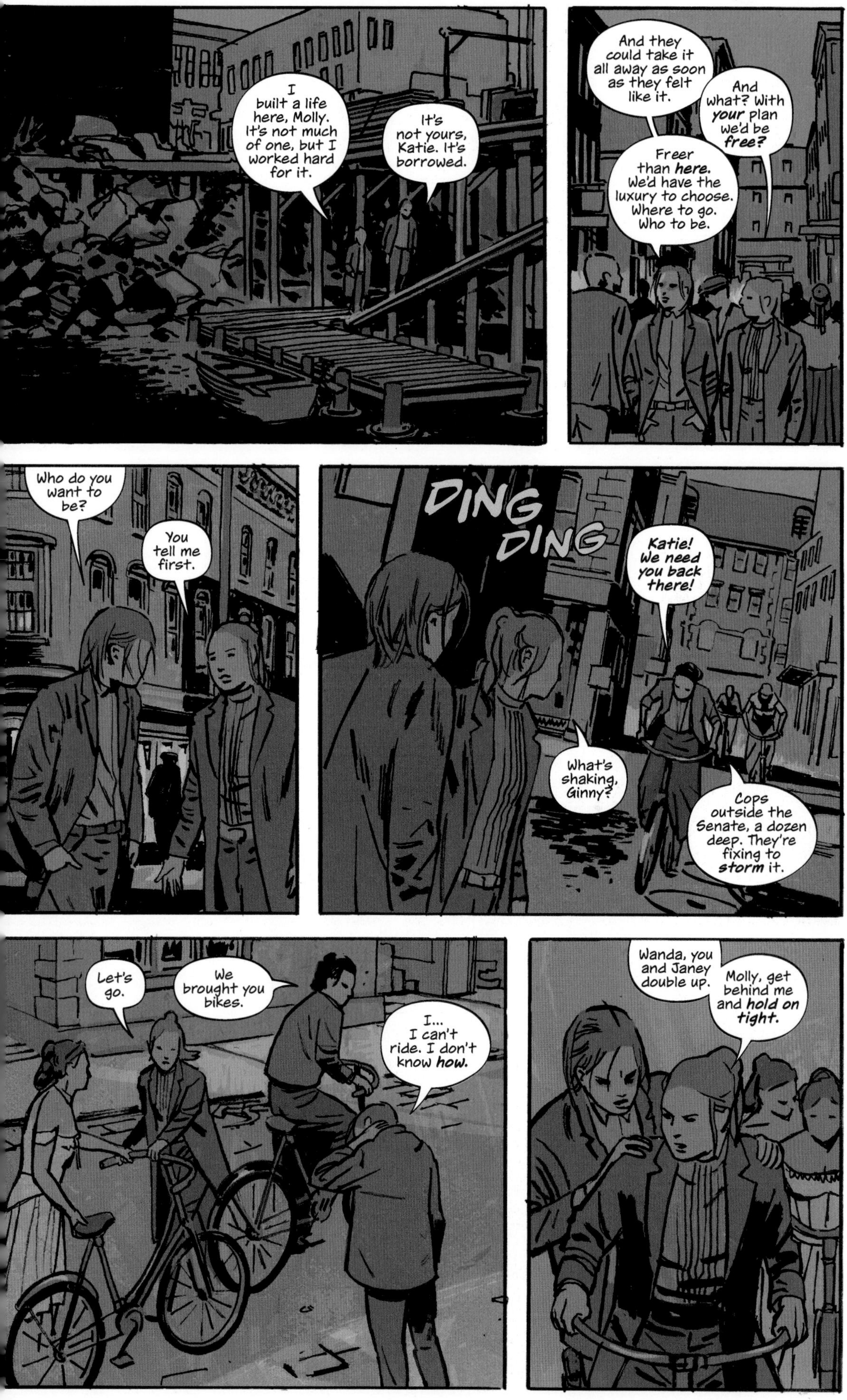

I built a life here, Molly. It's not much of one, but I worked hard for it.
It's not yours, Katie. It's borrowed.
And they could take it all away as soon as they felt like it.
And what? With *your* plan we'd be *free?*
Freer than *here.* We'd have the luxury to choose. Where to go. Who to be.
Who do you want to be?
You tell me first.
DING DING
Katie! We need you back there!
What's shaking, Ginny?
Cops outside the Senate, a dozen deep. They're fixing to *storm* it.
Let's go.
We brought you bikes.
I... I can't ride. I don't know *how.*
Wanda, you and Janey double up.
Molly, get behind me and *hold on tight.*

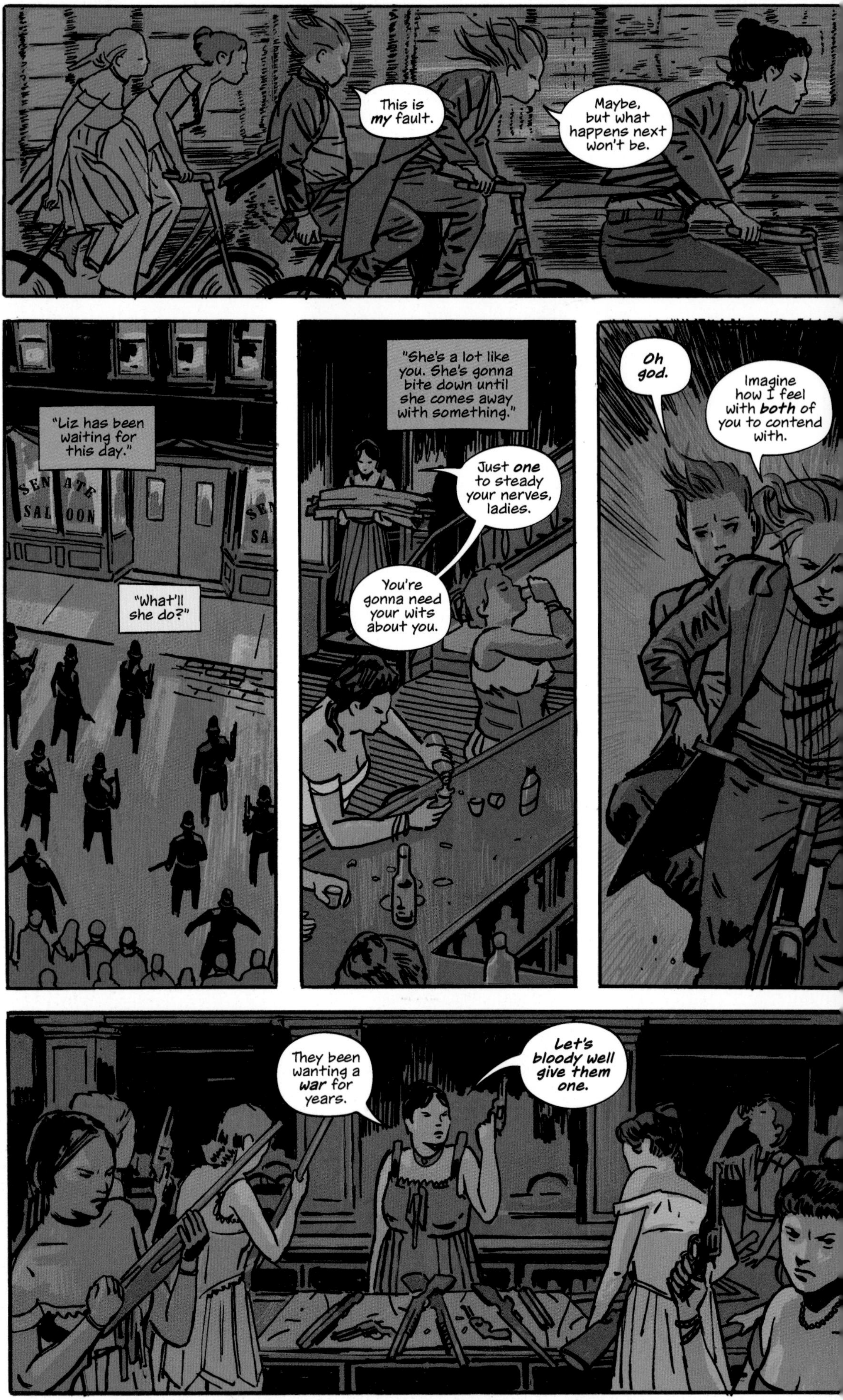
This is my fault.
Maybe, but what happens next won't be.
"Liz has been waiting for this day."
SENATE SALOON
"What'll she do?"
"She's a lot like you. She's gonna bite down until she comes away with something."
Just one to steady your nerves, ladies.
You're gonna need your wits about you.
Oh god.
Imagine how I feel with both of you to contend with.
They been wanting a war for years.
Let's bloody well give them one.

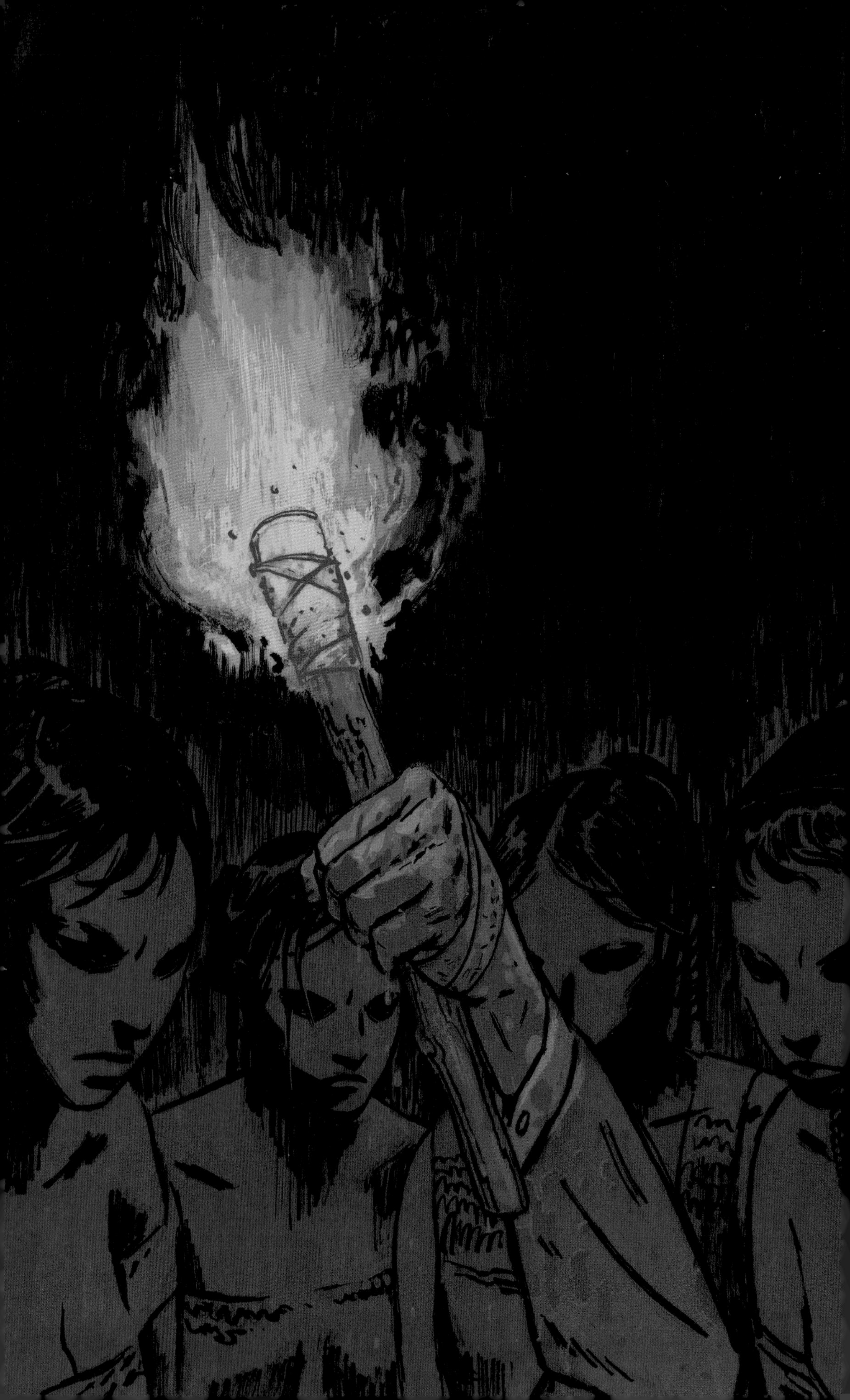

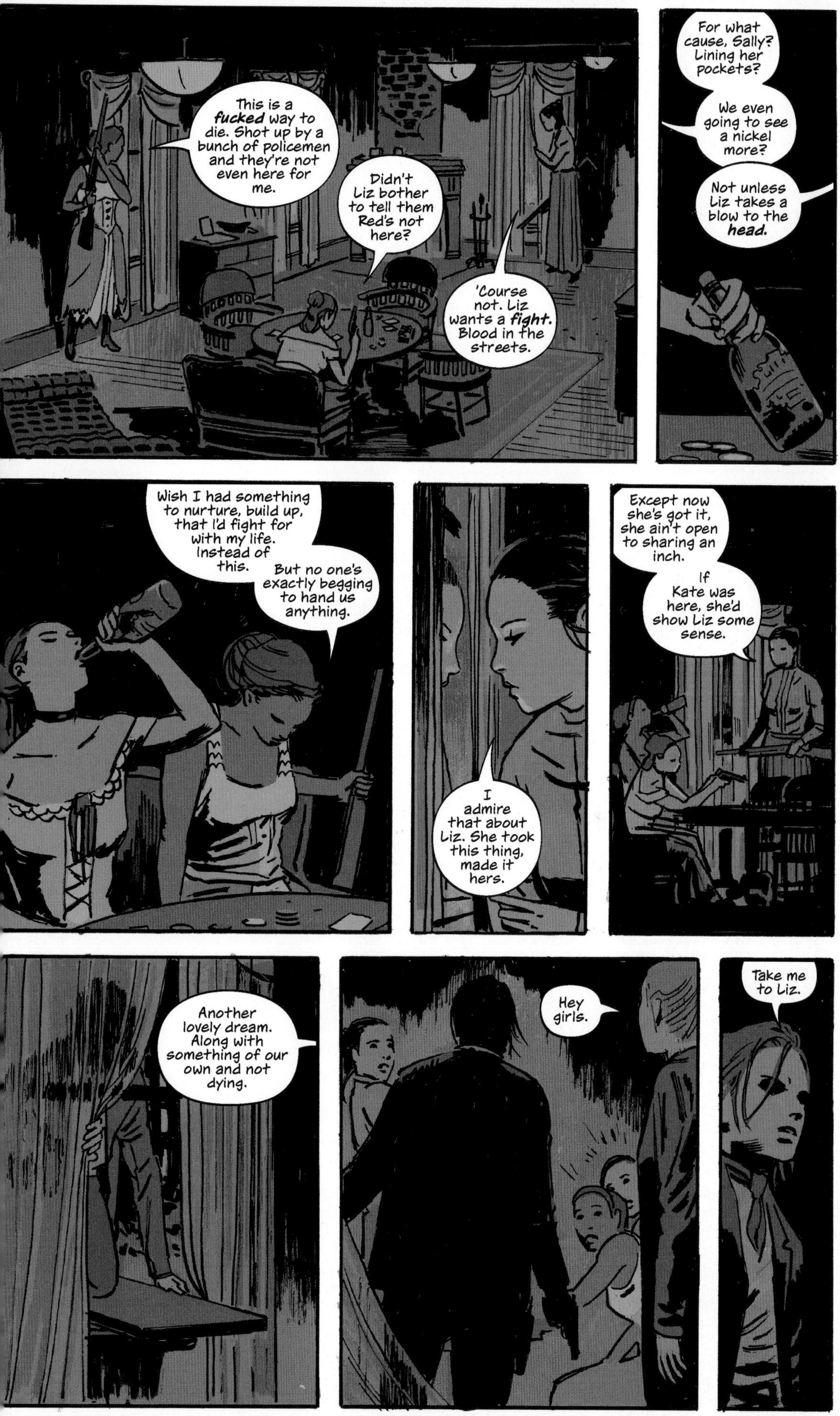
This is a fucked way to die. Shot up by a bunch of policemen and they're not even here for me.
Didn't Liz bother to tell them Red's not here?
'Course not. Liz wants a fight. Blood in the streets.
For what cause, Sally? Lining her pockets?
We even going to see a nickel more?
Not unless Liz takes a blow to the head.
Wish I had something to nurture, build up, that I'd fight for with my life. Instead of this.
But no one's exactly begging to hand us anything.
I admire that about Liz. She took this thing, made it hers.
Except now she's got it, she ain't open to sharing an inch.
If Kate was here, she'd show Liz some sense.
Another lovely dream. Along with something of our own and not dying.
Hey girls.
Take me to Liz.

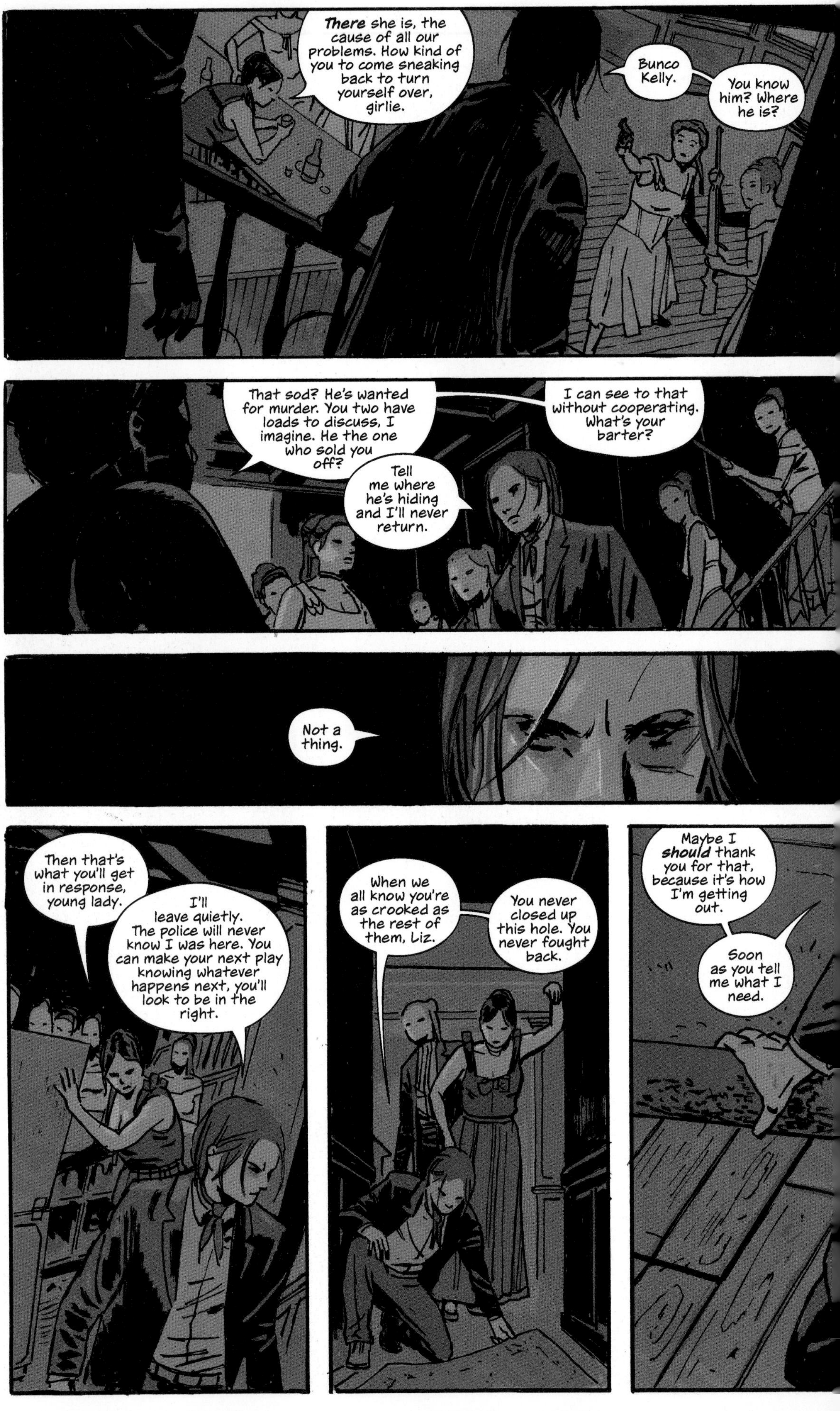
There she is, the cause of all our problems. How kind of you to come sneaking back to turn yourself over, girlie.
Bunco Kelly.
You know him? Where he is?
That sod? He's wanted for murder. You two have loads to discuss, I imagine. He the one who sold you off?
Tell me where he's hiding and I'll never return.
I can see to that without cooperating. What's your barter?
Not a thing.
Then that's what you'll get in response, young lady.
I'll leave quietly. The police will never know I was here. You can make your next play knowing whatever happens next, you'll look to be in the right.
When we all know you're as crooked as the rest of them, Liz.
You never closed up this hole. You never fought back.
Maybe I *should* thank you for that, because it's how I'm getting out.
Soon as you tell me what I need.

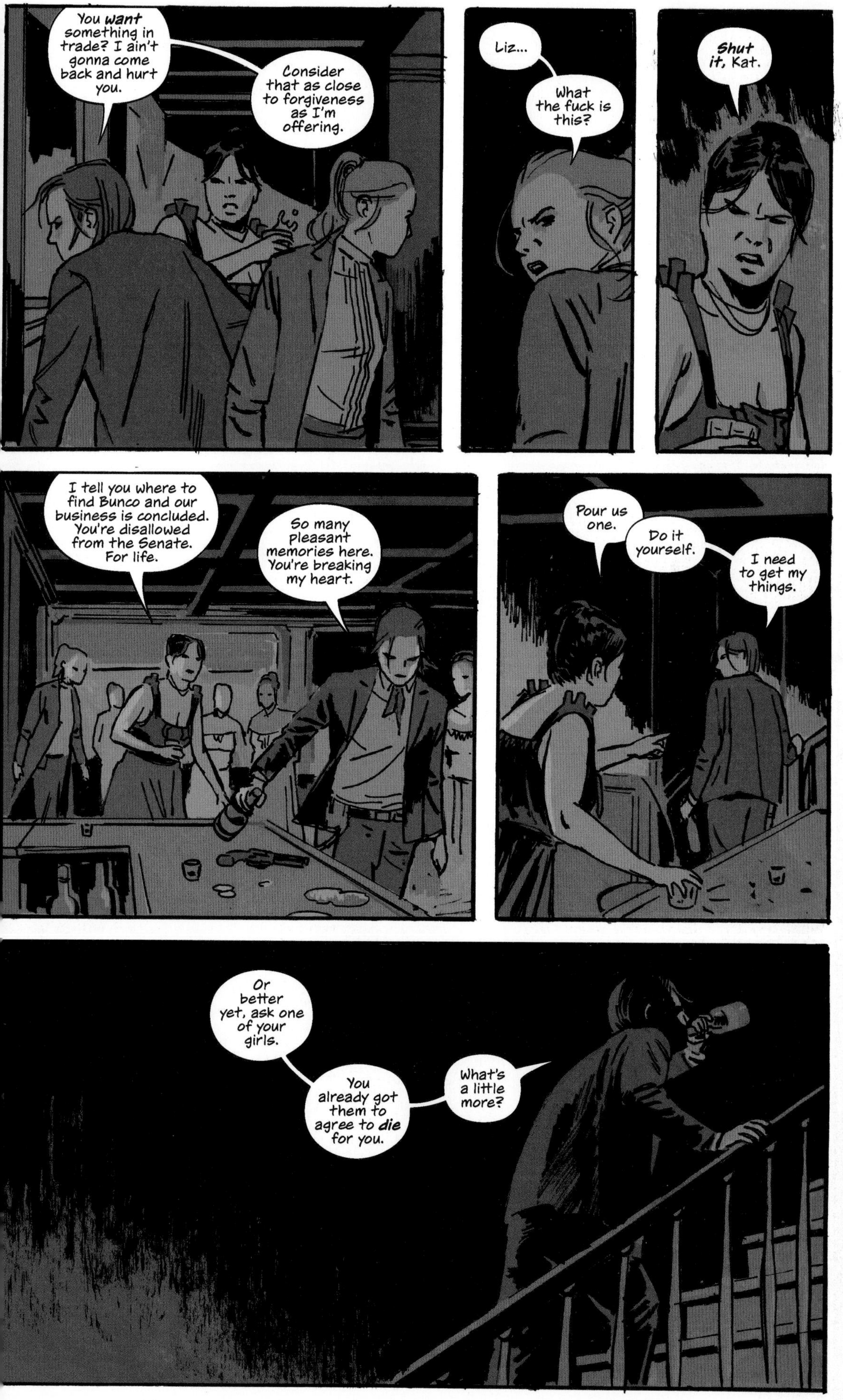
You **want** something in trade? I ain't gonna come back and hurt you.
Consider that as close to forgiveness as I'm offering.
Liz...
What the fuck is this?
Shut it, Kat.
I tell you where to find Bunco and our business is concluded. You're disallowed from the Senate. For life.
So many pleasant memories here. You're breaking my heart.
Pour us one.
Do it yourself.
I need to get my things.
Or better yet, ask one of your girls.
You already got them to agree to **die** for you.
What's a little more?

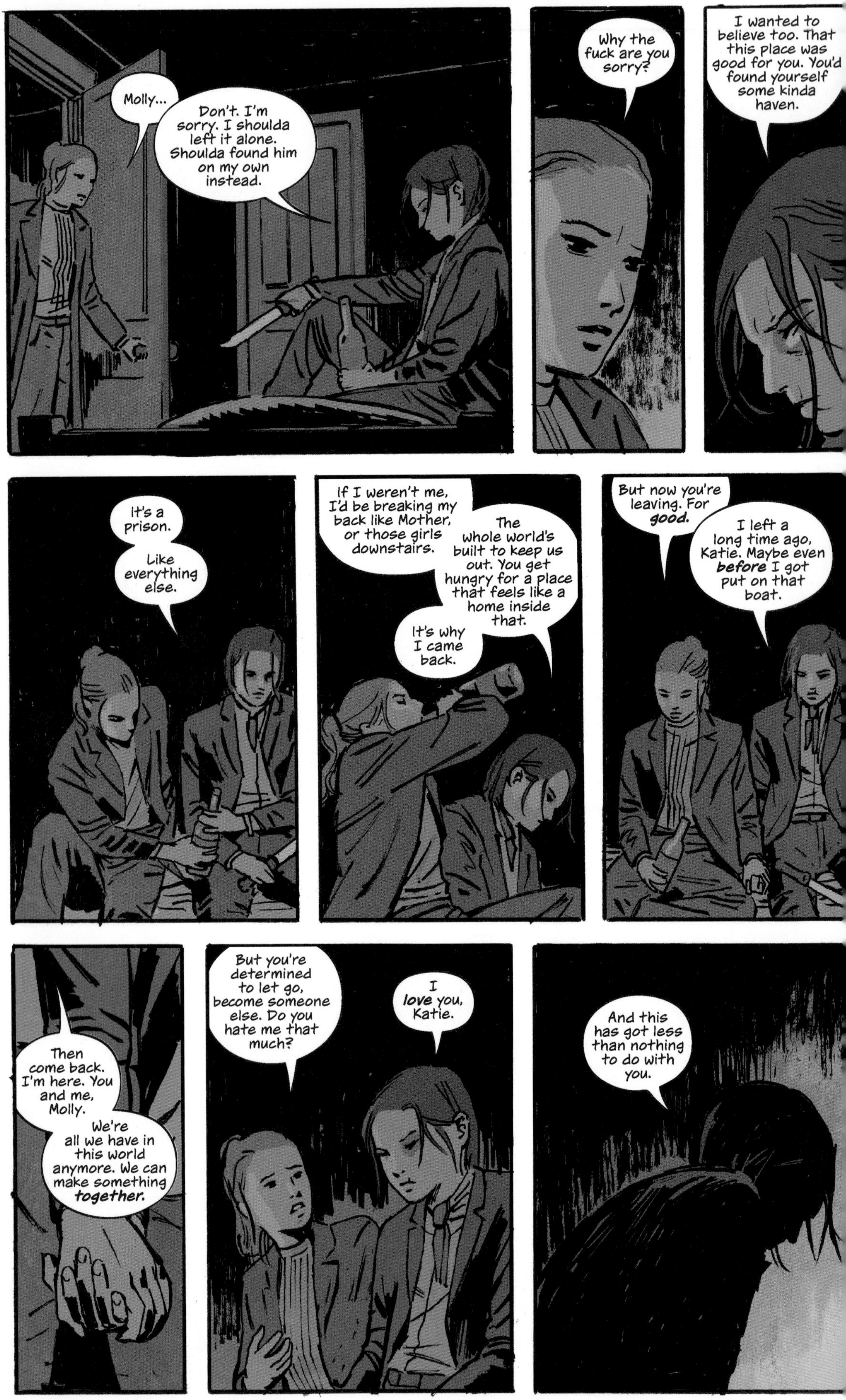

Molly...
Don't. I'm sorry. I shoulda left it alone. Shoulda found him on my own instead.
Why the fuck are you sorry?
I wanted to believe too. That this place was good for you. You'd found yourself some kinda haven.
It's a prison.
Like everything else.
If I weren't me, I'd be breaking my back like Mother, or those girls downstairs.
The whole world's built to keep us out. You get hungry for a place that feels like a home inside that.
It's why I came back.
But now you're leaving. For **good.**
I left a long time ago, Katie. Maybe even **before** I got put on that boat.
Then come back. I'm here. You and me, Molly.
We're all we have in this world anymore. We can make something **together.**
But you're determined to let go, become someone else. Do you hate me that much?
I **love** you, Katie.
And this has got less than nothing to do with you.

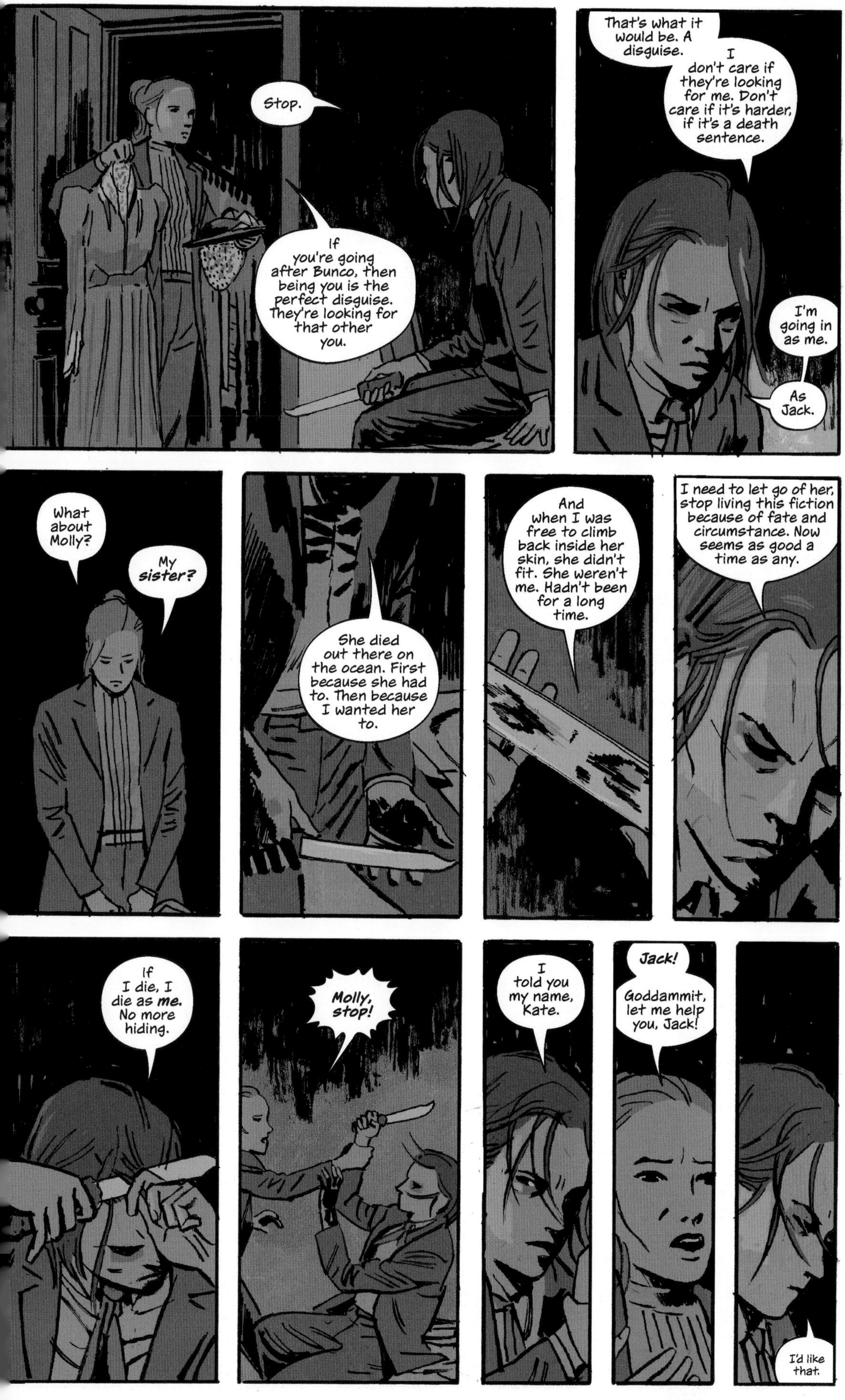
Stop.
If you're going after Bunco, then being you is the perfect disguise. They're looking for that other you.
That's what it would be. A disguise.
I don't care if they're looking for me. Don't care if it's harder, if it's a death sentence.
I'm going in as me.
As Jack.
What about Molly?
My *sister?*
She died out there on the ocean. First because she had to. Then because I wanted her to.
And when I was free to climb back inside her skin, she didn't fit. She weren't me. Hadn't been for a long time.
I need to let go of her, stop living this fiction because of fate and circumstance. Now seems as good a time as any.
If I die, I die as *me.* No more hiding.
Molly, stop!
I told you my name, Kate.
Jack!
Goddammit, let me help you, Jack!
I'd like that.

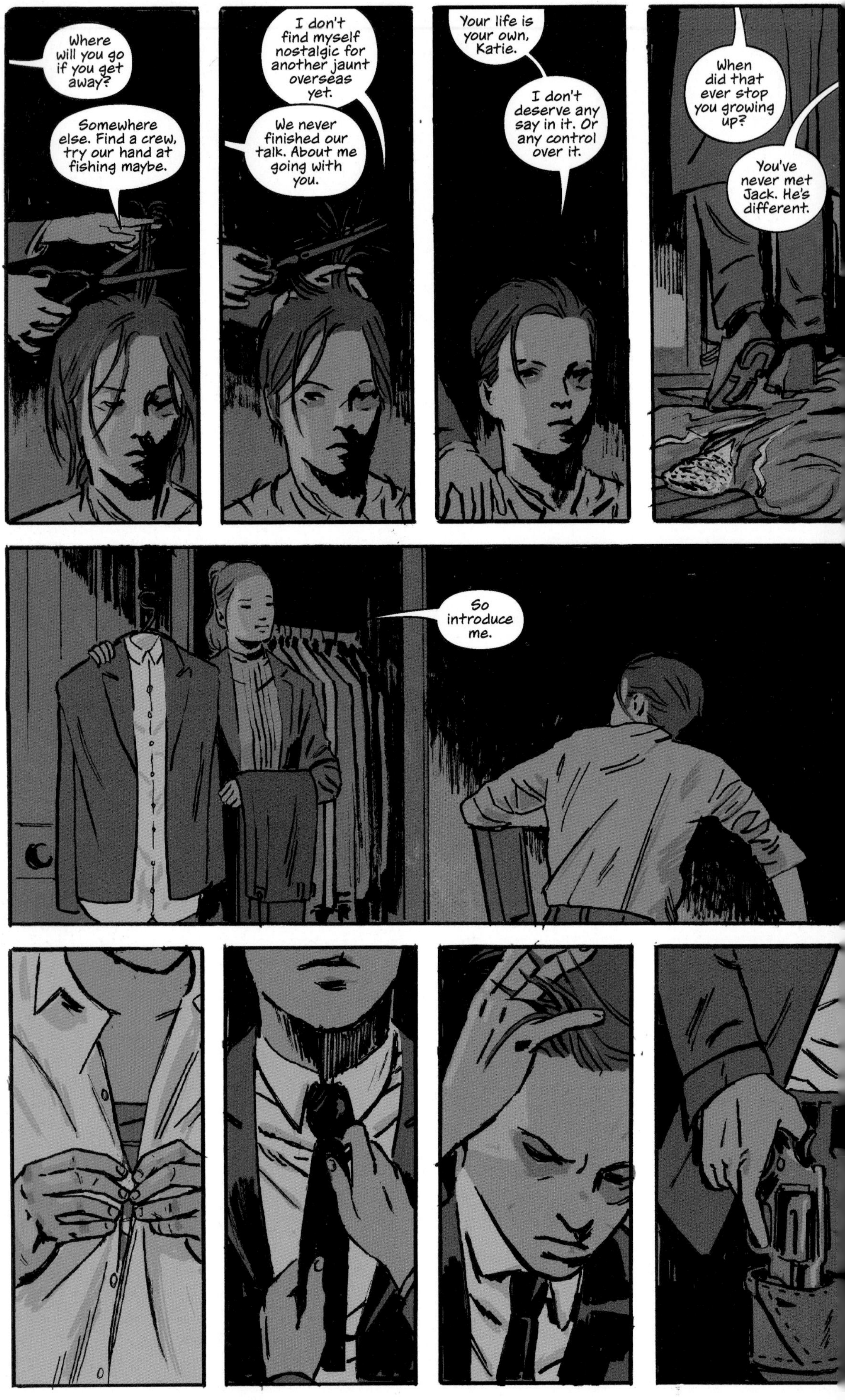

Where will you go if you get away?
Somewhere else. Find a crew, try our hand at fishing maybe.
I don't find myself nostalgic for another jaunt overseas yet.
We never finished our talk. About me going with you.
Your life is your own, Katie.
I don't deserve any say in it. Or any control over it.
When did that ever stop you growing up?
You've never met Jack. He's different.
So introduce me.

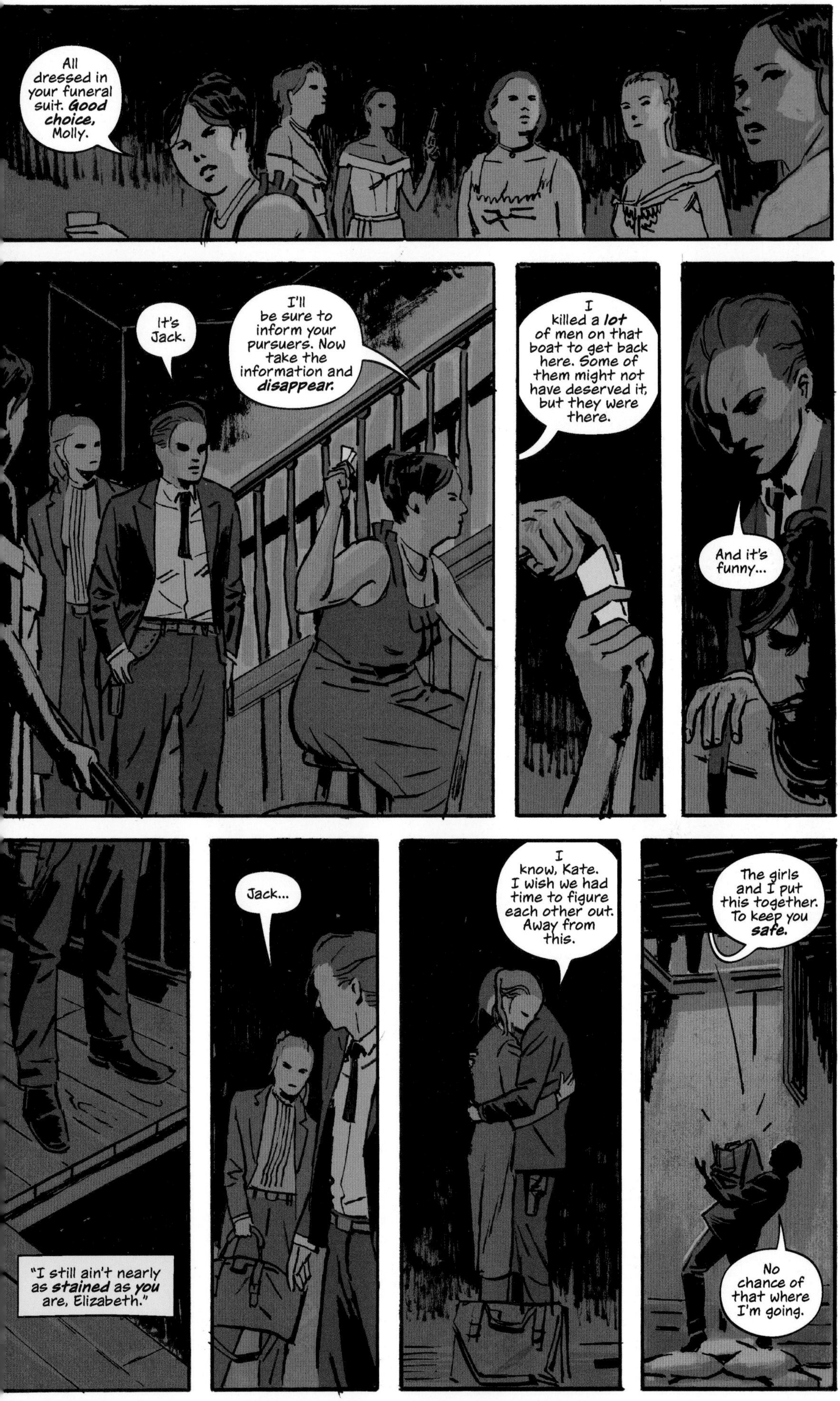
All dressed in your funeral suit. Good choice, Molly.
It's Jack.
I'll be sure to inform your pursuers. Now take the information and disappear.
I killed a lot of men on that boat to get back here. Some of them might not have deserved it, but they were there.
And it's funny...
"I still ain't nearly as stained as you are, Elizabeth."
Jack...
I know, Kate. I wish we had time to figure each other out. Away from this.
The girls and I put this together. To keep you safe.
No chance of that where I'm going.

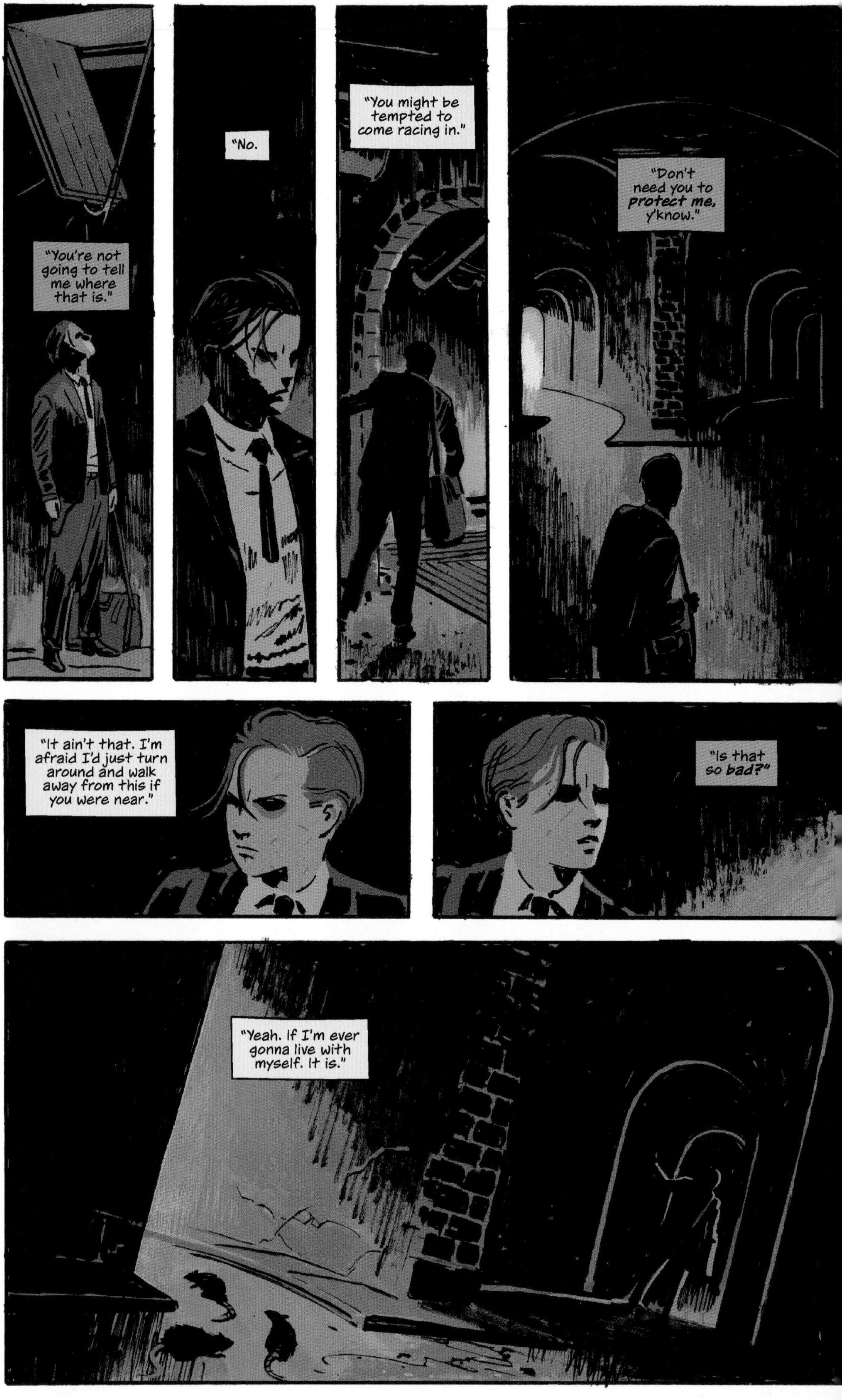
"You're not going to tell me where that is."
"No.
"You might be tempted to come racing in."
"Don't need you to *protect me,* y'know."
"It ain't that. I'm afraid I'd just turn around and walk away from this if you were near."
"Is that so *bad?"*
"Yeah. If I'm ever gonna live with myself. It is."

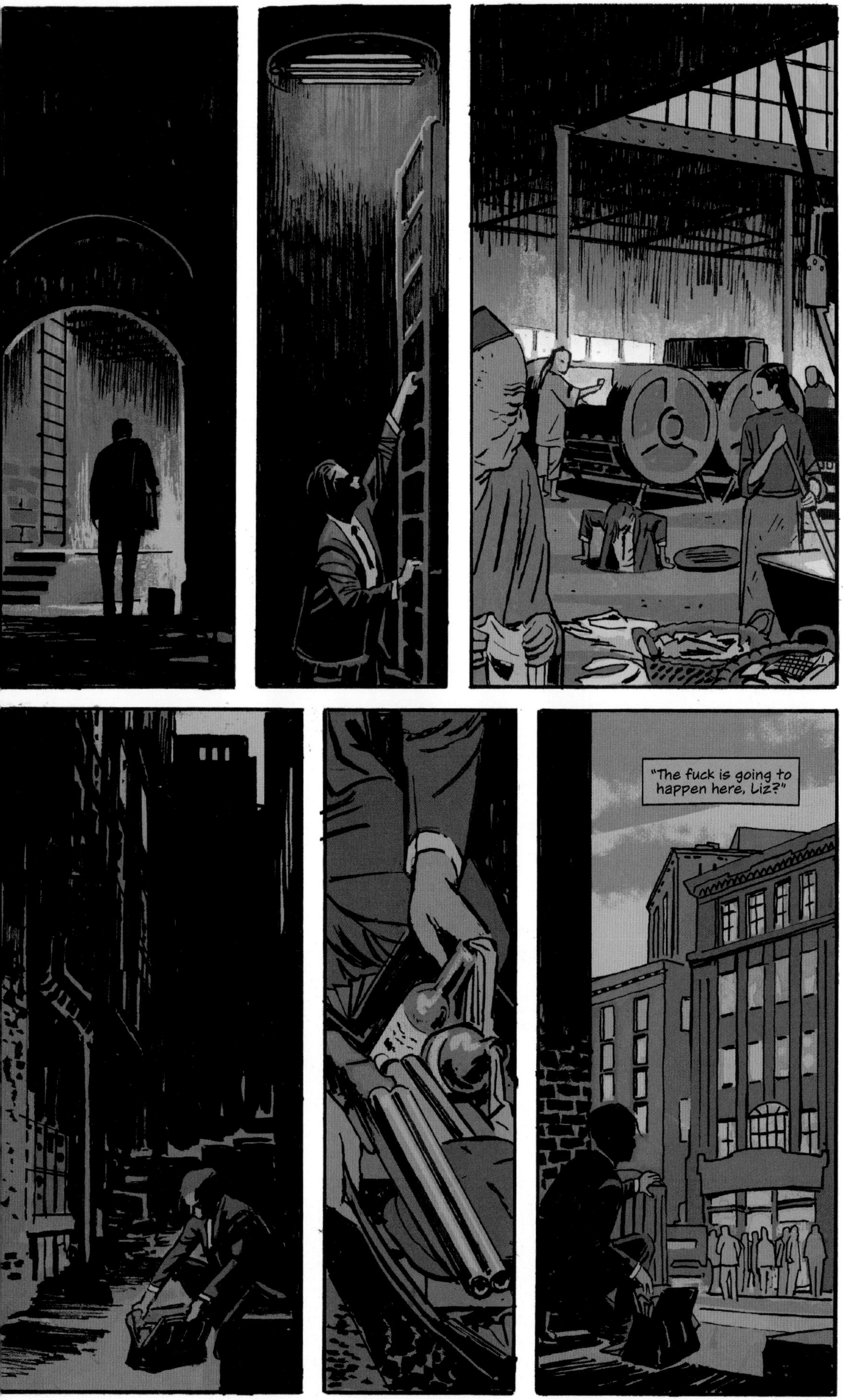
"The fuck is going to happen here, Liz?"

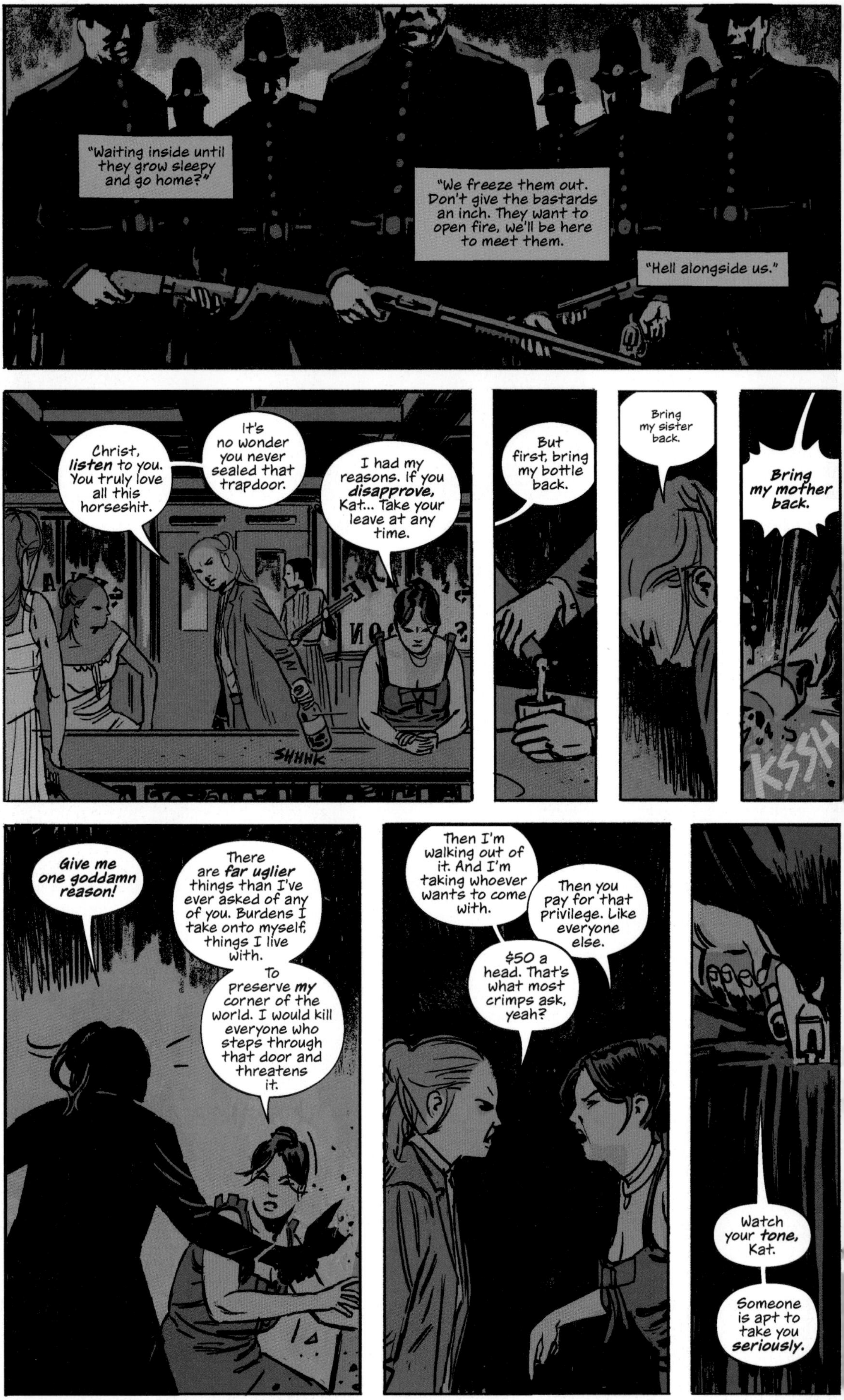
"Waiting inside until they grow sleepy and go home?"
"We freeze them out. Don't give the bastards an inch. They want to open fire, we'll be here to meet them.
"Hell alongside us."
Christ, listen to you. You truly love all this horseshit.
It's no wonder you never sealed that trapdoor.
I had my reasons. If you disapprove, Kat... Take your leave at any time.
SHHHK
But first, bring my bottle back.
Bring my sister back.
Bring my mother back.
KSSH
Give me one goddamn reason!
There are far uglier things than I've ever asked of any of you. Burdens I take onto myself, things I live with.
To preserve my corner of the world. I would kill everyone who steps through that door and threatens it.
Then I'm walking out of it. And I'm taking whoever wants to come with.
Then you pay for that privilege. Like everyone else.
$50 a head. That's what most crimps ask, yeah?
Watch your tone, Kat.
Someone is apt to take you seriously.

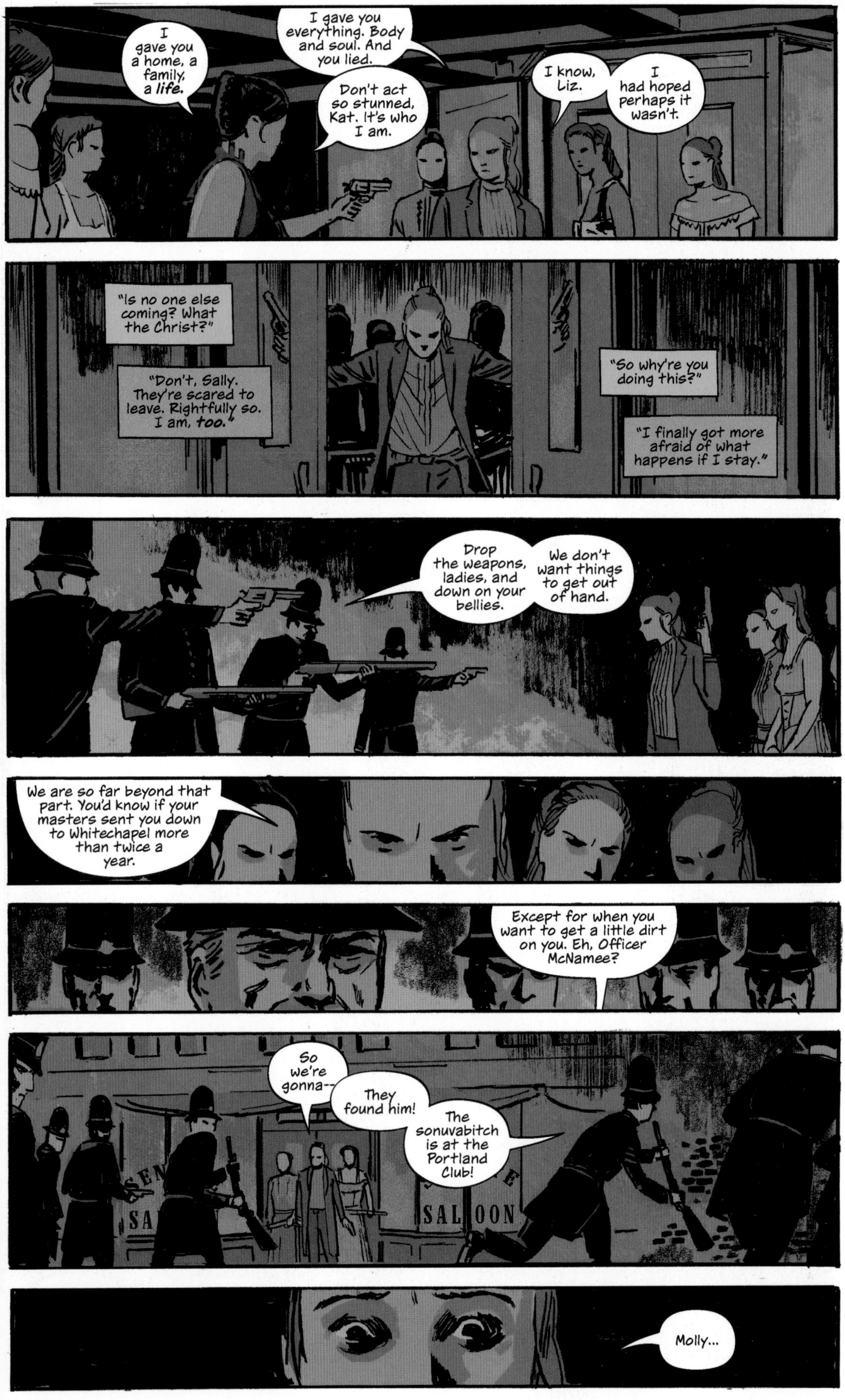
I gave you a home, a family, a *life.*
I gave you everything. Body and soul. And you lied.
Don't act so stunned, Kat. It's who I am.
I know, Liz.
I had hoped perhaps it wasn't.
"Is no one else coming? What the Christ?"
"Don't, Sally. They're scared to leave. Rightfully so. I am, *too.*"
"So why're you doing this?"
"I finally got more afraid of what happens if I stay."
Drop the weapons, ladies, and down on your bellies.
We don't want things to get out of hand.
We are so far beyond that part. You'd know if your masters sent you down to Whitechapel more than twice a year.
Except for when you want to get a little dirt on you. Eh, Officer McNamee?
So we're gonna--
They found him!
The sonuvabitch is at the Portland Club!
SALOON
Molly...

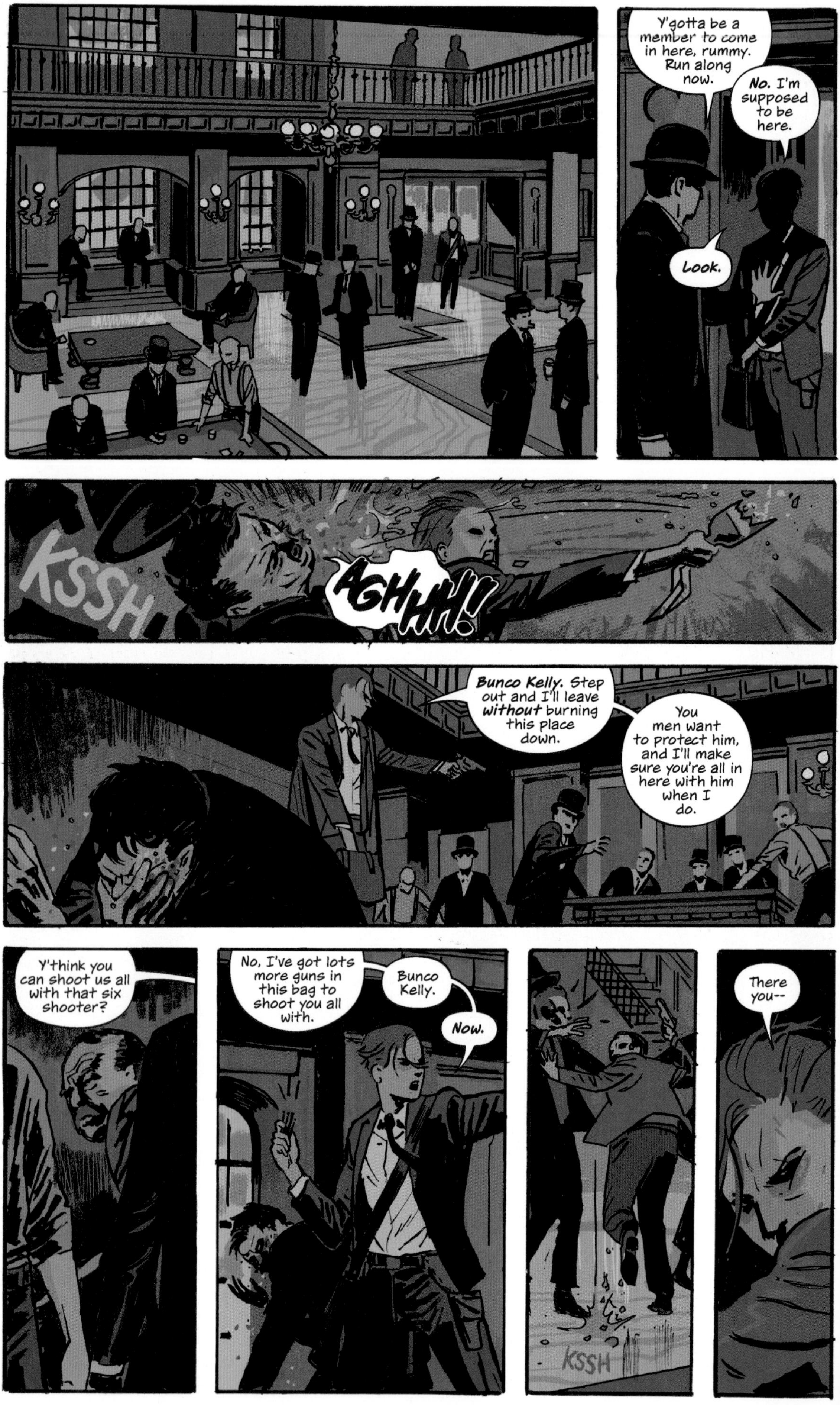
Y'gotta be a member to come in here, rummy. Run along now.
No. I'm supposed to be here.
Look.
KSSH
AGHHH!
Bunco Kelly. Step out and I'll leave without burning this place down.
You men want to protect him, and I'll make sure you're all in here with him when I do.
Y'think you can shoot us all with that six shooter?
No, I've got lots more guns in this bag to shoot you all with.
Bunco Kelly.
Now.
KSSH
There you--

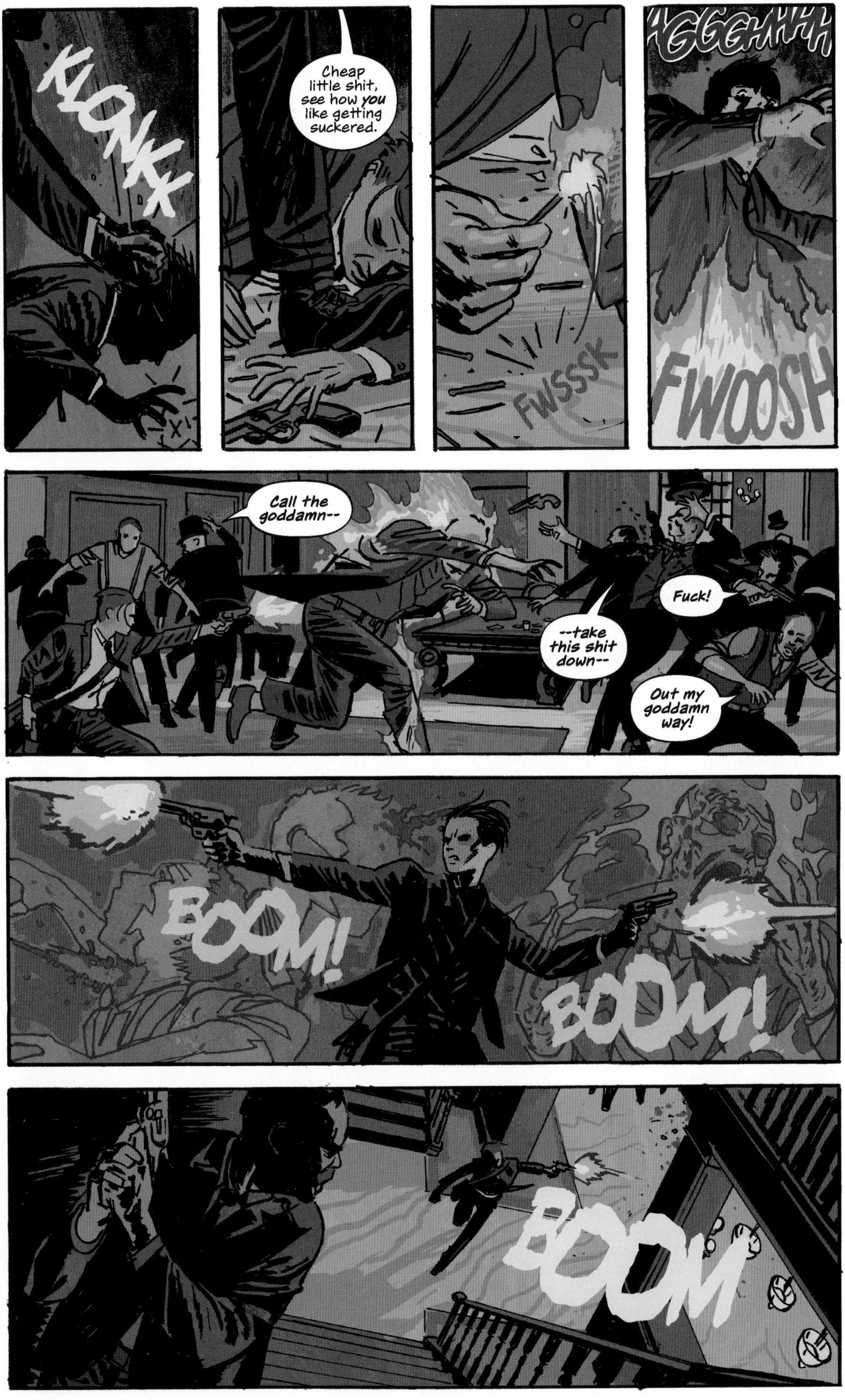
KLONKK
Cheap little shit, see how you like getting suckered.
FWSSSK
AGGGHHHH
FWOOSH
Call the goddamn--
--take this shit down--
Fuck!
Out my goddamn way!
BOOM!
BOOM!
BOOM

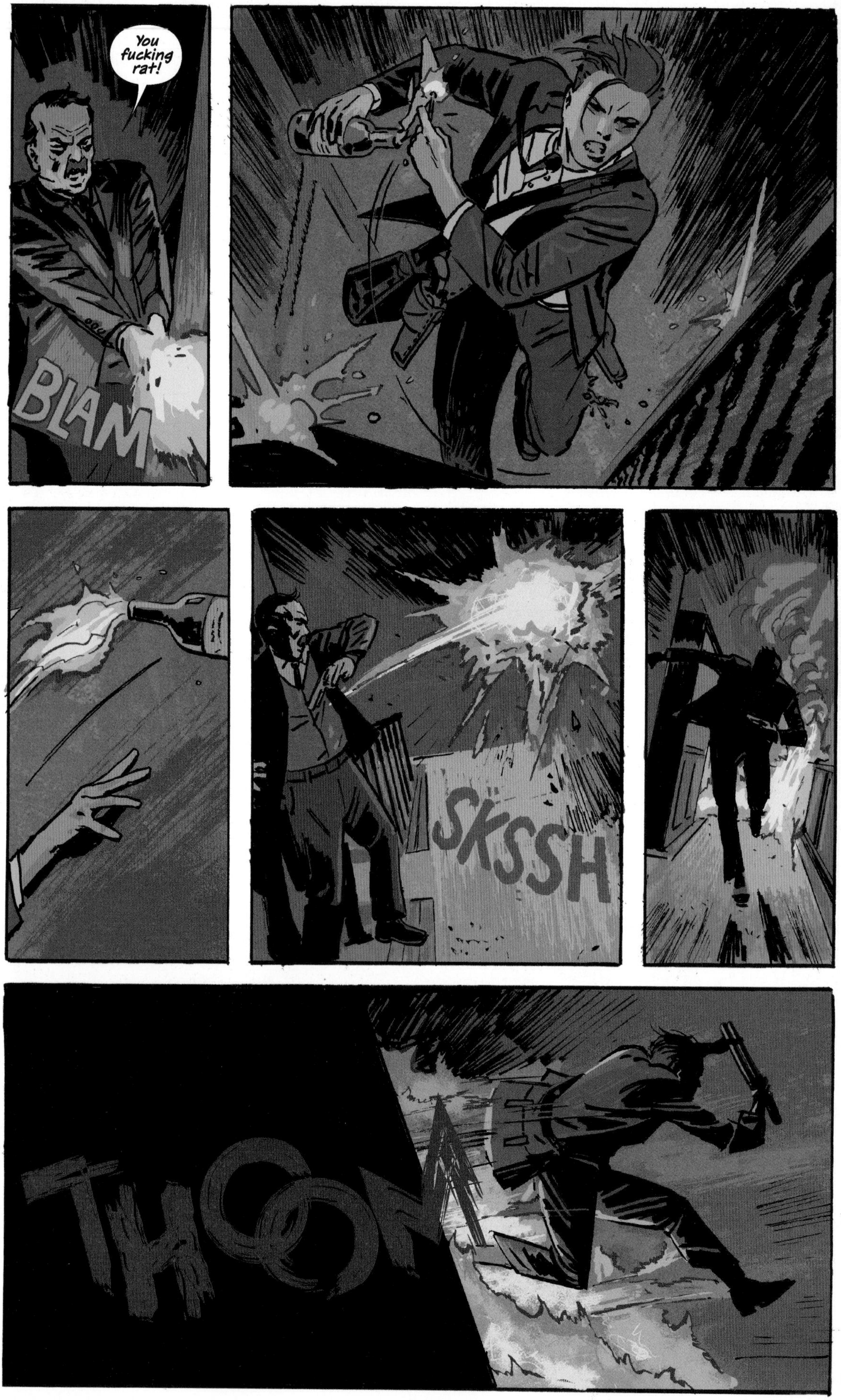
You fucking rat!
BLAM
SKSSH
THOOM

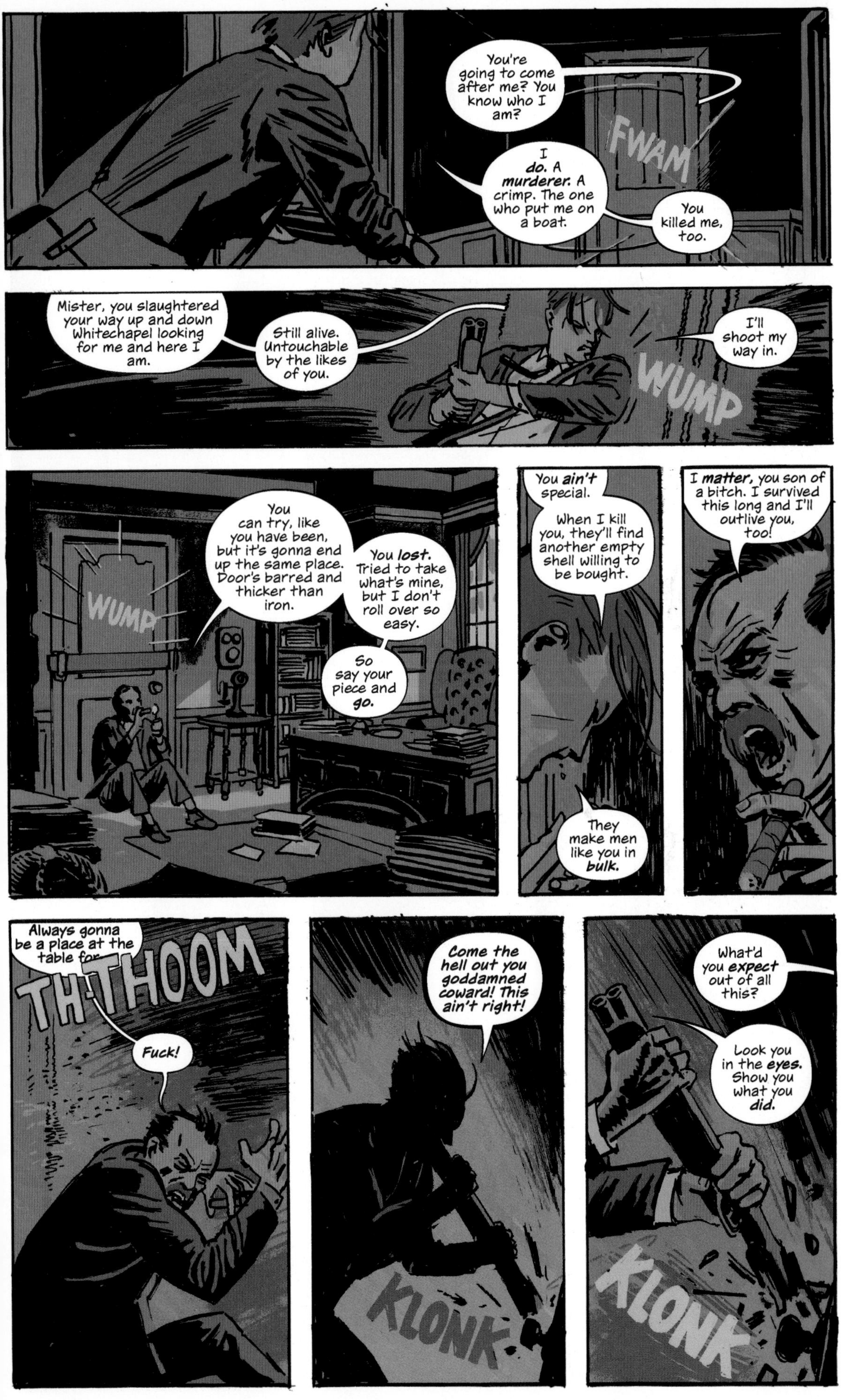
You're going to come after me? You know who I am?
FWAM
I do. A murderer. A crimp. The one who put me on a boat.
You killed me, too.
Mister, you slaughtered your way up and down Whitechapel looking for me and here I am.
Still alive. Untouchable by the likes of you.
I'll shoot my way in.
WUMP
WUMP
You can try, like you have been, but it's gonna end up the same place. Door's barred and thicker than iron.
You lost. Tried to take what's mine, but I don't roll over so easy.
So say your piece and go.
You ain't special.
When I kill you, they'll find another empty shell willing to be bought.
They make men like you in bulk.
I matter, you son of a bitch. I survived this long and I'll outlive you, too!
Always gonna be a place at the table for—
TH-THOOM
Fuck!
Come the hell out you goddamned coward! This ain't right!
KLONK
What'd you expect out of all this?
Look you in the eyes. Show you what you did.
KLONK

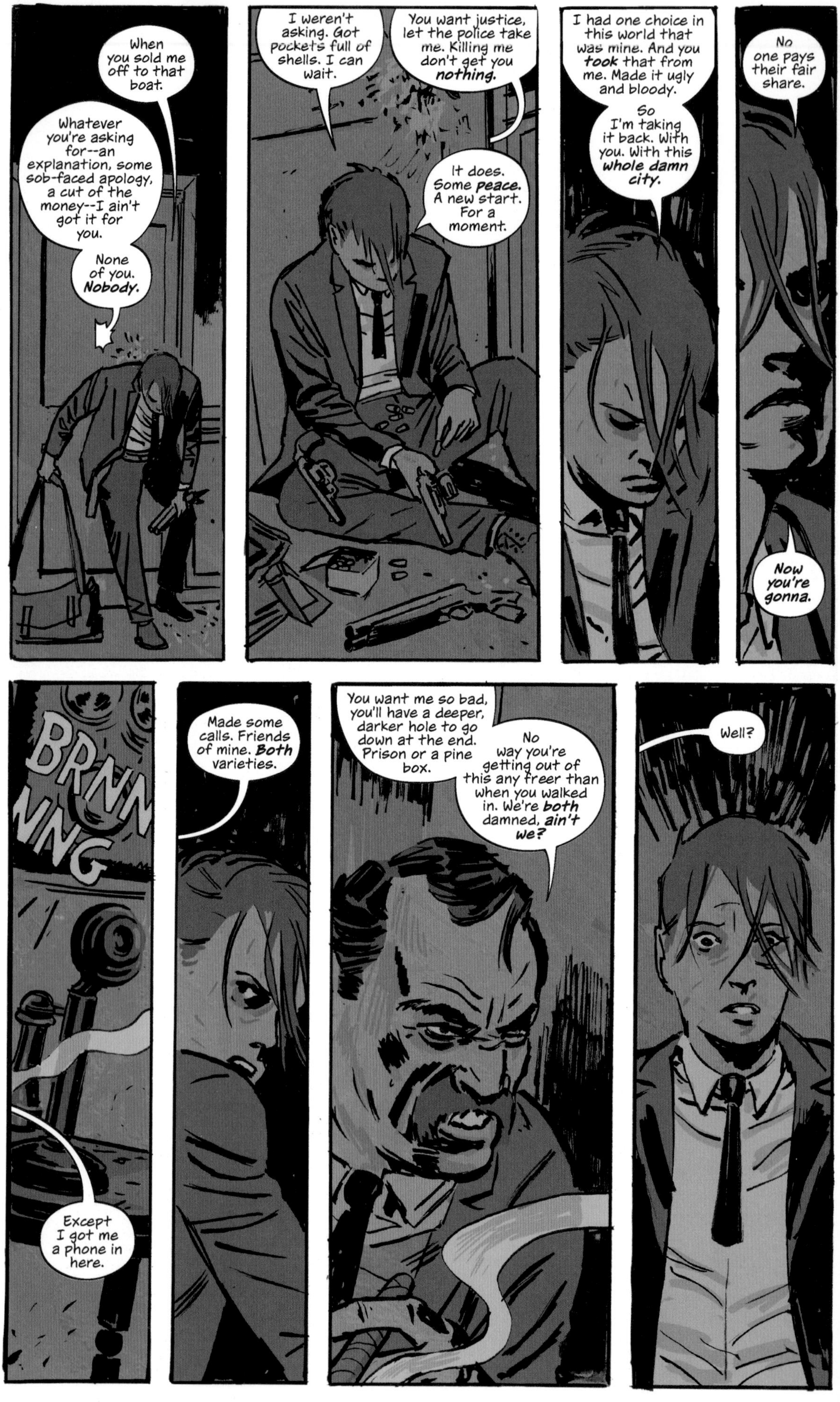
When you sold me off to that boat.
Whatever you're asking for--an explanation, some sob-faced apology, a cut of the money--I ain't got it for you.
None of you. **Nobody.**
I weren't asking. Got pockets full of shells. I can wait.
You want justice, let the police take me. Killing me don't get you **nothing.**
It does. Some **peace.** A new start. For a moment.
I had one choice in this world that was mine. And you **took** that from me. Made it ugly and bloody.
So I'm taking it back. With you. With this **whole damn city.**
No one pays their fair share.
Now you're gonna.
BRNNNNG
Except I got me a phone in here.
Made some calls. Friends of mine. **Both** varieties.
You want me so bad, you'll have a deeper, darker hole to go down at the end. Prison or a pine box.
No way you're getting out of this any freer than when you walked in. We're **both** damned, **ain't we?**
Well?

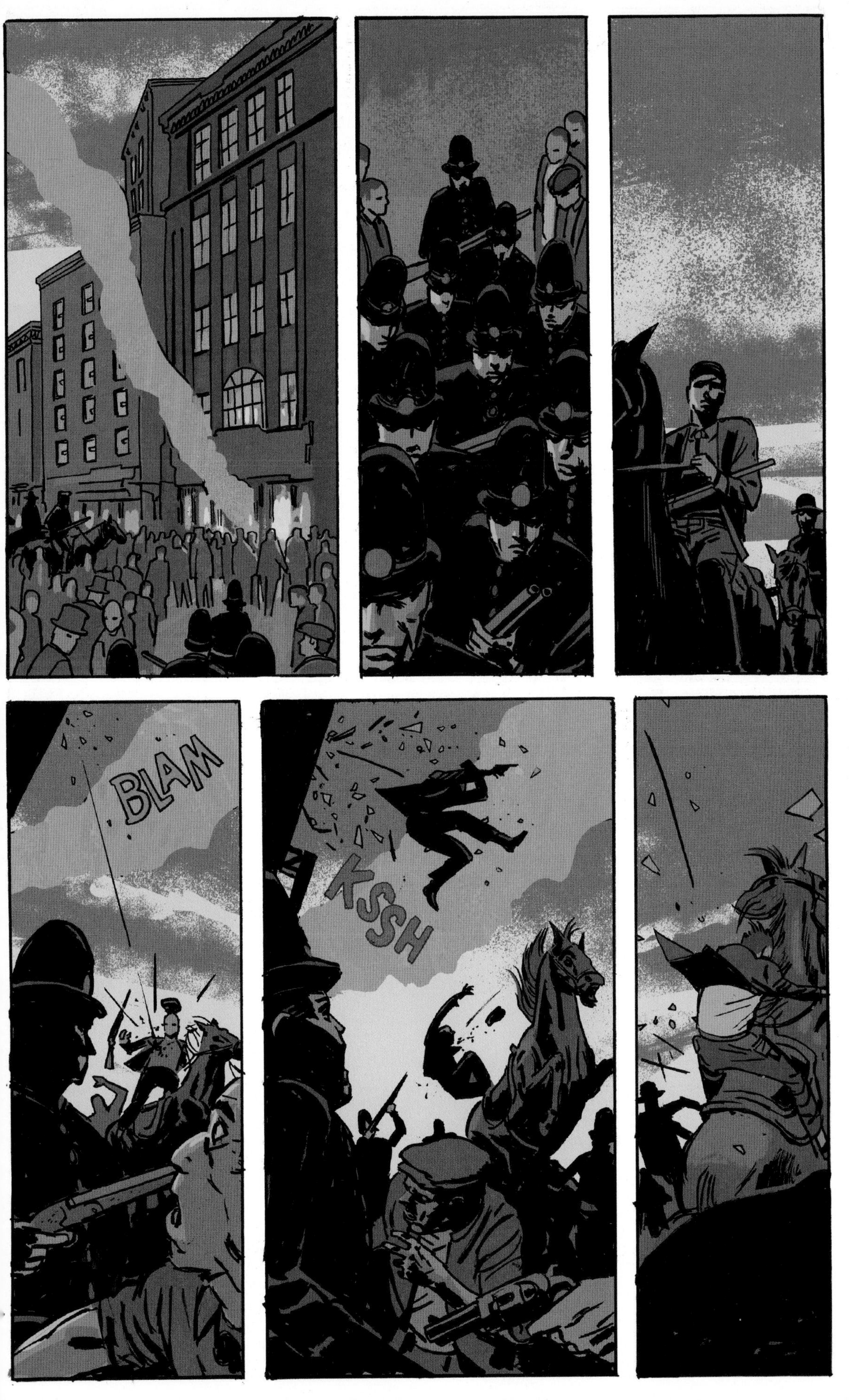
BLAM
KSSH

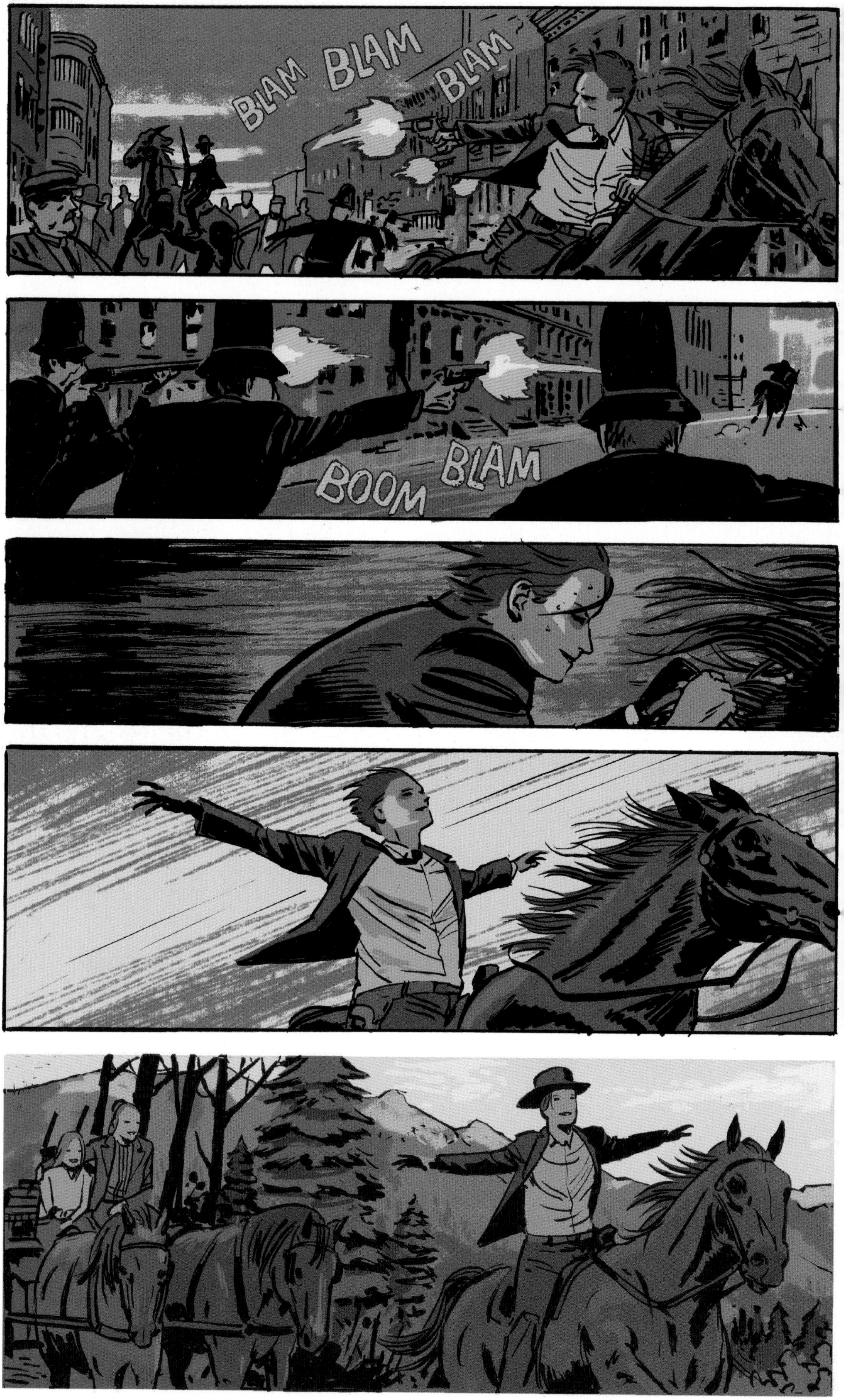
BLAM BLAM
BLAM
BOOM
BLAM

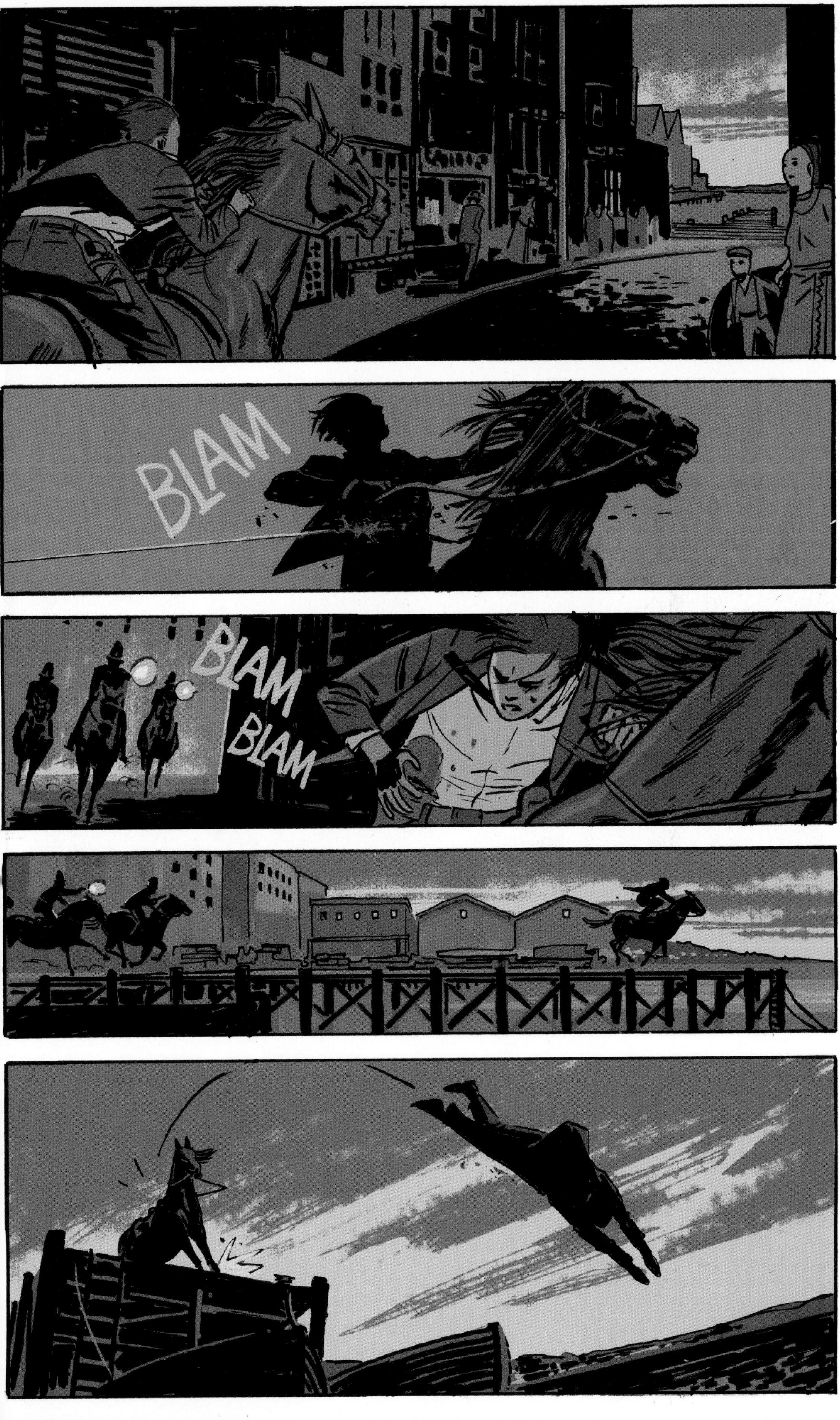
BLAM
BLAM
BLAM

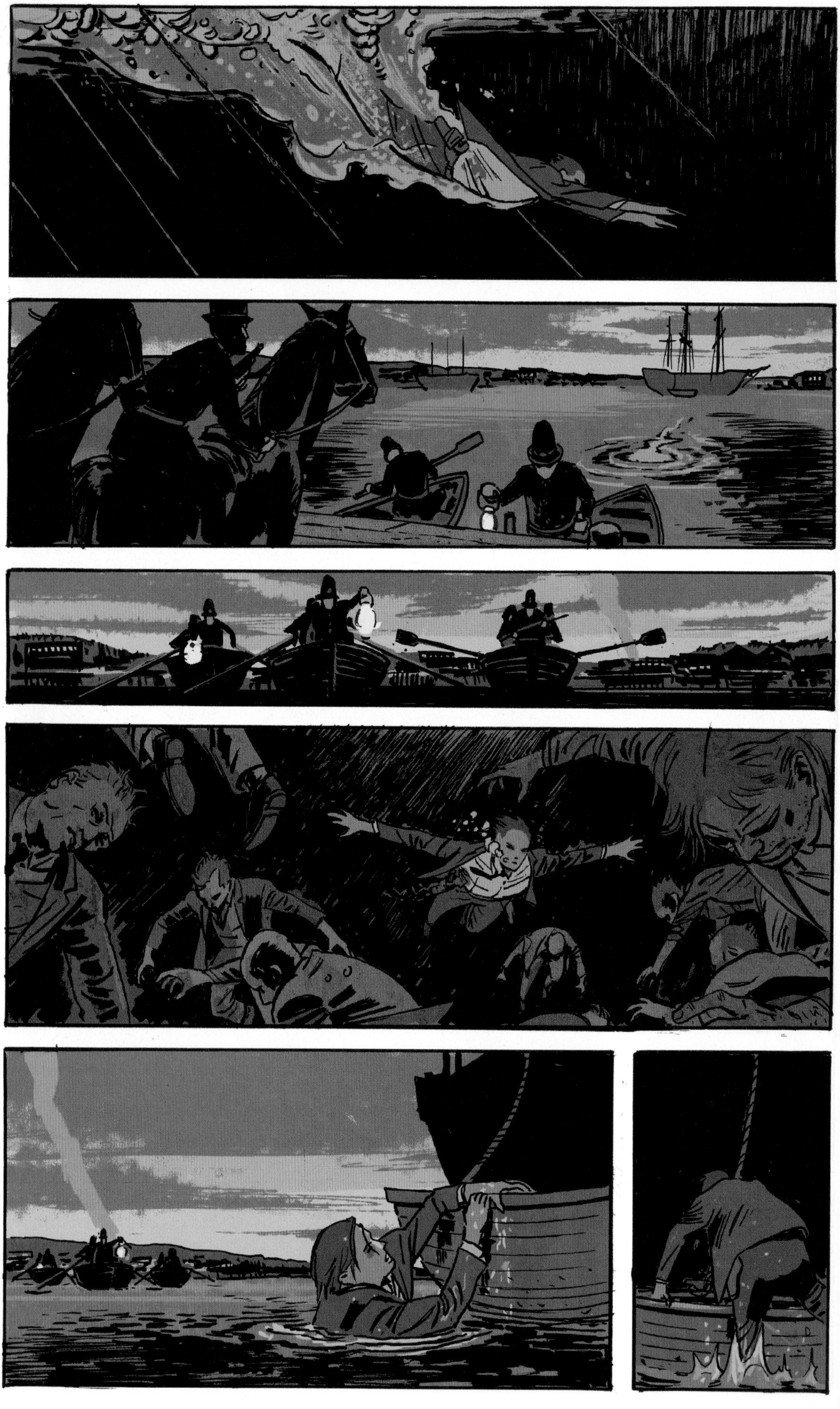

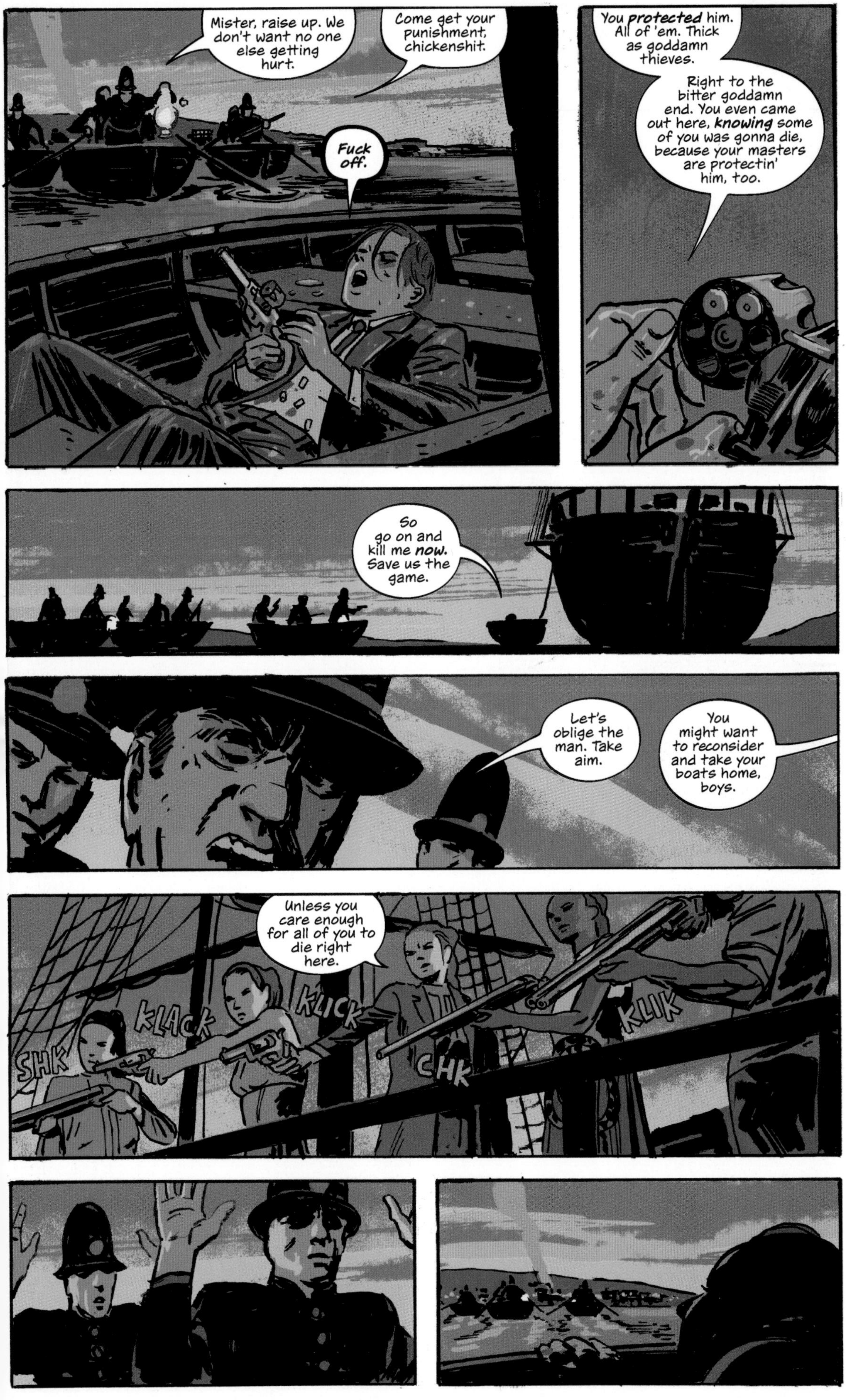

Mister, raise up. We don't want no one else getting hurt.
Come get your punishment, chickenshit.
Fuck off.
You protected him. All of 'em. Thick as goddamn thieves.
Right to the bitter goddamn end. You even came out here, knowing some of you was gonna die, because your masters are protectin' him, too.
So go on and kill me now. Save us the game.
Let's oblige the man. Take aim.
You might want to reconsider and take your boats home, boys.
Unless you care enough for all of you to die right here.
SHK
KLACK
KLICK
CHK
KLIK

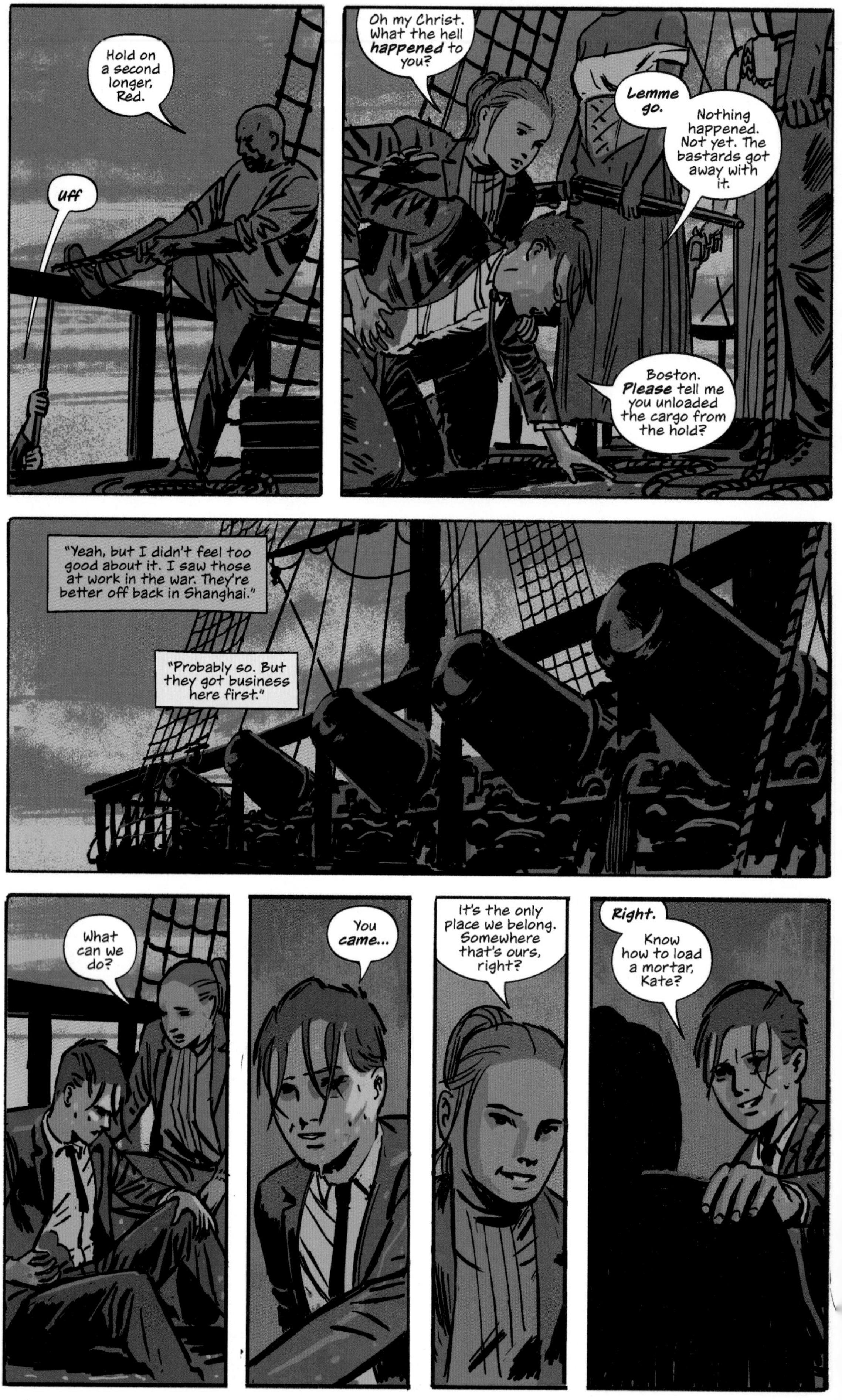
Hold on a second longer, Red.
Uff
Oh my Christ. What the hell *happened* to you?
Lemme go.
Nothing happened. Not yet. The bastards got away with it.
Boston. *Please* tell me you unloaded the cargo from the hold?
"Yeah, but I didn't feel too good about it. I saw those at work in the war. They're better off back in Shanghai."
"Probably so. But they got business here first."
What can we do?
You *came...*
It's the only place we belong. Somewhere that's ours, right?
Right.
Know how to load a mortar, Kate?

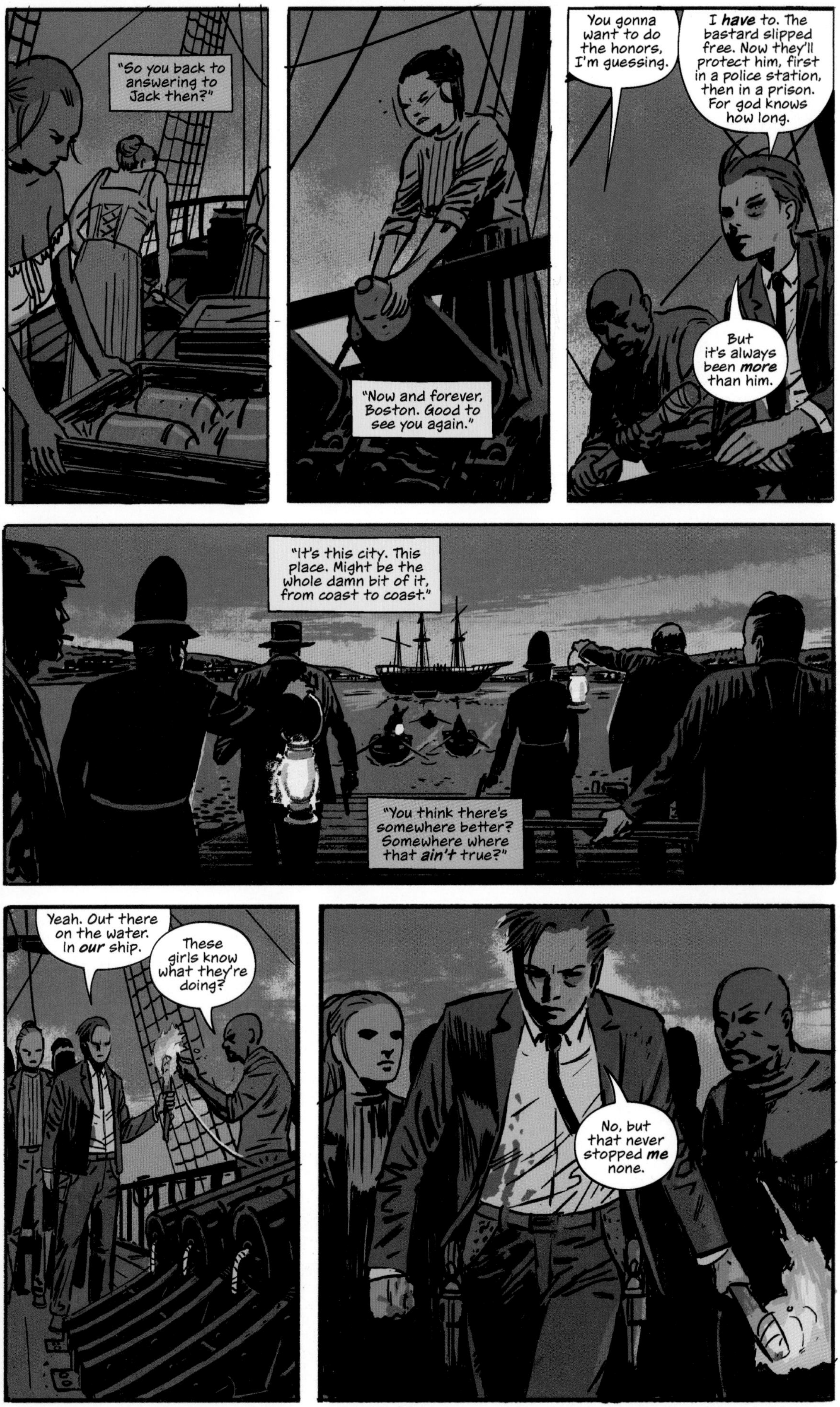
"So you back to answering to Jack then?"
"Now and forever, Boston. Good to see you again."
You gonna want to do the honors, I'm guessing.
I **have** to. The bastard slipped free. Now they'll protect him, first in a police station, then in a prison. For god knows how long.
But it's always been **more** than him.
"It's this city. This place. Might be the whole damn bit of it, from coast to coast."
"You think there's somewhere better? Somewhere where that **ain't** true?"
Yeah. Out there on the water. In **our** ship.
These girls know what they're doing?
No, but that never stopped **me** none.

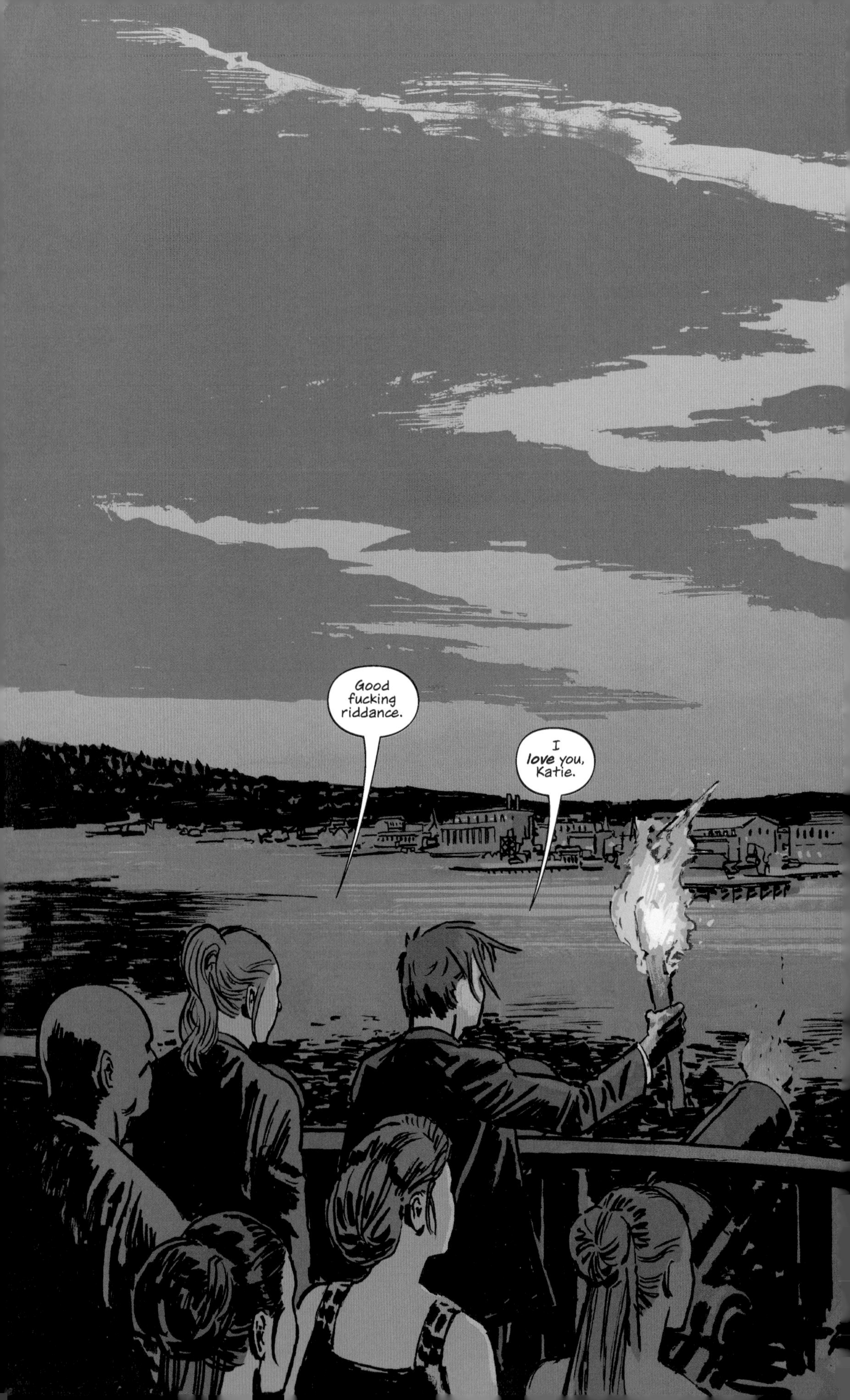
Good fucking riddance.
I *love* you, Katie.

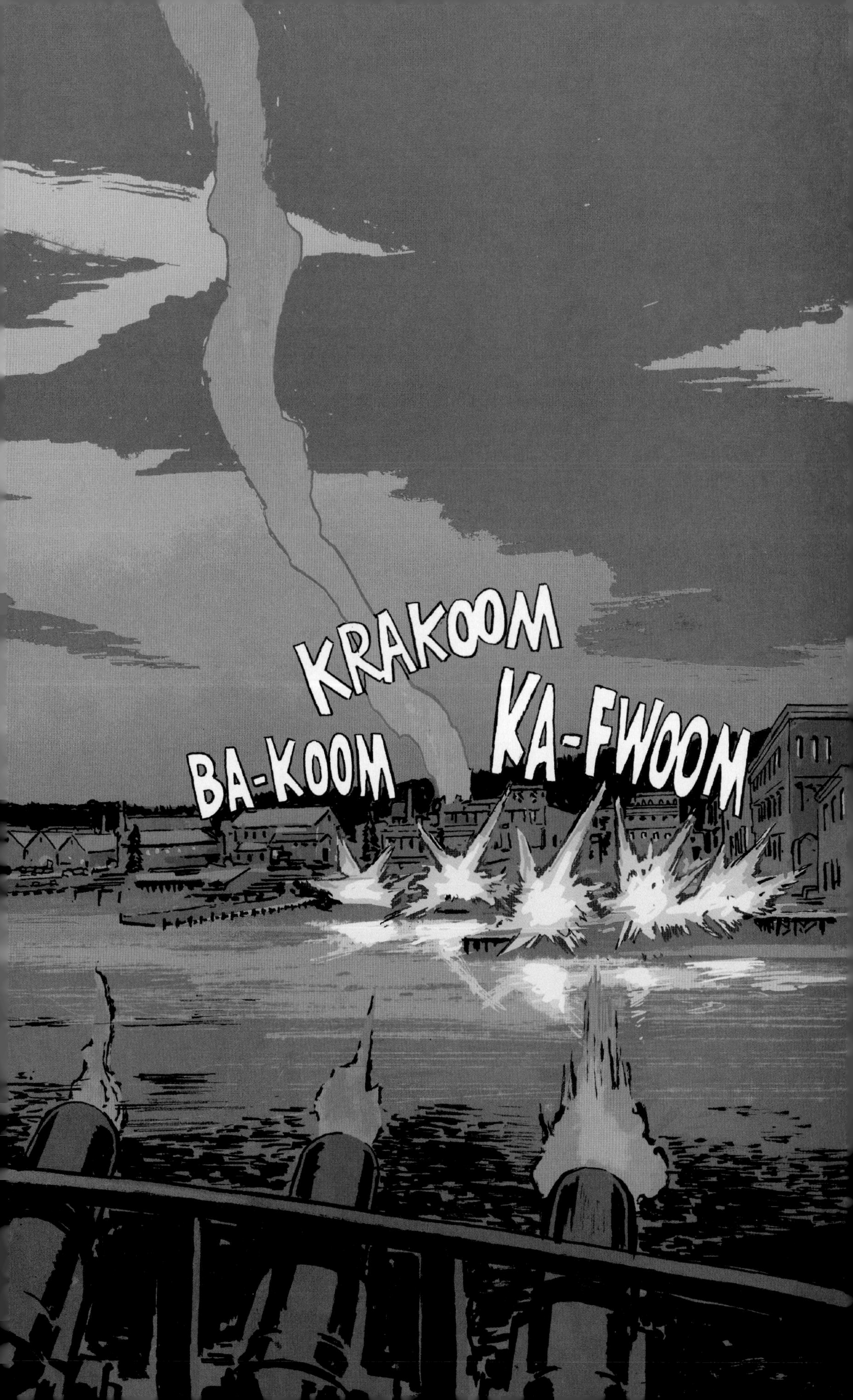
KRAKOOM
BA-KOOM
KA-FWOOM

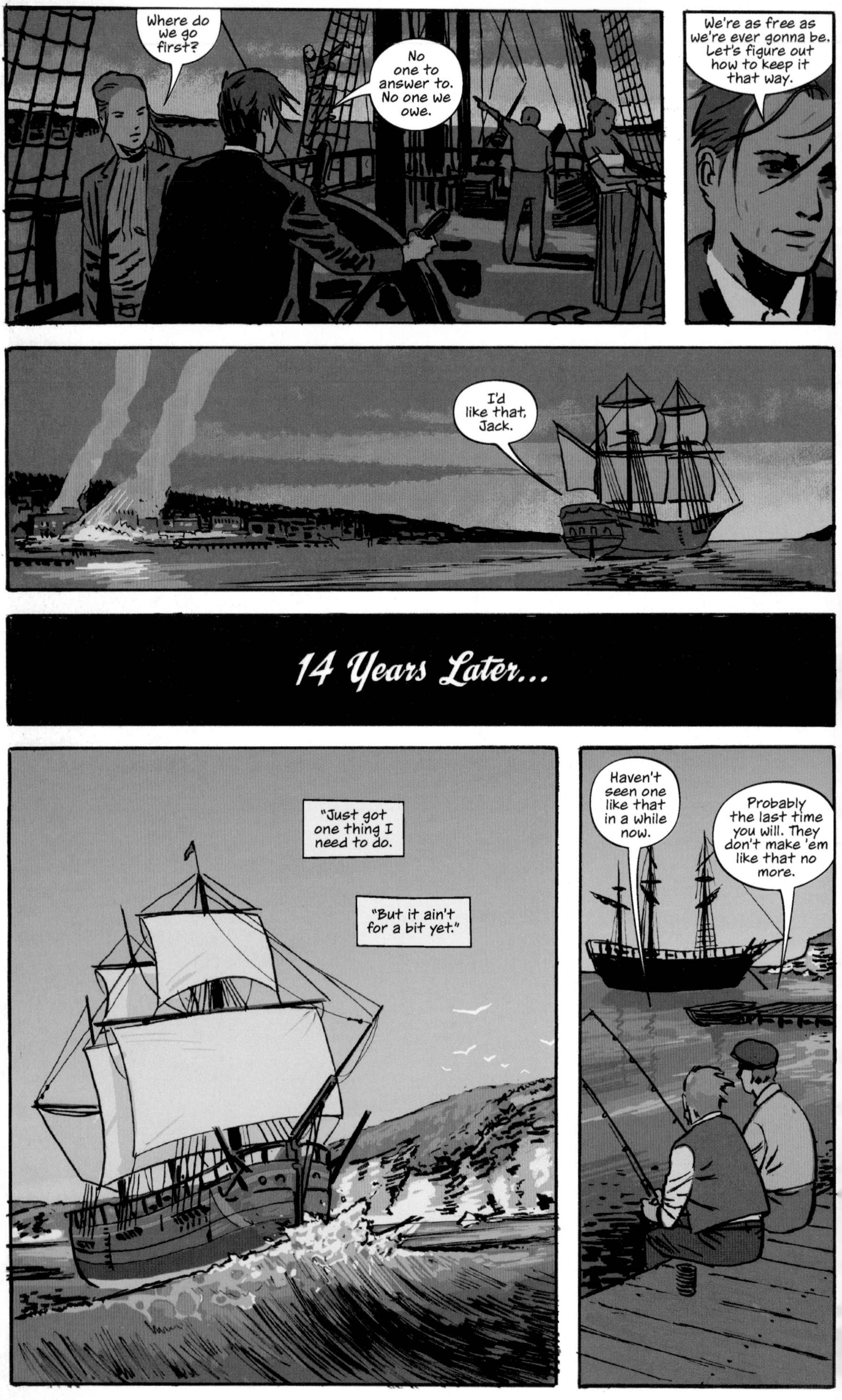
Where do we go first?
No one to answer to. No one we owe.
We're as free as we're ever gonna be. Let's figure out how to keep it that way.
I'd like that, Jack.
14 Years Later...
"Just got one thing I need to do.
"But it ain't for a bit yet."
Haven't seen one like that in a while now.
Probably the last time you will. They don't make 'em like that no more.

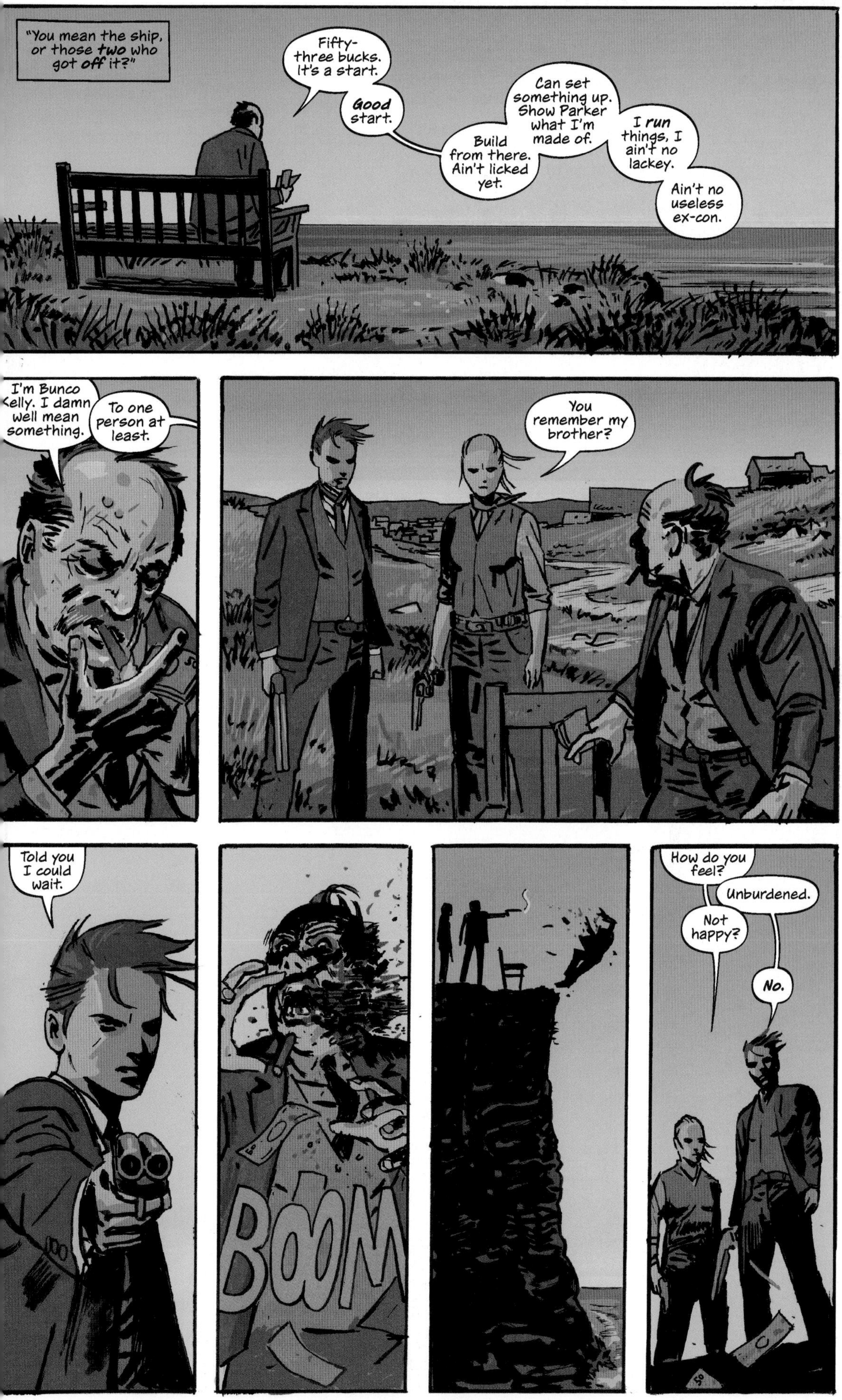
"You mean the ship, or those *two* who got *off* it?"
Fifty-three bucks. It's a start.
Good start.
Build from there. Ain't licked yet.
Can set something up. Show Parker what I'm made of.
I *run* things, I ain't no lackey.
Ain't no useless ex-con.
I'm Bunco Kelly. I damn well mean something.
To one person at least.
You remember my brother?
Told you I could wait.
BOOM
How do you feel?
Unburdened.
Not happy?
No.

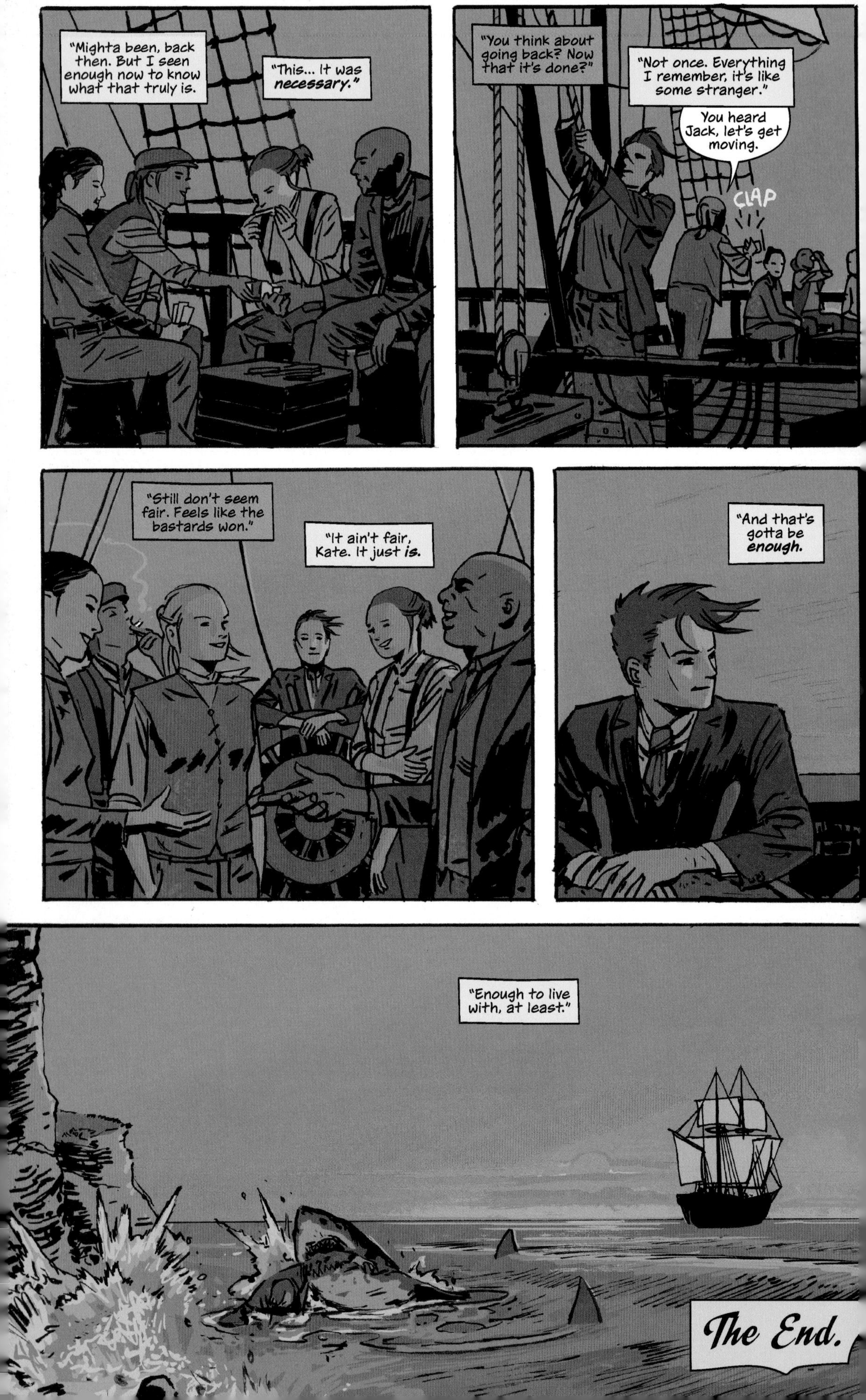
"Mighta been, back then. But I seen enough now to know what that truly is.
"This... It was *necessary.*"
"You think about going back? Now that it's done?"
"Not once. Everything I remember, it's like some stranger."
You heard Jack, let's get moving.
CLAP
"Still don't seem fair. Feels like the bastards won."
"It ain't fair, Kate. It just *is.*
"And that's gotta be *enough.*
"Enough to live with, at least."
The End.

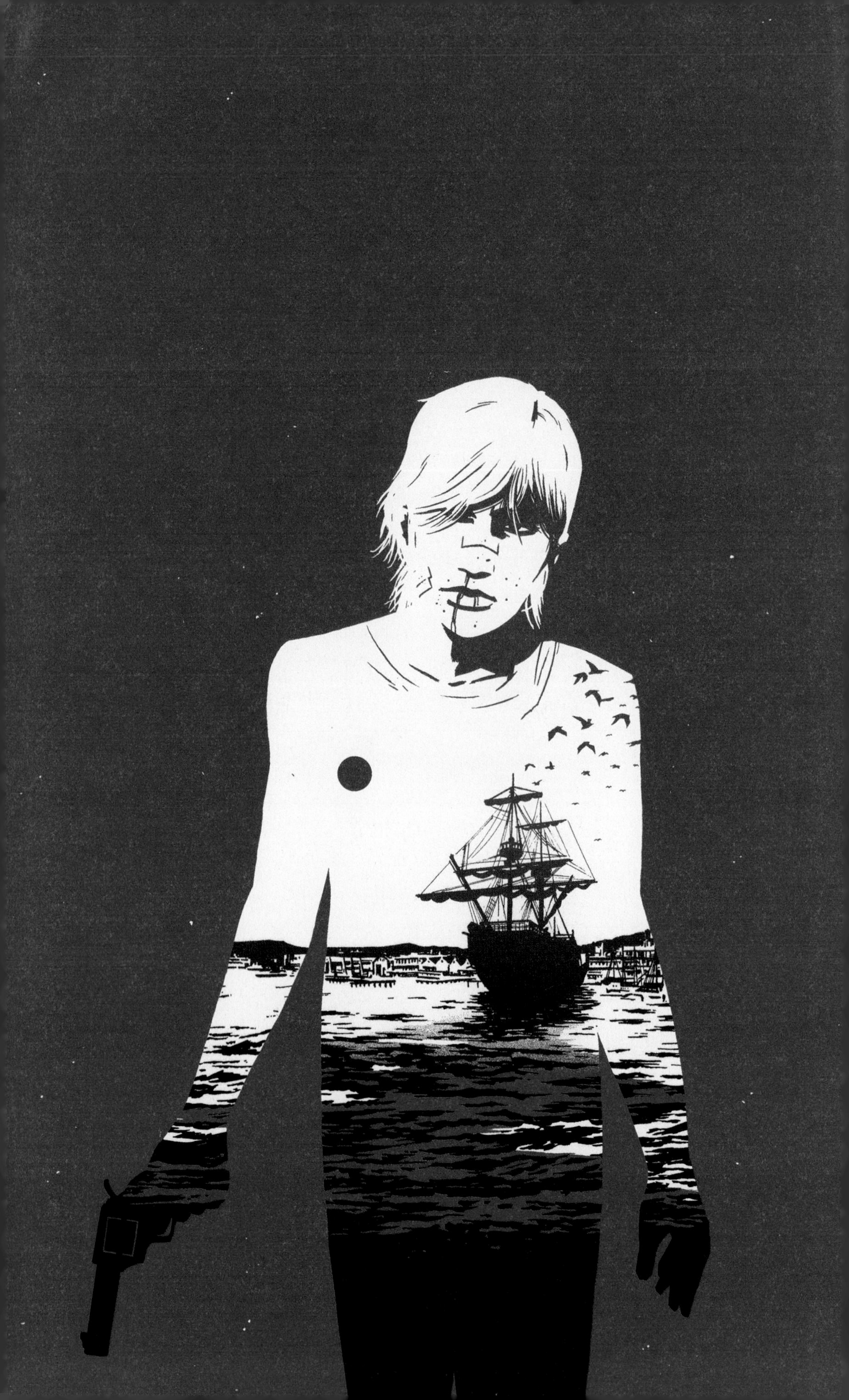

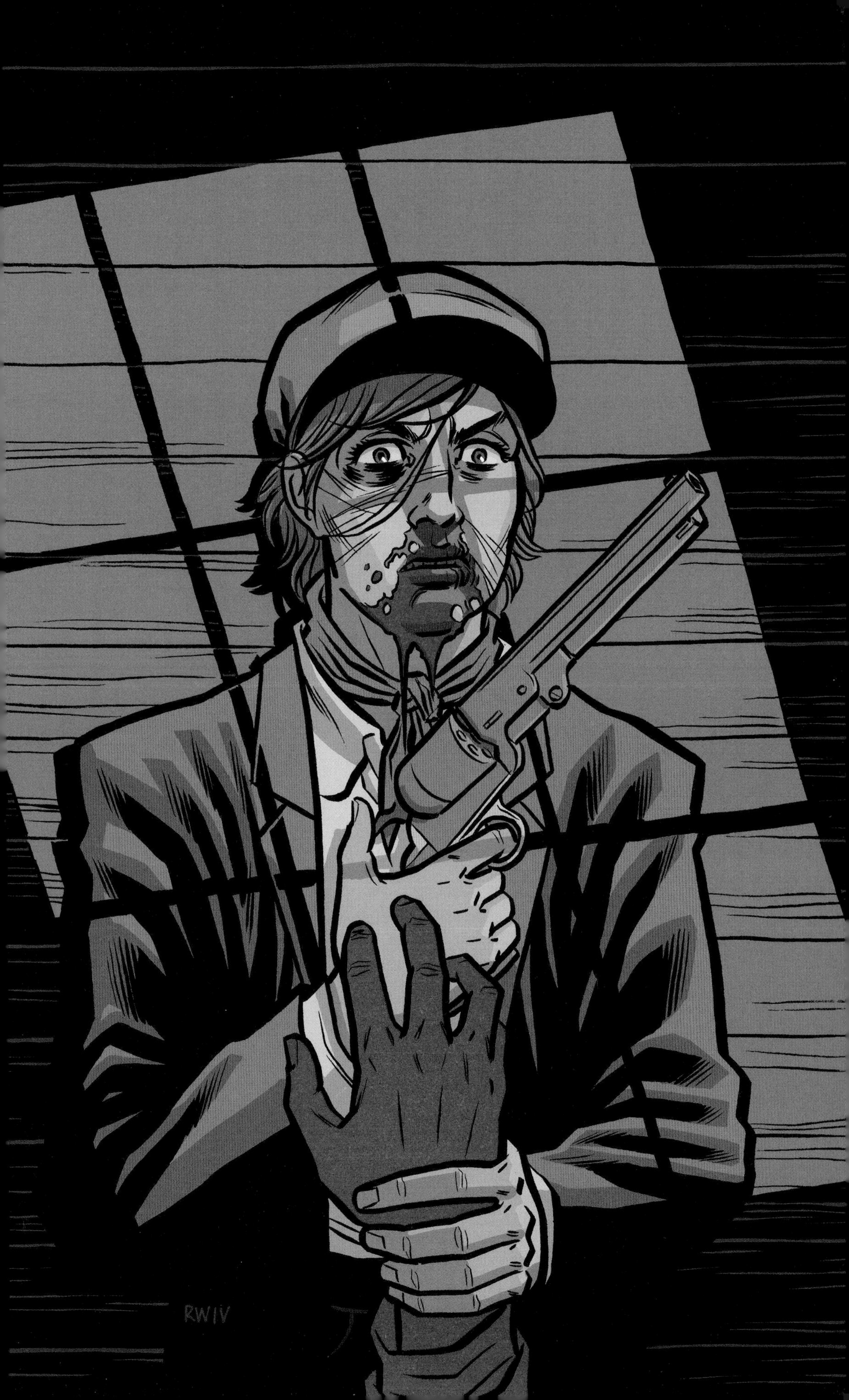
RWIV

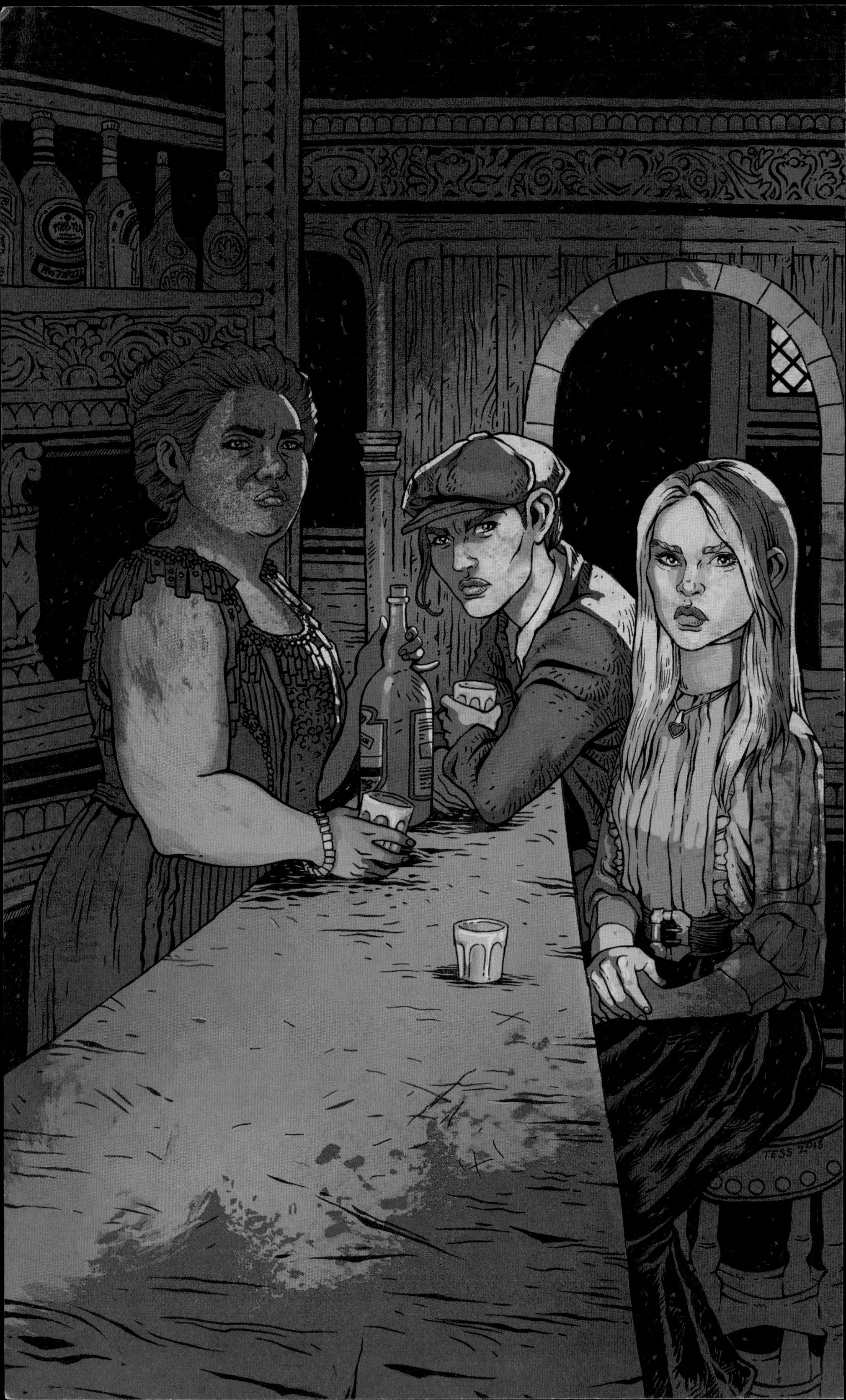
TESS 2018

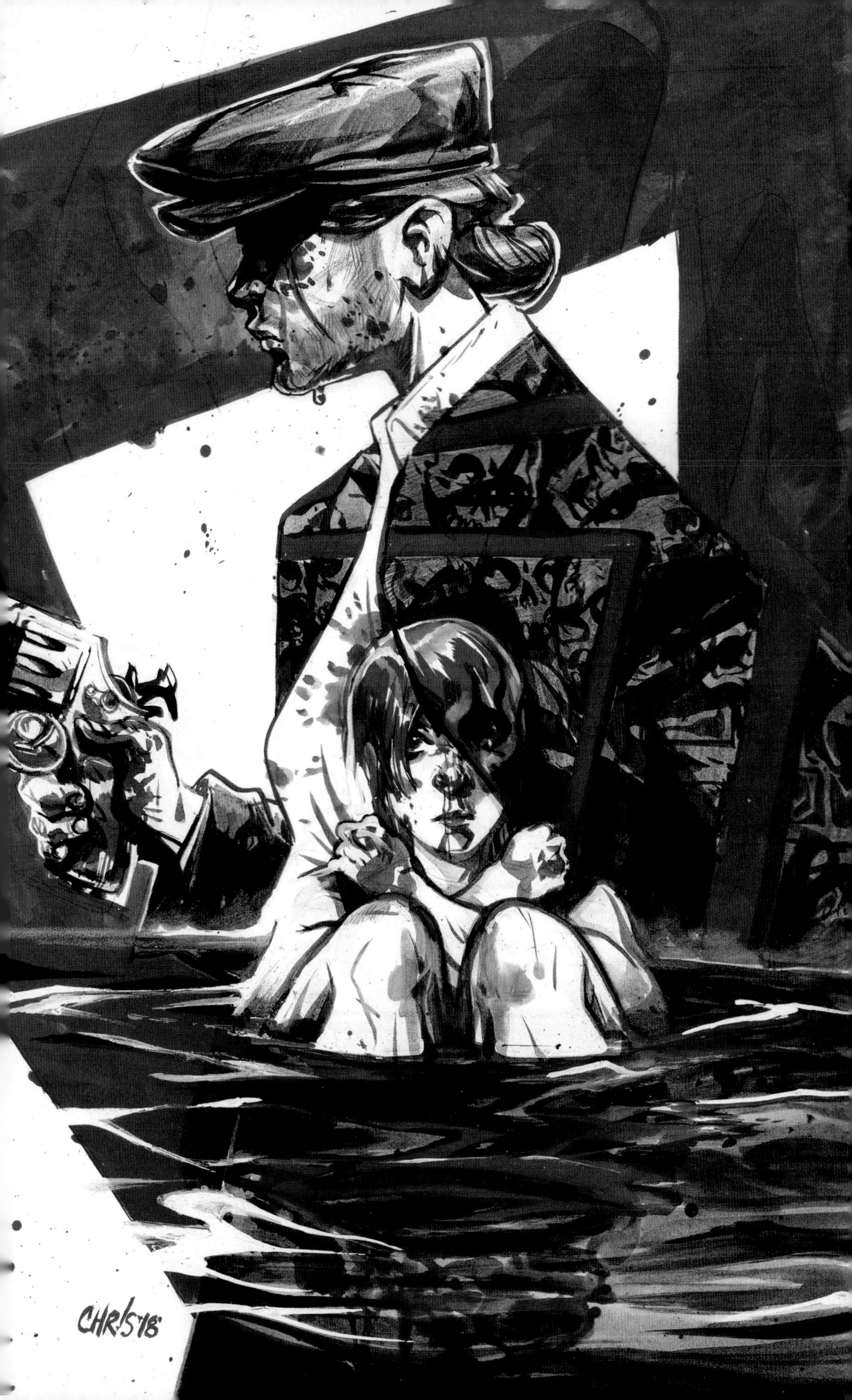
CHRIS '18

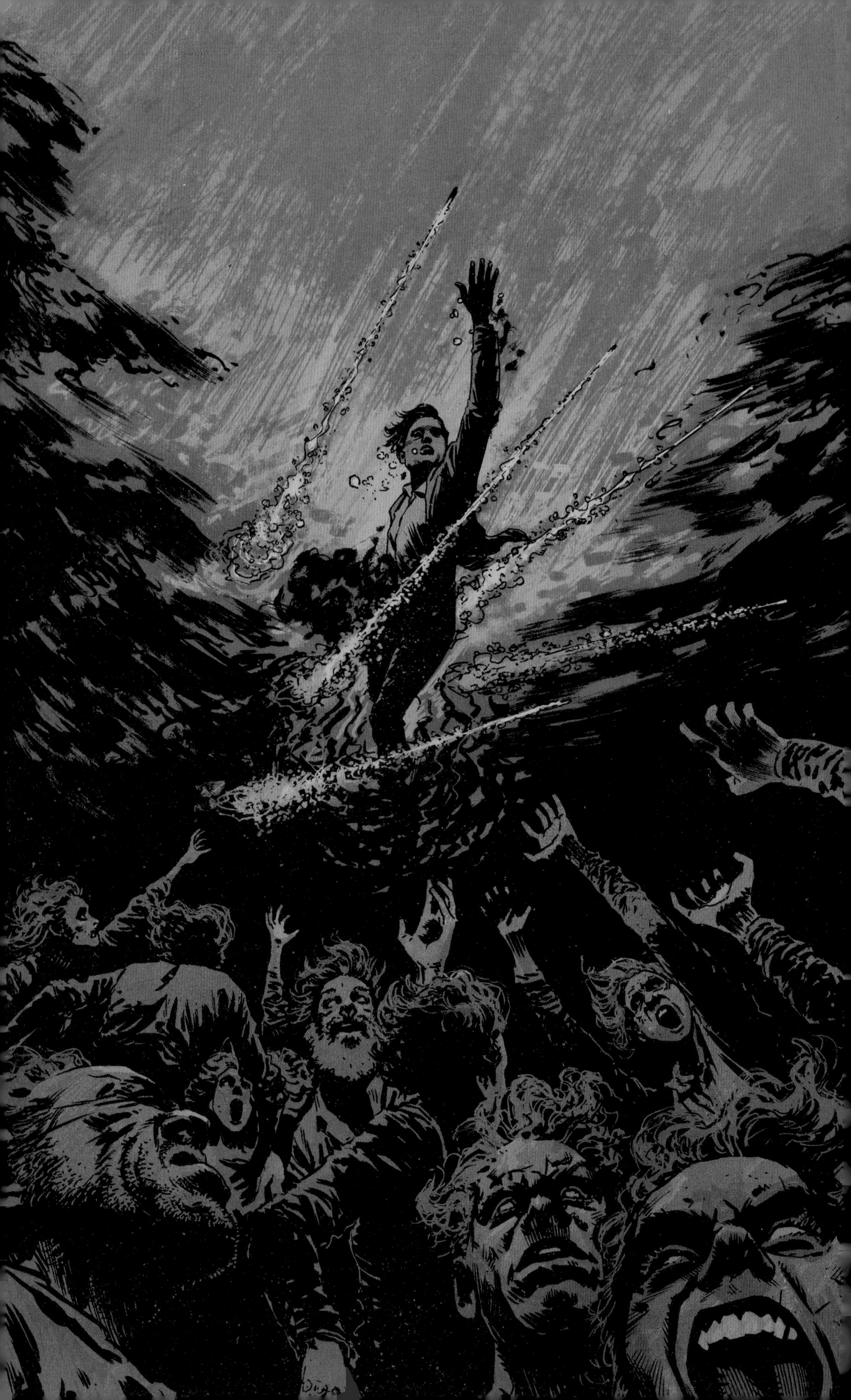

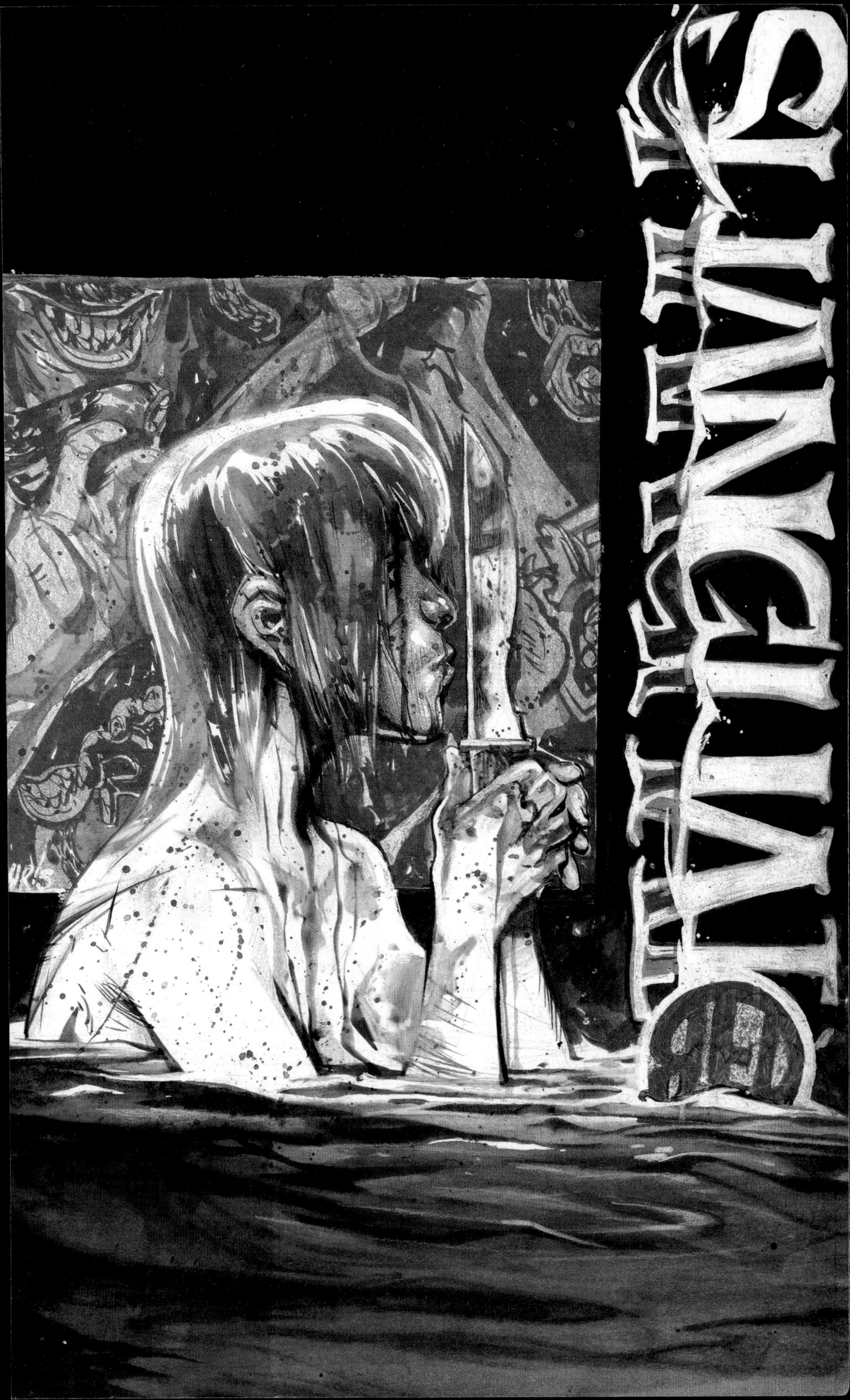

When Joshua and I started working together, the first thing I did was send him character descriptions of Red, Katie, Siobhan, Sullivan and Bunco Kelly. My character descriptions tend to be less about physical descriptions (tho I get into it some here, clearly) and more about the person themselves. Their lives, what they've gone thru up til this point and various other bits about them to give him a feel of what they're all about without saying "now draw this." The writing and grammar are occasionally atrocious and some of Red's story changed in the actual writing of the book, but these were always just vague directions that Josh took and turned into an actual living, breathing map of a person.

Molly (Red) Wolfram / Jack

Molly Wolfram is the firstborn of Herman and Siobhan Wolfram, German and Irish descent, respectively. She's in her early to late 20's through the story (22-27). Build-wise she's slender, slim-hipped, she'd almost be waifish except since she was a kid she's worked hard physical labor, and it's resulted in a layer of muscle stacked on top of her frame, bulking her up a bit. Because of her red hair, she was always called Red around the house and subsequently throughout her life.

Growing up on a farm in Oklahoma, Red was doing labor since she was old enough to walk. After her father, who dragged the family from New York to the middle of nowhere to build their own lives, disappeared on them (some say he abandoned them, some say he was killed), Red had no choice. She also helped raise her baby sister, Kat. But despite their efforts, the farm went under, preyed upon by men from the bank and land grabbers. Red and her mother plotted their route out west to look for work, ending up in Oregon. Red tried to find "women's work" and none of it suited her, and she saw the kind of money loggers were bringing into town every month, so she disguised herself. Cutting her hair short and dying it black (using walnut shells or printer's ink or whatever she can lay hands on), stealing some of her father's clothes he left behind, binding her chest, she signs up to be a logger, working 3-6 month stretches in the Oregon forest. She gives this male persona a name, an identity: Jack. Now she's full-time living as a man and making a good living at it, mailing money back to her mother and sister. When she's not working, she's wandering. Sometimes as Red, most times as Jack, never home for more than a few days, she's out enjoying life, having a lot of money in her pocket, freedom.

When we meet Jack at the beginning of her story (these will be flashbacks), she's 22, missing the tips of two fingers and her arms are covered in scrapes and light scars. Her face has several deep nicks in it. Flying splinters of wood, chains and rope burns, the occasional knife scar from a card game gone bad. She keeps her hair short and dyed black and she looks more than able-bodied with her endless stretches of logging. She looks dangerous and able bodied, a perfect catch for a crimp looking to shanghai someone. One of them does, slipping something into Jack's drink and dropping her through a trapdoor. She gets loaded on a ship and sold to the captain, both of them assuming Jack is a man. The ship sets off for Shanghai and ports beyond.

When we meet her at the beginning of our story, Jack is 25 and she's been working on a boat the last 3 years, living on crappy rations, no money given to her and nowhere to spend it, she's in servitude until her 3 year contract is up. She's grown gaunt, her muscles standing out more. She's kept her disguise, sawing off her hair with a pocketknife, dying it with engine oil. She binds her chest still and is constantly covered in a patina of dirt, oil, blood. Shanghai'ed sailors are worked to the bone and don't get the luxury of baths or clean clothes.

When we meet her at the beginning of her return to Portland, she's 27 now, having spent the last 2 years trying to get back home, her hair is grown out, red again, shoulder length. Once she slips off the boat, she stops binding her chest, buys some dresses and goes into disguise as herself, as Red.

Logos are the unsung heroes of comics. Luckily, we had logo designer Dylan Todd, who gave us several options to choose from for Shanghai Red. *According to my spotty memory, Joshua and I both loved the one on the front of the book right away, but we still dug the other two and in the interests of showing you all the possible ways this book could have looked, we wanted to include Dylan's other two designs as well.*

SHANGHAI ☠ RED ☠

Much of the look and uniformity of the covers for *Shanghai Red* were determined by the cover for the first issue. We knew we wanted it to be an image of our ship the Bellwood at sea and it took a lot of sketches of simple composition ideas until I figured out what felt best. As you can see in the color roughs, at first I was trying out colors that matched the interiors more with some moody bluish tones and a bit of red from the blood coming off the ship. But I scratched that when we landed on just going with reds and warm tones for the colors and I thought it could be cool to do the same for all the other covers. From there it was a matter of trying to figure out which moments from each issue would be best to focus on for the cover imagery. Below and on the facing page are some of the roughs I did for each issue.

When going through this process I usually picked the one I felt had the strongest composition and the image that fits the issue's narrative the most, and fortunately Chris was always on the same page with my picks. Chris was also great at reigning me when my ideas got too weird. My initial idea for the cover of 2 was just to have the burned up body of Murray in the bathtub but Chris pointed out how it was leaning too much towards horror, which he was totally right about. Luckily we still managed to get bathtub Murray in there along with Jack in the final version. For issue 3 I wanted to do something with the trap door Jack falls through. It's a crucial moment in the story and after trying several versions, I ended up liking the outstretched hand the most. My favorite of all the covers we did is issue 4. It's one of the simplest designs of all of them but I just love that we got to make a revenge comic with someone getting stabbed on the cover. But the most difficult to figure out was definitely issue 5. I couldn't find the right moment in the story to build the image around without giving anything away, I just knew I wanted to focus on the end scene with Jack and the torch. What we ended up going with was different from the previous issues in that it's just a pairing of images composed together rather than a scene from the story. I tried to avoid this in an effort to keep the uniformity but in the end I think it worked out for the better.

Joshua Hixson

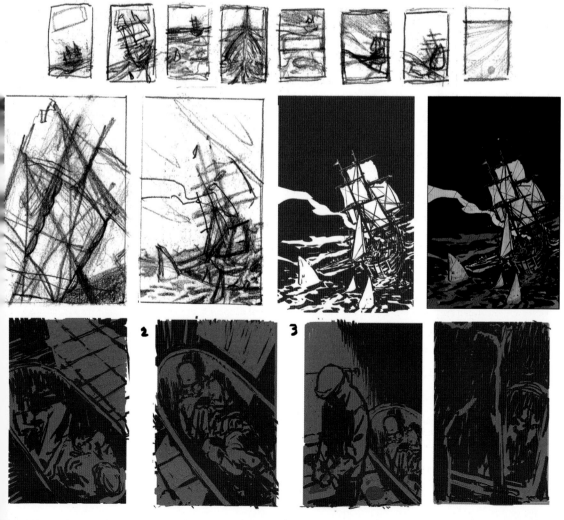

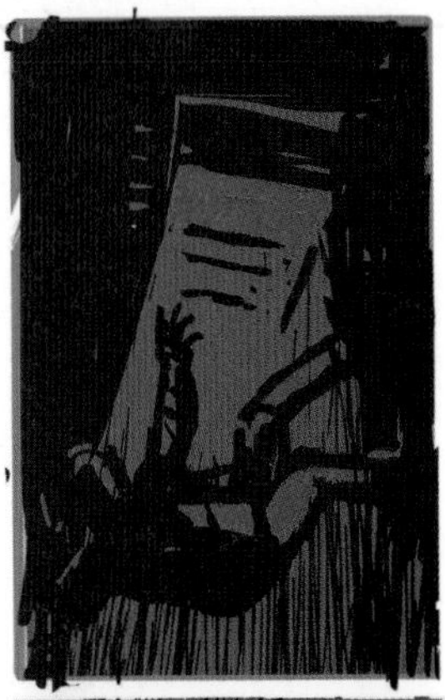
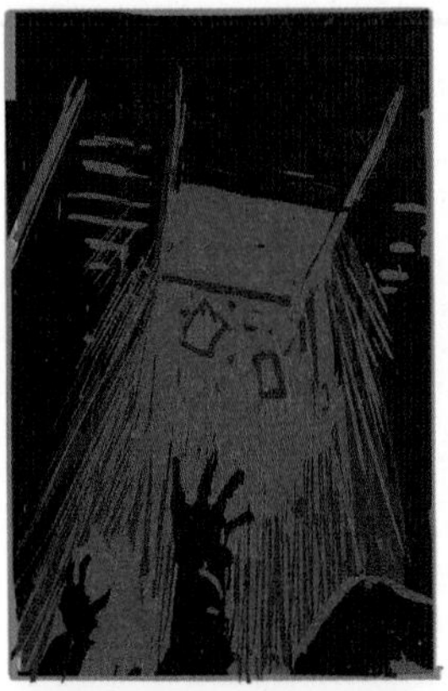
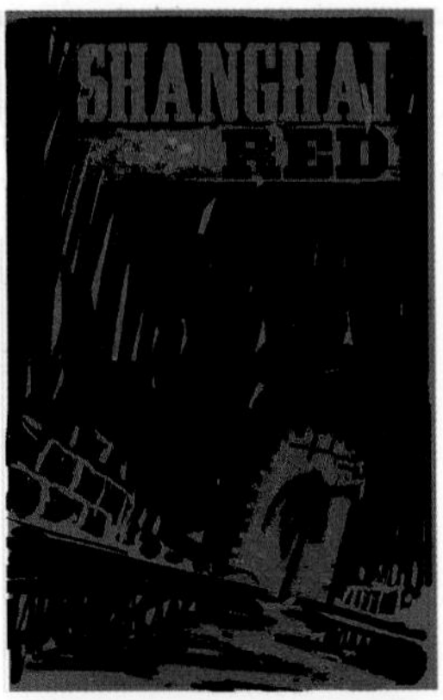
SHANGHAI
RED
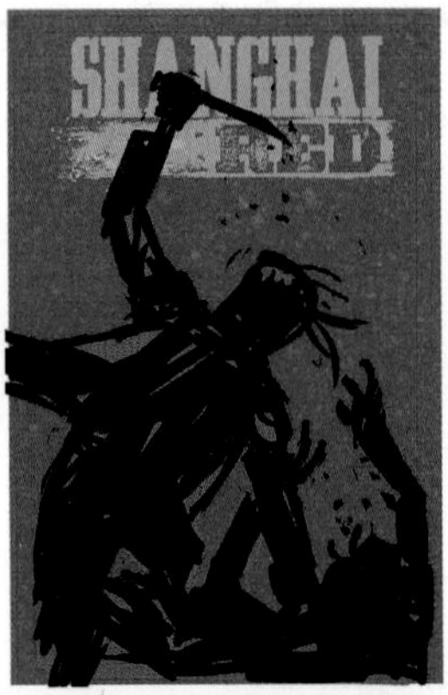
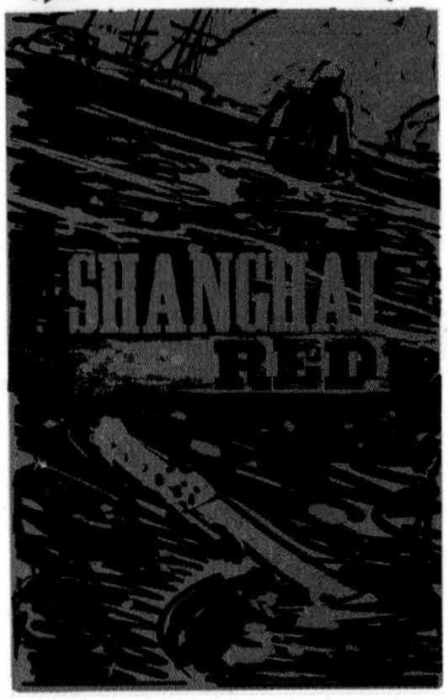
SHANGHAI
RED
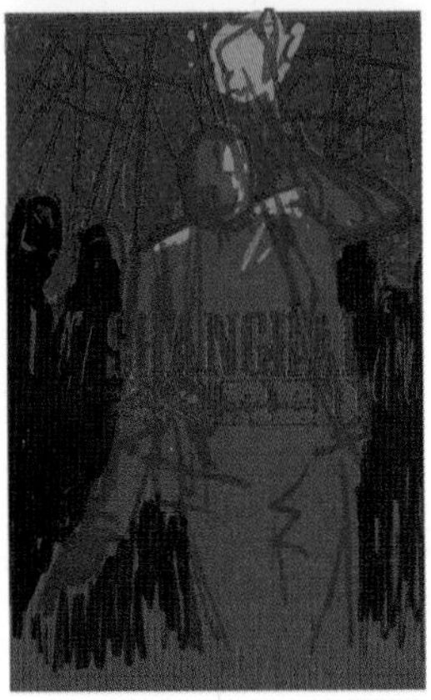
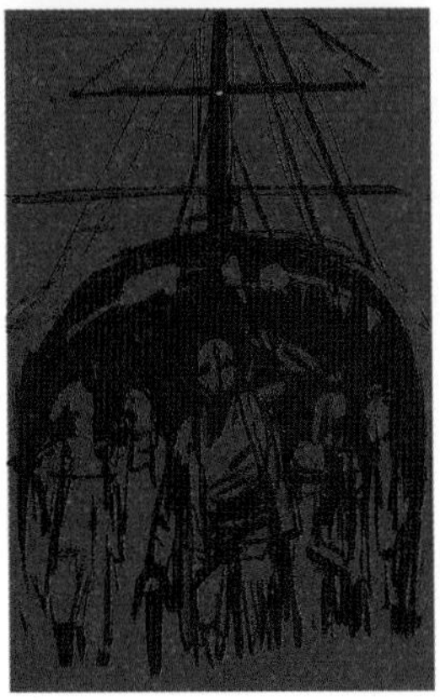
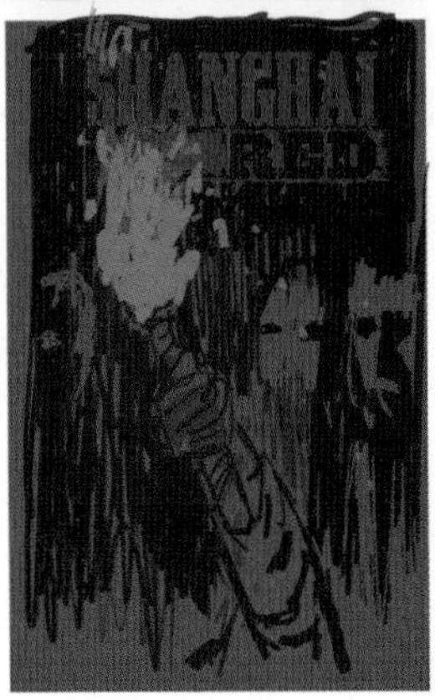

Shanghai Red was born from a well-told historical lie. One popularized in the 1930s, when a logger-turned-writer named Stewart Holbrook, looking for tales back from the old rough waterfront days, met Edward "Spider" Johnson. Spider, who had been a bartender at Erickson's — a workingman's saloon that took up an entire city block with gambling, stage shows, prostitution and a tsunami of alcohol — is the man whose stories more than anyone else's shape the mythos of what the shanghaiing days of Portland were like. He's the one who told the story of Bunco Kelly scooping up multiple (reports vary anywhere between 20 and 29) town drunks who had mistakenly drunk embalming fluid and selling their dying corpses to a ship captain, claiming they were merely drunk. He claimed to know all the major players like Larry Sullivan and Jim Turk and Spider was the one who told the stories of the tunnels being used to lock people up and ferry bodies to the boats. Lots of people say he'd talk to keep Holbrook buying him drinks.

Most historians have come to the agreement that the tunnels weren't used for shanghaiing purposes. Portland was a city with both hands in the pockets of the crimps and boardinghouse masters. No one needed to skulk around with bodies thru tunnels. They could just as easily load them into a wagon and roll them down the street. It was an accepted evil, along with the boardinghouses, which were designed to separate sailors on shore leave from their wages after a few short days, broke and owing enough that they would willingly step on board a new ship — sold for $50 to pay the bill. The tunnels' main use was to make it easier to move cargo from the boats docked on the Willamette without getting caught up in traffic. They also became a home for the Tongs and their illicit operations, a runaway chute when criminals needed to shake the law. But if you visit the tunnels, there are trapdoors leading from bars above down to the tunnels, small rooms with prison bars and piles of old shoes. History says one thing, but the tunnels whisper another story.

History is slippery. Fiction is even more slippery. Trying to hold on to both means sometimes you have to let one slide to keep a firm grip on the other. We tried to be as true to history as we could. I researched endlessly, Josh swam in what reference images he could find of the time and places. So that we could unleash something completely fictional and have it all feel effortlessly bound together. Whitechapel, Liverpool Liz, the Senate Saloon, the bicycle girls (Liz's living ads on wheels whose presence made it so that "proper" Portland women stopped riding bicycles altogether for years, lest they get mistaken for one of Liz's girls), Larry Sullivan and Bunco Kelly were all real, though much of them is lost to time and this city's quiet urge to bury its unseemly past, even as others literally dig it up and charge an admission fee.

The trickiest part in all of this was dealing with actual history refusing to be ignored that easily. Bunco Kelly, after making enemies of some powerful people like Larry Sullivan, was arrested for murder. He stood trial and went to prison for 13 years. Upon release he published a forgotten prison memoir and moved to California, becoming a flunky in a criminal organization. Then he disappeared without a trace. Incorporating that 14-year gap into our story was hard to wrap my head around — my grip on historical accuracy was rock solid while fiction was rope-burning my palm — but it felt perfect and sloppy in a way that real life usually is. None of us often get what we want when we want it, and when we do, it's usually not as advertised. What started as a revenge book became about the price of revenge, it became about identity and choices, it became about living people we'd created mingling amongst the historical dead. Nothing about this book was easy to make. It didn't take 14 years, but in the years we spent making *Shanghai Red*, like whatever Jack went off to do with his family on a ship of his own, we were capable of telling any kind of story we wanted. I'm grateful we got to tell this one. Lies and all.

Christopher Sebela
Portland, OR